THE WEAVER'S LEGACY

A FAMILY EPIC OF THE AMERICAN WEST

OLIVE COLLINS

A catalogue record for this book is available from the British Library.
ISBN 978-1-83853-754-8

www.olivecollins.com

This novel is dedicated to Tony 'Tip' O'Connor,
Roscrea, Tipperary − Boise, Idaho
(1941 − 2020)

GOLDIE O'NEILL

Born (circa) 1857

Interview Recorded by Midwest Radio, South Dakota:

August 30, 1936

If I could take a picture of my life and prop it onto my polished shelf, it would have been framed with two of America's greatest natural disasters. Both events were freaks of nature and occurred almost sixty-seven years apart, in 1866 and 1933. Between those years, the final shots of the American Civil War were fired, there were local wars and a world war, there were years of peace, and there were great floods and sweeping fires, yet it was the 1866 disaster that shaped my life. The sky blackened and a rasping gray-green mass blocked out the sun as millions of grasshoppers descended. They invaded our county and gnawed their way through our crops; they even ate the varnish from the tools. I can't recall that day without remembering my Spanish neighbor when she saw the handle of her ax and spat a litany of curses, *los hijos de puta*. At that stage I understood a little of several languages, German, Spanish, and the Indian Lakota language, but my thoughts continued to form in the native tongue my father would not permit me to speak.

Only with the 1933 disaster did it all make sense. On that strange day in April, I had a sense of finality that what I witnessed would change the landscape of the free world for decades. I watched as the mountains seemed to turn to dust. Slowly they edged across the plains and suffocated plants, farms, and dreams of prosperity to create the Dust Bowl.

I was old, vastly wealthy, and slightly infirm, and my only surviving child was a woman the Indians called Wakta.

CHAPTER ONE

Lucy O'Neill-Levingston
Fifth Avenue, New York
February 1937

The night Lucy O'Neill received That Call, she and her husband Harry had arrived home just after midnight. They had been to a concert in Carnegie Hall and afterward had dinner in the Persian Room at the Plaza Hotel. From there, they'd gone to a club on Lenox Avenue where their antics and conversation grew more foolish. Lucy had just arrived at their apartment when she heard the phone ringing. She was still wearing her fur coat, and her stockings were damp from New York's mist.

The operator put the call through.

"Hello, can you hear me?" The caller's tone was edgy. "Harry? Harry, is that you?"

Lucy recognized the voice.

"No, it's Lucy," she said, looking at Harry, who was standing in the center of the living room floor waiting to hear who was calling. "It's quite late, Wilbur," Lucy said.

At the mention of Wilbur's name, Harry raised his hands and looked up at the ceiling with exasperation. He pointed to the hall door, motioning to her that he was going to bed. Even as he left the room, he shook his head in bewilderment.

Wilbur Breen was Lucy's cousin. He was the mayor and local lawyer from her hometown, a small settlement on the border of South Dakota and Wyoming. He prided himself as the go-to man, the educated son of Four Oaks who was happy to help with everything from legal matters to family disputes. Occasionally his counsel was not wanted, but that didn't stop Wilbur.

"I've been trying to reach you all evening. I know it's late, but this could not wait one more minute." Wilbur paused and lowered his voice. "And you, sweetie, must hear it from me because this concerns you."

Lucy was cold and weary, and her feet were sore, and she was tired of Wilbur's antics. Even hearing his high-pitched voice accentuated her petty ailments. She flopped into the chair by the window without taking off her coat. "Is this about my land again?" she asked.

Lucy had inherited property from her late aunt, Goldie O'Neill, six months ago. The day of Goldie's funeral, Wilbur had expressed an interest in the land. Despite telling him she had no interest in selling, he had taken it upon himself to phone her regularly with reassurances that her old house was still standing, the woolen mill was ticking along nicely with its workforce of weavers, and the land she owned was still green. He regularly reminded her that he, her kin, was diligently keeping an eye out for her. With each call, he inquired if she had come to a decision to sell Goldie's land, which consisted of almost 2,000 acres.

Lucy's response remained the same—a resounding "No."

As time passed, his tactics changed. He'd offer advice or claim he had inside information. Recently, he'd suggested the entire parcel of her land was 'a maze of sinkholes.' Wilbur made it sound so catastrophic, Lucy had an image of the entire mountain suddenly inverting with a loud popping sound like in the recent TV cartoons. During their last conversation, ten days previously, Wilbur had told Lucy that he'd only speak to Lucy's husband about the land from now on. "Leave it to us men," Wilbur had said. "We don't have the sentimentality of women." Lucy had been incensed. She'd hung up on him. She knew the land was not valuable. Wilbur hoped to buy it so he would have more land to call his own. Wilbur Breen and his grandfather had come a long way since their homesteading years as illiterate, impoverished, Irish sodbusters. They were now the wealthy educated family of Four Oaks; however, the old Irish desire for land ownership had not faded. Lucy had seen the Irish mentality so often, that it was as evident in Wilbur and the Breens as if they had just stepped off the famine ship that had brought old Ned Breen to the American shore.

"About your land?" Wilbur asked as if he'd never considered it from one end of the year to the next. "When you hear the full story, it might well lead back to your land."

Lucy stifled a yawn; she was too tired to predict what conniving scheme was playing out behind Wilbur's bright, blue, calculating eyes. She slipped out of her shoes, put her feet onto the footstool, and sank deeper into the armchair.

"Are you sitting down?" Wilbur asked.

"Yes," she replied nonchalantly. She wouldn't confess that she was almost lying down from too many Dubonnets, and if he didn't get to the point, she'd be asleep before the call ended.

"This news will come as a shock to you," he continued.

"Wilbur, it's late!" Lucy needed to hurry this conversation along.

"Yesterday an elderly gentleman arrived in Four Oaks. He arrived on the train." He paused.

Lucy knew he was enjoying this.

"As yet, the old man's true identity has not been confirmed. He claimed he arrived on the three-thirty train, but…" Wilbur's voice grew quiet and sinister. "We don't know."

Lucy was beginning to find it amusing. Despite her deep suspicion of her cousin, most of the time she regarded him as a clown.

Or, to use Goldie's Irish expression, "an eejit." Albeit a clever, manipulative man, he was ultimately an eejit.

"He said he came from Denver, but…nobody is certain…" Wilbur's voice drifted off.

Lucy began to smile.

In a low, dramatic voice, Wilbur said, "He was first spotted looking in the window of Kelly's Store, then he was seen outside the school, but we just don't know for sure."

Lucy conjured an image of an apparition appearing out of nowhere and then slowly moving through Four Oaks while everybody stopped to stare at the hovering ghost.

"Then the old man drifted on down Main Street and wandered into Gallagher's Hotel," Wilbur continued.

The more Lucy thought about the apparition and Wilbur's sinister voice, the funnier it seemed.

"He had a drink at the bar…" Wilbur hesitated. "Lucy, are you there?" he asked, as his voice became his own again.

When Wilbur was met with howling laughter, his tone grew sharp, "Stop fooling around, Lucy, I've got something real important to tell you."

She found the sudden change of tone as comical.

"Lucy, you gotta listen to me!" There was an air of urgency in his voice. "Lucy, the man says he's Lorcan O'Neill."

Lucy's laughing subsided.

"Did you hear what I said?" he asked.

Lucy heard him but she still felt giddy, and asked, "Was he wearing a white sheet?"

"No, he was not," Wilbur answered as if Lucy had been serious. "Lorcan O'Neill," Wilbur repeated, knowing it would seem unfathomable. "Your father."

Lucy realized she was holding her breath. She had been told that her father was dead, that he'd gone to God on a battlefield on the other side of the world thirty years ago. He had died an honorable death for his country in the Philippines during The Battle of Bud Dajo. There were articles about his gallantry in the local newspapers, an enormous statue to commemorate his death and bravery, and on the very rare occasion, the mention of his name evoked a shrill silence that told a different story.

There was a moment's silence before Wilbur spoke. "What about the monument?"

The monument that Wilbur referred to was a life-size statue of a soldier in the center of Four Oaks. It was an ostentatious reminder to all of Lorcan O'Neill's death in a country very few people in Four Oaks could find on the map. Lucy had been raised by her aunt, Goldie O'Neill. She had no memory of either parent. Apart from the statue in Four Oaks, her only image of her father was a picture of a young man with a fresh complexion wearing a soldier's uniform. The photo which sat on the sideboard in her aunt's house, had been taken in the early 1890s when he'd been promoted to sergeant for his efforts during the last of the Indian Wars.

When Lucy didn't offer any words of consolation, Wilbur continued. "I had that monument erected in his memory and now he just waltzes into town like he's been doing it every day of his life for the past thirty years," he said, as if he were personally affronted with the deceased returning from the dead. "What are we going to do?"

"It's good of you to let me know," Lucy wanted to end the call.

"Is that it?" he asked.

Lucy was conscious that every detail of the call would be relayed to his mother, Frances. All of her vulnerabilities would be picked over by the Breens. She needed time alone to digest the enormity of the call.

"I'll discuss it with Harry in the morning," she said, and with that she thanked him for telling her and hung up.

Lucy felt suddenly alert and sober. On the console table beside her was a picture of her aunt, Goldie O'Neill. The frame was twenty years old. On the back was an eight-pointed symbol and beside it in distinct white writing was the word Wakta; it was the Lakota Indian symbol for hope. For a long time, Lucy remained sitting in her damp stockings and fur coat, staring out at the lights of Fifth Avenue.

CHAPTER TWO

1865

Grainne O'Neill was nine years of age when she set off on the longest walk of her life. Each day she noted the distance they traveled and the number of snakes they killed. She learned how to count the rattles in a rattlesnake, knew a scorpion could kill a man with its curled tail, and she knew she was going to the West because everybody called it that. It was a portion of America that had not been divided into states or plated with towns. It was so uninhabited that it had not yet been colored in on the map. There were thirty-seven wagons in their wagon train, each filled with provisions for the trip. One family had brought a piano, which seemed like a peculiar instrument to lug across the American plains, yet it happened. Each night, Ned Breen's wife played her piano as Grainne and the train of immigrants first gasped at the sight of a western orange sunset and sweeping vast lands.

During those evenings on the trail, the travelers sat around their campfires and pored over their government-issued brochure on the West to the sound of Mrs. Breen's piano. According to the brochure, not only were they promised fertile land by moving to the West, their lives would be long and healthy with matchless wealth.

Around the campfire in the flatlands of Nebraska, Ned Breen traced the wording with his index finger as he read aloud, "The land is beautiful enough to cause the angels to stop mid-flight and look down upon the soil and wonder if a new Eden had been born."

Those who listened were rendered silent at the wonder that awaited them. Each privately imagined the great farms they would own and wealth they would amass.

Aengus Kennedy broke their dreamy silence. "Who the hell writes that kind of thing!" he asked with a raised, incredulous voice.

Aengus Kennedy was their guide to their new farms. He was also Grainne's father's cousin. He was the reason why they had sold everything they'd owed and left all they knew to embark on this westward adventure. Aengus had lived in the West for almost twenty years and was the only man who knew what life in this new Eden entailed.

"It must be true," Sean Dwyer said with dancing, excited eyes.

Mr. Dennehy pointed to the brochure, saying, "It's there in black and white."

Ned Breen held the brochure up as if to prove its existence.

"Living in the West is hard work," Aengus said. He suggested they throw away the brochure.

Nobody took his advice. They wanted to believe everything they read from a bountiful government that had given them 160 acres for eighteen dollars. Some believed the great unexplored continent was waiting for their eager arms to harvest and cultivate the soil.

There were thirty-seven wagons in their train. Most were driven by people availing themselves of the Homestead Act. Those familiar with American politics said the Homestead Act gave the ordinary man an opportunity to prosper and self-govern. There were families who had brought their Bibles. They would serve their community in the greatest of ministries by spreading the Christian faith. There were Europeans fleeing their own wars. There were men of faith and no faith, and then there were the Irish. Eleven wagons belonged to Irish families, including Grainne's family. They were going west to be farmers and to form their own Irish Catholic colony in the abundant West.

They would be answerable to no Englishman or preacher, no boss or authority. "Only God," Ned Breen said, pointing his finger to the sky.

At night when they sat around their campfires, Grainne listened to their plans and dreams of freedom and self-governing. She was torn between the country she'd left and this new immense American West. As she trudged across the unclaimed landscape, she too was struck with its magnificence, sometimes beautiful, sometimes barren, and sometimes the scenes they stumbled on were so profound, Grainne could almost hear their amassed intake of breath. At times like that there were no words, only a sense they were all sharing something unexpected and as magical as the pretty angel on the brochure who pointed to their new Eden.

After a few weeks, Grainne stopped counting the days and the number of snakes they'd killed. Each morning, she checked the wagon for stray rattlers, cottonmouths, and scorpions. She no longer felt the need to scrutinize the scorpion's curled tail with a mixture of terror and excitement. Years later, she'd match events with the new sights she saw. She remembered the rise and fall of their hopes as they passed through miles of barren, sandy soil dotted with cacti as tall as trees. Some examined the brochure searching for references to deserts, lack of water, or the many treeless miles. They'd ask Aengus Kennedy how far away their destination was, hoping it was miles from the scorched land that altered their hopes.

On the edge of the desert they found one abandoned house. On the door of the shack the previous owner had inscribed the words, '30 miles to water, 20 miles to wood, 10 miles to hell and I've gone there already.'

They met a lone rider who was going to Cedar Rapids with news of an Indian attack. He spoke with disjointed sentences, saying, "Nobody left alive. Counted eleven dead. Everybody scalped. Woman and children taken."

On those nights when Mrs. Breen played her piano, the songs took on a melody of unknowing. They thought of the eagles feasting on the many rotting carcasses they saw on their path. They tried not to think of the white women taken captive by the Indians. Fear crept in; they saw only hardship and felt as poorly as their animals, who burned their hooves on the alkaline ground.

They passed landmarks where they wrote their names, their country of origin, and the date. Grainne always wrote her full name as Gaeilge, or Irish, Grainne Ni Néill.

They would always remember the first member of their party to die. It coincided with their first thunderstorm. It came in flashes lighting up the sky like a menacing God who was going to set the West alight. Some of the animals bolted. Mr. Lightfoot, one of the Bible-carriers from Boston who wanted to go west to spread the Christian faith, followed his oxen into the river and never resurfaced. The following day, Mr. Sean Dwyer's Spanish wife delivered a baby boy, and they called him Emilio. The day of Emilio Dwyer's birth, they killed a four-foot long rattlesnake with thirteen rattles. It was the one and only time Grainne ever remembered that number of rattles.

Grainne remembered her first sight of Indians. Aengus Kennedy got down from his horse and greeted them as if he knew them. When Grainne realized the Indians would not kill and scalp her, she stood beside Aengus for a closer look. As they traveled deeper into the West, she grew familiar with the sight of Indians. The men wore their large earrings and beaded decorations, some wore the uniform jackets of the Civil War soldiers, and some only wore a small cloth covering their groin.

"Savages," Mrs. Breen whispered, "godless, inhumane savages." She placed her hand on her chest and tilted her head back as if affronted at the mere sight of the men.

It was an English-speaking Indian who gave Grainne her name. He touched her hair, wrapped a lock around his finger, and smelled it. Gently he tugged the curl and released it. He was surprised to see it bounce back into place.

He called her Goldie. "Hair same color as the yellow metal the white man worships," he said, referring to the newly discovered American gold.

Some of the emigrants began to call her Goldie after that. Her father commented how still and fearless his Goldie had stood when the Indian had touched her hair.

"Were you not scared?" Goldie's sister Frances asked.

Goldie felt no fear. Aengus had told her that the Indians had lived in the West for thousands of years, yet it appeared as if they'd never lived here. They hadn't built big noisy cities or stone houses with big walls. Everything was as still and beautiful and wild as the day God made it. She likened the unstained West and the Indians to the stories of survival she had heard in her home parish, Mein, about the minority who lived and thrived, and would go on and on for thousands of years. Goldie even liked the new name the Indian had given her.

"No, I wasn't scared," she said to Frances.

Owen Breen tried to frighten Goldie. He claimed he knew everything about the West because he was born in America, not Ireland.

"I been here my whole life, not like you who hasn't lived here one wet day." Although he was the same age as Goldie, he told her that he knew more people in America than she did. He had lived in New York. He had seen real Indians in Kansas long before the Indian gave her the name Goldie, and he knew that the Indians wanted to scalp her. "You," he stressed pointing his finger at her, "more than anyone else on the wagon train. It's your white skin and orange hair."

She hadn't corrected him by telling him that her hair was red, not orange.

Since coming to America, Goldie realized her appearance and specifically her hair was a novelty. She was a tall child with a lily-white complexion, large green eyes, and red hair. It was her long, bright-red curly hair that people noticed and occasionally felt the need to reach out and touch. Some called her hair red, or orange or ginger. The long twisted red curls reached the small of her back.

Goldie's sister, Frances, was eleven months younger and had the same thick curly hair, except her coloring was different. Frances had black hair and brown eyes like their father, and her skin didn't burn as Goldie's did. They had one surviving brother, Lorcan, who was six years of age. His hair color didn't matter because people didn't admire a boy's hair.

Much to Goldie's delight, her new baby sister, Miriam, had a crown glossed with the same red as Goldie's hair. Baby Miriam was three months old and had the beginnings of two bottom teeth. Goldie adored her new sister. When they saw their first herd of buffalo grazing in the valley beneath them, she hoisted Baby Miriam up to see them and whispered in Irish, "Seo í ár n-Iarthar." *This is our West.*

CHAPTER THREE

1865

When they were six weeks into their trip to the West, they camped on the bank of a wide river with a steep embankment. Goldie knew from the sound of the crashing piano that Ned Breen had finally dumped his wife's furniture. The weight was too much for the tired oxen that pulled the wagon. Mrs. Breen's screams of protest were heard as Ned Breen tossed her books and sheets of music into the wind. She kicked up such a fuss that her husband said he'd like to fling her down the embankment after her piano, if she didn't shut up.

After supper, Goldie found one of the music books in the grass. She looked at the pages of the music but couldn't understand the strange dots on the lines with the accompanying letters. Later, when everyone sat around the fire, Goldie saw Mrs. Breen standing alone on the steep bank of the river. She seemed to hover indecisively, reminding Goldie of her dog in Ireland who hesitated at the wide gullies in the bog.

During their first few weeks on the trip, Goldie heard her

parents say that Mrs. Leonora Breen had notions. However, Goldie felt she was entitled to her notions, not only because she wore beautiful dresses; she was also nice and pretty, far prettier and better dressed than the women she'd glimpsed in the elegant part of the ship they had taken from Ireland. Goldie heard that Mrs. Breen's family was wealthy. Her father and brothers worked in a large bank in New York. She spoke three languages and had been educated until the age of sixteen in a school that had a music room solely for piano lessons. Goldie's parents couldn't fathom how the young, pretty, affluent, educated American girl had married the gruff Irishman.

Mrs. Breen told Goldie's mother she'd married Ned Breen because he was strong and filled with adventure.

When her parents heard that, they didn't refer to Mrs. Breen's notions anymore, they only said she was naïve.

Goldie handed Mrs. Breen the music book. "I found it in the grass," she said, "I thought you'd like to have it back."

Mrs. Breen looked sadly at the proffered music book, saying, "You keep it. You'll probably need it before I do."

Goldie kept the music book, believing that someday she'd understand the dots and lines, and she too could make music like Mrs. Breen.

The next morning Goldie saw Mrs. Breen's piano wedged in a tree on the steep bank of the river. One of the Indians was seated on Mrs. Breen's large soft chair, banging the keys, while the rest of the Indians gathered round and laughed hysterically.

"When you're on the road, you begin to realize what's important and not important," Aengus Kennedy said, as he passed the scene. "And a piano in a sod house is just not that important."

It wasn't only Ned Breen who was shedding layers by dumping the excess weight from his wagon, Goldie's father was discarding something else. He mixed not only with the Irish during the evenings but the Americans, Germans, and Russians. He was interested in their lives, their native countries, and the stories that revealed what had pushed them westward.

"The Irish aren't the only persecuted nation," he concluded after hearing their stories of war and genocide.

Even at that stage, her father's disdain of the Irishman recounting his catalog of woes irked him.

He corrected his family when they lapsed into Gaelic. "English, speak English," he'd say impatiently.

When asked his name, he no longer gave the Gaelic name Bearach O'Néill, but the English translation, Barry O'Neill.

Goldie pointed out that their colony in the West would be Irish, asking, "Surely we'll speak Gaelic?"

"Not every Irish person speaks Gaelic," he said. "Anyway, there are only eleven families, some may not stay in the West. Some may not even survive," he said dismissively.

"But your name in Gaelic is your right name," Goldie insisted. At that stage Goldie's thoughts continued to form in the Irish language. She'd translate Gaelic to English and hope the words that left her mouth made sense.

"What's the point in using an Irish name in a country that speaks English?" he asked her.

Goldie was sitting with her father and her sister, Baby Miriam, on the side of a hill. The sun was setting, and the sky was streaked with oranges, blues, and purples.

"Out here there's nothing in a man's formal name," Barry told Goldie. "We're going to a place where there is no history, only beginnings. There are no towns and nothing to root us to its past, only the future we make for ourselves."

"What about Mein?" Goldie asked of her home parish.

"Forget Mein," Barry said, irritably, "and forget the language. Imagine it never existed. Mein, Leith, Kilflynn, Aulane, the Stacks," he listed off place names to reiterate his point, adding emphatically, "none of them ever existed."

Goldie knew her father was happy to leave his native language, his name, and the windswept country in that corner of the Atlantic Ocean. According to Goldie's grandmother, Barry had a sickness —greed.

Goldie's father could read and write in Irish and in English. He'd read aloud the letters his cousin Aengus Kennedy posted from America. Aengus told Barry about the American West where he'd worked as a fur trapper and claimed 160 acres to farm. Aengus described the mountains and land that were as old as Mein but legally didn't belong to anyone. Nobody held the fishing rights to the streams or rivers in the West. Anybody who was willing could hunt and sell the fur from the animals that roamed the land that belonged to nobody. Everything in the Western part of the United States of America seemed as if it were there for the taking.

"All free," Barry said.

What started as a small idea in her father's mind grew. At times he could be found drifting through their cottage in Ireland adding up the value of their possessions, right down to the price of their turf for the winter. He made enquiries, once taking the horse and trap to the English people whom he allowed onto his land to paint pictures. Eventually he told Goldie's mother that the English man wanted to buy the land for the view. Goldie's mother, Neasa, reminded Barry that the land and the sheep that grazed it also belonged to his brother, Ruairi. Barry had talked to Ruairi, who had no interest in America. They'd bargained and then Barry pleaded for more money for his share; finally, they fought. Barry claimed that the land was rightfully his. The deed rested in his hands as the oldest son. Goldie heard her father and Uncle Ruairi several times, then she saw them early one morning after they'd returned from fishing. Her father was shouting and wildly gesticulating with the skillet knife in his hand. Barry had sold everything they owned except her mother's spinning wheel. When Ruairi went to the mart in Listowel, her father sold their forty acres on Mein to the Englishman who wanted their land to paint pictures of the view. They'd left the same day.

"This land speaks of new beginnings," Barry said to Goldie, pointing at the infinite lands laid out beneath them.

Barry turned his attention to Goldie's sister, Baby Miriam. He picked her up and put her on his lap. "Little Miriam was born on the wild waves of the Atlantic Ocean and survived to see her first beautiful sunset on her way to the West," he said, referring to Miriam's birth on the ship they'd taken from Ireland. "That girl will have great stories to tell her grandchildren," he added, stroking Baby Miriam's head.

Goldie didn't know if Baby Miriam was better off not knowing about Ireland. There would be no Mein, or grandmother, or Irish language in her memory, and no terrible loneliness for those gray stone walls that once encased her entire life.

Baby Miriam was preoccupied with a picture on the blanket on which she sat. It was a picture of a wagon that Goldie had stitched onto a blanket woven by her mother.

"Everything we once knew is no more," her father said.

For the rest of his days, Goldie's father never again mentioned their home parish of Mein. Years later, he was vague about his origins and always disapproved of the Irish lamenting the country that had given them nothing.

When they came to the last landmark onto which they would write their name, in big bold letters, Goldie etched her new name in English and the date. "July 4, 1865, Goldie O'Neill."

On July 11, the families began to disperse until there were only the O'Neills and Aengus Kennedy on the final stretch to their new property. They were nearing the mountains they'd spotted weeks beforehand. They were so big and dense with forest they appeared black in the distance, with their peaks stretching into the clouds.

"They call them *Hĕ Sápa*," Aengus said when he saw Goldie looking up. "The Black Hills."

"Is our farm up there?" Goldie asked Aengus, pointing to the highest tip of the mountain.

"No," Aengus shook his head.

"Who owns that farm in the Black Hills?" she asked.

"The Indians," he said.

When they were close to their land claim, Aengus rode ahead and stopped in a clearing. He turned his horse and smiled back at them.

Barry O'Neill drove the oxen faster, knowing the end was at last in sight.

When he reached the clearing, Barry jumped down from the wagon and extended his arms. "We're home," he declared. At which point, Goldie's mother, Neasa, began to sob uncontrollably.

CHAPTER FOUR

1866

Their first year in the West was measured by the changing seasons and the improvements they made to their farms. Women, men, and children plowed the fields that had never been turned since the beginning of time. They were awestruck at the fertile soil that opened as easily as if they were cutting a cloth with a sharp knife. When the sun sizzled every part of their exposed body, the men used scarves and wide-brimmed hats while they built barns, paddocks, and cabins. When temperatures cooled, Goldie's father caught a wild mustang. At least once a day, Goldie's father entered the mustang's paddock only to flee twice as fast. Goldie watched the mustang buck with rage at his confinement. She wished he'd kick his way through the fence to find his freedom again.

When at last it felt like Irish weather had arrived, with cloudy skies and sporadic downpours, Goldie saw where Aengus lived. She rode out with her father to Aengus' farm. His solid barns and tilled land were testament to the fact that he'd lived in the West longer than anyone else. They passed a paddock where a boy was breaking a horse. She watched as the horse trotted in circles, kicking up dust in its wake. The boy didn't acknowledge them, but Goldie saw how he looked after them as they passed.

"Is that Aengus' son?" Goldie asked. She'd never considered the possibility of Aengus having a family.

"He's an Indian boy who works for Aengus," Barry explained.

As Goldie got down from the wagon, she again saw the boy watching them.

Close to the front door there was an Indian woman on her hunkers washing clothes. Goldie asked her father if she also worked for Aengus.

Barry hesitated, responding, "Yes, sort of."

Aengus' cabin was cozy with a bed in the corner, a shelf with lots of books, and a loft. There was a stone fireplace with a large black-and-white feather pinned in the center of the mantelpiece.

Goldie stroked the feather. It was like two feathers; the bottom half was white and the top was black.

"It's an eagle's feather," Aengus said when he saw her looking at it.

Aengus was sitting at the table eating. He cut a slice of bread, then coated it with something that looked like honey and passed it to Goldie. When she bit into the bread she was surprised at how soft and sweet it was.

"Isn't it tasty?" Aengus said.

Goldie nodded as she ate.

When she finished, she licked the syrup from her fingers and watched enviously as Aengus cut another slice of bread and began to slowly coat it with the same syrup.

"Is it as nice as apple pie?" Aengus asked playfully.

"Nicer," Goldie said.

"As nice as honey?"

Goldie laughed, saying, "Nicer."

"As nice as the crispy fat from a sow?"

"It's nicer than anything I've eaten in my whole life," she said, matching his excited, raised voice.

Goldie loved Aengus. On the wagon train to the West, she loved the way he used to hoist her onto his horse when he thought she was tired of walking. He'd tell her stories about trapping animals and the names of the Indians, *Black Shawl, Blue Thunder, Walks Tall, Red Cloud.* She loved that he was kind and knew everything about the West. She loved seeing his house and eating bread and syrup with him. Aengus was handsome; he had blond hair and green eyes. Although Aengus was her father's first cousin, they didn't look alike. Barry was dark. He claimed he got his looks from the handsome side of the family. Aengus called him a liar, and at that they both laughed.

"Maple syrup with pecan nuts on cornbread." Aengus held up the bread that was lathered with so much syrup it dripped over the side onto his hand. "One meager slice is never enough," he said, passing it to her.

Her father sent her outside to let them speak. Goldie saw the Indian boy drinking from Aengus' well. As she ate, she walked toward him.

She stood in front of him. Quietly they regarded each other.

Goldie was the first to speak. "This is the nicest food in the West," she declared.

The boy didn't reply.

"Do you want some?" Goldie held it out to him.

He shook his head.

"Do you speak English?" she asked.

He didn't answer her, but instead, he pointed to her hair. "Real hair?"

"Is my hair real?" Goldie repeated. "Of course, it's real. Did you think my hair was a hat?" She thought the idea of wearing a hat that looked like real hair funny and began to laugh.

The boy smiled.

She removed her bonnet and went closer to him. "Here," she said, holding up her hair, "it's real."

He rubbed it between his fingers. "Real," he repeated.

A few years later during the Great Indian War, he would tell her it was his first time to see hair the color of a red sun, and he'd compared her curl to the coiled spring in a gun.

When the green leaves in the trees began to turn rusty browns, yellows, and purples and fall from their branches, Baby Miriam learned to crawl. The O'Neills sat around their fire and urged her to try again. She pushed herself onto her arms and knees before landing on her belly and rocking. Her family applauded.

Barry taught Goldie how to use the gun and make bullets with lead and powder. Each morning her first chore was to collect water at the stream and twigs for the fire. She'd fill her bucket and stare into the hills owned by the Indians. They were forbidden to enter these hills. Owen Breen told Goldie that the Indians in the Black Hills painted their faces for war, raided homesteads, and scalped everyone. Goldie couldn't reconcile the helpful Indians she'd met on her journey to the murderous Indians that Owen Breen talked about.

"Don't worry," Aengus said when she asked him, "more white people die from accidents or disease than being killed by Indians."

Despite Aengus' reassurances and Goldie's father insisting to his fearful wife that the Indian problem was irrelevant to them, Goldie wasn't convinced her father believed it himself. The first time he ventured into the forest that bordered the Indian Territory, he took with him two guns and Aengus Kennedy. Goldie asked how he knew when he was stepping onto the Indian land. She imagined a stone wall encasing the Indians and keeping out the whites.

Her father shrugged, saying, "Best to avoid the forest for now."

Aengus suggested taking the wood from the edge of the forest and emphatically warned the O'Neills and all the visiting children never to venture into the forest.

Goldie did go into the forest on the hill. She took ten steps and stared at the trees. There was no stone wall to indicate where the Indian Territory began or where her father's land ended. The day after, she took fifteen steps and found the biggest tree she'd ever seen. The inside was hollow, and at least five men could have sheltered there. Before returning home, she walked around the circumference of the tree. It took twenty-three steps. She wished she could tell someone about the best hiding place in the world, but then they'd have known she had disobeyed her father by entering the forbidden hills.

When the remaining leaves blew from the trees and the temperatures dipped further, Goldie saw the Indian boy on their farm. He was standing at the mustang's paddock staring in at the horse.

"Are you going to set him free?" Goldie asked hopefully.

He didn't reply. She wasn't sure if he understood her.

Chaytan was his name. He came to the O'Neill house each day for one month to break the wild mustang. The first time, Chaytan only stood outside the fence looking in at the horse. The O'Neills watched, expecting Chaytan to perform some miracle that would see him trotting around the paddock on the wild beast by evening. It didn't happen. After a while they grew bored and carried on as if Chaytan were not there, all except Goldie. After a week, Goldie saw Chaytan standing beside the horse. Slowly he extended his hand and scratched the horse's nose before feeding him a handful of oats. For a long time, he stayed next to the mustang, quietly stroking it.

"Is Chaytan a real Indian?" Goldie's brother, Lorcan, asked their father. Little Lorcan idolized Chaytan, who was older, bigger, and brave enough to feed the wild mustang by hand.

"Yes, he's a real Indian," her father replied.

As a treat, they were eating the special syrup with pecan nuts that Aengus brought them.

"Why doesn't he live in the Black Hills with the other Indians?"

"His father took him away from the tribe to live here," Barry told them.

"Has he murdered and scalped white people?" Lorcan continued.

"Only bold boys who spend half a day searching for the chicken's eggs," her father said.

"So, he *has* murdered white people?" Lorcan asked

Barry was cutting another slice of bread and buttering it with the syrup. "No, he's too young."

"But his father and his uncles probably did?" Lorcan persisted.

"Probably," Barry agreed.

That evening Goldie took twenty-five steps into the forest. She passed the giant tree but found no other tree as big or remarkable. She returned to the tree and pulled a branch in front of the entrance. It was a perfect place to hide something valuable, although she couldn't think of anything valuable that she owned.

CHAPTER FIVE

1866

The day Chaytan rode the mustang for the first time, they'd had their first big freeze. Everything was covered in white frost. Ned Breen and Sean Dwyer were at the O'Neill farm with their children. Everybody stopped to watch Chaytan ride the mustang around the perimeter of the paddock. Goldie thought it was such a great accomplishment that she applauded, then Aengus and the rest of the children joined her.

During those early days when they worked together, they learned their neighbor's oddities. Small jealous remarks were made that set the scene for resentments that lasted for decades and were passed onto subsequent generations.

When Ned Breen saw the location of Barry's farm, which bordered the Indian Reservation, he said, "Only a crazy Kerryman would live so close to the Indians."

Barry countered that his farm was the best farm, "Because I'll always have water trickling down from the hills. In the freezing depths of winter, I'll have trees to keep me warm, and when the sun shrivels your streams in the summer, mine will still flow."

Ned Breen had little to say to that one.

On the same day that Chaytan first rode the mustang, Ned Breen said to Barry, "It's all well and good now, but it might be a different story when you ride the mustang."

"We'll see," Barry said, then added, quietly enough that he wasn't heard, "you begrudging cute Limerick whore."

The same day, the adults convened in the O'Neills' cabin and left the children alone. Owen Breen used a stick to flick ox dung at Chaytan as he passed.

"We'd get five dollars for his scalp. The government is offering a reward for every Injun we kill," he told the other children, then he flicked the dung a second time. "My dad says the only good Injun is a dead Injun."

When he was about to do it a third time, Goldie scooped up a handful of hard frozen mud. As Chaytan was about to pass and Owen had his stick in the fresh dung ready to flick it, Goldie fired the muck as hard as she could at Owen's face. He screamed and staggered backward, clutching his eye. Chaytan continued elegantly trotting the mustang as if he were oblivious to the small foray at the other side of the corral.

When Owen regained his composure, he picked up a spade and Goldie ran. At the side of their cabin, Owen threw the spade, hitting her on the head. She stumbled and fell. Just as Owen was on top of her, Aengus appeared.

"That's no way for a young man to behave," Aengus said.

"You see what Goldie done to me?" Owen said, pointing to his face.

"And I saw what you did to Chaytan." Aengus said. "Go dip your face in water, or you'll have a big shiner tomorrow."

As Owen walked away, he said quietly enough not to be heard, "Aengus Kennedy is nothin' but an Injun-lover."

That evening Goldie entered the forbidden hills again. She lost count of the number of steps she took this time. She came to an opening where there were no trees. At the verge of the barren area, she found a large rock on which were a series of circular carvings. She noticed a small opening at the top of another rock leading into a cave. She contemplated entering but was too frightened to squeeze through the tight entrance. Instead, she said her name in Irish, Grainne Ni Néill, and was disappointed to hear no echo.

Despite her father scolding the children if they lapsed into Gaelic, Goldie found various opportunities to return to her native tongue.

When the first of the snow fell, Baby Miriam spoke her first word.

"Hing, hing."

Goldie spun around to see if anyone else had heard. There was nobody there, but her mother was just outside the cabin door.

Miriam repeated it, "Hing."

She was asking Goldie to sing.

Goldie put her finger to her lips, "Shush," she said, wishing Miriam would stop.

Each day Goldie sang her favorite Gaelic song to Miriam. It was a little game that was repeated at the same time every evening. Goldie would take Miriam to check on the animals. They'd amble through the paddocks with Goldie pointing out the animals, the horses, the sheep, and the pigs, and then into the barn, where they'd count the hens. Each evening they'd end the game the same way, with Baby Miriam sitting on Goldie's lap inside the open door of the barn. Baby Miriam would look up at Goldie expectantly.

Goldie would ask, "Will I sing?"

Baby Miriam would smile, and Goldie would begin to sing in Gaelic, Mo Ghile Mear, *My Gallant Darling*. For those few minutes, Miriam would sit in absolute silence, looking up at Goldie as she sang in Irish. Sometimes, Goldie sang the song only to hear herself speak her own language; other times she sang it for Miriam's amusement, and sometimes she sang it as a reminder of those she had left in Ireland. She pretended that her grandparents and aunts were with her, that they too had accompanied her family across the Atlantic and into the West to this new unfamiliar country.

Each evening Goldie's repertoire ended the same way. She would clap her hands and Miriam would imitate her, then Goldie would stand and take an elaborate bow, with Miriam bending her body forward following suit. It was their secret little game.

"Hing," Miriam said again.

Goldie looked out the window and noticed the snow billowing down. She picked up Miriam and stood at the door to show her baby sister their first sighting of snow in the American West. They could see their father cautiously mounting the mustang. Nervously, he rode out of the paddock and trotted away as the plains turned white.

The O'Neills expected the white snow to turn into dirty gray slush and be gone like the brief snowfalls in Ireland. Despite Aengus warning them that the snow had no notion of going anywhere, each morning they peered out the window and were surprised that the snow remained. Some mornings it was so deep they thought it would come in the window of their cabin. During daylight hours, they'd occasionally look out the small window and glance at the sky, marveling at the clouds that kept pouring out great white, fluffy flakes. During those winter evenings they made candles and soap. Their father taught them the basics of reading, writing, and arithmetic. Frances and Lorcan were good students, but Goldie was not. She continuously confused the order of the letters and when she got the order right, she wrote some of the letters backward. Frances was pleased that she was better than Goldie in one area. Her father praised Frances so much that she suggested writing a letter to their grandmother in Ireland. Barry became so angry she never again mentioned it. Instead of trying to master her reading and writing skills, Goldie turned her attention to weaving on her mother's crude warp-weight loom. By the fourth week of the snow, Goldie had woven her first adult-size blanket. At night she slept under it with Baby Miriam. She whispered her dreams and made plans for the spring as the snow softly fell on their cabin.

Eventually the snow melted and gradually the landscape turned to a lush green. By spring the O'Neills had six new lambs and a kitten they found by the river. Barry sheared the sheep and Goldie's mother, Neasa, got to work on her spinning wheel.

Neasa would gladly have remained in their wet corner of Ireland instead of following her husband's dreams to this lonely outback. Neasa was a shy woman who blushed easily. The only time she came into her own was when she sat at the spinning wheel and churned out her wool. She appeared confident and unperturbed, not in the least daunted by the great differences in her new country so far removed from her clannish flock of sisters in Ireland.

One day in early spring, Aengus took them to pick berries. At the other side of the river they spotted a long cortege of Indians. There were more than 200 of them, some mounted on horses that were pulling sleighs.

Neasa took a step back when she spotted them. She put her hand on Goldie's arm and glanced over her shoulder at their cabin as if she were about to flee.

"They're only passing through," Aengus reassured Neasa.

"Where are they going?" she asked.

"They're going to their summer home in the hills," Aengus said.

"Do they have winter cabins and summer cabins?" Neasa asked.

"No, their cabins are tied to their horses." He told them that the sledge attached to the horses contained their worldly possessions.

"Why don't they stay living in the same place?" Goldie asked.

"Because they're tied to the seasons. Each spring and autumn they take down their tepees, pack their belongings and head north to hunt deer and ice-fish. By spring, the deer grow scarce so they move south, ice-fishing for pike and bass. And then they come back to the Black Hills to hunt buffalo and harvest the crops they set in the autumn."

Goldie watched them until the last Indian left her sight, admiration brewing for a people who could drift so easily around the West.

When the scorching sun returned and the haze of heat quivered over the countryside, they realized a year had passed since their arrival in the West. The rivers shrank and the insects returned. They discovered grasshoppers. Aengus told them that the hoppers were good bait for fishing and tasty to snakes. The syrup and pecan nuts arrived again. Barry sold his mustang and captured two more. The process of Chaytan coming each day resumed, and life found a routine once more at the foot of the Black Hills.

During one of those hot summer days in 1866, the women and children of several families were gathered on the edge of the forest collecting wood for the coming winter that seemed an eternity away from the sweltering heat of summer. Barry O'Neill had cut the trees on his land that bordered the Indian Reservation. Then Barry dipped into the abundant forest on the Reservation, despite Aengus advising him against it.

"The red fellas won't miss the odd tree," Barry said when Aengus was absent.

Ned Breen agreed, "It's unlikely they'd have counted them."

They left the chopped wood to be gathered by the women and children and placed on the wagon.

Early in the afternoon, the women returned to the cabin to prepare food, leaving the children alone to continue working. As Goldie was the oldest girl, she was responsible for the children, and as Owen was the oldest boy, he'd see that the wood was stacked tightly.

Once alone, Owen Breen told Goldie that she looked like a ghost.

"A ghost who'll scare the Indians," Owen said.

Goldie had a scarf wrapped around her head, and there was only a small opening for her eyes. She didn't explain that her skin was so fair, even a light breeze on a cloudy day would burn her white skin.

"You look like a ghost that's been dead for years," Owen continued.

Since the day that Goldie had thrown frozen muck at Owen, he had not forgiven her and took every opportunity to execute his revenge.

"The Indians will scamper when they see you," he said as he walked behind her and jostled her.

Goldie didn't know if there was an English word for *eejit*, so she explained it to Owen. "An eejit is an Irish word for someone who's a fool in every way," Goldie said. "A dunce, a clown, the village idiot," she emphasized, "and you, Owen Breen, are an eejit," she concluded.

Owen called her a bigger eejit and tossed a handful of clay at her. She knew he was about to do something to hurt her. She'd seen the same mean expression when he taunted the young Dwyer boys until they cried with frustration and fear.

As she brushed off the clay, Goldie noticed a harmless orange and brown fox snake. It was slithering toward a grasshopper, one of several Goldie had seen that day.

"You're a bigger eejit who'll never find a husband, Goldie O'Neill," Owen said. This time he tossed a piece of wood at her.

With her back to Owen, Goldie bent down to watch the snake gobble the grasshopper. Aengus taught her that a coiled snake with a quivering tail was a sign that it felt threatened, whereas a contented snake was stretched out. Goldie guessed this was a contented snake with a belly full of grasshoppers.

"Only dirty old Injuns like Chaytan will marry you," Owen continued.

He threw a heavier piece of wood at her. It hurt, but she pretended it didn't.

"Or his uncles who go around the West killing and scalping good white folks," Owen continued.

Keeping her back to Owen, Goldie hunkered down and picked up the snake as Aengus had shown her.

She glanced over her shoulder at Owen, who was looking at her suspiciously. Suddenly she turned and threw the snake at him. "Rattler," she called out and ran.

She jumped over Baby Miriam who was sitting on a blanket in the shade and ran into the forest. Despite knowing that Owen was going to do something brutal, Goldie found herself laughing at the horror on his face as the snake soared through the air toward him.

"Goddamn you, Goldie, I'm gonna flay you to hell," Owen hollered after her.

She could hear Owen's voice approaching.

Goldie ran up the hill into the forest toward the giant tree.

"I'm gonna punch your goddamn head till you're dead," Owen continued, chasing after her as the rage in his voice broke the whispering stillness of the forest.

Goldie removed her scarf to see clearer but couldn't find the tree. She ran higher, skipping over branches and stray rocks. She thought of the cave and hoped she'd fit through the opening before Owen caught up with her.

When Goldie arrived at the area where there were no trees she suddenly stopped. Something had changed. The sky darkened as if it were suddenly dusk. Owen was no longer shouting. Goldie looked up at the approaching gray thick clouds. They appeared to descend. The clouds came lower and lower until they fell into her hair and onto the ground. They were grasshoppers, thousands and thousands of grasshoppers snapping their wings all at once. She tried to go back the way she'd come but couldn't. They crunched beneath her bare feet when she stepped forward and crawled up her ankles when she stood still and nipped her white flesh. She wanted to scream but couldn't find her voice. She looked back the way she had come.

Who'd take Baby Miriam home?

"Frances," she called loudly to her sister, but the sound of the grasshoppers' clipping wings were louder. "Frances," she said in a quiet, suffocating, tearful voice, "take Miriam home." Goldie knew Frances would not hear her.

She ran for shelter beneath a tree. The grasshoppers fell from the branches like raindrops during a downpour. Goldie brushed them from her hair and placed her hand on her head. The only place that would save her was the cave. She looked through the blizzard of grasshoppers. She saw the outline of the trees behind the cave and then she thought she saw something approach. She wasn't sure if the trees were moving and coming toward her or if her eyes were playing tricks or if there was really somebody approaching. She began to move in the direction of the cave. She felt a hand at her back, as if someone were guiding her. When she stumbled, something pulled her up, preventing her from falling. Then she felt something cold and hard. She recognized the rock guarding the cave, and her fingers were on the circular indentions on the rock. She squeezed through the narrow opening, leaving the frenetic forest at the mercy of a million grasshoppers. Once inside the cool darkness of the cave, she found another world, a place that told a story that captivated her for the next seven decades.

CHAPTER SIX

February 1937
Fifth Avenue, New York

Lucy awoke abruptly. Lying perfectly still and staring wide-eyed at the fan on the ceiling, her first thought was of Lorcan O'Neill, her father. She recalled her phone conversation with Wilbur Breen the previous night. She thought of his theatrics and sinister tone, how she'd poked fun at him and asked if the man he talked about was wearing a white sheet, and then the bizarre revelation that Lorcan O'Neill had returned to Four Oaks.

Lorcan O'Neill is alive, Lucy whispered. *He is alive and well, and probably eating his breakfast in Gallagher's Hotel as I lie here in my bed.*

She felt foolish whispering the information aloud, yet she felt it necessary to help her absorb the outlandish yet wonderful news. *He is not dead,* she continued in the same vein, getting happier with each utterance. *He is alive. My father is alive.*

Lucy knew very little about her father apart from the fact that he had been killed in the war fields of the Philippines. The Battle of Bud Dajo, which occurred in 1906, had taken twenty-one American soldiers, including her father, Lorcan O'Neill. Lucy had been three

at the time of his death. When she became old enough to understand what it was to die for your country, she remembered being
proud of the selfless act of giving his life in a war against
communism.

Lucy sat on the side of the bed as she considered the great
news. What was he like? Would they share interests? She tried to
imagine what he'd look like now. Would she resemble him?
Abruptly, Lucy got up. She'd drive herself insane if she sat on the
side of her bed much longer trying to imagine a man she didn't
know.

She washed and dressed quickly before going to the dining
room. Lucy's husband, Harry, was eating his breakfast and reading
the newspaper.

"Morning," he said without raising his head.

Immediately, Harry began to comment on the news. There was
a shooting on Lexington Avenue, there was a new musical on
Broadway, and something about the President and the Supreme
Court justices. "I'm beginning to question President Roosevelt's
motives," Harry said.

Lucy massaged her temples. Harry was a morning person, one
of those who bounced out of bed brimming with energy. He was
vocal and had staunch opinions; he had theories and ideas and
unbendable solutions, all of which were aired before the clock struck
eight.

Lucy had breakfast with Harry only on the weekends. She was a
not a morning person and preferred to allow the day to begin slowly
and silently. On weekdays, when she ate her breakfast alone, the
hum of the traffic eight floors below on Fifth Avenue and the quiet
feet of the maid puttering about were enough noise.

"Can you believe it!" Harry continued talking about the President and the Supreme Court. "I expect there will be more about
this—."

Lucy interrupted him; she couldn't wait one more minute. "I
had a call from Wilbur Breen last night."

"What did that three-ring circus clown want this time?" Harry
asked, a clear irritation in his voice.

"According to Wilbur, Lorcan O'Neill returned to Four Oaks yesterday."

"Remind me again," Harry said as he skimmed through the baseball results. "Which O'Neill is he?"

Lorcan was somebody who belonged at the forgotten beginning. His name was so rarely used that it didn't register with Harry.

"Lorcan O'Neill, the great sculpture in Four Oaks. The war hero," Lucy said.

Harry slowly lifted his head from the paper. "Your father."

Lucy nodded.

"He is dead," Harry stated in that emphatic tone he used on his mother, who occasionally lapsed into forgetfulness.

"Not according to Wilbur Breen," Lucy said.

Lucy gave Harry a brief account of Wilbur's call, although she didn't mention Wilbur's theatrics. It was too early in the morning, and Lorcan O'Neill returning seemed a more pressing issue than entertaining her husband.

When Lucy finished her account, Harry sighed loudly. He pursed his lips and traced his finger around his mouth.

Lucy poured a cup of coffee.

After a few moments of silence, Harry said, "There are two vital questions. A," he held up his index finger, "is it really him?" He left the question hanging before moving to the middle finger, "And B, what does he want?"

"I expect it is him because Wilbur wouldn't have phoned at midnight without being certain that it is him," Lucy said.

Harry agreed. "Then, what does he want?" Harry asked.

"Maybe he's dying and wants to see Four Oaks one last time, or maybe he came to see me."

"He left you in that place," Harry said, referring to the orphanage.

"He was at war when my mother died."

Lucy vaguely remembered the orphanage in Denver where she'd spent a year. When she was five years of age, Goldie had taken her from the orphanage to live with her in Four Oaks. One of Lucy's earliest clear memories was a train ride. Goldie had sat beside her with her handbag on her lap and her freckled fingers pointing out the passing landscape. Lucy didn't know if she was remembering the day she'd left the orphanage in Denver where Goldie had found her, or if it was an outing with Goldie after she went to live in Four Oaks. She only remembered the excitement of the train and Makawee, a local Lakota Indian woman sitting opposite them sharing the thrill of the day. Lucy later asked Goldie about it. "Yes, I remember," Goldie had confirmed, "that was the day I went to Denver and collected you at the orphanage." For years, Goldie rattled off the same story; how she'd gone all the way to Denver, Colorado on the ten-thirty train when she realized that her dear sister-in-law had died and her only child was ensconced in an orphanage. "The same day a storm was blowing so strongly, I thought the train would be lifted off the tracks and bounced into Nebraska." Goldie was a big expressive woman. When she was animated, she emphasized her point by waving her hands. She described how she'd found Lucy living in a lovely orphanage with pumpkins growing in the garden. She formed a big circle with her arms. "Enormous pumpkins," she'd said. "You needed a bath, but you were well fed," Goldie told her informatively. Then Goldie described taking Lucy home on the train, "And we all lived happily ever after," she'd chime in an uplifting voice.

Lucy had never considered the family unit until she went to live with Goldie. At school she saw that the other children had a mother and father. It was Wilbur Breen who told Lucy about her father's death. He told Lucy that her father had been killed at war. "You got no dad because he was blown to a thousand pieces. Now all he's good for is fodder for the wild animals in a country where yellow people live." Wilbur Breen was three years older than Lucy, and as a child he took every opportunity to tease her. All those years ago in the grounds of Four Oaks' one-room school, Wilbur went as far as imitating a bird plucking out her dead father's eye and eating it. The scene was impaled on Lucy's memory forever. When Goldie heard that Wilbur Breen had been taunting Lucy, the first thing she did was to pull Wilbur Breen by the ear into her buggy and threaten to shoot him "between the eyes" if he teased Lucy again. Then Goldie sat Lucy down and told her a wonderful love story about her parents. "They met before Lorcan went to war. Your Mom was a schoolteacher. She was small and so pretty, every man wanted to marry her. Your father, Lorcan, was a great war hero. They were both so beautiful you'd stop to stare at them. Then Lorcan went off to fight a war and was killed when you were four years of age. Almost a year later, I heard that you were in the orphanage, and my legs couldn't carry me fast enough to find you."

Goldie contradicted Wilbur's account. She told Lucy that Lorcan was indeed in one whole piece. "Your father was shot once, so quickly he'd never have felt a thing." Goldie went as far as telling Lucy that Lorcan had been given a war hero's funeral, with the other soldiers playing songs as they lowered his coffin.

Now as an adult in her New York apartment many miles and years removed from Goldie's rustic kitchen, Lucy almost laughed aloud as she thought about Goldie describing the finer points of a funeral that she couldn't have known about. If pressed, Lucy had no doubt that Goldie would have told her the song the other soldiers sang during Lorcan's funeral and given a rendition if invited.

"Where has he been for the last thirty years?" Harry said, interrupting her sweet memory.

"I've no idea," Lucy said.

"What about your mother's people?" Harry asked. "Maybe Lorcan was in contact with them over the last number of years?"

"I don't know anything about my mother or who she was apart from the fact that she died soon after my father was killed," Lucy said vaguely.

Goldie admitted that she knew very little about Lucy's mother; however, she did know her cause of death. Goldie told Lucy that her mother was so lonely after her father's death, she died from a broken heart. Years later, when Lucy pointed out that people couldn't die from a broken heart, Goldie remained steadfast. "I suspect she just lay down crying all day long and got some sickness because she wasn't able to cook for herself. Then her heart just stopped." Only with age, did Lucy realize that Goldie was an unreliable narrator. Goldie skimmed over truths with dramatic story-telling. Sometimes she believed the best truth was hiding the truth, or dressing up the truth, or digressing from the truth. Goldie once admitted that sometimes it was best to tell anything but the truth. Lucy had always suspected that her beginnings were not as heart-warming as Goldie claimed, although Goldie never deviated from her account, even the death-from-a-broken-heart account.

"So, you have nothing that can shed light on any of this?" Harry asked.

"There might be documents in Four Oaks, I don't know."

"You don't know!" Harry repeated with a raised voice.

Harry was a black-and-white man. He liked facts and figures, he hated speculation, he liked certain people and detested others, he never tired of praising the Republican politicians and spewing vitriolic hatred about the Democrats. People were either alive or dead.

"I do know," Harry said in the same irritated tone. "Somebody is lying."

Lucy hated when Harry went on like this. Dogmatic. Aggressive. Biased.

She got up from the table and went to the bay window that overlooked Central Park. This morning there was a mist, so dense it obscured the entrance to the park and the street below them. The only clear items that she could see were on her balcony: a cast-iron table, two chairs, and one lonely plant. It was an arrowwood plant with white petals that seemed to shiver in the February wind. Lucy had brought the plant back from Goldie's garden in Four Oaks after her funeral. Each day she'd look out at the white flowers on the plant that sparked another memory from her last days with her aunt. Sometimes Lucy didn't know if the sight of the plant accentuated her grief or comforted her. Lucy was told that the Lakota Indians believed that the soul went to the happy hunting ground, a realm that resembles the world of the living, but with better weather and more plentiful animals that are easier to hunt than they are in the world of the living.

Although Goldie's days of hunting were long over, she'd never allowed age or creaking bones to stop her attending events. Lucy was pleased that she'd spent the last day of Goldie's life in her company. They'd gone to Mount Rushmore to see President Roosevelt unveiling Jefferson's head. There was plenty pomp and ceremony. The American flag was draped across the top of the mountain. When they removed the flag, behind it was the biggest, most modern sculpture any of the spectators had ever seen in their lives. President Jefferson's head was carved into the rock. It seemed an impossible feat, to carve the features of the third president of the USA into the face of a mountain. The visiting dignitaries, local politicians, and business owners were seated closest to the front. President Roosevelt sat in his big shiny car and gave a speech about nature and honor. They applauded, stood, cheered, and waved their hands like fevered children unable to contain their excitement at the sight of the President of the United States of America on their home turf, with the Jefferson sculpture overseeing the fanfare. Goldie, however, sat throughout the proceedings without smiling and noiselessly broke wind. It was her small gesture in protest at the ugly sight in what she called her "beautiful wilderness."

The same day, a man from the local radio station put a microphone under Goldie's nose. She gave a brief interview and spoke about the grasshoppers and the Dust Bowl. During the car ride home, Lucy remembered Goldie's peculiar silence. That night the silence was only broken when Goldie put her hand on her chest and complained of indigestion. She died a few hours later. That had been six short months ago.

Lucy missed Goldie so much, it was as if her grief clouded everything she did. Although she tried to hide her despondency, Harry must have noticed. He suggested they go on a holiday, somewhere hot where they could relax by a pool. He mentioned the Caribbean. Lucy suggested a location closer to home, as she wanted to return to Four Oaks to sit in the old familiar house and allow the death to settle around her more comfortably. Harry dissuaded her. He said it would make her feel worse, "and think of the cold in that old house." He made a play at shivering. When she suggested it again, he said they'd go the following month, and each month after that he found an excuse to defer their returning. Finally, he told her to sell the land and the house. He had said it casually, as if it were an item she was eager to offload. He told her it would be best to break free from all her ties with Four Oaks. She couldn't comprehend the idea of breaking free from her home. Each year for the month of August, Lucy had returned to Four Oaks. She spent her days with Goldie, visiting friends and going on daily excursions to remote towns, if only to admire the décor of a hotel. Lucy still had friends there. Some of Goldie's friends were like aunts, especially her old friend, Makawee, and Winona. It wasn't only the people: it was the landscape. The old hills formed the backdrop to who she was.

Harry wouldn't hear of it. "New York's skyline is your backdrop now. There's nothing there for you anymore," he gently reminded her.

Lucy ignored the pull to return, and each time she went along with Harry.

"This is a mess," Harry sighed, breaking the silence. "There are some friends I could talk to, a few legal professionals who could point me in the right direction, but who can I call on a Sunday morning?"

Lucy hadn't thought about the legal implications, if there were any.

"I've never heard of a case like this," Harry continued. "How long has he been gone? Thirty years?"

"Thirty-one years," Lucy clarified.

"Thirty-one years," Harry repeated, "he'll still be recognizable."

As a child, Lucy had compared her features to those of the man from the picture that hung in Goldie's house. Lucy had large eyes and an oblong face. She was pleased that she'd inherited Goldie's high cheekbones but not her cleft chin. When she was young, Lucy had deemed her cleft chin manly. Lucy's coloring differed from Goldie's, as Lucy had black hair and brown eyes. According to Goldie, she had the same coloring as her father, Lorcan.

Harry continued, as if talking to himself, "There is a lot at stake here, he could be entitled to your inheritance or a nice fat chunk of it. We need professional advice," Harry continued, "somebody to establish the legal implications. For all we know this man could have an ulterior motive."

Lucy was disappointed that Harry saw her father's return as a threat. She was the sole benefactor of Goldie's estate. Although Goldie had been married, her husband was long dead, and her only child had not survived. Not only did Goldie leave Lucy the house and almost 2,000 acres of land, she'd left her enough money to last her several lifetimes. Most of it was tied up in investments that Harry looked after.

"An Army pension is nothing to write home about," Harry added. "That's probably Lorcan's only means of income."

Lucy saw two white petals blow from the plant on the balcony. The swirl of wind raised them higher and higher until they were blown over the terrace and lost in the thick mist.

"I'm going back," Lucy said.

"We won't go yet," Harry cautioned. His tone was firm but kind. "We can do the groundwork here. I'll speak to a few people tomorrow morning."

Lucy put her forehead against the cool glass.

"Once I've established his legal entitlements, then we'll return to Four Oaks." Harry said.

"I'm going back with or without you," Lucy declared in a quiet, even voice.

CHAPTER SEVEN

1866

The day of the grasshoppers, Goldie had cried while she hid in the cave. She said a prayer to God that the grasshoppers had not devoured her family in their quest to satisfy their insatiable appetite. She prayed for her own survival, for Aengus and Chaytan and the mustang, and when the sound of the insect's wings intensified, she even prayed for Owen Breen's family.

When she stopped crying and the noise of the grasshoppers faded, the sun reappeared and a shaft of light fell on the wall of the cave. Goldie saw drawings of bears and tepees, of men with arrows, shapes that didn't appear to mean anything, small and large interwoven circles and one drawing of two people upside down. Goldie thought she might have imagined the pictures she saw, as she imagined that someone had led her through the swarms to the cave. Other times she thought it might be her own terror, so that her eyes made her see something that wasn't really there.

When Goldie eventually left the cave, the grasshoppers were still there but only on the surface. As she ran home, her naked feet barely ruffled them, and they rose and descended as quickly to finish their banquet. At the bottom of the hill nobody was there. For a fleeting moment she thought everybody had been eaten, even Baby Miriam and the blanket she sat on.

Goldie ran home as fast as she could, trying to escape the image of her brother and sister being eaten alive by the hungry swarms of hoppers. At the back of her cabin, Goldie met Sean Dwyer's Spanish wife. She was holding the spade and looking disbelievingly at the rough handle. They'd eaten the varnish.

"*Los hijos de puta*," she screamed, *sons of bitches*, and beat the ground. "*Putas sucias*."

When Mrs. Dwyer saw Goldie, she rushed toward her and began to cry. "*Donde esta* Baby Miriam?" *Where is Baby Miriam?*

Baby Miriam was gone. Eaten by the grasshoppers? Or carried into the sky and discarded at their next green feast?

In her small cabin, there was a melee of voices all talking at once. Her father was sitting at the table with his head resting in his hand.

"Was Baby Miriam eaten?" Goldie asked about the worst scenario.

Nobody heard her question. There were suggestions that she could have crawled into the forest and been taken by a bear or a coyote or an eagle. There was a suggestion that she was taken by the Indians. It was reported that the Indians had been seen passing through the area an hour prior to the grasshoppers' descent. They'd stolen an ox that was grazing by the river and raided the cabin of one of the homesteaders. They were seen heading in the direction of the O'Neill farm on their way to the Black Hills. Someone else said it was more likely that she'd crawled to the stream, her little body taken to another part of the West. That day, there were plenty of suggestions but little consolation in any of them.

Frances sidled up to Goldie and told her what happened in her absence. By the time the other children had returned to the cabin, their parents were lighting fires to stave off the grasshoppers. The children pitched in where they could. Time lapsed. After three hours, they'd asked after Goldie and Baby Miriam. "I told them that

Owen threw wood at you and you threw a snake at him and ran away."

Goldie stood still, looking from her father to her mother while Frances' voice shook as she spoke. "Dad went back to the edge of the wood but Baby Miriam wasn't there." Frances' voice wobbled as if she were about to cry, but she continued, "Dad knew you were alive because he said it would take more than a swarm of grasshoppers to kill you."

Goldie saw Mrs. Breen put her hand on her mother's back. She too was crying.

That evening, at dusk, Goldie watched as the men established a search party. They gathered at the O'Neills' cabin and some made a performance of loading their guns and noisily leaving to search for Baby Miriam. Even as they left the farm, most knew it was pointless. They rode up and down the banks of the river, but none were brave enough to go into the Black Hills, an area that was 120 miles deep and 45 miles wide.

"It's a lot of ground to cover," said one.

"If we go in, we might never come out again," said another.

Aengus was the only one who went into the forest. He went alone, taking his dog and horse. When his search yielded nothing, he went to the fur traders' post to meet his Indian friends. He returned that night empty-handed. Early the next morning, the same men combed the river. That too yielded nothing.

Baby Miriam had been gone three days when Owen Breen apologized to Goldie. She was standing outside the paddock watching Chaytan break a new black mustang.

"I'm sorry," Owen said, appearing beside her.

When she looked at him, she saw he had a black eye. Goldie had heard that Ned Breen allotted some of the blame to Owen. The idea that someone might share the responsibility never lessened Goldie's unyielding guilt.

"I'm really sorry," Owen repeated in a quiet voice.

Goldie never asked if he was sorry for chasing her, or if he was sorry Miriam was gone, or sorry that everyone was so sad and angry.

She nodded that she'd heard him before looking back at Chaytan.

She could hear Owen's step as he walked back toward the cabin where Ned Breen and some of the other men had gathered.

Goldie's mother didn't speak for days and didn't cry aloud or wail like Mrs. Dwyer. Her mother's loss was mourned quietly. Goldie noted her wet red eyes each day. One week after Baby Miriam's abduction, she saw her mother sitting alone at the back of their cabin staring into the hills.

Lorcan was the only one who seemed pleased at Baby Miriam's abduction. "I didn't like when you all made such a fuss over Baby Miriam. It's not such a bad thing that she's gone," he declared. "I'm the most important person in the family again."

Goldie's father shook his head in bewilderment.

They spent days speculating. One minute her father believed that Miriam had crawled to the stream that was only a short distance from where she was last seen. As quickly, he'd blame the Indians.

One week after the event, Goldie's father said that Chaytan was not wanted by the Indians or the whites, "And I don't want him either."

When he said that, Goldie knew he'd come to the conclusion, only at that moment, that the Indians had taken her.

"Nobody wants Chaytan," Barry said in the rushed angry manner he'd developed since Baby Miriam had gone missing. "He can break in the horses and leave once the job is done. Those Indians are a different breed. I hate them."

Goldie didn't hate the Indians. In fact, she believed that they had taken her sister as much as she believed an Indian had guided her to the cave, yet she'd never dare say that aloud. One of the visiting men said the swarm of grasshoppers could probably have killed Baby Miriam. He said they'd eat her eyes first, and the grasshoppers would attack the softest part of the body. Goldie couldn't bear to think of the grasshoppers feasting on her sister's green eyes. She was so sure the Indians had taken her, she said a prayer that they'd return her now that the grasshoppers had gone.

"Why don't the other Indians want Chaytan?" Lorcan asked her father.

"Because his father is a scout for the Army," Barry said.

"What's a scout?" Frances asked.

"It's an Indian who tells the Army where the other Indians are hiding. He helps the Army track them, and sometimes the scout negotiates. Basically, he's a traitor."

"So, the rest of the Indians won't let Chaytan or his family live with them?" Goldie asked. "Because his father's a traitor?"

"Yes," Barry confirmed. He stopped speaking and moved his boot on top of a long hopper on the floor.

Although the swarms were long gone, the odd grasshopper lingered. For weeks afterward, when they'd see the glowing wings of a grasshopper in the dark, they'd stop what they were doing to vengefully crush the insect between their fingers, relishing the crack of their nemesis' shell.

Her father stood on the grasshopper and twisted his foot, grinding on the insect before speaking, "He turned against his own. Men who have a divided nature are no good."

Although nobody blamed Goldie for Baby Miriam's abduction, and nobody pointed their finger and said aloud *it's your fault*, Goldie believed it was her fault. When the O'Neills rehashed the events to visiting neighbors, Goldie heard their voices laced with accusations. It was retold how Goldie had run from Owen Breen and hid, leaving the other children behind, how she was the oldest girl and should have taken better care of Baby Miriam. She should not have thrown the snake at Owen, because boys would always want retribution. She should not have entered the woods; she should have returned as soon as she saw the grasshoppers. Frances was not blamed. Although she was only eleven months younger than Goldie, Frances was smaller and prettier. People spoke differently to Frances, as if she didn't have the capabilities of Goldie. Lorcan was a boy, and boys were not responsible for children.

In the weeks after the event, they tried to resume their lives. Goldie wove a blanket on her mother's warp-weighted loom using the wool from a sheep that grazed in their paddock. According to

Neasa, Frances did not have the aptitude, whereas Goldie had a natural flair for weaving. Each product that Goldie made was appraised by her mother. There was one small blanket that Goldie didn't show anyone. It was made for a child, using wool from a sheep she called Hope.

Today, she took the blanket and a slate and returned to the hills. For the first time since Baby Miriam's disappearance, Goldie retraced her steps, hoping to find some indication that Baby Miriam had passed through. She checked the big tree with the hollow interior. She looked inside, but there was nothing except the small carcass of a bird. Then she continued to the cave. Goldie had her own plan.

Unlike the men who rode up and down the outskirts of the reservation making noise but doing nothing more, she'd try talking to the Indians. On a slate, she wrote a message to the Indians. 'Plees leeve Baby Miriam heer n the cave. I wil com and find her.' She placed the slate outside the cave. She picked bright yellow and purple flowers and laid them at both sides of the slate. She hoped the bright flowers would attract the attention of an Indian. Then she folded the blanket neatly for Baby Miriam and tucked it behind the slate and under the rock to keep it dry.

Goldie peered into the cave before squeezing through the small opening. She stood in perfect silence in the dark and stared at the wall, waiting for the sun to shine through the crack and light up the walls. When at last a glimmer of sunlight appeared, Goldie saw a picture of a tepee on the wall of the cave. As the clouds moved, the light poured onto another picture of two figures, and beside that a picture of an arrow. She sighed with relief that she hadn't imagined it.

"You're real," she said, tracing her fingers over the etching and drinking in the paintings as if they were the only great fragment of life that remained in the West.

In early August, two soldiers called at the O'Neills' cabin. One of them was an Irish soldier, Captain Gallagher. He'd heard about their fledgling Irish community.

He shook hands with the men and expressed his delight at

meeting his own people. "'Tis great to hear a nice Irish brogue as thick as my own."

Goldie heard Captain Gallagher tell the men that he'd come to America ten years ago and joined the Army straight away. "Got to see every corner of America in the Army. Carolina, Mississippi, Louisiana, and right up as far as Boston and New York. There are places in Leitrim ten miles from where I was born that I've never been." For the last two years he'd been posted to Wyoming, Colorado, and Idaho to deal with the Indian situation. "We do our best for the folks traveling west, but sometimes it don't do any good. This damn Indian War is a long way from being fixed when we're dealing with the Injun."

It was the first time Goldie had heard about an Indian War.

"Red Cloud won't lead nor drag," Captain Gallagher said about the chief of the Indians. He told them how the Indian tribes had been at war with each other for centuries, but now the Indian tribes were united in a new war against the white man.

"Are they really as barbaric as we've been told?" Barry asked.

"They sure are," Captain Gallagher confirmed. "They've got the best shot I ever did see. They can fire arrows from a galloping horse, and they don't spare the ax." He described the Indians springing from the long grass with hatchets raised and pointed arrows. "I seen one dead white man in Crazy Woman Creek with fourteen arrows in his body. He'd been stripped and scalped." He recounted what he had seen in an informative, indifferent manner, yet there was a note of admiration for the Indians' fighting abilities. "They could hunt down a battalion of armed soldiers and kill everyone with their crude bows and arrows. When I first came out here, I was told to save the last bullet for myself. Best die from my own hand than allow them to cook me slowly, and boy, do those Injuns know how to torture a man to death." Captain Gallagher removed a pouch of tobacco from his pocket and began to pack his pipe. "Me and the boys came across their camp down south. We found the charred remains of a man hanging over the ashes of a fire. He was so burned we could only tell he was white from the little tufts of brown hair on his sizzled scalp. They roasted him alive."

Goldie's mother cautiously set the food on the table.

"Roasted him alive!" Barry repeated in a whisper.

"They start at the bottom with the feet," Captain Gallagher said. "When your feet been burning for a while, you lose the feeling. So, the Injun moves the flame to a different part of your body, so the pain starts all over again." Captain Gallagher paused to light his pipe. "When they give chase you better hope you got a sturdy mule that'll move fast 'cause they don't give up too easily. And nobody knows this land like they do. They can survive on the driest stretch of dirt-land. They've been doing it for thousands of years," he concluded, before offering his tobacco to the men.

Barry accepted. Slowly, he packed his pipe. He commented on the moist tobacco, and he sounded as if he wanted to move off the subject of Indians and tortured whites.

Captain Gallagher held up the tobacco pouch, "That there pouch is a squaw's tit," he told them. "I must have killed twenty Indians the same day I got that pouch. Happened in Sand Creek, it only took two hours to kill more than 150 Indians." He let the pouch drop onto the table. "Old Harrison there," he pointed to one of the other soldiers, "he had a pouch made of a baby he cut out of a squaw. He lost it to me at poker, then I lost it the same day," Captain Gallagher said, laughing as he recounted it.

"Mostly women and children," Aengus said. "You attacked the village when the men were away."

"We sure did," Captain Gallagher said unapologetically. "One hundred and fifty fewer Indians in two hours. We done to them what they done to a woman and her three children about fifty miles from here. They hunted them like they were wild hogs, and then killed them and put wood up the woman's private part and done the same to the men."

Aengus stopped him, saying, "I think we should stop talking like this." He indicated Goldie, Frances, and their mother.

Lorcan was standing beside Captain Gallagher, his young excited eyes on the soldier's gun as he listened.

Immediately, Captain Gallagher stopped speaking, his tired eyes looking at each of the ladies. "I'm so sorry," he said, sounding genuinely apologetic. "I spent so long out here with soldiers and war, I forget my manners around good women."

Goldie's mother smiled uneasily.

A silence followed before Captain Gallagher spoke again, "Sometimes you gotta wonder, where is God in all of this?"

Everybody appeared to ask the same question.

CHAPTER EIGHT

1866

Although Chaytan became more comfortable in Goldie's company, most of the time she guessed that he only tolerated her. Many times, she likened him to the flighty, captive mustangs he tamed. By befriending and taming the mustangs, Chaytan was teaching them how they too could contain their disdain at the new immigrants who brought ideas of land-claiming and dominance. Chaytan did not have friends his own age; he didn't fish with the Breens or Dwyers as her brother Lorcan did. Many times, Goldie recalled her father saying that nobody wanted Chaytan, not the Indians or the whites. Sometimes she'd like to have told Chaytan that she wanted him. She'd like to tell him that when he rode the mustang it was one of the most beautiful sights in the West. And Goldie would like to tell him that she knew he was nice. When Pedro Dwyer's wheel fell off his wagon, she had seen Chaytan helping him fix it. Each day he'd bring the mustang to the edge of the corral so Lorcan could get a closer glimpse of the wild horse. If Chaytan had been interested, Goldie would have told him that she wanted him to come to her farm every day even if every white man in the world hated him and every Indian shunned him. Goldie never told him any of that; instead, each day she placed his lunch outside the mustang's corral and stayed with him while he ate it. Goldie didn't know if he'd prefer to eat alone.

"I need to know something," Goldie spoke slowly to Chaytan.

She sat on the ground and smoothed out the sand with her hand. Chaytan watched her inquisitively.

She drew two figures in the sand. Then she led Chaytan to the other side of the drawing so he was seeing it upside down.

Chaytan stopped eating. He looked at her suspiciously.

One of the drawings that Goldie saw in the cave was of two people drawn upside down. Initially, she'd tilted her head, thinking the artist had made a mistake. When she'd realized the artist had deliberately inverted the figures, instinctively she knew it meant something bad.

"What does this mean?" she asked.

Chaytan looked at her and then at the drawing.

"The day of the grasshoppers, I hid in a cave," she said, feeling the need to explain. Apart from giving her parents that factual account, nobody knew what she'd seen.

"Where?" Chaytan said. "Where you see?"

"I saw this in the cave," she said.

"Cave, where?"

Goldie pointed toward the hills, saying, "Close to where we get wood."

He nodded.

"It's a secret," Goldie said. To ensure he understood the seriousness of it, she put her finger to her lips. "A secret," she repeated, and then shook her head. "Don't tell anyone."

He appeared to understand.

"I'm not allowed go into the hills," she explained.

"How do you see in the cave?" he asked. "Dark?"

"I can only see the pictures when the sun shines through the opening," she said using hand gestures as she spoke. "The sun shines on the wall."

He nodded that he understood.

"What does it mean?" she asked.

Chaytan looked at the drawing, saying, "People go away."

That was his explanation.

Twice a month, Captain Gallagher visited their cabin and brought news of the ongoing Red Cloud War.

"In Fetterman, Red Cloud killed 100 soldiers," he told them, adding that the soldiers were hacked to death.

Aengus was quick to point out that the army and white men never tired of provoking the Indian.

"They roast men to death," Goldie's father said. He'd never quite gotten over that snippet of information.

"And the Indians learned how to torture from the Spanish," Aengus said.

Ned Breen was always ready to spit his fury at the Indians and praise the Americans. "The American government gave them reservations in the last treaty. They get money from the government for doing nothing," Ned said. "I sure would like to loll on my behind and get money and whiskey and food for doin' nothin'."

Aengus disagreed, "The Indians were promised food and money, and given land so scorched that it's only good for sand snakes." He pointed out that some of the Indian agents spent the money and sold the supplies. "When the Indians were starving and their people were dying, they went to the agent, who told them that if they were hungry, they could eat grass," Aengus said.

"You know what they did to that Indian agent?" Captain Gallagher asked.

"They killed him," Aengus said, "and stuffed his mouth with grass."

When Goldie heard talk of war and fighting Indians, she wondered what Red Cloud would do to her if he found her sitting alone in his cave? Would he scalp her? Maybe nail her to a tree and roast her alive?

Goldie decided that she'd explain to Red Cloud what she was doing. She was looking for her sister. She'd tell Red Cloud what she couldn't speak of in her own home. She'd explain to Red Cloud that each day she thought of Baby Miriam alone on her blanket when everybody ran away. She imagined her crying for someone to pick her up, for some consoling hand to stroke her red head. She might even tell Red Cloud that each day she almost cried over Baby Miriam but didn't. If she were feeling brave, she'd ask Red Cloud to kidnap her too, just for a while so she could be reunited with her sister.

Sometimes when Goldie returned to the cave, she'd rewrite her message to the Indians with improved spelling. Each new message was addressed to Red Cloud. Sometimes she hoped the sign and flowers would be gone, taken by the Indians who'd tell Baby Miriam that her sister was looking for her, news that would keep alive in Miriam, the knowledge that one day they would be reunited.

With the arrival of the first winter snow, it didn't deter Goldie from trekking up the hill to the sound of crunching snow beneath her feet. When Goldie was close to the tree with the hollow inside, she thought she heard movement behind her. She stopped walking and looked over her shoulder. She held her breath and peered into the woods, waiting to see if someone was really following her or if she had allowed Captain Gallagher's tales of war to scare her.

Goldie was adamant she wouldn't be scared. "Red Cloud," she called out.

There was something mysterious about him. So many times, she tried to imagine what he looked like. Saying his name aloud made her feel brave. "Red Cloud, are you following me?"

Goldie saw nothing, only the falling snow from the branches of the trees overhead and her footprints in the snow.

She continued toward the cave, looking over her shoulder every few minutes. Goldie had overheard Captain Gallagher tell her father that the Indians only stole children but scalped and killed adults. If it came to that, she'd tell Red Cloud that she was still a child.

When Goldie arrived at the tree with the hollow inside, she sat down. She tried to imagine life as a captive during the cold winter months. If Baby Miriam were alive, she'd be two years of age by now. She'd probably help the older children with their chores of collecting kindling for the fire or water from a stream. Although

Goldie had only seen one tepee on the wagon train, she thought their tepees were cozy with layers of warm fur blankets. Then she thought of the Indians who were starving, the hungry children who cried for food because the Indian agents had kept the supplies or sold them. Goldie said a prayer that her sister had been taken by a tribe with an honest Indian agent.

So engrossed in her thoughts, she suddenly heard crunching snow outside the tree, then a pair of moccasins appeared.

"Who are you?" Goldie tried to sound assertive.

Chaytan appeared at the opening. "Take me to the cave," he said.

"Damn you," she swore. She remained sitting until her racing heart had calmed. "Damn you," she said again, "I thought you were Red Cloud."

He didn't respond, only stood at the tree waiting.

She was so accustomed to seeing Chaytan in the mustang's corral, she thought the sight of him in the forest wearing his moccasins and a fur coat with a satchel over his shoulder was unusual. As they walked up the steep incline toward the cave, she told him that.

At the cave, Chaytan was too big to fit through the opening. In the snow he found a branch of a tree that he snapped in half. Fervently, he began hacking at the clay above the rock and scooping it out with his hands to widen the opening. Goldie joined him; breathlessly they dug and tossed the snow and clay away until the opening was wide enough that Chaytan squeezed through. Once inside the cave he made a small fire, then removed a rag that had been dipped in kerosene from his satchel. He lit it, and the cave opened up. Using the torch, they began inspecting the pictures.

"Summer," he said pointing at a series of upright lines. "Sickness," he indicated another symbol, then, "our family are home."

The pictures conveyed the stories of a people who'd lived in the West long before Goldie's wagon train hobbled across the plains to this remote outback. They were Chaytan's people, and as she watched his eyes hungrily move from each picture to the next, she realized it was the history of his people.

Chaytan began to move deeper into the cave. Goldie hesitated, as she had not considered that there was more to the cave than what she had seen.

Chaytan stopped, and he extended his hand toward her.

Only when his hand held hers did she realize that he wanted her with him. Under the light of the torch, they dipped further into the cavity of history.

CHAPTER NINE

February 1937
Lucy O'Neill-Livingston

Harry Livingston didn't like Goldie O'Neill. He didn't like her red hair that remained as vivid in old age as in her youth, or her choice of politics. He didn't like her vague Irish accent that became more pronounced when she was animated or her anecdotes that made everybody laugh except him. Lucy was all too aware of his litany of dislikes toward Goldie. Judging from Harry's clenched jaw, she also knew that he didn't like the fact that his feet had just touched Wyoming soil, and the taxi driver was extolling Goldie.

"I sure have fond memories of your aunt," the taxi driver said to Lucy.

It was late afternoon. Lucy and Harry had just flown into Wyoming. They had returned to the West to meet Lucy's father, Lorcan O'Neill. As soon as the taxi driver recognized Lucy, he began to talk about Goldie.

"She was mighty generous," the taxi driver added.

Harry was in the front seat. Lucy could see his chest rise as he took a deep breath and slowly exhaled. If Harry had been seated beside her, she could have reminded him that the trip would be over before it began, and they'd be back in New York in no time. Instead, she looked out the window at the open road and quiet countryside. They drove for miles without seeing man or child; the only sign of life was an abandoned cabin. The little homes that had once teemed with families were now used as shelter for livestock. The crumbling homes were testament to the hard life as a pioneer, as so many came and fled as quickly from the unkind extremes of the West.

"Every year Goldie gave her workers Christmas boxes, and she gave 'em to the colored folks too," the taxi driver added.

Lucy knew about Goldie's generosity. She'd built a theater, sponsored festivals, gave money to the town's committees, and helped families on the brink of starvation. The only area she didn't sponsor was education. Goldie deemed it a long harrowing pointless chore.

"Not much happening in these old towns no more," the taxi driver continued. "I tell my son about the days when Four Oaks was busier than Chicago or New York with workers. Hard to believe it now," he said, staring ahead. "The machines are replacing the workman."

Lucy agreed with him.

"The world is changing," he added. "Look at you folks, you just hop on a plane from New York to Wyoming. Who'd believe that you could do that?"

Lucy agreed, "Yes, it's a different world."

There was a silence, as if each were considering the world that became more convenient for every generation.

"They say sitting on a plane is like sitting in your living room but you're miles up in the sky," the taxi driver said, then leaned forward in his seat and looked up at the sky as if expecting to see a plane. "Although, it ain't no good being up there if you got a problem with the accelerator," he added with an air of caution.

Lucy smiled. She enjoyed listening to his ramblings. She had an image of him and his son sitting at their kitchen table discussing the old days and the workings of a plane. There was something primitive and unstained about the people of the West. There was an acceptance in most. They didn't harbor the same desires as the city folk, or the likes of Harry, who couldn't sit still. Lucy was guilty of it too. Since Goldie's death, Lucy had wanted something more, but she couldn't put a name on exactly what it was that she wanted. Sometimes she thought she wanted something less, a simple life like the taxi driver and his son. Or a husband who was content to return to his wife's hometown, or even a husband who didn't need to take the lead role in every decision.

"You're the man on the radio," the taxi driver said to Harry.

Lucy saw Harry's features soften slightly. He said he was and gave the taxi driver a brief smile.

"Round here we all know that Lucy married the man on the radio," he said.

It appeared as if Harry was someone. He had a weekly slot on an economics program on the radio that reached the residents of Four Oaks. He was also a partner in an Investment firm, and he wrote a weekly article on finance in the *New York Times*. People seemed more impressed with the radio than his business or article. Harry liked it when people thought he was a man of importance, a local celebrity in Four Oaks.

"Don't know much about finance," the taxi driver said, "money comes in one hand and goes out the other. Ain't that the truth!"

"Sure is," Harry said.

At forty-five years of age, Harry was still handsome. At parties she saw other women stand close to him, too close for another man's wife. Harry enjoyed it; he even encouraged it. He was lean and tall with fair curly hair. He had strong features and almond-shaped eyes. He took great pride in his appearance and exercised daily. He was a subscriber to the new fitness craze by employing the services of a fitness instructor. It made no sense to Lucy. Who would pay a man to tell you what to eat and instruct you how to move and then measure your body once a week? "That boyo is as vain as a dirty old peacock," Goldie said when she first met Harry. Goldie never realized the extent of his vanity. He wore cream on his face, and recently he'd bought a heat-emitting thermocap that he sat under to promote hair growth. Lucy found it so funny, that Harry had stopped using it. Secretly, she suspected he used his heated thermocap when she wasn't there.

The taxi driver began to talk about Goldie again. He mentioned her knowledge of the local area. "I heard she knew every inch of those hills, and she knew about Wind Cave long before anyone else," he said, referring to the most famous cave.

Harry emitted a long, exasperated sigh.

"She found the cave when she was looking for the baby who went missing. Ain't that right?" The taxi driver looked at Lucy in the rearview mirror.

"Something like that," Lucy half-heartedly said.

"Some say the baby fell into a stream, and then others will tell you the Indians took it. Nobody really knows the truth, only God Himself."

"Do you reckon the Indians took the baby?" Harry asked.

The Breens had told Harry the story about the day of the grasshoppers, and Lucy confirmed the little bit she knew.

"Don't rightly know," the taxi driver said. "Back then, the Indians roamed all these parts when there was only a handful of homesteaders. There were no lawmen and no laws."

"Only the gun," Harry said.

The taxi driver agreed, "Only the gun and a belly full of courage."

Lucy saw Harry look out the window at the landscape.

These were stories of the West that people wanted to hear about. They wanted to know about the lawless men, the shoot-outs, and cruel Indians. The stories that Hollywood told of barbaric wars and slow deaths at the mercy of the Sioux. Lucy saw the tourists arrive each year to reenact their ideas of the first pioneers. These visitors would shoot bears and buffaloes as if their life depended on the meat for survival. Harry fell into that bracket of man, those who were impressed with the stories from the West. It was Harry who told Lucy that President Lincoln began his days in a homesteader's cabin and ended his days in the White House. New York City-born President Theodore Roosevelt used the myth of the West to get elected, and Hollywood never tired of churning out gunslinging heroes on horseback. The reality of the West was far less glamorous than most imagined.

"Only last week, Mrs. Kelly tried to tell me the baby was Goldie's child," the taxi driver said.

"What year did the baby go missing?" Harry suddenly asked.

"It happened when the grasshoppers came, '66 or '74," he said.

"Goldie would have been seventeen or eighteen," Harry said. He looked over his shoulder at Lucy. "It could have been Goldie's child."

Lucy knew that Harry would like nothing more than to think that Goldie had a child out of marriage. It would be another reason to vilify her, but he was wrong. The baby had gone missing in '66, a year after the O'Neills arrived. Goldie had been ten.

"It wasn't Goldie's child," Lucy said. "It was her sister."

There were very few families who survived to tell the story of Baby Miriam's disappearance. At an early age, Lucy had known that Goldie didn't want to talk about it. It wasn't a secret, just one of those family stories left alone. Instead, Goldie taught Lucy the magnificent old fables about the spiritual significance of the Black Hills for the Native Indians. She told her that the Lakota believe that the Black Hills is where life began. Beneath the hills, there is a labyrinthine cave network that is the densest in the known world. The Indians believed they and the buffalo originated from Wind Cave. They entered the world together, and this was where they'd lived for centuries, with the Indian dependent on the buffalo for survival. Although some of the caves were only discovered in the 1920s, Goldie told Lucy that she'd stumbled on them as a child, "long before that old explorer gave up searching for the end to the caves," Goldie said, referring to a man employed to map the caves, and who had been unable to complete his task because the cave was so complex.

In the distance, Lucy could see the hills, their peaks stretched into the clouds. They were enigmatic, powerful, overbearing -- they were home. She felt a tingling of excitement as the taxi began the climb toward Four Oaks.

As soon as they arrived in town, the taxi driver slowed down and began to comment on the locals.

"Gallagher's Hotel is doing mighty fine." he said. "Bertha knows how to feed hungry men with big dinners and sweet apple pies."

Lucy leaned forward to admire the two-story hotel. Blazed across the front was the name and at both sides of the name she read Billiards and Dance Hall.

"Who could forget the old Captain Gallagher!" the taxi driver remarked.

"Yes, I remember him," Lucy said.

He was an old Irish soldier who had played his part in the Indian wars and had been a great friend of Lucy's grandfather. His heroics garnered him as much respect as his longevity. After he left the Army, he bought land from the Breens and used the timber from the O'Neills to build the first saloon in Four Oaks. Captain Gallagher lived into his nineties. Each Sunday, Goldie and Lucy had dinner in the hotel, and there was always an exchange with Captain Gallagher. Lucy remembered his old shriveled body sitting in the shade outside his hotel. His eyes were so hooded, she wasn't sure he could see anything. Goldie assured Lucy that he saw her. "He sees everything," Goldie said in a nice way.

As they drove slowly down the main street, the taxi driver continued to comment on the locals. Lucy was reminded of Goldie at every juncture; she saw her sitting outside the ice-cream store, leaning across the counter of Kelly's Store extracting all the news from Mrs. Kelly, and later coming home to tell Lucy the latest.

"Mayor Breen is doing his best but sometimes it's no good," the taxi driver said as they passed Wilbur's office. His shiny car was parked outside.

"He's still got his Model V-8," Harry said, referring to Wilbur's Ford, which was as much a focal point in the town as Gallagher's Hotel and the statue of Lorcan O'Neill.

Just then, John Dwyer crossed the road in front of their car. Lucy watched him walking into the strong wind. He took long strides, his blond hair swept back from the breeze. The Dwyers had come west on the same wagon train as Goldie's family. John's father,

Pedro Dwyer, was a lifelong friend of Goldie's. The last time that Lucy had seen John Dwyer was six months ago at Goldie's funeral. His sympathies were genuine and heartfelt.

"Ah," Harry said in mock surprise when he spotted John Dwyer, "the sheep man is still wearing his father's coat."

John was wearing a sheepskin coat. It looked warm on this cold afternoon.

"It's not his father's coat," Lucy said. She saw him enter Kelly's Store.

"You're right, it's not his father's coat," Harry said. "It came from the sheep he killed and ate this morning."

There was a time when Lucy would have laughed at that.

Apart from Harry, John Dwyer had been Lucy's only other boyfriend. When she was nineteen, Lucy and John had talked about marriage and children and a house with a three-sisters vegetable garden, a system the Indians had taught the settlers, in which three main crops grow symbiotically to deter weeds and pests, enrich the soil, and support each other. Their garden would be as harmonious as their union, or so she'd thought at the time. Over the last few months, Lucy had thought how different her life would have been if she'd stayed put and married John Dwyer as planned. She'd be living on his farm, and she'd probably have brushed the coat he wore this afternoon. Only now, at the age of thirty-five, and sixteen years into a childless marriage, Lucy had time to dwell on the what-ifs and sometimes indulge her regrets. It was all irrelevant, as John Dwyer had married a girl from Chicago, had three young daughters, and according to Goldie, had a three-sisters garden.

They passed the school, the Catholic church, the enormous statue of Lorcan O'Neill, and then they were back into the countryside, where they passed the Breen farm. Wilbur's family was also one of the founding members of Four Oaks. The O'Neills and Breens had traveled together on the same wagon train to the West as the first homesteaders in Four Oaks. Wilbur loved to mention his family's pioneering history in his political speeches. His family was the first generation that staved off lawless men, built churches and jailhouses, irrigated the land, and according to various accounts, fought the Indians. They also made money and built a mansion befitting a man with his family's high notions. Wilbur lived in the family home with his mother, Lucy's Aunt Frances, and her husband, Owen Breen. Quietly, Lucy speculated on Aunt Frances' thoughts on Lorcan returning. She was very proud of her brother, and could often be seen looking forlorn at the statue of Lorcan. "My brother, the war hero," she'd say. Goldie would raise her eyes intolerantly, and sometimes she'd mutter the odd profanity under her breath, "Bloody Godforsaken eejit of a woman." Lucy knew Frances would be sitting in their living room in her wine velvet armchair where she always sat and drove her maids crazy with orders. Her husband, Owen, would be sitting across from her. Owen was all but dead after a stroke left him wheelchair bound. Despite his disability, he was mentally alert. His eyes would follow visitors as they came and went; nothing went unseen by Owen Breen.

As they drove higher into the hills, Lucy's childhood home came into view. She could see the old colonial-style house nestled on the side of the hill. She smiled and leaned forward as if she couldn't get there fast enough. Behind the house was the farm, the barns, paddocks, and stables, while behind that was the woolen mill, and higher in the hill was the land where the sheep used to graze and grow thick coats of wool. Although Goldie had made money in livestock and investments, her pride lay in the wares produced in her mill, Wyoming Tweed. It wasn't only Wilbur Breen who used his family history to further his political career. Goldie often used her family history of weaving that dated back to the seventeenth century in Ireland to promote her business. Goldie had left the mill and her many looms to Makawee and her daughter, Winona, although Wilbur and most of the town's folk thought that Lucy also owned it.

"Ain't never will be anyone like her again," the taxi driver said as they approached the entrance.

"No," Lucy agreed as they advanced down the drive toward the house.

Just then she thought about Goldie's life and the events that had shaped it. She thought about her beginnings in Ireland, her sea voyage to America, followed by the trek across the West to arrive as a young girl in an unfamiliar open country. She thought of her contradictions, as Goldie was obstinate and brutal, generous and empathetic. She was the child who endured and became the woman who thrived. Lucy thought of all that was unsaid, the conditions she'd overcome to allow her Irish Catholic colony to survive, the grasshoppers, and her absent sister, Baby Miriam. In the end, Goldie went to bed with her gun like someone who was expecting one final caller.

When the taxi driver stopped at her home, Lucy thanked him and looked toward the front door, half-expecting Goldie to appear with open arms and shouting an array of excited greetings. Her absence tore at Lucy so much, the pain was almost physical.

Harry whispered, "At least the old battle-ax isn't here to pick holes in me."

CHAPTER TEN

1937 February

While Harry brought the bags upstairs, Lucy walked around the rooms downstairs. Everything stood in the same place as the night Goldie had died, yet the house yawned with her absence. Knowing she was dead didn't stop Lucy from looking at her empty chair in the living room or expecting Goldie's voice to break the silence. The house was warmer than she had expected. The fires were lit in each room. Lucy knew her neighbor, Winona, had been there and gone. Lucy had sent a telegram from the airport in New York, letting her know that she was on her way. Winona had left fresh milk and supplies in the fridge. There was also maple syrup with pecans and cornbread. Lucy smiled and was suddenly hungry.

She made coffee and cut a large chunk of the bread, coated it with syrup, and returned to the living room. It was a long, large living room, big enough for several armchairs and sofas at one end, which faced the hill behind the house. Along the wall there was a sideboard with a lifetime of reminders, photographs, an ornament from Dallas, an eagle's feather encased in glass, and a snow globe from New York. Behind the sofas was a dining room table and eight chairs, and at the other end of the room was a loom. It was placed by the window that overlooked the town.

Lucy lit three lamps and sank into Goldie's old comfortable armchair, which faced the hill. Goldie had told Lucy about her early days in the West when the Indians owned the Black Hills. There were stories of men going into the hills and never returning. Sean Dwyer was one such unfortunate man. He went panning for gold and never returned to tell them what he'd seen. However, in the 1900s, two hunters found a stone onto which was carved, 'Got all the gold I can carry, I've lost my pistol. The Indians are hunting me.' It was dated the same year that Sean Dwyer had vanished. The rock had been displayed in Gallagher's Hotel for years. As a child, Lucy would gape with macabre fascination at the last sighting of Sean Dwyer.

Lucy finished eating and sat back. Then she was struck by the silence; it was as if she were the only occupant of the immense West. For a moment, she sat still, savoring the calm until Harry's feet on the wooden floor above made her look up. He was in Lucy's old bedroom.

Most nights Lucy had fallen asleep to the hum of voices below her. Goldie's house was rarely without visitors or old friends who were passing through town and needed a bed. Goldie was a wonderful host who fed and watered her guests with genuine hospitality. She'd talk into the early hours, never appearing to need as much sleep as most people. Lucy often lay awake until she heard Goldie's step on the stairs. Goldie's bedroom was directly across the hall from Lucy's, and as a child, Lucy found great comfort in their close proximity. There were many nights when Lucy had crept from her own bed and climbed in beside Goldie.

Lucy could hear the clip of Harry's heel leave her bedroom. He paused on the landing. She heard him enter Goldie's bedroom; it sounded as if he was walking around the bed.

After a few minutes she heard his feet on the stairs.

"Look what I found," he said, appearing behind her with a gun. "Goldie's gun was still under the pillow. Look at the size of it," he said. He held it in his open hand to demonstrate its size. "Is it real?"

"Yes," Lucy said, watching him as he pointed it toward the window.

When Lucy had initially come to live in Four Oaks, the house terrified her. Sleeping alone in a room was frightening after sharing a dormitory with dozens of children in the orphanage in Denver. When Goldie realized that Lucy was afraid, she took Lucy into her bedroom and picked up the pillow, showing Lucy the tiniest silver gun she'd ever seen. "A Derringer," Goldie had announced, "it's the smallest gun in the world and does exactly what a Colt .45 will do." Goldie had picked up the gun, "Now, I'll blow the head off anyone who comes in here. I'll splatter their brains until my walls are covered in their gray matter." It was not the language of reassurance for anyone, least of all a child, yet it did bring a degree of reassurance. Although it didn't stop Lucy from occasionally creeping across the landing to climb in beside Goldie. She'd watch the rise and fall of Goldie's chest and marvel at how her hairnet stayed in place for the night.

The night that Goldie died, Lucy woke after midnight. It was one of those soundless nights. Lucy didn't know what had prompted her to leave her own bed and go to check on Goldie. She'd touched her cold face and knew she was dead. Lucy curled up as she had done as a child and studied the outline of her features. As the minutes passed and Goldie's chest didn't rise and fall, she felt something die in her too. She cried like a wailing child. The memory brought that same disbelief she'd experienced since Goldie's death. She really is dead.

"It's engraved," Harry said, holding the underside of the handle to the light. "To G from C, 1890. Was C her husband?"

"No, it was from her friend, Chaytan," Lucy said, looking at one of the photos on the sideboard with Chaytan and Goldie together.

Harry stood in the center of the floor pointing the gun at various ornaments, then he pointed it at Lucy, "Hands up," he said in a fake Southern accent.

"The gun is loaded," Lucy informed him.

He ignored her and continued playing his imaginary role. "My name is Harry," he said, switching from a Southern drawl to an exaggerated deep voice that Lucy could only assume was meant to be menacing, "and I'm going to accost you, my little prairie girlie."

Lucy was amused.

Slowly he walked toward her with Goldie's gun cocked. He bent down and kissed her.

"My prairie girl tastes mighty fine," he said, standing up straight and narrowing his eyes in another attempt at playing the womanizing gunslinger from the movies. "Maybe I'll steal another kiss," he said.

There were times when Harry was amusing and playful, but recently it was a rarity. So much had happened without being said. Over the last few years, Lucy noticed how Harry needed reassurance and validation. He liked when Lucy listened to his radio program and commended his show, and it was even better if she could mention some part of the show during which he had spoken particularly well. He liked to be liked and found unwarranted faults with those who didn't like him. He told her every detail of his working day, and each account was filled with praise for his principles or his integrity or his leadership. He liked it when Lucy agreed with him and would commend his characteristics that everyone else lacked, but it took more and more effort to listen and respond to the events of his day. Lucy didn't know if he had always been so needy; or if his neediness had been there all the time and she'd only noticed it recently. Sometimes she thought it was another side effect of her grief, one of Harry's many little nuances that she'd suddenly noticed and found tiresome. In the last few years, she hadn't been as soothing or agreeable. Periodically, Lucy felt sorry for Harry, and she knew exactly how to soothe him. Occasionally, watching him struggle with insecurities was satisfying. Her own behavior made her feel guilty, so she'd appease Harry, and the cycle continued before she withdrew again. Lucy had long suspected he'd gone elsewhere, to other women, for approval and the attention he craved. As she'd never aired her suspicions, Harry had never asked why she distanced herself from him. It was a marriage of unaired grievances.

Now, Harry kissed her and Lucy went with it. She'd often

wished they could go back to the first few years before it got so difficult and complicated. She missed the days when he was calm and
fun-loving. She welcomed his hands as they ran over her hips.

Suddenly he stopped. "Jesus Christ," he said as he stepped back.

Lucy looked at his rounded startled eyes.

"A mouse," he shrieked, "or maybe a rat, it just ran across the
room." He took another step back. "It just caught the corner of my
eye," he continued as if she doubted him.

Lucy looked over her shoulder where he pointed but couldn't see
anything.

"Right there," he said pointing the gun at the floor beneath the
dining table.

"You're not thinking of shooting the mouse?" Lucy said, taking
Goldie's gun from him.

"This house is crawling with mice," Harry said, still distressed
about the offending mouse, "probably crawling with rats and dust
and...."

"Spiders and creepy crawlies!" Lucy said, making light of his
complaint.

This was one of the issues Goldie had had with Harry.
According to Goldie, Harry was a new breed of American, a city
boy who had the solutions to all their rural problems from drought
to diseases, yet he was afraid of a mouse.

"You're not listening to me," Harry continued.

"For goodness sake, every old house has mice," she said, getting
impatient with his hysterics, "especially a house without occupants."

"This is why I hate visiting country houses; you people think it's
all right to share a house with mice."

Lucy rolled her eyes at that. Although she didn't like to think
that there was a nest of vermin under the sideboard, she made a
mental note to borrow Makawee's dog, as the terrier would rid the
house of all mice within a day.

"Have you any idea how they spread disease?" he added,
looking around him with real fear.

"It's only a mouse," she said.

"It's high time you sold this house," he said, returning to the source of his discontent. He'd never liked the house because it belonged to Goldie, one of the few people who did not approve of Harry. "The floorboards creak, the wind whistles through it, and it could very well cave in on us tonight while we sleep in our beds," he continued, his tone getting angrier with each utterance. "Not that anybody would buy it. The only thing to do is knock it down."

Lucy had no notion of knocking down the house. Apart from needing a paint job, the house was as sturdy as when it was built by Goldie's husband in the 1890s. At the time, it had been modern, with verandas downstairs and upstairs; their outhouse was situated in-house and had a flush toilet to boot. Now, in the 1930s, it was a big old-fashioned imposing country house filled with her fondest memories.

"It's a big, useless, creaking, cold historic house." he reiterated.

"It's my useless, creaking historic home," Lucy replied.

"You're welcome to it." Harry continued. He wouldn't let up.

She saw him peering at the seat of the armchair. His clean light-colored trousers were a contrast to the dark upholstered armchair.

"There's fresh coffee in the pot," she said.

Harry didn't respond.

Lucy poured a fresh cup and sat down again. She thought of Goldie's excited bellowing voice when she talked about Lucy's future. Many times, Goldie had told Lucy that the world was her oyster and that she could become anything she wanted. She told her she was lucky to be born in a time when women could go to college and enter professions that were previously open only to men. "You can be a doctor or lawyer or cowgirl," Goldie had said, making the profession of *cowgirl* sound as reputable as doctor. "You can be anything," she'd say in her customary excited voice, as if Goldie were also young with a world of opportunity laid out before her. Now, as Lucy watched Harry's pathetic fussing, she was pleased Goldie was not alive to see it.

Harry sat down and crossed his legs. He pointed at the armchairs and rug on the floor. "They're crawling with almost half a century of dust." he said.

"Actually, they're crawling with more than half a century of dust," Lucy corrected him. Some of the rugs dated back to the 1890s, and one rug had been woven in 1866. "I'm quite proud of my old rugs and seventy-year-old dust mites," Lucy added.

"Yes, Ms. Havisham," he replied sarcastically, "you won't be happy until you're found dead with dust and cobwebs hanging from your eyelashes, alone in your primitive house with nothing for company except scurrying mice," he said, referring to the Dickens novel.

Lucy ignored him.

Harry wiped the arm of the chair before resting his elbows on them. They sat in silence for a few moments before Harry sat forward and squinted into the distance, saying, "There is a car in the field."

Lucy saw headlights circle the field and stood up for a better look. It was John Dwyer, the man they'd seen in town earlier. He rented all of Lucy's land that Goldie had left her.

"Who is it?" Harry asked.

"John Dwyer. He's probably checking on his sheep." She squinted into the dusky evening, hoping to catch a glimpse of him. She stayed watching the headlights until they left the field and drove down the hill and passed the house.

"Aren't you lucky I saved you from him, a life of toil and probably darning socks and weaving blankets to sell so you could feed your children?"

The Breens had told Harry the stories about Sean Dwyer, but they never gave Harry the updated version of their story, how Sean's son, Pedro, had improved the land that was untouched during his father's time. The rest of the Dwyer children were lawmen and sheriffs. Emilio, who had been born on the wagon train west, had become the hangman. And the present sheriff in Four Oaks was Emilio's grandson.

"Pedro Dwyer's children have never gone hungry," Lucy said, "they have a few thousand sheep to kill at the first hunger pangs."

Lucy took her dirty dish to the kitchen.

Until she met Harry, Lucy's world had begun and ended in Four Oaks. At nineteen years of age, she'd worked side by side with

Goldie and her team of weavers in the mill. Her evenings were spent with her first boyfriend and the only man she'd considered marrying, John Dwyer. It appeared as if she'd forgo the cowgirl or high-brow professions of doctor or lawyer to become a housewife when she'd marry John Dwyer. She'd live twenty minutes' drive from Goldie's front door on the Dwyer farm. Lucy told Goldie of her plans, and she described the house that she and John had discussed. They'd have a painted front door as opposed to the ordinary timber door; they'd have a living room like Goldie's with views from the front and back and a three-sisters garden. Goldie thought it a fine idea, such a fine idea it would appear she was more in love with the idea than Lucy and John were. "And on Sundays I'll treat you and John to dinner at Gallagher's. Pedro Dwyer and I can talk about sheep and wool and farming," Goldie had said, referring to John's father. Goldie and Lucy were like a couple of girls who'd tumbled out of a romance novel. They discussed the best time of year to get married, and who they'd invite. Goldie even mentioned having a big tent, "Like they had in *Every Woman* magazine." Lucy was too carried away with the excitement to interrupt Goldie by asking where had she seen *Every Woman* magazine. "We'll fill this tent to the brim with everyone we know," she'd enthused, her voice growing louder and more excited with each utterance.

Lucy told John her plans. According to John, it was a given that she'd look after the wedding and Sunday dinners at Gallagher's were fine by him, but he couldn't have Goldie paying; John would insist on paying for dinner. Each evening, John and Lucy pored over their plans in the soda bar looking onto Four Oak's main street.

John's father, Pedro Dwyer, was a forward-thinking farmer who believed that education was the only way farmers could progress. Pedro Dwyer would take advantage of the college grant by sending John to Dakota Agriculture College, so that when he'd return, he'd take over the farm. He'd learn how to bring the farm into the future with modern machinery and clean ideas. Lucy remembered Goldie raising her eyes with irritation when she heard about the Dwyer's educational plans. Goldie, who could barely write, thought an education a waste of time and a waste of good money. Many times, she'd point out men with fine educations who were as poor as church mice. Nonetheless, John left for Dakota, and Goldie did her best to console Lucy. During the first month of his absence, Lucy wrote reams of letters. Goldie said Lucy would give herself cramps in the fingers from all her letter writing. When she wasn't writing letters, she was waiting for the postman to arrive with John's letters. John, in turn, wrote long letters describing the city, the house where he boarded, how many sheep he'd sheared to earn extra money, and the subjects he studied. He told her he missed her, he missed home, and he missed Goldie. When Lucy finished reading the letter, she put pen to paper and wrote him a long romantic letter, all of which was read aloud to Goldie before it was placed in the envelope, sealed, and sent with a thousand kisses. Similar to the wedding plans, Goldie got caught up in the romance of it all, and she too attempted to write a letter to John, but the spelling and writing were so illegible that Goldie then dictated the letter, which Lucy wrote. In Goldie's letter she told John Dwyer he was missed terribly by everyone. She told him about the lambs she'd bought and the first signs of the winter approaching.

"Anything else?" Lucy had asked.

"Yes, there damn well is," Goldie said, "John, if you're lonely, don't be bothered wasting another minute on this education malarkey. Everything I own will be yours and Lucy's. Tell him that," Goldie said, pointing at the letter.

"We'll stick to describing the new sheep and winter," Lucy decided.

While John Dwyer was 400 miles away in Fargo, North Dakota, with his nose in the books, planning to return to Four Oaks with improved ideas of farming, a different kind of man came from New York to visit his aunt, Leonora Breen.

Harry Livingston was ten years Lucy's senior and divorced. He lived in an apartment in New York, and according to his cousin, Wilbur Breen, there was a picture of Harry in his New York apartment with the actress, Mary Pickford. Harry worked in stock and shares; although Lucy wasn't entirely sure what that involved, it seemed apt that Harry Livingston would work at something that required a great brain. He was vastly different from the other men in Four Oaks. He wore fashionable clothes, and he was very hand-some. He was confident, polite, and charming. He'd seen the world and had that manner of a man who could achieve just about anything. He did the unthinkable back then, he went running for exercise. Only he was so handsome and educated they would have said he was soft in the head. But a man like Harry Livingston was not soft in the head. He'd been to Europe and Hawaii, he went to fashionable restaurants, and he knew how to salsa dance.

Lucy met him at the Harvest Festival in Four Oaks. He taught her the basics of salsa dancing and, there was something exotic in the movement of their hips. He placed his hands on her waist to demonstrate. With each erotic movement, John Dwyer's romantic letters and notions of a spring wedding and a three-sisters garden edged away.

Harry stayed an extra week in Four Oaks. One month later he returned and the salsa lessons continued.

"This. Must. Stop," Goldie had finally bellowed one night, banging her hand so hard on the table that the cups bounced.

Lucy told Goldie that Harry could salsa dance, he lived in an apartment, and he'd had his picture taken with Mary Pickford. Goldie said she'd find someone else to teach her salsa. As for his apartment in New York, Goldie said, "Who the hell wants to live in the sky? You don't even have a front door or a garden." And she claimed that it was easy to get your picture taken with Mary Pick-ford. When asked how easy it was to meet Mary Pickford, Goldie couldn't really say. "I expect she walks around the streets of New York all the time."

On the quiet, wide, dusty streets of Four Oaks, Lucy and Harry talked about their future together in New York. He told her they'd go to new plays on Broadway and concerts in Carnegie Hall. They talked about waking up together in Harry's apartment, how they'd take a boat ride out to see the Statue of Liberty and shop in depart-ment stores. She made plans with a similar air of optimism as she had done with John Dwyer. Lucy noted that Harry was even confi-dent about asking Goldie for Lucy's hand in marriage. He told Lucy that he remembered Goldie from his childhood visits to Four Oaks. When he did come to ask Goldie for Lucy's hand, he brought her a bunch of flowers and a box of chocolates. For an hour he talked about his life; he told her about the countries he'd seen, that he was educated at Harvard and worked in finance just like his father. He mentioned the radio slot and made himself sound like the best catch in the West. He told Goldie the same story he'd told the Breens, that he'd eaten frogs' legs in France. It was exotic then, a world removed from the one-horse town.

"It's a delicacy," Harry told Goldie.

"And what about your wife?" Goldie asked. "Was she eating those frogs' legs with you?"

Harry explained that the marriage was nullified because she had left him.

Goldie refused to taste the chocolates, and a few weeks later when Harry returned to ask Goldie for Lucy's hand in marriage, she refused that too.

Afraid that Harry would return alone to his apartment with his picture of Mary Pickford, Lucy begged Goldie to give the wedding her blessing.

Goldie accused Lucy of being as naïve as Leonora Breen. "You won't be a wet week in New York when you'll see the real boyo beneath that Brill-Creamed head. You'll end up like Mrs. Breen and that imbecilic sister of mine."

Goldie had finally relented and given the marriage her blessing, but in the same breath she thanked the Lord that divorce was legal in Wyoming.

Her final words of caution on the matter were expressed the morning of Lucy's wedding, "In a few years' time, that boyo will be an old, cranky, wrinkled man, and you will still be elegant and beautiful."

Lucy and Harry had been married in New York sixteen years ago. Goldie cried throughout the ceremony.

All these years later, Lucy didn't see Harry as being old, and she couldn't determine if he was cranky. She could only admit she found his company wearisome and saw flaws that were accentuated with each passing year.

Lucy dried the dishes and put them on the sideboard. She went to the front door and opened it to look into the night. There was nothing to see at this hour, only the silhouette of the snowy mountains against the indigo sky. All that happened now took place on the floor of the forest, where the nocturnal animals came out to hunt. It was the teeming unseen that she thought about then. The badgers and bats, the cougars and coyotes, all vying for survival.

"What are you doing?" Harry called from the living room. "There is a gust of freezing wind making this damn house even colder," he shouted.

Lucy looked over her shoulder and down the long corridor to the light from the living room. She couldn't see him, but she did see the mouse. It zigzagged across the hall, then stopped outside the living room door. Much to her surprise, the mouse sat on its hunkers and looked at her, as if regarding her.

Lucy crept towards the mouse. She lightly tapped her foot on the floor, and the mouse rose from its pensive pose and retreated into the living room.

"I'm going out for a breath of fresh air," she called.

When she closed the door behind her, she heard Harry's screams piercing the silence.

Lucy smiled.

CHAPTER ELEVEN

1868

Red Cloud's War ended with the Lakota Indians and their allies as the victors. There was a new agreement. The 1868 Fort Laramie Treaty ceded all rights of the Black Hills to the Indians for the rest of their lives. President Grant promised never to interfere with the new Indian Territory again. Goldie was jubilant for the victors, Red Cloud and the tribe she'd never met. It appeared that the sacred hills would remain unstained without dirt roads or smoke drifting into the sky from settlers' cabins.

"The treaty won't last," Captain Gallagher declared in his offhand way. "Them boyos in Washington have written hundreds of treaties, and every last one has been broken."

Captain Gallagher was sitting at their table counting out money. When he had four notes and two neat piles of coins, he slid them toward Goldie's father. "Payment for three blankets and two mustangs."

Captain Gallagher proved to be a steady source of income for Barry O'Neill. He bought the blankets that Goldie wove, which he sold to the soldiers. He had also promised to buy the mustangs after

Chaytan broke them. In turn, he'd sell them to the Army after taking another cut for himself.

Captain Gallagher tucked the neatly folded blankets under his arm. "Something cozy to cling to during these cold nights while we wait for this damn peace to end."

Since the arrival of peace, Captain Gallagher said the soldiers had a new war to fight— boredom.

"Is it that bad?" Goldie's father asked.

"For thirteen dollars a month we ain't got nothing to do but battle the dreariness and the cold."

"Will the peace end soon?" Lorcan asked.

Each time Captain Gallagher visited, Lorcan would sit in on their conversations, his imagination spiraling at the thoughts of a being a man at war. At that stage, he sensed from the Breens that the Indians were the enemy, yet he didn't see Chaytan as an Indian. Ned Breen and each of the Breen boys hated the Indians, though Goldie never knew why. If anyone should have had a reason for hating them, it was Captain Gallagher, yet he seemed to admire them as survivors and warriors. Goldie's father didn't hate the Indians. In a peculiar way, Barry understood the natives' struggle, but it was not his struggle. Goldie could never hate them. Regardless of the many theories about Baby Miriam's disappearance, Goldie believed the Indians had taken her and in doing so, they'd spared her the worse kind of death. Equally, she believed that an Indian had guided her to the cave on that day. Everything was unfair for the Indians; it was unfair that they lived on reservations and starved, unfair that the Army wanted the war to end because they were bored and wanted to kill more Indians, and unfair that the Americans made countless promises and broke each one. If she were an Indian, she would probably steal everything from white settlers, their oxen and food and horses, without any hesitation.

"Of course, peace will end but not so soon after this new treaty." Captain Gallagher said. "For now, we've a lot of free time and cold nights ahead of us. Keep the blankets coming," he said to Goldie with a wink.

Goldie learned to weave on a Navajo Indian loom in Aengus'

cabin. Up until then, she only knew how to spin wool on a spinning wheel and weave on a warp-weighted loom. But she learned so much more from Chaytan's mother, Makawee, who was also Aengus' wife, although her father said they weren't husband and wife like white people. He told her it was an arrangement like a married couple.

Each Wednesday and Saturday, Goldie spent all day in Aengus' house with Makawee teaching her how to use the traditional vertical loom. It appeared much more complex with so many rods and crosspieces, but Goldie quickly mastered it as Makawee guided her through each step. Makawee had learned all she knew from her own mother who was a Navajo Indian. In her twenties, Makawee's mother had been taken captive by the Lakota. She continued to weave and passed on the great secrets of her tribe's skill to Makawee.

"Oyáte weave for óhiŋniyaŋ," Makawee said, waving her hand over her shoulder. "Best Oyáte in makȟá to weaving that last forever."

Makawee spoke a mixture of English and Lakota flavored with Irish expressions she'd learned from Aengus. "Her mother's tribe has been weaving forever," Aengus interpreted. In the early days, when Makawee and Goldie conversed, Aengus filled in the gaps. "The Navajo is the best tribe for weaving. Their wares last for hundreds of years."

Aengus told Goldie about an Indian massacre in the south. "The Navajo fled to a fissure between the rocks with their wares. Then, the Army fired at them, killing every one of them. For over a hundred years, their remains lay untouched because of the Navajo taboo about disturbing the dead. Then 100 years, later a European trader found them. There were a dozen skeletons with textiles that remained as good as the day they were woven."

"Now I teach níš," Makawee said, pointing at Goldie. "All our anáȟmA."

"Now she'll teach you all of her secrets," Aengus interrupted.

"Do it wašté, then the blankets and rugs be wašté for your life and your wakȟáŋheža life and their wakȟáŋheža life."

If she did it well, the blankets and rugs would last for her life and for the lives of her children and grandchildren.

Makawee was young and pretty. She had long black hair that she kept in braids and a small pretty face with large brown eyes. She was small and appeared delicate, but Goldie had seen her lugging sacks of wool from the barn and knew she was anything but delicate. When she worked at the loom she frowned.

Goldie loved her days in Aengus' cabin, especially when Aengus was home and told stories about his life in the West as a fur trapper, how he'd spent months without meeting a white person until he went to the nearest fort to sell his fur.

"The only people I met were Indians," he said.

He told her that there were several Lakota tribes, the Sisseton, the Teton, and the tribe of Makawee's father, the Yankton.

"The Lakota were great horse thieves, they were called Little Snakes by their enemies the Chippewa tribe," he explained. "The whites lumped them all together using the Chippewa slur, Sioux, which means Little Snakes in English."

Aengus was a little different from the rest of the men in Four Oaks. He read books, and he talked about things that the other men didn't talk about, like the spirit of the Black Hills and the great significance of the eagle feather that was pinned to his mantelpiece.

"It was given to me by a Lakota chief," he told Goldie, "a gift of an eagle's feather from a Lakota Indian is a great honor."

"Why did they give it to you?" Goldie asked.

Aengus unpinned it from the mantelpiece. "Because I helped them," he said, rotating the feather between his index finger and thumb.

Sometimes Aengus didn't tell stories or talk; he read aloud from the books he kept. He would read in English and translate the words that Makawee didn't understand. Once, he read about two ladies in a London hotel having afternoon tea with scones and cakes. He read about pink and blue icing and described the linen tablecloth and how the London ladies picked their delights from a three-tiered plate. It sounded so lovely that Goldie and Makawee asked him to read the passage again. The following

Saturday when Goldie returned to Aengus' cabin, Makawee had laid the table with a sack as a tablecloth and had fashioned a three-tiered plate from wood that was laden with fresh bread and syrups.

"Afternoon tea for you and me," Makawee said mischievously.

As Aengus and Makawee and Chaytan talked, Goldie copied the graceful movements of Makawee's hands. Makawee generously shared the great nuggets of wisdom that made the Navajo wool and weaving the best in the world. She told Goldie which diet for a sheep produced the best wool, the plants to use for dying, dried sediment to produce brilliant white wool, and the yucca root that gave a luster to the wool.

For the rest of her life, Goldie referred to the secrets that Makawee had taught her. She learned to count in Lakota and decades later when the American government had all but rinsed the language from its people, Goldie could be found at one of her many looms muttering her accrued reminders in Makawee's tongue.

Once a week, Chaytan and Goldie trudged up the mountainside to the cave. Goldie always ensured that the slate was visible with her message to the Indians. When she mentioned her fears for her sister, Chaytan consoled her with stories of his days when he lived with his tribe. He told her they were his happiest days.

"Every woman is my aunt, and every man is my uncle. We all sleep in our tepee. We are safe and warm," he said. "Then the men go to war and we wait, all day we look out for their return. Then when the men come home, we have a big dance and feast..." he hesitated.

Goldie knew he was searching of the word.

"How you say everybody is happy and lights fires and eats?"

"A party," Goldie said. "You have a big party."

"Yes, we have a big party."

Each day, Chaytan asked Goldie to interpret his actions for the English word. He never forgot it once she told him.

"What happens at your party?" she asked. She loved hearing stories about his days when he lived with his tribe.

"The men march around the camp with the scalps on sticks and the legs and arms of the enemy." When Chaytan told her that, he held his hand up as if he were holding a stick with a limb attached.

"It would be nice if we could live there again. You and me, Aengus and Mama."

Goldie agreed, although she didn't like the idea of seeing arms and legs and scalps affixed to sticks, but then, they'd be the enemy's limbs and not hers.

When Chaytan told her about his father, there was no warmth or fondness in his voice. He recalled being taken from the tribe to live close to the Army fort where his father worked as a scout. His father was regularly gone and eventually he remained away.

"It was better when he was away," Chaytan admitted. "He needs to fight all the time, fight with me and my Mama and the other women and soldiers. Always fighting for no reason."

He told her that Aengus called often to buy blankets. Sometimes Aengus would eat with him and his mother, and sometimes he'd bring the food that his mother cooked.

"We were hungry many times," Chaytan said.

When Chaytan's father didn't return and the approaching winter would have killed him and his mother, they moved to Aengus' cabin.

"Aengus is a better man and a better father than my blood father," Chaytan said. "My father is *puŋpúŋ*." Rotten.

Goldie and Chaytan went deeper into the cave that told the true story of the West, each time exploring new tunnels and noticing different drawings. She particularly liked the symbol for hope.

"Wakta," Goldie said, using the Lakota word. It was in the shape of a star.

On the tree closest to the cave, Chaytan etched the symbol for hope. It represented the fragile peace and hope during those years.

When the spring arrived, Makawee moved the looms outside. They were sitting in the shade weaving when Goldie saw three men on horseback appear from the forest. They were riding at a steady pace toward Aengus' house. As the men came closer, she noticed the piebald horse and a shirtless man, and when she realized they were Indians, Goldie rushed to the barn to warn Aengus. Instead of reaching for his gun, he stepped outside and squinted into the distance. He watched them come closer and then smiled before going to greet them. Goldie sat in Aengus' cabin with the Indians while they talked and ate. She enjoyed tasting the buffalo meat they brought. As Goldie watched them, she thought of Captain Gallagher's barbaric stories and Ned Breen's vitriolic hatred at the mention of the savage Indians, and how they cut up their enemies and affixed their limbs to sticks. That night, as she observed these men in Aengus' cabin, she believed they too would kill and burn their enemies alive, but none of the visiting Indians were their enemy.

"Lila Was'te," Aengus said appreciatively, as he sampled the food.

They spoke in Makawee's language. The older Indian had long gray hair and seemed as if he were angry all the time, but when everybody laughed at something he said, Goldie realized it was only the way he spoke. She'd misinterpreted his frowning, worn face and the guttural language.

The youngest of the Indians was called Blue Feather. He grew bored at the men's conversation and wrestled with Chaytan. She thought him playful and nice and wished that someone like Blue Feature was among the tribe of Indians who had stolen her sister.

At dusk when there was nothing more to say, the Indians left. She watched them disappear into the forest until they were out of sight.

Goldie didn't know why she didn't mention the visiting Indians to her parents. Maybe she was *puŋpúŋ,* rotten like Chaytan's father, with a divided loyalty. When she contemplated telling them, she knew her father would disapprove. He might stop her going to Aengus' cabin. She also knew that he'd tell Ned Breen, who hated every single Indian, even a nice Indian like Blue Feather. It was easier to say nothing.

There was so much she didn't tell her parents. She didn't tell them that several nights she woke up with a sick feeling. She'd lie awake listening to her family's nocturnal sounds. Goldie had heard Father O'Brien say during Mass that all prayers were answered.

Goldie prayed at night. She implored God and the saints and martyrs to return her sister. Some nights she prayed so hard, she thought it must have worked, and the Lord would answer her prayers. A few times, she crept out of bed and looked out the window, thinking God would surely have heard her fervent pleas and some kind Indian had returned Baby Miriam. But Miriam never appeared outside the window, and her absence made room for a brutal sadness that weighed on Goldie's shoulders.

Quietly she'd climb back to bed and will daylight to come.

CHAPTER TWELVE

1872

On Easter Sunday, 1872, it was the O'Neills' turn to host the weekly Mass in their cabin. They moved everything they could outside the cabin so everybody could fit inside. Goldie liked Sundays. It was the only day of the week when she didn't work from sunrise to sunset. Every chore was completed by noon, when they'd be washed and wearing clean clothes as they bobbed along in their wagon to one of the cabins to hear Mass and meet their own people.

Goldie had just finished sweeping the cabin when Captain Gallagher arrived. "Afternoon, Goldie," he said as he peered into the cabin, "No sign of the Padre yet?"

"Not yet," Goldie said.

"Good, I've time for a quick coffee," he said as he wiped his feet.

Goldie's mother said she didn't know why Captain Gallagher came to Mass because he spent most the time looking around him or standing outside smoking his pipe. Goldie's father said he was only there for the social element. "Maybe he's looking for a wife," Barry had said. Goldie's mother said it would be about time.

The Kellys arrived next. They'd only joined their town in the last year. Although the Kellys were Irish, they had very different Irish accents from the O'Neills and Breens, as if they scooped the words from the pit of their chest, making them longer and more affected. Goldie's father said it was a Cavan accent. He pronounced it Caaaavaaaan.

The Dwyers arrived next. They were a source of ridicule for the Breens and O'Neills. The Dwyers were poor farmers, and Sean Dwyer was also a poor immigrant. He pined for the old country he'd left. Each day he alluded to his home in Tipperary, the damp weather, the home cooking, the smells of Ireland. Sean Dwyer drank often and cried easily. His mind was rarely on his new home. His farm remained largely untouched and nobody in the West knew hunger like the Dwyers. Owen Breen liked to remind the Dwyer boys just how hungry they were. "You'll always be hungry, 'cause your dad is useless." The Dwyer boys were an easy target for Owen Breen, and as time passed, Lorcan, also joined in the ugliness of young men. "Reckon you should get on the ship and go back to Ireland to starve," Lorcan said to Pedro Dwyer, who was small for his age, "'cause you'll die of hunger out here," he added, using the same slur that Barry had used when he referred to the Dwyers.

Goldie greeted each of them. She was particularly fond of little Emilio, who had been born on the wagon train to the West. He was now six years of age and smiled shyly when he saw Goldie. He had big gamey brown eyes like his mother. Goldie brought a chair into the cabin for Mrs. Dwyer, who was Spanish. Her youngest child was three months old, and despite spending twenty years in America, her English remained poor.

"Gracias," she sighed, flopping into the chair with the new baby in her arms.

Then the Troys arrived, and the Donnellys and the Ryans and then the Dalys. According to Goldie's father, the Dalys brewed the finest whiskey he'd ever tasted. "I thought Poteen was alright until I tasted this," he said of the elicit Irish homemade whiskey. "The Dalys whiskey has a good bite and hits you softly," he told Captain Gallagher.

The only notable absence was Aengus. He never came to Mass. When her father asked him why he didn't attend, he said, "There are other ways to speak to God." It made no sense to either of Goldie's parents, yet they accepted it.

By the time Father O'Brien arrived, it appeared as if every Catholic in the West were crammed into their cabin, waiting to hear the word of their Irish God.

Mass had started when the Breens arrived. Goldie was standing near the door, and she stood aside to allow them in. The only other family in their community to drive their family as hard as the O'Neills were the Breens. They too never sat still. While Goldie's family stopped work on Saturday evening to wash the week's clay from their skin, the Breens often arrived for Mass with the mud still stuck to their bare feet.

Father O'Brien talked about the importance of Easter in his Irish-American accent, saying, "On this very day almost 2,000 years ago, Jesus Christ rose from the dead providing us with hope for eternal life."

Everybody was listening intently except for Captain Gallagher, who was cleaning his fingernails with his knife.

"Easter is a time that gives us peace; it restores our souls, mends our brokenness, and helps us to conquer our struggles, especially when we are overwhelmed."

Goldie glanced over at the Breens, as they were the only family who looked overwhelmed just then. She saw Owen with his eyes closed as he swayed slightly. Anyone would think he was in tune with this peace that Father O'Brien referred to, but she knew he was only exhausted. She'd heard her father say that Ned Breen was determined to build their new barn if it took them until six in the morning. Goldie guessed that the weekly Mass was the only respite for the Breens.

When Father O'Brien began the consecration, everybody knelt and bowed their heads. "Take this, all of you, and eat of it. This is my body, which will be given up for you." Father O'Brien held up the host.

Ned Breen was on one knee with his closed fist reverently held to his chest, and his wife was on both knees beside him with her hands joined.

Ned Breen ruled his family with his fist. Nobody said aloud that they suspected life for his wife was difficult. With each passing year, Mrs. Leonora Breen became a shadow of the striking woman who had played her piano on the wagon train. Her once colorful dresses were now used as shirts for her sons. She didn't talk about her life in New York where she'd lived before moving west, or her music lessons or the great house where she'd grown up as the daughter of the esteemed banker, Jasper Livingston. The only time she expressed herself was through singing.

Father O'Brien continued, "This is the chalice of my blood, the blood of the new and eternal covenant, which will be poured out for you and for many for the forgiveness of sins. Do this in memory of me."

There was a long pause, and the only sound was from Minnie, the milking cow.

Slowly, everyone gathered round Father O'Brien to receive the Eucharist. There was restlessness building up, as the Mass was almost over. Lorcan stood with Timothy Breen, and they nudged each other lightly. Captain Gallagher began to pack his pipe. Bertha Daly, the big, capable daughter of the newly-arrived Irish family, stood at the door. She had to deal with the orders for their whiskey.

Father O'Brien scanned the faces in the cabin until he spotted Mrs. Breen, saying, "We'll end in the usual way."

Mrs. Breen stood up.

At the close of each Mass, Mrs. Breen sang a hymn. Nobody ever knew the name of her hymns and very few could say what the hymns were about. It was her voice that they heard. The rise and fall of her singing calmed the restlessness of the few previous minutes. She sang about abundance and angels, God and good tidings. Goldie saw her father, his head tilted to one side, lost in thought, and her mother with her eyes closed. Captain Gallagher stopped packing his pipe and looked out the open door of the cabin. There wasn't a sound until she finished.

"May God go with you," Father O'Brien said and made a sign of the cross.

Everybody followed and blessed themselves hastily before pouring out of the cabin.

The table was laid with food. Most families brought some small contribution and left their offering on the table—bread, tarts, strawberry jam, roasted mutton. The table was cleared of food as quickly as it was set. A few men followed Mr. Daly and his daughter Bertha to his wagon to buy jars of his homebrewed whiskey.

Goldie drifted between groups, refilling cups of coffee for their guests. She heard Mrs. Kelly gave her mother the recipe for her jam, with a secret ingredient. Ned Breen had hammered the last nail into his new barn this morning at daybreak, and Lorcan was talking to Captain Gallagher about killing.

"Did you kill anyone this week?" Lorcan asked.

"No, son, we got peace now," Captain Gallagher said.

Lorcan remained ordinary in most aspects. By the age of twelve, he could read and write as well as his peers. He showed great horsemanship, he was tall for his age, and he was handsome, with black hair and big green eyes. Handsome he was, but a worker he was not. When he did his chores, they were never done right. He poured too much seed into the soil and left other areas seedless. He'd hang the tools in the barn without washing them. When he fished and hunted, he never arrived home with a big bounty, and sometimes he arrived home with nothing at all. "Indians had everything gone," he'd complain.

"You reckon peace will end soon, and you'll be killing again?" Lorcan asked.

They were outside leaning against the wall of the cabin. Lorcan looked up to see where his father was before taking a pistol from his pocket, and then he began to rotate it on his index finger. It was one of a pair of pistols that Captain Gallagher had sold to their father. There was a gun belt that went with it. Lorcan wasn't allowed to take the pistol from the cabin without permission, and he wasn't allowed to wear the gun belt. Goldie knew that when Lorcan was alone he wore the belt with both pistols. She'd seen him looking in the small mirror by the door and pointing the pistol at his reflection.

"Peace never lasts," the Captain replied.

From the moment that Lorcan had learned that Captain Gallagher spent years chasing and killing Indians, he never tired of hearing his gruesome war stories.

"What's it like to kill a man?" Lorcan asked.

"Killing ain't easy, but you get used to it," Captain Gallagher said, watching Lorcan as he breathed air on the long barrel of the pistol and wiped it with his sleeve. "First killing is the worst, you think you've committed a terrible sin, you can't make sense of it. You feel empty and strange. Then after a few days you think it's all over because there's something else to think about."

Most times Captain Gallagher enjoyed Lorcan's adulation. When Lorcan was a boy of seven or eight, Captain Gallagher would allow Lorcan to try on his Army jacket, hat, boots, and gun belt. Their father and Captain Gallagher would holler with laughter at the sight of him marching up and down in the jacket that touched his knees. While it was endearing when he was boy, it was barely tolerated when he turned twelve, yet when he thought he'd get away with it, he tried on Captain Gallagher's jacket again.

"Then you kill again?" Lorcan asked hopefully.

"Maybe not right away," Captain Gallagher said, "because then you begin to remember the person's eyes just before you kill them. You see the anger or their determination and you're thinking you're lucky 'cause your determination was better than theirs."

"Then what?" Lorcan wanted to hear it all.

"Then you see the men and women in your sleep, and you're not sure if the sweats are from the whiskey, or the killing, or just plain old imagination."

Lorcan didn't want to hear about the remorse or the dead men who stalked Captain Gallagher's dreams, he only wanted to hear about his bayonet wet with blood and his gun hot from firing.

"Reckon I'd make a good soldier," Lorcan said, as he looked up to see his father approach. Quickly, he jammed the gun into his pocket.

Barry had seen him twirling the pistol on his finger. In three long strides, Barry was beside Lorcan. He reached into Lorcan's pocket and pulled out the pistol and then slapped him in the back of the head.

"I told you not to play with it," Barry said as Lorcan edged away. "Sometimes I wonder about that boy," Barry said as Goldie watched Lorcan join the Breen boys and the older Dwyer boys.

Barry could not understand Lorcan. He often pointed to his head when he tried to understand his only son, saying, "There isn't one grain of sense up there." Barry regularly said that Lorcan's mind was never on any job. "He's a dreamer, away with fairies," her father said in the same frustrated tone. He compared Lorcan to the Breen boys, who brought home at least a fish or a wild bird after a day by the river. "Lorcan only brings home wild stories about bears and Indians," Barry said. Their mother tried to assure him that Lorcan was still only a boy at twelve years of age. "It's no excuse," Barry said.

As time passed, Barry honed in on his son's work. The stakes he planted were not at regular distances. Barry called him out to tell him. He stood over Lorcan as he replanted the stakes at the right distance. The tools were left on the floor of the barn, so Barry sent him out to hang them in the right place. The hoe was not cleaned after it was used, so Barry stood over Lorcan as he washed it. When the new stakes were planted for a corral, similar to the first round of stakes, they were not at regular distances. Barry moaned that he was wasting his time. He compared Lorcan to Chaytan, "The Injun in the corral makes me more money than the sale of the yearly oats, even though he's an Injun, and his father is a turncoat," Barry listed all of the parts of Chaytan's poor background, "yet he's more of a man than you."

The greatest insult for Lorcan was when Barry compared him to Pedro Dwyer. "Little Pedro comes from the most embarrassing Irish family in the West, his father is useless, and his mother can't even speak English, but Pedro is doing a better job than you are."

Occasionally, Sean Dwyer and his oldest son Pedro did a day's work for Barry. Goldie agreed with her father that regardless of

Pedro's small size, he was a mighty worker. The first night that Barry compared Lorcan to Pedro, Lorcan objected so fiercely that Barry was taken aback. Lorcan told his father that he knew he was lying. Since then, every time Barry was frustrated with Lorcan's work, he'd remind him that Pedro could have done a better job. Lorcan didn't retaliate like he did the first time, but it was clear that he seethed.

As the afternoon progressed and conversation dwindled, the families began to round up their children and leave.

The Breens and the Dwyers were the last to leave. Goldie was sent to the barn to fetch the children. She'd seen the boys huddled in a group a while earlier.

The barn was empty, and she noticed that the horsewhip had been left on the ground. She picked it up and followed the sound of voices to the side of the barn where she saw Pedro Dwyer tied from a branch of a tree by his hands. The Breen boys, the Kelly boy, and Lorcan were standing back looking up at him. Most of the boys were sniggering at the sight of a pleading Pedro while Lorcan stared up with his arms folded.

Goldie ran at them. They took flight after she flayed them with the whip, connecting with those closest to her. She followed them as far as the corral and then stood breathless, watching them running to the cabin for safety.

She returned to Pedro and let him down.

He told her in a subdued tone, that it was only a game. "Maybe a bit of fun," he'd said.

"Maybe," she said. She didn't tell that she'd seen the wet patch on his trousers where he'd wet himself.

That night when everyone had gone and Goldie was alone with her parents, she heard them discussing the day and gossiping about their guests.

They talked about the Dalys and their whiskey. "Seemingly, it's the daughter, Bertha who makes the homebrew whiskey." Barry said.

Neasa nodded. She was washing the pans.

They talked about Captain Gallagher. "Did you give him a pie to take to the fort?" her father asked.

Captain Gallagher said nobody could make a pie like Neasa O'Neill. Every time he tasted it, he licked the bowl clean and said the same thing. "If I'm ever facing the hangman and they allow me a last meal, I'll take Mrs. O'Neill's pie."

"I did," her mother said and smiled. She was fond of Captain Gallagher and secretly pleased with his compliment.

They talked about Ned Breen and how he'd finished the barn in record time. "The last nail at sunrise!" Barry said.

Then they talked about the Dwyers. "Don't you think Mrs. Dwyer would learn English?"

Neasa agreed.

Then they talked about matters closer to home. Barry heard what Lorcan and the Breens had done to Pedro, but Barry was more perturbed that Lorcan had left the ax out in the rain overnight. He'd also toyed with the pistol when it was forbidden. And the strangest of all was his thirst for war stories from Captain Gallagher.

"There's a bit of a want in him," Goldie's father said to their mother about Lorcan.

"He's still only a boy," Neasa said, "he'll grow out of it."

"He is twelve years of age," their father reminded her. "Sometimes I wonder about him," he sighed.

When there was nothing more to discuss, her father lit his pipe and stood at the open door of the cabin, sending blue smoke into the still evening.

"Mrs. Breen has a way of making you think when she sings," he said.

Goldie's mother stopped what she was doing and considered it.

"It makes you think about…" her father hesitated, "about memories, and the future, and us," he added.

"The voice has remained beautiful throughout everything," Neasa said.

Mrs. Breen's voice remained as pure as the clear days in the West. It seemed a contradiction to Goldie that such a sad, beaten woman had within her the ability to subdue their small flourishing congregation. Goldie likened it to the West, a land that was pocketed with as much ugliness as it was with beauty and bounty.

CHAPTER THIRTEEN

Four Oaks 1937

Goldie's old car started on the first try. Lucy knew it was another job that Winona would have done. She would have sent one of her sons to recharge the battery and wipe the dust from the seats. Lucy revved the engine and drove down the avenue. She turned right and then left. Lucy couldn't wait one more minute. For her, home was more than Goldie's house, it was also Makawee's home. Makawee and her extended family were those who formed the backdrop to Lucy's life. It was her second home. Only they could bridge the gap that had opened since Goldie's death. As she drove down their avenue, she began to smile at the prospect of finally sitting with them to discuss all that had happened. She pressed harder on the accelerator. When she arrived at the house, Winona's dogs began to bark aggressively, and the smaller terrier snapped at her heels until she spoke.

"It's only me," she said, bending down to pat the three dogs, who wagged their tails and licked her hand.

When Lucy looked up, Winona was standing at the door. Lucy walked toward her. With each step her joy was replaced with sadness. It was their first meeting since Goldie's funeral. When Winona opened her arms to greet her, Lucy was unable to fight the tears. They stood on the veranda holding each other, as the icy wind went unnoticed.

Winona stepped back to look at Lucy. "Time, we'll give it time."

Makawee was sitting by the fire. Her head was cocked in the direction of the door, waiting to see who had arrived.

"Lucy's here," Winona announced loudly.

Makawee greeted her in Lakota. "Tan yan yahee," she said, pushing herself to her feet and extending her hand.

Lucy hugged her before taking a seat beside her. Although Makawee was in her nineties, she had more working faculties than women twenty years her junior. Makawee was a small woman with long gray hair and brown skin. She wore thick glasses, and although her hearing was fading, she was capable of holding her own in a conversation. On Makawee's lap were several strands of yarn leading into a tight strong rope. Even at this stage of her life, she continued to do whatever chores her age allowed. She made ropes from yarn and gave them to her grandsons or friends.

"Tea, coffee, or something stronger?" Winona asked.

"Something stronger," Lucy said and thanked Winona for getting the house ready and recharging the battery in the car. "Harry was very grateful that the house was warm."

"I'm pleased I could help," Winona said. She had the cupboard open and was standing on her tiptoes as she peered inside to retrieve a bottle of whiskey. "For the night that it is, we'll have a little of Goldie's brand," Winona said. Goldie always kept a bottle of Irish whiskey at Makawee's. "It hasn't been opened since Goldie's last night here," Winona said, looking at the bottle before opening it and pouring three small whiskeys.

Lucy noted that Winona diluted hers and Makawee's with too much water. They rarely drank.

"I hope you haven't spoiled this good whiskey with water," Lucy said, imitating Goldie.

Winona smiled, saying, "Possibly," as she handed Lucy and Makawee their drinks.

"Good health, girls," Lucy said, and raised her glass.

Makawee and Winona smiled and followed suit. Makawee wet her lips and left the drink on the table beside her. Her fingers continued weaving the rope.

"So, how's it all going?" Winona asked.

Lucy sighed, admitting, "It's strange. It will take a lot longer than a few hours to get used to Goldie's absence."

"Every day I pass the house I still look, hoping I'll see her in the garden." Winona looked in the direction of Goldie's as she spoke.

They talked about their last day with Goldie.

"And the ballyhoo at Mount Rushmore that had her seething," Winona said.

Then they erupted into fits of laughing, recalling Goldie's stench from breaking wind and how people began to turn and look to see who the culprit was while Goldie sat poker-faced. On the way home in the car, Goldie admitted it was her. She said she gave the occasion the flavor it deserved. Goldie was appalled at the sight of the President's head as much as she was appalled at the clapping and waving. "Nobody will question it," Goldie had said about the new sculpture. "They'll come and gape at the President's head and drive away thinking they've been told a happy story."

Lucy and Winona began to talk about Goldie's death, and how the news had hit them. Since Goldie's death, Lucy had no time with Makawee and Winona. She'd phoned from New York, but it wasn't the same. Only now, in their living room, did they share their grief. Lucy found it a relief to talk to someone who knew Goldie, about the shock of her death and her gentle and eventual exit.

Winona listened to Lucy recount the day of her death, their last conversation, and how she'd found her dead that night. They talked about the funeral and the crowd who came to pay their respects.

"It's good that she has a resting place for townsfolk," Makawee said, and then added in a quieter voice, "and then she went our way." Makawee paused and nodded toward the skies.

Lucy and Winona agreed.

Lucy had laid Goldie out at home. When it was time to move her remains from the house to the Catholic church for Mass and burial, Lucy closed the doors for a few moments alone with Goldie's nearest friends and family. Lucy, Makawee, Winona, and Blue Feather's sons were the only people present. Unbeknownst to the rest of the mourners, they took an empty coffin to the church, where it was buried in her family plot with her husband and child. Later that night, Blue Feather's sons returned to Goldie's house. While Harry slept, they took Goldie's remains to the high ground, where they placed her body on a scaffold to return her to nature and allow her spirit to rise. Goldie had left instructions years earlier.

They remained silent as they thought about it.

"How is New York?" Winona asked.

Lucy rattled off the same response to friends and acquaintances who asked, "It's wonderful, I'm so busy with various parties and friends, I never have a moment. Harry is so well-known, we're privileged to get so many invitations."

Lucy saw that Winona was waiting for something more. Lucy's usual rehashed upbeat response didn't wash with Winona or Makawee the way it did with others.

Lucy sighed. "It's probably Goldie. I miss her. The parties and New York lifestyle don't hold the same fascination that they once did," she confessed. "Sometimes everything seems so different. I never knew grief like this," she said, then began to cry.

Just then Makawee's old mahogany, agile hand grasped Lucy's. When Lucy looked at Makawee, she was surprised to see a tear roll through the creases in her lined face.

"I'm sorry, I've upset you too," Lucy said.

"We're all sad," Makawee said.

"I miss home, maybe that's it. I wish I could live here, for a while, anyway," Lucy sighed. "Sometimes I regret not coming home more often. I regret not phoning more often," she admitted.

There were periods during her marriage when Lucy had almost forgotten about Goldie and Four Oaks. She'd phone once a week, each Friday morning before the weekend began with a social report of outings and dinners. Sometimes she had little to say, and there was a time when she'd had little interest in the local news of Four Oaks. She saw her home and Goldie as Harry saw it, as a sleepy backwater she was happy to have left behind. For a period, she thought she was more informed than Goldie, and she'd poke fun at Goldie's accent. All the while, Goldie never got annoyed. "It's great to be as informed as you," she'd say dryly. "Ring me next week and tell me all your news." In the last few years, she'd developed an interest in Four Oaks again. Even prior to Goldie's death, she'd often thought how nice it would be to spend more time there. And now that she was lost and lonely, she wanted to stay in Four Oaks forever; she wanted to sit on her veranda staring at the hills for the rest of her days.

"You can come back anytime. If Goldie's house is too lonely, you can stay here," Makawee said.

Lucy thanked her. She knew that their door was always open. "Harry wants me to sell the house or knock it down," Lucy said. "He's thinks it's too old and cold, and he's afraid of mice."

Lucy heard a small chuckle from Makawee.

"Do you mind if I borrow Reggie for a few days?" Lucy asked, referring to the terrier. "I think there might be a problem with mice."

"Sure," Winona said. "Are you home for a few days or longer?" Winona asked.

"I don't know. I presume you heard the news?" Lucy said.

Winona shook her head. Makawee stilled her hands and cocked her ear.

"Lorcan has returned."

They were silent. Winona's head inclined forward and blinked slowly. The rope that Makawee was weaving slipped from her lap onto the floor.

"Lorcan is home!" Winona repeated.

"Yes, that's the reason I came home. He's in Gallagher's at the moment."

None of them spoke.

"Do you remember him?" Lucy asked, only because she wanted to hide this new, uncomfortable rising silence.

"Yes," Winona said, her tone neutral.

She didn't offer any fond memories, Lucy noted.

"I expect we'll have dinner tomorrow or the day after, a special dinner to get to know him and welcome him home. You're welcome to join us," Lucy said. Goldie always invited Makawee and Winona to her gatherings. Just then, she enjoyed the idea of Goldie's kitchen bursting with atmosphere and smells of cooking.

"No," Winona answered quietly. "Thank you, but no."

They moved the conversation along. They began to talk about Bertha and Gallagher's Hotel and other local news but Lucy noted that they were distracted. It was as if something unpleasant had descended on their gathering. Lucy had long suspected that there was more to her father than heroic stories of war and bravery. Years earlier in the Dwyers' house, his name had elicited the same unpleasant undercurrent. Makawee and Winona's reaction confirmed what she'd long suspected. Lorcan was not always the gentleman that she had been led to believe.

Lucy left shortly after nine with Winona's dog. When she pulled up at Goldie's house, the dog was sitting on its hunkers looking at her expectantly. "What is happening that I can't see, Reggie?" she asked the dog. It began to bark and wag its tail. "Come on. Scare the mice away," she said in a playful, excited voice that increased the dog's yapping.

CHAPTER FOURTEEN

1937

The following morning, Lucy found three dead mice, which she discarded. She patted Reggie, who followed her from room to room as she lit the fires in the living room and Goldie's office where Harry was working.

"Do we really need the dog?" Harry asked. He was in Goldie's office with the receiver in his hand. This morning, he said he'd find the name of an attorney who specialized in inheritance law, and then they'd go to town to meet her father.

"It's the mice or the dog," Lucy said.

"Take him out of here, I'm about to make a call," Harry said tilting his body away from Reggie as if he were a monster about to snap the receiver out of his hand.

Lucy left with the sound of Reggie's nails clacking on the wooden floor behind her. One of the things that Lucy missed in New York was a dog. There was something incomparable to a dog greeting her first thing in the morning. Apart from the occasional barking, a dog was mostly silent. As she prepared breakfast, she could hear Harry on the phone. He was not silent in the morning. His voice bellowed down the long corridor.

"We'll organize a meeting next week with him. Yes, I know. I'm out west for a few days." There was a moment's silence before Harry gave one of those insincere, loud guffaws. "You've said it in one, old chum."

Old chum, Lucy said quietly and lifted her eyes. She looked down at Reggie, who was sitting on his hunkers looking up at her expectantly as she cooked.

"You're my main chum," she said. At that Reggie's tail wagged faster. "My mouse-slaying chum." She tossed a crust of the bread to him.

A dog did so much, yet it expected nothing in return. A dog was easy company. As she cooked, she couldn't help comparing Harry to the terrier. A dog didn't expect a commendation with bells and whistles for everything it did. Lucy divided the omelet in three. A dog was loyal. When Lucy thought about Harry's lack of fidelity, she moved the knife slightly to her right. She picked the bigger portion of the omelet, put it onto a plate, and mashed some bread.

"You get more because you're better behaved," she said to Reggie as she put the plate on the floor. She was amused with herself for speaking to the dog and even giving it part of Harry's portion. She put Harry's breakfast onto a tray with a fresh coffee and took it to Goldie's office. She noticed that Harry had put on his long woolen overcoat and hat. Last night, he'd worn two vests and his pajamas to bed. He'd said he was freezing. First thing this morning, she'd woken to the same rhetoric.

Lucy took her own breakfast to the living room. Harry was still talking to his business partner. He had just asked for the name of a lawyer specializing in inheritance law.

"Oh, does he?" Harry said.

There was a long pause, then a few more oh's and ah's.

"Ah, I remember meeting him," Harry said. "Ah, a short, stout chap. I don't know him, but he'll probably know me."

Lucy sat in the chair closest to the window and ate slowly.

In the office, she heard Harry ring the operator and ask to be put through to Johnson & Davy Lawyers in New York.

"Harry Livingston here, I'm with Livingston and Kilmer Brokers. I got your name from my associate, Bartley Kilmer."

She guessed from Harry's tone that he was speaking to the short stout lawyer who specialized in inheritance law.

There was a pause. "Yes, that's me, the one and only," Harry said, giving his little humble chuckle. There were a few more pleasantries exchanged before he got down to business. "I believe you're the expert in inheritance law, and I have a case that may be somewhat unusual."

As Lucy listened, she wondered how he'd get around this one. When Lucy had first told Harry that Goldie had adopted her from an orphanage in Denver, he'd thought it best that she should never mention the orphanage to their New York friends or members of his family. There was an air of scandal about it, the idea that his wife had spent a year in an orphanage before an aunt rescued her. Harry's people believed in knowing the pedigree of their family, and any links with an orphan were best left unsaid.

"Hypothetically speaking, if a man who was assumed dead returned alive, what are his entitlements?" Harry asked.

Lucy listened as Harry reverted to the oh's and ah's.

"Ah, that would make sense. I'm looking into the matter for one of my clients." Harry explained it briefly. "It seems a dead relative returned, or there is a suggestion he was dead, he's obviously living or possibly pretending to be living."

Even Lucy was getting confused at that stage.

"My client?" Harry asked.

Lucy waited to hear his response.

"Yes, she's overjoyed that her father is alive, but we just need to doublecheck his legal entitlements to her estate."

Lucy looked at the picture of Lorcan that sat on the sideboard. He had been handsome in his day. It appeared he had it all; bravery, selflessness, and the looks to go with it, yet Lucy couldn't ignore Winona and Makawee's reaction last night, or the same uneasy silence that occasionally accompanied his name. Lucy knew that Lorcan had been commended for his role in the Indian Wars, particularly the Battle of Wounded Knee. She'd found an article in her local library that said Lorcan had pursued Indians to a ravine, where he'd directed his fire at the hostiles. The account left Lucy cold instead of proud.

"There is a substantial estate at stake here," Harry was saying. "There is land, roughly 2,000 acres, and a sizable amount of money that is tied up in investments."

Lucy got up and closed the door. She'd rather not listen to that now. She finished her breakfast and gave the crust of her bread to Reggie. She sat back and looked into the early crisp morning. The snow was melting on the hill, and the winter sun glared across the glistening landscape. Lucy had forgotten how beautiful the scenery was in Four Oaks. Each time she returned, she had a glorious gratifying moment of appreciation, and it hit her now again. The contrast with the view from her Manhattan home was not lost on her. The landscape of her home was more dominant, as the mountains and many dips and valleys emitted a sense of a presence far greater than New York's architectural feats. Slowly, it began to sink in that she was home at last. Home to all that was familiar, with little Reggie on her lap. Lucy sat very still savoring the moment until Harry bounded into the living room waving a notepad.

"I was right, I was damn well right all along," he said, taking a cigarette from the box. "According to my attorney, your father is entitled to a share in your inheritance. He is going to check a few details and ring me back this evening," he continued in a loud, adamant tone.

"Why don't we wait to see what my father wants?" Lucy said. "He may not want anything from me."

Harry didn't answer her. Instead, he pointed to Goldie's empty chair. "We'd have no issue if that..." he paused as he searched for the right word while his finger shook with anger, "that woman," Harry said in his customary angry tone when he referred to Goldie, "had done the respectable thing in the first place instead of treating me like a free-loading criminal, we would not be in this predicament."

"We've been over this before," Lucy said, raising her opened palm to him and turning her face away.

"Her red mane and quaint Irish goings-on," he said in a sneering voice. "If she had left a solid, decent, normal will without complicating things, we could pretend the money was gone. Instead, it's all in your name."

Harry's issues with Goldie were not only her red hair or even her occasionally affected Irish accent. Each year, their mutual abhorrence of each other had gone deeper. After Harry and Lucy were married, Goldie accepted Harry. "Warts and all," as she said. She extended the great country hospitality to Harry and his family. She was so hospitable Harry thought that Goldie had come full circle and was now one of his ardent admirers. He suggested to Goldie that she change the house and build something fashionable, maybe add a greenhouse for her gardening. Goldie told him to stay in Gallagher's Hotel if he found her house too unfashionable. Harry realized his mistake and instead talked about the investments he made for his clients. He told her how he made money through property and that only poor people worked. "Money begets money in our modern world," he said, as if she were as green as the grass outside her window. He encouraged Goldie to give him money to invest. Goldie refused to do business with him. "I might be penniless, for all you know," she said.

There were small tit-for-tat comments, Goldie making light of Harry's radio job, and Harry suggesting that Goldie learn to read. Eventually, when Goldie and Harry realized that they'd never like each other, they presented their worst versions of themselves to each other. Harry told Goldie how he'd bought his apartment in New York from a widow who needed the money, saying, "That old lady needed to pay her husband's bills. She practically gave it to me." Goldie would dwell on the plight of the poor woman. Harry knew this. He excelled at playing the role of the unscrupulous greedy vulture waiting to take advantage of the penniless widow. For her part, Goldie overdid her Irish-eens that aggravated Harry. "God bless us and save us, you createreen, I'll pray for you," she'd say to a visitor. Goldie knew and disapproved of the fact that Harry's family had changed from Catholicism to Presbyterianism, and that they

had anglicized their Gaelic name and deliberately distanced themselves from the Irish, whom they thought were beneath them. When
Goldie would introduce Harry, she used the same countrified Irish
accent that Harry detested. "This is my son-in-law, Harry, he's one
of us, Irish and proud of it, his people are from the Bog of Allen."
Harry's family was not from the Bog of Allen. Goldie admitted that
she'd no idea where the Bog of Allen was. After Goldie's comments,
Harry would start it all again by discussing modern and fashionable
business deals.

Three short years ago, Goldie had made a will. She told Harry
that she had made a "fashionable will," and she used all the same
words that Harry used. "It's our current way of making wills in the
West. We're more modern than you New York folks. I'm leaving
everything to Lucy. As a woman, she'll have the lot in her name."

Harry pretended that he agreed with Goldie's will, but in truth,
he was apoplectic. For months afterward, every time Goldie's name
was mentioned, Harry assumed a pose of indignation. Finally, when
he did refer to it, he spat such fury by calling Goldie every unwhole-
some name; vagabond, criminal, thief, outlaw, disingenuous, alco-
holic, and general low-life. Since then, at every given opportunity
over the last three years, the subject of Goldie's will was enough to
make him fly into a rage.

The day of Goldie's funeral, there was further insult added to
injury. Goldie had stipulated in the will that if Lucy died before
Goldie, her estate was to go to charity, bypassing him entirely. After
the details of the will were disclosed, Harry's name-calling went to
new level—mutant, drunkard, sadistic.

"She showed nothing but contempt for me," Harry said,
marching across the living room and flinging wood onto the fire,
"making fun of me with her 'modern' will."

"You didn't do anything to help the situation," Lucy retorted,
"telling her about your investments and making it sound as if you'd
swoop down on the first poor widow you met."

"Why not! She was an insulting, cold-hearted, manipulative,
coarse, drunken country hobo."

Lucy put her head back and closed her eyes. It was too early in the morning to have to listen to this again.

"None of this would have happened if she'd done the right thing like every other person and left me in charge," Harry said. "Now I'm left doing the dog's work. No, she didn't think of that when she was ridiculing me." To reiterate his point, he waved his notebook at her. "I'm the one spending my time to protect your interests."

Lucy remained silent.

"Tomorrow morning, at the very latest, we will be out of here."

"I won't be ready—"

He interrupted her. "We'll return again in the summer when you can sort out Goldie's belongings."

"In the summer, you'll find an excuse not to come back. I would rather do it now," Lucy said.

"You haven't the time now," he said with a raised voice.

Lucy remained calm. "Why don't you return to New York, and I'll stay for a week, do what needs to be done here," she noted Harry's features growing sharper with anger, yet she continued. "When I've finished here in a week or so, I'll return to New York."

"What! You'd stay here alone!"

"Yes, it's only a week. I'll survive alone, and I'm sure you'll manage too," Lucy said.

"Maybe I'll allow you to speak with the attorney in New York alone, and maybe I'll allow you to deal with the enormous legal implications alone?"

"We'll see what Lorcan wants first," Lucy said. "Then we can deal with the legal implications."

Harry opened his mouth and inhaled. He was ready to fire another round of ammunition at her when they heard the front door banging. Both looked toward the door in unison.

"Hello, Harry? Lucy?"

"Wilbur Breen," Harry spat through clenched teeth. "How could he have known we're home?"

Lucy shrugged.

"In here," Harry called, his eyes closed in protest against the intruding guest.

CHAPTER FIFTEEN

1873

In 1873, Goldie's name and date of birth were changed. The government passed the Timber Act, which allowed anybody over the age of twenty-one to claim 160 acres, the only stipulation being that they must plant forty acres with trees. Barry O'Neill put in two claims, one claim in his name and the other in Goldie's.

"Why is the government giving away more land?" Lorcan asked.

"Because the government knows that nobody can live in the West without timber," Barry said, before turning his attention to Goldie. "From now on, your official name will be Geraldine Nile, no O, and we've moved the e," he said, emphasizing the O and the E. "Remember, it's Nile, not O'Neill."

"That's a queer name," Goldie said.

Her father didn't answer.

"And your date of birth is 1852."

"But I'm only sixteen, so that makes me twenty-one."

"You could easily pass for twenty-one," he said. "It doesn't really matter; it's only a formality."

"Why not put my name or Lorcan's name?" Frances asked.

"Because you must be over twenty-one years of age and look the part," he said. "And," he raised his head and pointedly glared at Lorcan, "you must have a bit of sense between the ears."

Lorcan had been scolded for taking the horse to Parker Falls "for a look about."

"Will I be moving to my new land?" Goldie asked hopefully. She enjoyed the idea of having a cabin all to herself. During the dead of night when she woke, she wouldn't have to lie still waiting for daylight. If she owned her own cabin, she could get up and make as much noise as she wanted and slurp her tea, if she pleased. She could also spend as much time with Chaytan as she wanted. She'd act like they did in the books that Aengus read and have afternoon tea with cornbread and ask Makawee for some sugar to make scones. She might even have Blue Feather, Aengus' Indian friend, over for afternoon tea.

"No, you'll live here. I've already marked the land, but you'll have to come to the Land Registry Office with me and fill out the forms. Remember, you're twenty-one and sign your name Geraldine Nile and your date of birth 1852," he raised his finger, and continued, "do not put 1857."

"Lying is a sin," Frances piped up.

"We'd still be stuck on our poor mountain in Ireland freezing and hungry if we didn't tell the odd white lie," Barry said.

"Will the land be mine?" Goldie asked.

"The land will be yours only in name. It'll be mine and then your brother Lorcan's," Barry said.

"He'll be the wealthiest man in the West," Frances said, looking at their thirteen-year-old brother.

"Nothing is set in stone," Barry cautioned. "A man needs to show he's worthy of the lands he'll inherit."

Lorcan looked at their mother and smiled. Neasa raised her eyebrows slightly, as if amused by Barry's threat. Each of the O'Neill family knew their father had no notion of leaving every square inch of his land and every possession to anybody other than his son. Even if it meant that Barry had to spend the rest of days trying to rectify what he called that 'peculiar quirk,' Lorcan would get it all.

Barry continued to despair over Lorcan's behavior. There were times when Lorcan worked as diligently and as hard as the Breens and Pedro Dwyer. He'd do everything he was asked and more. But like an animal with an unfixable quirk, he inevitably regressed to his old behavior. Neasa retraced Lorcan's steps to ensure he'd completed his jobs to Barry's satisfaction. Many times, Goldie saw her mother and Frances finishing the job he'd half done. Both would plead with Lorcan to do as he was asked. As recently as last week, he'd been scolded for disappearing for a full afternoon and most of the night. He claimed that he got waylaid helping a passing wagon train going west. Later, Barry heard that he'd spent the evening in Parker Falls, and he was genuinely perplexed

Ned Breen did not have such trouble with his six sons. He was the only other Irishman to prosper as much as Barry O'Neill. Ned also put in two claims, one in his name and the other in his son, Owen's name.

The day their documents arrived confirming their new claims, Ned Breen and Aengus convened in the O'Neills' cabin. Sean Dwyer was also there. They listened as Barry and Ned talked with elation at all they'd accomplished since coming to the West.

"We left the walking dead," Ned said, referring to the famine-stricken country he'd fled in 1847, "to become our own masters."

"With more land than Lord Stratford-Rice," Barry said, referring to the local English landlord in Ireland.

That night both men oozed with so much pride it was almost too much to contain in their small cabin. They talked about the future, the great harvests they'd yield and money they'd accumulate. They discussed giving Four Oaks an official name rather than the name given by early trappers who'd used their small crossroads as a meeting point.

Barry thought O'Neill Town had a better ring to it than Breen Town. In Barry's opinion, Breen Town sounded too whiny.

"What's whiny about Breen Town?" Ned asked.

"It's the name, Breeeeen Town," Barry repeated, dragging out the name and raising his voice to a whine.

"And what's better about O'Neill Town?" Ned asked.

"It's a name with strength," Barry said, unabashed.

Aengus appeared amused as he looked from Barry to Ned.

"O'Neill Town," Ned repeated, "O'Neillyyy Town," he continued matching Barry's whiny voice.

Aengus broke the tension by laughing loudly.

They decided to leave the name as Four Oaks for now. They'd plant their trees on the new land, continue with their harvest, raise livestock, and prosper.

Aengus was not always amused by their antics. When Barry and Ned plotted how to get more land, Aengus called them greedy. Aengus' lack of interest in putting in a claim for forestry baffled them.

"Someone else will take it, why not you?" Barry asked.

Aengus said he didn't need it. "I have plenty enough in what I have."

"But it's free," Barry persisted. "Remember it was you who told me it's all free."

"How much do you want?" Aengus asked Barry and Ned. "Is it 300 acres? 600 acres? Maybe 2,000 acres?"

Barry's eyes danced wildly. "I want as much as I can get," he replied, his tone matching Aengus' incredulous raised voice.

"You'll kill your family from work and want," Aengus said, looking from Ned to Barry. "What good will it be to your sons when your family is dead or their bones are buckled from work, or they can't stand up from pain?" he said. "There isn't a tribe of Indians who drives their family as you do."

The O'Neills and Breens knew there was a price to pay for their hard labor. Goldie's mother, Neasa, had developed a peculiar way of standing. Her body was tilted to one side. Goldie couldn't remember when Neasa had started to walk with her hand on her hip. When she was tired, she dragged her leg. Barry was not immune to suffering either, as he complained of pains in his neck and shoulder. Regardless of Barry's ailments or his wife's tilted body or his children's bleeding hands, Barry was irked by Aengus' accusation.

With Aengus' disinterest in land, Barry formed a strong alliance with Ned Breen, whose greed for more was as torturous as Barry O'Neill's.

Later, when Barry and Ned were alone, Ned Breen said, "'Tis the influence of the squaw that has him like that."

Barry agreed. They saw his contentment as an affliction.

During those years their town changed slowly. They were drip-fed news from the outside world. They learned that the railway going from east to west was finished. Trekking across the country was no longer a six-month survival test.

"Now a man can climb aboard and snooze all the way to the West Coast," Barry O'Neill said when he heard it.

The railroad brought new arrivals. Goldie felt old and wise at the sight of them hobbling into town with their government brochures and big dreams of prosperity. Occasionally, the extremes of the West drove them back to the crowded cities they'd fled or further west to chase a different dream. Some brought newspapers from Chicago and Kansas City that were passed around Four Oaks like the coveted gold that the '49ers sought.

There was talk in the papers of a global recession and how a new gold-find would lift the country out of the recession. One in eight men in the United States was unemployed, the banks were corrupt, and the papers that passed through the O'Neills' cabin increasingly referred to shortages.

At night, when there was a lull in the conversation or there was nothing more to say, Goldie's father and Ned Breen would look toward the hills and speculate about gold. They heard about gold seekers venturing into the hills to investigate and never returning to tell their tale.

"We've got gold in California, Montana, and if I were a betting man, it only stands to reason that the Hills are dripping with it," Barry said to Ned Breen.

"The Treaty forbids white men to enter the hills," Aengus reminded them.

"World is a different place today than it was six years ago when they signed over the Black Hills," Ned Breen said.

Captain Gallagher agreed, "That depression ain't goin' anywhere too soon."

Barry and Ned stopped talking about the gold when Aengus was present. Occasionally, the railway brought drifters, men who'd work on the O'Neill farm for bed and board. They slept in the hay barn, and Barry saw to it that they earned their food.

One drifter told them about the price of gold. "I seen nuggets the size of my finger that could buy you a hotel in New York, and I seen flakes that seem worthless that could get you enough oats for the year."

Barry's and Ned's minds became alive with the idea.

"Gold seekers will come," the drifter said. "And I'll be the first one with them when they go into the hills."

"Imagine someone else coming in and taking our gold," Ned said, his eyes fixed on Barry as he spoke.

Barry remained silent, staring at Ned with the same intensity. "'Twould gall you all right."

Sean Dwyer offered to investigate. They paid him and the drifter three dollars to go into the hills. Ned Breen told Sean all he had to do was confirm where the gold was and come straight home.

Barry told him to draw a map. "A detailed map," he emphasized. They gave him a pan and a pick. For once, Sean Dwyer was not lonely or oozing with homesickness for Ireland. He didn't seem at all unhappy or fearful of going to meet his death. He and the drifter left the O'Neills' farm in such good spirits that Barry and Ned Breen laughed with them.

It was their last sighting of Sean Dwyer, and within a few days, nobody could remember the drifter who'd accompanied him.

Barry O'Neill built more barns and corrals and filled them with livestock. In spring, he bought 100 sheep and sent them out to pasture on the land that bordered the reservation. He looked up at the hills and figured how much he'd make if he had another thirty acres from the Indian Territory. Sometimes, he estimated how much he'd make with another fifty acres, or what he'd do if he had another seventy acres.

"It seems such a waste," he said to Ned Breen, "all that idle land."

Ned agreed. "And all that timber just waiting to be cut."

They cut the trees and set traps on the boundaries of the reservation but were reluctant to stray too deeply.

When the first crisp morning of winter arrived, Barry went as far as the cave where there were no trees. Still haunted by Sean Dwyer's disappearance, he stood on the verge, staring up at the high rocks.

Chaytan and Goldie saw him. They were hiding, lying flat on their bellies on a rock so old and smooth that a tree grew out of the top. They saw Barry standing on the edge of the clearing with his hands on his hips, surveying all he could see.

Chaytan pretended his finger was a gun. He closed one eye and pointed his index finger. "Bang," he whispered, "greedy Wašícu!" *Greedy white man.*

Goldie knew her father was a greedy white man. His recent behavior reminded her of the time before he'd left Ireland, when he'd added up the assets he shared with his brother, sold their land on the hill, and fled with money that was not rightfully his.

"You have enough," Aengus moaned that night when her father and Ned Breen raised the subject of the luscious, idle, virgin vegetation that belonged to the Indians.

"Seems an awful waste," Barry sighed. "All that land and not a sinner working it."

"Nobody comes onto your farm and points at your land and says, 'We'll take this back because he's not doing what I'd like him to do,'" Aengus replied.

"It's not the same," Barry said with an edge to his voice. "This is the West, everything is for free. You said it yourself."

Barry's talk of wealth and gold increasingly irked Aengus.

Aengus realized the West he'd fallen in love with was not the same West that his cousin wanted to build. The early letters that Aengus had written about the sun and sky and buffalo were lost on

Barry. He had little appreciation for the beauty that Aengus saw unless it held a monetary value. Aengus told him, "My West and your West are vastly different countries. You could have everything if you stopped being so greedy."

"A man could get rich out here," Barry said.

"And a man could get shot or die from want quicker," Aengus retorted.

"Die from want!" Barry repeated. "I never heard such foolishness."

That night was the first time that Goldie remembered her father castigating Aengus. When Aengus went home, Barry likened him to Sean Dwyer. "That old Irish mentality that they have enough," he said, raising his lip sneeringly. "Men like him are too backward to fight for more. He's spent too long around those Indians; he even set up housekeeping with a squaw and treats her like his wife."

They were so surprised with his rage at Aengus, each of the O'Neills stopped what they were doing to stare at him.

"Bloody fool thinks he's an Indian," Barry shouted. After a few minutes he calmed, then said in a quiet, suspicious voice, "Captain Gallagher says the Indians call to see him."

"I wouldn't be surprised," Neasa said. "He's been here a long time."

"Did you ever see Indians at Aengus' farm?" Barry asked Goldie.

Goldie knew that too much time had passed to tell the truth. She was pleased that she had never told her father that the Indians were regular callers. She never mentioned the fact that they knew Goldie's name, and she kept secret that her favorite visiting Indian was Blue Feather, who spoke a little English and was more playful than his friends. Initially, she had been tempted to tell her parents that Blue Feather had a habit of humming that irked the older Indian. "Sing or shut up," the old Indian had said in Lakota. Goldie had expected a fight. Blue Feather didn't appear scared. Instead, he stood up and began singing at the top of his voice and performing an idiotic dance. Everybody laughed uproariously except the old Indian, although eventually he too found it funny and smiled.

Goldie never told anyone that she'd asked Blue Feather if he'd ever seen her sister. By the well at the front of Aengus' cabin, Blue Feather listened intently as Goldie described Baby Miriam. She suppressed the rising lump in her throat and didn't stop describing Baby Miriam until Blue Feather put his hand on her shoulder. His hand rested there long enough for her voice to taper away. When there was silence, he shook his head, and he told her that he hadn't seen a captive among the tribes matching that description. He promised her that from now on he'd look for her. Goldie had remained perfectly still until the urge to cry had passed. Blue Feather removed his hand from her shoulder. He joined his index finger and thumb, and then he pretended to look through it like a telescope. "If I see, I will tell you." When there was nothing more to say he splashed her with water. She filled a bucket and chased him around the yard until their laughter brought Aengus and Makawee to the door of the cabin to investigate. Eventually everybody was laughing, even the cross old Indian.

"So, you didn't see anything strange?" her father asked.

"No," Goldie said, "only this week I learned to do the Diamond Twill Weave."

He looked away. He'd no interest in the different weaving designs for her Navajo rug, only the accumulation of money, the gold that was waiting to be picked from the streams in the forbidden hills, and the idle vegetation on his doorstep.

CHAPTER SIXTEEN

1874

Talk of gold and fortunes came and went during the ensuing months. Most were too preoccupied with the hard grind of work to develop dreams of anything other than a good harvest. There were few outward signs of change for the adults apart from their offspring, who stretched and bounded into adulthood. Those who had come to the West as children were the new generation who would nail their roots further into the landscape of the American plains. They made plans and saw a future on which their names were engraved. In the spring of 1874, Barry built a new house with a large kitchen, a veranda, and an upstairs.

Aengus came to help, but there was little talk or warmth between him and Barry.

There were new arrivals in Four Oaks. Some Irish families came to live among their own. Lorcan could often be heard boasting about the size of their farm and offering advice on how to make good in the West.

Barry's patience with Lorcan waned with each passing month.

"God love the families advised by that eejit," he said about Lorcan.

That same spring, their community felled timber from the O'Neill and Breen farms to build a schoolhouse and a church. When the church was finished in June, Father O'Brien said his first Mass, and the congregation was ordered to remain motionless while they posed for a photograph. It was the first time most had had their photo taken.

Afterward, there was music and a party. Some of the community elders set their sights on the small patch of land at the back of the church where they would eventually be interred.

"Maybe I'll be the first to be buried here," Neasa said as she looked at the bare patch of newly consecrated land. "It could be sooner than later," she added.

Neasa's back and hip trouble had worsened. Her spine was as curved as the hook they used to hang meat. At night, they'd hear her moaning in pain. When she walked any distance, she had to be helped by another person. She did whatever she could from a sitting position and rarely ventured far from their new house.

"You can't die from being a hunchback," Goldie retorted as she linked arms with her mother.

Neasa was not convinced. A few times when the pain was too severe she grew angry, and she concurred with Aengus. "Maybe it's the work out here. The stooping, and the clawing for more."

Barry listened without comment.

Captain Gallagher brought them news that General Custer had marched into the Black Hills. The Captain sat in their new kitchen and unfolded a newspaper with the story and an accompanying photograph of General Custer.

Barry read the article aloud. "The expedition comprised ten companies from the Seventh Cavalry, one from the Seventeenth Infantry and one from the Twentieth Infantry, three Gatling guns, and a Rodman rifled cannon." Barry stopped reading. "How many men is that?" he asked Captain Gallagher.

"About 1,200 men, and it doesn't say that he also has three journalists and a sixteen-piece band."

"So General Custer can play music to the sound of slaying Indians," Ned Breen said, taking his turn to examine the newspaper photo.

It was reported in the paper that General Custer was in the Black Hills looking for a location for an Army fort, but Captain Gallagher said that was unlikely. "You don't need 1,200 men or three newspaper men to find the best place to build a fort."

"What's he doing, then?" Ned Breen asked.

"Looking for gold," Captain Gallagher said.

"Will he find it?" Barry asked.

"Reckon he will," Captain Gallagher replied, "and then everything changes."

"How does it change?"

"Then the gold seekers will come and find more gold. Then America will become rich again and the recession will end, the Indians will go to war for a while, the Army will subdue them and take back the Black Hills, and we'll live happily until the next war," he said before tucking into the meal that Frances placed in front of him.

Captain Gallagher called once a week, sometimes to attend Mass and other times on a Saturday night to play cards. Ned Breen and his sons and the Dwyer children were always there, eager to hear the latest from General Custer. They wanted to know everything about the General, from his breakfast to the type of horse he rode. Goldie found it peculiar that grown men had such a boyish fascination for another man.

Captain Gallagher fed their curiosity and even told them facts that didn't concur with their idea of General Custer.

"He tends to his hair like a woman," Captain Gallagher told them. "Every morning he doesn't leave his tent until his hair is right. He looks this way and that in the mirror," Captain Gallagher said, turning his head from right to left and tugging at his hair. "He don't do a thing till the hair is right. There isn't a woman as fussy."

Ned Breen refused to believe it.

"I seen him with my own eyes," Captain Gallagher said. "Last

Tuesday I was dispatched with post to his camp, and I seen him riding by with his locks flowing in the wind."

"Stop it!" Ned Breen said.

"Sure as I'm sitting here," Captain Gallagher said, "the Indians call him Long-Hair,"

When Captain Gallagher called again, he told them that General Custer had shot a grizzly.

They lapsed into silence as they considered it.

"Shot a grizzly and had his picture taken with it," Captain Gallagher clarified as he handed out the newspaper with the picture.

Everybody took their turn to look at it.

"Did he find his gold yet?" Barry asked, passing the paper to Ned Breen.

"His men are panning for it as we speak," Captain Gallagher told them.

Much to Goldie's annoyance, it wasn't only the men who were in awe of General Custer. Frances regularly looked at Long-Hair's photo and compared him to Owen Breen.

"Owen and General Custer have the same hair, and they're about the same height. They're both handsome." Frances had a dreamy quality to her voice. "If Owen were in the Army he'd be just as famous as General Custer."

Goldie couldn't believe what she was hearing. "Are you off your rocker?" she asked.

As Owen grew into a young man, he inherited his father's protruding jaw. There was a crease at the top of his nose joining both eyebrows. He filled out into a stocky bulk of a man. However, never in a million years could Goldie say he was handsome.

"Can you not see the resemblance?" Frances said, holding up a picture of General Custer. "I reckon Owen is every bit as clever as General Custer," Frances continued.

Their mother didn't voice her opinion, while Lorcan thought the comparison was just about right.

Goldie had heard enough. "Owen Breen is nothing but a brute. Same as his father."

"Stop that," Neasa chided.

Goldie would not stop. "The same as his brothers. All the Breens are brutes. Every darn one of them. And," Goldie paused, "his father flogs his wife."

"Enough," Neasa said, raising her voice. Nobody dared say aloud what everybody knew.

"I've seen the marks on Mrs. Breen's arms, and so has everyone else," Goldie added.

"I said, enough," Neasa said.

"She came out here a fine-looking woman and now she looks like a beat-up old nag from her life with Ned Breen and his bully boy sons."

"I said, stop it," her mother raised her voice.

"And you'll end up like Mrs. Breen," Goldie continued. "Any woman who goes within an asses' reach of those men is gonna end up like Mrs. Breen."

"You might be a law unto yourself and behave like a man by…," Neasa forced herself up from her chair and hobbled across the kitchen to Goldie, and continued, "coming and going as you please, but I said enough…." She pushed Goldie toward the door.

Goldie continued to shout out her objections, "And you'll end up with…" The front door closed behind her. Goldie finished her sentence by shouting through the corner of the closed door, "with bruises and flogged until you can't even raise a smile."

That summer, Goldie was seventeen. Her appearance changed dramatically. Since they had come to the West, Frances had been the beauty of the family. She was smaller and prettier than Goldie; she had long black hair, dark eyes, and a small, pretty heart-shaped face. People had a different way of speaking to Frances; it was as if her beauty brought out the softer side of people. Captain Gallagher always said that Frances had "the stuff that fellas stopped to stare at."

But that summer, Captain Gallagher sat at the O'Neills' table and declared Goldie the new beauty, saying, "Now she's the one that strangers stop to stare at."

Goldie's face was more handsome than pretty. She had the

strong chiseled features of her father, high cheekbones, and a wide smile. She had a cleft chin and the bright red hair of her mother that remained as vivid as the first days when she'd come to the West. However, it was her eyes that people noticed. Her every mood was conveyed in her large, expressive green eyes.

Owen Breen claimed that he could tell what she was thinking from her eyes. "I can tell that you're sweet on me," he told her.

Goldie was alone in their house preparing Sunday lunch when Owen Breen appeared at the door wearing his good Sunday clothes. He held his hat to his chest and appeared almost shy.

"Admit it," Owen continued in a peculiar quiet voice. "You like me too."

Over the last few months, Goldie had noticed him but not in the way he assumed. She'd seen him staring at her at Mass. At the "Neck-Tie" festival to raise funds for the town, boys bid for the priv-ilege of eating supper with the girls. Owen bid to eat with Goldie. She thought it very odd. At a party hosted by the Dalys where there was music and dance, she caught him looking at her several times.

That Sunday, when he appeared in the kitchen, with his cap in his hand and his play at being refined, Goldie gaped in disbelief. She was holding a plate of bacon in one hand and a jug of milk in the other.

"I saw you looking at me at the Dalys' party," he continued. "You're real sweet on me too."

"Owen Breen," Goldie began, closing her eyes in admonish-ment against the mere thought of it. She didn't know how she could explain her real feelings for him. "You are a pig," she began. "You were a pig on the wagon train out here, you are a pig to the young Dwyer boys, you are a pig to Chaytan, you are a pig to take my sister home from the Dalys' party and then come into my kitchen on this Sunday morning while I'm making lunch and tell me that I have feelings for you."

Owen blinked with disbelief.

Goldie continued. "You have the manners of a pig, the look of a pig, and the smell of a pig," she concluded.

Owen's expression went from shock to anger, "Nobody is gonna want you," he said, pointing his finger at her. "You'll end up with that Injun, only Chaytan who knows nothing other than mustangs."

Just then Goldie was reminded of the day of the grasshoppers. His childish taunt brought her to a different place.

"I come in with a good proposition," he continued, "and maybe it just might be the best offer you…"

Afterward, Goldie couldn't remember what she threw at him first, the bacon or the milk.

When Goldie relayed the story to Chaytan, she saw the funny side of it. She omitted what Owen had said about Chaytan, but she told him the rest.

"The milk was splashed all over his good Sunday shirt. The plate of bacon hit him on the nose," she told Chaytan. "Then he left with his Sunday clothes ruined."

Goldie and Chaytan were sitting together on the beams of the mustang corral. Each week, Chaytan came to the O'Neill farm to break the mustangs that Barry continued to sell to Captain Gallagher. Goldie brought Chaytan his lunch and waited while he ate.

Chaytan smiled and shook his head, saying, "You called him a pig, and then you threw the pig at him."

"Something like that," she said, keeping secret the fact that she'd spent the rest of the day feeling out of sorts over Baby Miriam.

She looked at the mustang. It stood in the center of the corral looking toward them as if waiting for Chaytan to return to it.

"Did you name this one?" she asked, referring to Chaytan's habit of giving each mustang a name that reflected its personality.

"Maybe I will call this one Goldie," he said. "She is wild and bold and does whatever she wants."

Goldie laughed.

On the other side of the corral, Lorcan, Owen Breen, and his younger brother, Timothy, were loading feed from the barn onto a wagon She saw the boys looking over their shoulders at them. Owen Breen said something that Goldie couldn't hear. The three boys began to laugh.

Goldie recalled the time when Lorcan and the younger Breens

had idolized Chaytan and the magic he worked while taming mustangs. As they grew, they adopted the hatred and misgivings their parents harbored about the Indians. Added to that, Goldie knew it was a little more than hereditary bigotry, as Chaytan had come to a new agreement with Barry. For each tamed mustang, Chaytan earned ten dollars. Barry sold the stock to Captain Gallagher for three times that, and Captain Gallagher took another slice. Lorcan was seething when he heard how much money "The Injun" as he called Chaytan, was making. It was all the more frustrating when Barry never tired of praising Chaytan and reminding Lorcan that he could do nothing right.

"One of these days I'll be gone from here," Lorcan said to Neasa, "and then he might want me."

Neasa did her best to console Lorcan. "He wants what's best."

There were times when Lorcan wanted to please Barry. He was a good horseman and thought he could do as good a job breaking the mustangs as Chaytan.

"It takes dedication, and that my boy, you do not have," Barry said.

Lorcan went into the corral only to get kicked in the thigh. He hid his limp from Barry.

"Do the day's work, and he'll be happy with that," Neasa advised Lorcan.

Lorcan couldn't do the day's work. He was easily distracted, his sights set on faraway stories of gold strikes and Army adventures. He was constantly aggrieved that Chaytan was seen as a better man in his father's eyes.

Goldie heard Lorcan discussing how much Chaytan made with the Breens. She also guessed that Lorcan wildly exaggerated Chaytan's cut.

"Should be a crime to give an Injun that kind of money," Owen Breen said.

Ten dollars was a fortune to the Breens, who were barely fed. Every red cent that Ned Breen earned was spent on material to go back into the farm.

"They can't be white unless they hate me," Chaytan said with a guarded expression, looking to the other side of the corral at them.

Goldie looked at Chaytan's profile. He had a high forehead and brown, cautious eyes. He had full lips, and when he smiled, his appearance changed. He looked younger, almost mischievous. She couldn't remember when she'd noticed he'd grown into a man, but it was recent, as recent as the snow that had melted on the mountain peaks three months ago. There were times she'd liked to have reached out and touched his face. Just then she had the urge to put her hand on his cheek and trace his long arched eyebrows with her finger. Instead, she took his empty plate and returned to the cabin. She could hear the barn door closing. Lorcan and the Breens were leaving. She looked over her shoulder to see them passing the paddock. Timothy Breen was sitting with Owen and Lorcan on the top. As they passed Chaytan, Lorcan stood up, leaned to his right, and spat into the corral.

CHAPTER SEVENTEEN

1874

During that summer of 1874, as General Custer and his men camped in the Black Hills and panned for gold, Aengus and Goldie's father's relationship grew more strained. Barry's preoccupation with the gold became more incessant, and all the while Aengus grew cautious and guarded in their company. During one of Aengus's last visits to the O'Neills' home, Captain Gallagher, Ned Breen, and Barry were playing cards. They discussed the killing of the buffalo. The rotting carcasses of buffalo had become a common sight. Close to the new railway tracks, Goldie found a woman's hat and a leaflet offering excursions to *shoot the buffalo from the passing train.* There was a picture of a man and woman leaning out of the window of a railcar, both smiling gaily behind their shotguns. Goldie brought home the leaflet. While Ned Breen and Barry regretted not finding the buffalo before their carcasses rotted, Aengus was appalled at the idea that a company could promote a trip offering tourists the opportunity to shoot buffalo for sport.

"It's a waste," Aengus said as he looked at the leaflet. "Killing a magnificent beast for no good reason other than a bit of sport seems immoral."

"Some city folks have too much money," Ned Breen said.

"It doesn't say much about city life if the wealthy people want to pay money to ride the railcar and shoot from the windows. It's plain stupid," Aengus quipped.

"Killing the buffalo is all part of a bigger plan," Captain Gallagher interrupted them. "When the buffalo are gone, then the Indian will have nothing, no food, no clothing, no tepee. Nada. Those rich folks don't realize that they're paying to play their part in the big plan."

"That's very clever," Barry said.

"These lads in Washington are no fools," Captain Gallagher said.

"Sooner the Red Man realizes that America is not going to stand still for the Sioux, the better," Ned Breen said.

Their conversation moved onto gold. Once again, they speculated about the location of the gold and wondered which streams deposited the coveted yellow flakes and nuggets that would make them wealthy for the rest of their days.

"How do they know where to pan for gold?" Barry asked Aengus.

"I don't know," Aengus said, "I've never panned for gold."

"We know there's gold; it's just a matter of time before General Custer finds it," Barry said.

Aengus didn't respond.

"Aengus, is there gold there?" Barry asked, laying his cards on the table. He sounded as if he were tired of talking in circles.

"Suppose there is," Aengus said quietly.

"Would you tell us where to find it?" Ned Breen joined in.

"I just said, I've never panned for gold, so I don't know."

His reluctance to reveal all he knew was another new indication of his distrust of Barry and Ned.

"Maybe we should take a look," Barry said.

"That'll remove your greed once and for all," Aengus retorted.

"You'd probably tell your red friends we'd gone into their territory," Barry said.

Angus didn't answer immediately. "I might do that," Aengus said without denying that the Indians were his friends.

Aengus left that night without eating the prepared food.

Ned Breen laid down his cards and leaned toward Barry, saying, "That man will be your enemy yet."

Four weeks later, in late August, a newspaper arrived at Four Oaks. The headlines declared the discovery of 'Gold and Silver in Immense Quantities.'

Ned Breen stomped the floor and flapped his hands. "They'll come from every corner of America to claim our gold. We have to do something," he whined, as if it were his money the masses were coming to pluck from his hideaway.

Barry had something new to contend with. Neasa's face had changed; her mouth appeared to twist, and her eyes drooped. The O'Neills took turns sitting with her at night.

In early September, when everyone had gone to bed and it was Goldie's turn to sit with her mother, Neasa surprised Goldie by speaking about Baby Miriam.

"I been thinking," Neasa said, "maybe it's not such a bad thing if Baby Miriam was taken by the Lakota."

Goldie was astounded, first with her mother mentioning Baby Miriam by name and then by her reference to the Indians. She was unable to reply.

"Those people are good to their children," her mother said.

She then curled up in her chair and moaned for three days before yielding to death.

The O'Neills gave Neasa an Irish wake. They laid her body on the kitchen table, killed three lambs, bought bottles of liquor, and opened their house to all. The townsfolk came to pray and comment on her peaceful remains. They drank to her death and willed her soul to rest in peace.

"She has all the answers now," Mrs. Breen said, looking sadly at Neasa's remains. "I've lost a dear friend."

Aengus and Chaytan called to sympathize. There was little to say. Barry didn't say that the West was too much for his wife or admit that he'd worked her too hard. Instead, they did what all the Irish did at funerals, Aengus shook hands with Barry and offered his sympathies.

Goldie watched the interaction between Barry and Aengus.

"Thanks for coming," Barry said before moving onto the next sympathizer.

It was not the time for Aengus to tell Barry than Makawee was expecting their baby; she was three months along.

In the spirit of the Irish wake, nobody was allowed to go hungry or thirsty. Lorcan O'Neill and the Breens had their first taste of liquor. When Goldie heard their exaggerated laughter, she was quick to realize they'd found a new sustenance.

Late in the evening, Goldie found respite in the quiet barn with only the hens picking quietly at the grain. Owen Breen appeared behind her holding his hat in his hand, and she presumed he had come to sympathize.

He didn't offer his sympathies; instead, he stepped closer and raised his hand to her hair. He smiled as he toyed with a strand of it. His eyes were glassy. "You're as pretty as the morning," he sighed.

Goldie could smell the liquor on his breath.

"Prettiest girl I ever did see," he added, stepping closer to her.

Goldie stood still, only aware of the revulsion toward him intensifying with each utterance. Of all the times to come and act maudlin around her. *Prettiest girl I ever did see!* She couldn't wait to tell Chaytan the update.

Owen continued in the same slow-moving, sleepy drawl, "I know I been stepping out with Frances, but you're really the girl for me."

"You're a beast," she said. "The wild hog is more of a gentleman than you."

Suddenly, he lunged forward and grabbed her. "You're gonna kiss me this time," he said. He pinned her arms to her side, and she couldn't wriggle free. She began to scream, while the hens took flight, cackling at the melee.

"You ugly, horrible boar," she screamed louder.

"Just give me one little kiss," he said, winded at the strain of trying to hold her.

He pressed his body against hers. He held her so tightly she felt overwhelmed by his strength.

"It ain't no use," he said breathlessly. "Promise me you'll be mine," he said, leaning in for a kiss.

She tried to turn her face away.

Suddenly it stopped.

Chaytan was there. He had one hand around Owen's neck, and his free hand punched Owen in the face twice. Owen staggered and fell against the side of the barn. Some of the tools fell from their hangers. Chaytan hit him again, and on the fourth punch Owen lay prostrate on the ground.

Chaytan turned to Goldie. He pushed her hair back from her face to examine her.

Goldie was so indignant about the attack that she remained rooted to the spot. Her earlier revulsion was now replaced with a simmering rage.

After a few moments, she nodded. "Yes, I'm all right."

They heard voices approaching. Goldie recognized Lorcan's voice.

"You should go," she said to Chaytan. "If they see Owen, they'll think they have a reason to hurt you."

Chaytan hesitated.

"Quickly, go," she said as the approaching voices came closer.

He left through the back of the barn. Goldie stood perfectly still for a moment. The sight of the tools askew on the floor of the barn intensified her fury. The only tool that remained on its hanger was the ax. Goldie took the ax from its hanger, and then she went to Owen and toed him in the ribs with her boot. He opened his eyes and looked up at her. There was a neat stream of blood trickling from his nose down his cheek.

She raised the handle of the ax and rammed the butt into his mouth.

Lorcan, Timothy Breen, and the Dwyer boys appeared at her side. Owen rolled over and spat out a tooth.

They boys looked at the sight before them with glassy, disbelieving eyes.

The following morning, Neasa's body was the first of their congregation to be interred in the consecrated soil at the rear of their new Catholic church.

CHAPTER EIGHTEEN

1937

Wilbur Breen was a small, dandy little man, unlike the other burly men of the Breen family. He had small blue eyes and a boyish freckled face. He always dressed immaculately. This morning, he was wearing slacks with a crease so sharp, Lucy thought of the old expression, 'they'd cut butter.' He wore a crisp white shirt and heavy overcoat.

He shook hands with Harry and when he turned to Lucy, he opened his arms as a father would to a child. "Lucy, how are you?" His expression of caring was overdone, she thought.

"Hello, Wilbur," Lucy replied, without rolling into his opened arms. She stood up and shook his hand.

"You're looking mighty sophisticated, even at his hour of the morning and under these circumstances," Wilbur said.

Lucy had taken extra care doing her hair and choosing her clothes this morning. She was wearing a coffee-colored woolen skirt and a cream, silk bow-necked blouse. It wasn't every day she would meet her father for the first time.

"I could say the same for you," Lucy said. She was going to say something about the sharp crease in his trousers but didn't. "How is the family?"

"Great, all are doing great. The boys are in college, both doing law. Mom is good, and poor Dad, he's still hanging in there."

"Yes, he's remarkable," Lucy said, thinking of Owen Breen and his unending will to survive after his stoke.

"He's made of great stuff," Wilbur summarized.

"And Harry, how is business?" Wilbur asked.

Lucy noticed his voice went a little deeper when he spoke to Harry. They were cousins, although Harry hated to have it pointed out, whereas Wilbur was impressed with Harry.

"Great," Harry smiled. "We're kept busy. And how is business with you?" Harry asked.

"I'm doing so well I cannot keep up," Wilbur said, taking the seat beside Harry. Once seated, Wilbur looked around him, surveying the large room. "Place looks fine," he said with surprise.

Although Goldie was Wilbur's aunt, their relationship had been broken after the statue of Lorcan was erected. When Wilbur suggested having the monument erected for Lorcan, he was only entering politics at twenty years of age. He'd asked Goldie to sponsor the statue. He led her to believe it would be a small plaque on a stone, his words were "something dignified and discreet to honor our fallen heroes." Goldie was reluctant. "And something little Lucy will be able to admire, Lorcan being her father," Wilbur said. Lucy was seventeen at the time. "It would finally silence the gossips," he added, referring to those who insinuated that Lucy was an illegitimate child unrelated to Goldie and the O'Neills. "We'll also include Ciaran Dwyer's name," Wilbur said, referring to one of the Dwyer boys who had been killed in the Great War. "It'll commemorate all of our local heroes," Wilbur concluded.

Goldie agreed. When she saw the scale of the life-size copper sculpture she was enraged. She burst into Wilbur's office and flayed him with her walking cane. His screams could be heard in Gallagher's Hotel. Since then, Wilbur had only been in Goldie's home once, and that had been for her funeral. Now, Lucy thought it peculiar that Wilbur had arrived uninvited this morning.

"How did you know I'd returned?" Lucy asked.

"I met your taxi driver in Gallagher's, and he told me that our very own Miss Four Oaks had returned," he sang the last line as if she were a child.

Lucy had won the title of Miss Four Oaks when she was seventeen, and Wilbur loved to remind her of it.

"I hear you came by plane from New York," Wilbur said. "Aren't you a pair of high-flyers!"

"It's the easiest and fastest method," Harry said.

"So, you're home to meet the man himself," Wilbur said.

Lucy nodded.

"We got ourselves a mighty problem here," Wilbur said, changing his tone.

She noticed his inclusive 'we.' He stretched his arms across the back of the sofa and hoisted his leg on top of his knee. He appeared comfortable at once. As a politician, Lucy assumed he was probably used to sitting in people's living rooms and talking to them as if he were part of their daily lives.

"I've been thinking about our little problem," Wilbur continued. "You two being a recognizable couple and all, this return of Lorcan O'Neill could affect your..." he scrunched up his mouth trying to find the right word, "your persona."

"Our persona?" Lucy said, glancing over at Harry, who had an amused smile.

"That's right. Your persona, your ego. We all got an ego," he said, informatively looking at Harry. "You know that?"

This was why Wilbur would never be a politician anywhere except Four Oaks. He was a clown. Certain members of the electorate believed everything he said, and others knew he was a clown. However, he was their clown. Despite his nonsense, Wilbur was the man who appeared to get things done in Four Oaks.

"You gotta remember," Wilbur continued, "the fact that your picture has been gracing every magazine all over America, and Harry is a famous personality, this could potentially be a deadly situation for you."

Their picture did not grace the pages of every magazine all over

America. Occasionally, they attended events and had their picture taken, which then appeared in newspapers and magazines. For a brief period, Harry had taken an interest in the woolen mill and used his connections to promote it. It was a rare period during which Harry and Goldie were united. There was a Hollywood actor who'd identified his favorite winter coat as Wyoming Tweed, and the *New York Times* had run a feature on the mill that included a photo of Lucy. It was a wonderful coup, and all down to Harry. It appeared exotic in Four Oaks. Lucy didn't contradict Wilbur or tell him that some of the features in the magazines cost a lot of money and favors.

Harry got straight to the point. "Where is he?" he asked of Lorcan O'Neill.

"He's staying at Gallagher's Hotel. I spoke to him briefly last night, told him who I am," Wilbur said, as if the arrival were under no illusion about who was the most important man in town. "I gave him all our news about my sons and nephews. I told him about you," he said, looking at Lucy, "that Goldie took you in and that you'd married my cousin." Wilbur looked at Harry. "My cousin the financier."

Harry cut across this comment, as he was clearly unable to listen to Wilbur this morning. "Have you seen him today?"

"I called at Gallagher's Hotel this morning, but he was asleep."

"Asleep," Harry repeated, checking his watch. "It's ten o'clock."

Wilbur shrugged, "He's old."

"Have any of the old folks seen him, the likes of your mother or that old Dwyer man?"

"My mother is returning from Montana tonight. She spent the last three days with Kate," he said, referring to his sister. "Bertha Gallagher is the only one who's seen him, and rightly enough," Wilbur said in a singsong voice, "she confirmed," Wilbur looked from one to the other, "it is he," he announced with perfect enunciation.

"Did he explain where he had been?" Harry asked, "or explain why he'd returned now?"

"He said he was curious," Wilbur said.

"That's it? He got curious after thirty-odd years?" Harry asked.

"More or less," Wilbur said. "He wanted to know all about the old families, the likes of the Dwyers and Kellys, all about us Breens." Wilbur looked at his fingers as he spoke. "He said he knew we'd always come out on top. Actually," Wilbur turned to Lucy, saying, "he was mighty surprised to hear your old beau, John Dwyer, is one of the biggest sheep farmers this side of the Missouri River."

Lucy didn't know if she should be flattered.

"Lorcan said we'd come a long way since some Kennedy man." Wilbur hesitated. "I can't remember his first name; it's a peculiar Irish name, anyway, we've come a long way since that Kennedy man led our kin to the West."

Lucy looked at Goldie's ensemble on the sideboard, where Aengus' eagle feather was kept in a glass case. Many times, Goldie had referred to Aengus Kennedy, her father's cousin, who was also Makawee's husband. Aengus Kennedy had taught her people everything about living in the West, all of which he'd learned from the Indians. According to Goldie, he was generous and kind, and in the end, her people had looked for more than he could give them.

"Does he plan on staying long?" Harry asked.

"You know, I asked him that," Wilbur said. "And you know what he told me?"

"What?" Harry asked.

"He said he doesn't like to make plans too far into the future. Said he'd take it day by day."

"We'll know more when we meet him," Lucy said. She was beginning to get a little nervous as she thought about meeting him.

"You know this kind of thing really happens all the time?" Wilbur said. "We got fellas rolling into towns all over the country, claiming to be dead people and then taking money and land that was never theirs."

"Sure, Wilbur, only in Hollywood movies," Lucy said. She didn't want Harry to become even more suspicious than he was already.

"Remember the Newcastle case!" Wilbur reminded her of a case in which an elderly gentleman had returned to the family farm after a twenty-year absence. He claimed to be the rightful owner of the land. Both sides battled it out in court. Costs for the court case took a substantial amount of the farm. Eventually, the elderly gentleman won. Bit by bit, he lost the farm over various card tables.

Lucy held up her finger, saying, "One incident."

For a long minute they remained silent. The only sound was the wind.

"What are we going to do?" Wilbur asked.

"We'll probably call at the hotel at some stage this afternoon," Harry said vaguely.

"I'll come with you," Wilbur offered immediately, "best thing to do is, you and I go to meet him," Wilbur said to Harry. "When we've established what's what, we'll have dinner and invite the ladies." As if that settled the matter, Wilbur asked, "What time shall I pick you up?"

"We won't make any arrangements yet," Harry said. "I'm expecting an important business call shortly."

Just then, Lucy was grateful for Harry's diplomacy. She didn't want Wilbur Breen sitting in on her first meeting with her father. She'd like time alone with him on their first encounter. If Wilbur were present, he'd spend the time butting in and talking about himself and his own importance. Equally, Lucy knew that Wilbur would rush home to tell his parents all the trivial details, and the Breens would scrutinize her every utterance with a critical eye.

Wilbur spent a few minutes speculating about Lorcan O'Neill's life after the war, where he'd lived, how much he remembered. "That war in the Philippines was pretty rough." As he spoke, his foot toyed with the carpet and he slipped his toe under the corner.

Lucy watched his foot and noted that if he were a child, the closest adult would slap his thigh as an indication that you do not do that.

"The papers were full of horror stories about torture and killings and the thousands who were butchered," Wilbur continued. "Lorcan is probably a class of," Wilbur paused again, "a maniac."

"A maniac?" Harry asked. Lucy could see his amused expression return.

"Yes, a kind of a lunatic," Wilbur clarified. "Somebody like Old Kathleen Daly," he said, referring to Bertha Gallagher's insane sister, who was married to Timothy Breen. She appeared in their town every few years. Kathleen Daly would roam the streets, terrifying women by trying to take their babies and other odd behavior until her antics became too problematic. She was always returned to the asylum for another few years before reappearing again.

When there was nothing more to say, Wilbur began commenting on the house, the old furniture, and the rug on the floor.

"Those side tables are quite old; I'd say Bob Clancy's father made them. Look at the detail in the legs, the curve and foot, it's good craftsmanship," Wilbur said, rubbing his finger over the grooves.

Wilbur reminded Lucy of a man who worked in the radio station with Harry. It was rumored that he was a homosexual. He loved to talk about colors and fashion and house designs. Wilbur had similar interests and mannerisms. Unlike most men she knew, Wilbur noticed and commented on the texture of clothes and the colors of rugs and upholstery. Wilbur had the same womanly way of walking, and when animated, as he was now, he held his head to one side and pouted.

"I'll bet you this is one of Goldie's rugs," Wilbur said, bending down to take a closer look.

Lucy had forgotten how ignorant Wilbur was as she watched him pull back the corner of each side of the rug until he found what he was looking for.

"Look at that," he said, pointing to the underside corner closest to Lucy.

There was a picture stitched in white thread. Wilbur bent forward to take a closer look.

"Well, I'll be damned," he said, rubbing his finger over it. "It's a grasshopper. This sure is one of Goldie's old rugs. You know every house in Four Oaks had one of Goldie's rugs or blankets at some stage."

Goldie was known for stitching pictures into her wares. Some said it was her own version of the Lakota Winter Count, which was a record kept for thousands of years by the Indians. Each year they documented the main event of that year. Goldie did the same thing with her blankets and rugs.

"I'll bet you that this rug was made in 1866 or 1874 when the grasshoppers invaded," Wilbur said.

Lucy wished he'd take his paws off her aunt's rug and stop being overly familiar.

"Last summer my boys went fishing at Buckhorn. They found an abandoned cabin and inside there was an old coal-oil lamp and other paraphernalia." Wilbur stood up but continued to look at the rug as he spoke. "Poor boys thought they'd stumbled on the biggest historical discovery of the century. A few days later, I drove out with them. There was nothing much to see except tin cups and a few of Goldie's old blankets. I knew it was Goldie because I'd heard how she used to stitch a different picture each year into her woolens."

"What was on the blanket in the cabin?" Lucy asked.

"It was a star," Wilbur said.

Lucy quietly guessed that the blanket had been woven in late 1870s. Goldie had told her that she needed more courage than ever after her mother had died. The morning star was for courage.

"I asked Mom and Dad but neither of them knew."

Wilbur left the rug peeled back. He took his car keys from the coffee table. "We'll have dinner tomorrow," Wilbur said. "I'll have Molly prepare something nice and gather all the old clan together for a party."

"I don't think we'll be here too long. This is a flying visit," Harry said.

"You'll be here for two days at least. I'll call you this afternoon to make plans," he said to Harry.

Lucy and Harry remained silent until they heard the front door close.

"Was he right?" Harry indicated the rug. "Was it made in 1866 or 1874?"

"It was 1866," Lucy said before placing her foot beneath the rug and flicking the grasshopper out of sight.

CHAPTER NINETEEN

1937

It was after two o'clock when Lucy and Harry drove down the hill to meet Lorcan.

"Shouldn't we phone ahead?" Lucy asked.

"No, I'll use the element of surprise and catch him unawares," Harry said. "I won't give him any time to prepare or rehearse, then I'll ask him a few discrete questions in such a way he won't realize he's being questioned. I'll allow him to walk into his own booby trap."

"You're making this happy occasion sound like some covert military maneuver," Lucy said, annoyed that he continued to be so suspicious.

"And that's exactly what it is," Harry said as he drove down the main street and pulled up right outside Gallagher's Hotel. "I'll treat this like an armed operation until I know exactly what his mission is, and if I have to get down and dirty with him, so be it."

Harry's militaristic talk was making her more nervous. She looked at the entrance of Gallagher's to see Bertha at the door. Lucy would have preferred if their first meeting could have happened in a less public place than Gallagher's Hotel, but Harry had insisted. He said there would be plenty of time later for chitchat.

Bertha walked toward them as they got out of the car. "I spotted Goldie's old motor, and I knew it would be you," she said, fluffing her arms excitedly. She bent forward to kiss Lucy on the cheek. "You're very welcome, dear, and Harry," she said, as she put her hand on her large chest and tilted her head back slightly as if in awe at the sight of them, "you're both as handsome as ever and as welcome as the flowers of May."

Lucy liked Bertha. Over the years, Lucy heard that Bertha had sold home-brewed whiskey when she first came to the West. It was said she had some secret ingredient that brought buyers from miles around. Lucy also heard the disapproval in other quarters when Bertha's name was mentioned. It was rumored to be a brothel in the early days of the West. Aunt Frances was Bertha's most ardent critic, her condemnations were mainly targeted at Bertha's liquor. She said that Bertha was so hungry for money she'd serve men who were lying prostrate on the floor, comatose from her lethal concoction. She also said that Bertha used to try new brews on local men. Bertha was no longer a whiskey brewer and her hotel wasn't a brothel; it was, indeed, the finest hotel for 200 miles in any direction. Now that Bertha had found respectability, she liked to hammer home the point by boasting about her clientele, like the judge from Chicago who came each summer for a month, as did a Hollywood executive. Bertha loved to name-drop and claimed she had inside information on Hollywood gossip. This new clientele put a distance between the brothel and her home-brewed whiskey. For all of Bertha's silly name-dropping and nosiness, Lucy liked her, but didn't like her enough to reveal anything personal. She was a hopeless gossip.

Bertha extended her hand to shake Harry's hand.

"Where's my kiss?" Harry said jokingly. He leaned forward and kissed her on both cheeks.

Harry loved to overplay the role of the gentleman when in Four Oaks.

"Oh my, two kisses and it's only midday," Bertha joked and

waved her hand in front of her face as if she were going to faint. Then she turned to Lucy again, asking, "How have you been?"

Lucy knew she was referring to Goldie's death. "I'm all right. It'll take time."

"It sure will," Bertha said. "As the Captain used to say, 'ain't nothing is more certain than death.'"

Lucy agreed. Bertha went on to tell them how shocked she was at the news. "I was there, right there behind my bar," she said, putting her thumb over her shoulder and indicating the bar. "Next thing I heard from Emilio Dwyer that Goldie was dead. I just couldn't believe it." Bertha clapped her open palm on her chest and shook her head as if she'd just heard the news again.

"A surprise for all of us," Harry said. Lucy could see he was impatient to get on with his military mission.

"Now Lorcan comes home," Bertha said in the same disbelieving tone.

"Maybe Goldie sent him to me," Lucy said.

Bertha's expression changed from disbelief to skepticism. "No, I don't think Goldie would have sent him to you," she said.

"Is he here now?" Harry asked.

Bertha nodded slowly.

"Is it the real Lorcan O'Neill?" Harry asked.

Bertha nodded slowly again.

Lucy waited for her to say something sweet about Lorcan, maybe that it was a pleasure to see an old face, or even mention how handsome he had been. A lot of people who knew him mentioned his good looks. She didn't say anything, she just took Lucy's arm and guided her inside. Lucy deduced that Bertha was in the camp of those who didn't like Lorcan.

As Lucy passed through the bar, she noted some of the regulars, husbands and fathers of friends whom she'd love to catch up with during her stay.

Bertha tightened her grasp on Lucy's arm, then nodded toward a man who was standing at the bar. Bertha's eyes widened as if the encounter were something to be dreaded rather than enjoyed.

Lucy noticed that Lorcan was taller than most of the other men.

He was holding a drink in his right hand, and his hand was curled with the glass resting against his heart. He wore a beige suit, not the usual choice for men from these parts. The dust in their West would quickly darken it.

As they approached him, Lucy saw that Lorcan had spotted them too. He was watching them in the mirror behind the bar. When Harry tapped him on the back, he turned slowly to face them.

Harry began the introduction, "Good afternoon, I'm Harry Livingston, and this is my wife, Lucy O'Neill. I believe we are connected."

Lorcan looked from one to the other before accepting Harry's proffered hand.

Bertha guided them into one of the private snugs, where the three of them sat alone at a table. "Can I get you anything before I go?"

Harry ordered two gins, then looked at Lorcan's half-empty glass. "And whatever Lorcan is drinking."

While they waited for Bertha to return with the order, Harry and Lucy surveyed Lorcan, who in turn sized them up. Harry broke the silence, asking, "Is your room comfortable?"

"It is," Lorcan said.

"And the food in the hotel is renowned," Harry added.

"Sure is," Lorcan said.

When the drinks arrived, Harry raised his glass in a toast, "Bottoms up."

Lorcan nodded and raised his glass slightly. "Thanks."

Lucy noted Lorcan's features. He had a shock of thick white hair and a large bony face that was knitted together with a thousand lines. Age and life had made his eyes small; they were as small as peas between the curtains of two droopy eyelids. His appearance didn't convey kindness or malice. His only resounding feature was hardship.

"It must be nice to be home?" Harry said.

"It is," Lorcan said.

"Well now, this is very nice," Harry said.

Lorcan didn't make any attempt at idle chat. Lucy began to form the opinion that he was the strong silent type, a decorated soldier who didn't need to make small talk.

"All of us together," Harry added.

Harry was normally so suave that Lucy was surprised he was finding the conversation so difficult.

Lucy noticed Lorcan's calloused hands holding the drink. The two smallest fingers were bent at an unusual angle. She couldn't imagine the pain he had endured.

"We live in New York," Harry began.

Lucy knew what Harry was doing now. People in Four Oaks were either impressed or curious about New York.

Lorcan nodded that he'd heard him.

"On Fifth Avenue," Harry added.

So much for Harry's war tactics and getting down-and-dirty.

"We flew from New York to Wyoming," Harry said.

Lucy assumed Harry was hoping to get a reaction similar to that from the taxi driver and Wilbur.

"By plane," Harry added.

For the first time, Lorcan's expression changed. He looked at Harry and tilted his head to one side, and then the long, deep lines in Lorcan's face changed direction; he appeared amused. "Well, I sure hope you weren't gonna tell me you flew with wings."

Harry blushed before he quickly regained his composure. "Of course not, that would be stranger than a dead man returning to town after thirty years," Harry said.

"It surely would," Lorcan said.

"How long has it been since you've been in Four Oaks?" Lucy asked. She thought it would be best to warm up with a few personal questions before he told her all about her mother's family.

"Over thirty years," he said.

"You must have found a lot of changes since you were last here?" Lucy asked, trying to keep the conversation going.

"Sure, different country from when we first rolled out here. It was nothing but a crossroads. We built this town."

"I can't imagine how difficult times were then," Lucy said, encouraging him to continue.

"We sowed the timber and chopped the wood to build the sidewalks and our church and school," Lorcan said, "Not many can say that about the things they've done." He told them about irrigating the lands and digging wells. "You spend so long with a shovel it feels like an extension of your arm. The dust goes into your eyes and mouth. For months you can taste nothing but dust. People don't know how hard life was."

"You were probably more suited to the military life than farming?" Harry said.

Lorcan tilted his head back and looked at Harry before considering it. "Probably. I left lots of times, I used to shoot the buffalo and got two dollars for every one of them. Then I came home and dug some more wells and plowed fields and dug more holes to set more trees and left again to fight the Injuns in the south and communists in the east."

Lucy had an image of him digging and tossing the clay from the hole, his small soft hands turning into the coarse, scarred, thick fingers that delicately wiped the condensation from the glass. He was no longer the young man who had earned two dollars to kill buffalo.

"Then you come back and you see it's not very different," Lorcan said. "I've met a few boys from the old days, Emilio Dwyer for one."

"Yes, I know Emilio." Lucy smiled. During her stay, she hoped to call at the Dwyers' home.

"Emilio was born on the wagon train out here," Lorcan continued. "We had to listen to him bawling the whole way across the quiet prairies. Then he became the hangman and strung up every sort of villain, from the crazy killer to wild Injuns."

Lucy noted that his second reference to the Indians was as degrading as his first.

"He was always a bit of a crier," Lorcan continued, "his father was useless, a useless drunk who was only good for making babies with his wife. Emilio," he said his name and gritted his teeth, "he was in Goldie's pocket."

Lucy was perplexed and annoyed by his statement. "They were old friends," she said.

Harry moved the conversation along, "A lot of your old crew have passed on. Goldie died; I presume you heard that?"

"Sure did. Who'd have believed Goldie went first? Thought she was so tough she'd outlive us all." He cleared his throat. "She was tough, toughest women I ever did meet."

Lucy and Harry remained silent.

He cleared his throat and added in a voice so low that Lucy had to strain to hear him, "She gave money to the divorce campaign."

Harry was too fixed on finding Lorcan's motives to enjoy a good old moan about Goldie and her lack of morals in advocating divorce. "So, after all this time, what brings you back?"

Lorcan gave a long, labored sigh, "Sometimes a man gets curious. I wanted to see what had happened to everyone."

"And have you been curious for some time, or is it only a recent curiosity?" Harry asked.

"When you get old you start to wonder. I guess I got tired of wondering."

"So, Denver, was it Denver you came from?" Harry asked.

"Yes, I came from Denver. But I lived in lots of places, Kansas, Nebraska, Texas."

"Were you stationed at those places while in the Army?"

"I was posted to a lot of different locations, Fort Steele, Fort Niobrara, Fort Logan. I was at Fort Laramie and was one of the last soldiers to leave when it was abandoned."

"Wow, Fort Laramie is one of our greatest historical forts," Harry said.

Lorcan nodded. "Sure is. I was proud to serve there."

"Have you been living in Denver for the last number of years?" Harry asked.

"Yes, I own a small farm there."

She waited for him to say something about her mother. Where had she fit into this past? Would he reveal any clues to suggest that there was a grain of truth in Goldie's love story and that her death from a broken heart was indeed true? Lorcan didn't mention her; instead, he talked about his life.

"My Army days have been over for a few years. My health ain't what it used to be," he sighed.

"And have you seen the statue they made in your memory?"

"Sure did," he said with a smile. "And Goldie paid for it!"

"Goldie was very generous," Lucy said.

"So I hear," Lorcan agreed. "I hear she built the theater and hired blackies and Indians."

"And she adopted me," Lucy added.

"That she did," Lorcan said. "What age were you when she adopted you?"

"I was five years of age." She gave him a brief account of her life.

Lorcan didn't say anything. Slowly, he took a cigarette from his box and rolled it between his thumb and index finger as he listened.

"And she brought you up like you were her daughter?" Lorcan asked.

"Yes, I wanted for nothing," she said.

"Did she send you to school?" he asked. "She could hardly read or write. I guess you knew that."

"Yes, I used to write her correspondence for her," Lucy said. "I went to school until I was seventeen. I had violin lessons, dance lessons." As she spoke, he looked at her differently, she saw him glance at her hair, and then he seemed to take her in feature by feature. "There were regular doctor and dental checkups, birthday parties, Spanish and French lessons, piano lessons." Lucy said.

"That's good," Lorcan said.

"Did my mother give me the name Lucy?" she asked.

Lorcan seemed surprised by the question. "My wife? Yes, that's about right."

"What was she like?" Lucy asked.

Lorcan considered it. "She was pretty. She had fair hair. She was a widow with two sons when I met her." He looked up toward the ceiling as if trying to recall Lucy's mother. "She was a school-teacher," he added as if he'd only remembered it then.

"How did she die?" Lucy asked.

"Don't rightly know," Lorcan said as if he were referring to an old brief acquaintance, not his wife or the love of his life as Goldie had led her to believe.

"What was her name?" Lucy asked, trying to conjure an image of her mother.

"Marissa," he said.

"Who were her people?" Lucy asked.

"I don't know, I never met them. They were from Oklahoma," Lorcan said, as he lit the cigarette. "She was a fine cook, I remember that. She made pies almost as good as my own mother. But she wasn't strong; she had a bad chest," tapping his own chest when he said that. "And she was small." He stopped speaking then and stared at the ashtray on the table as if he were recalling a memory.

"Lucy got her height from you," Harry said, breaking the silence.

"From me?" Lorcan said. He looked confused.

"Her father! She got the height from you," Harry said.

"Oh yes, from me, her father," he nodded as if he only remembered then that he was her father.

Harry and Lucy exchanged glances.

"What happened to her two sons?" Lucy asked.

"They were hardy when I went to war, so I expect they found their own way," Lorcan said dismissively.

"And did you have other children?" Lucy asked.

"None that I know of," he said to Harry and laughed.

There was another silence. Lucy waited a moment before asking her next question. "How long ago did you return from the Philippines?"

He gave a long, labored sigh, "Few months after the war ended. Our men had gone home. I went to the American Embassy and they brought me back in early 1907."

"Why leave it until now to come back to Four Oaks?" Lucy asked carefully. "You know, to look me up."

He considered the question. "The war was a bad one. I..." he hesitated. "I knew Goldie had adopted you, and I knew you were being cared for. Thought it best to stay away," he said. He looked at Lucy, "Nothing more to say about it. All those days are gone. People are gone, life is changed. You live in New York now; even you're gone."

Judging from his dismissive tone, Lucy realized that Lorcan hadn't returned to develop a relationship with her.

CHAPTER TWENTY

1875

There was a complex branding system that was only recognizable to those who kept livestock in the area. There were letters bleeding into numbers, numbers and letters with lines and dots, as each unique brand belonged to one family. The Breens used the letter V with a line at the top and bottom. It was the same branding iron they'd used to brand Chaytan.

Two hours after it had happened, Frances returned home and told Goldie in a quiet terrified voice how the blacksmith's son, Lorcan, and Timothy Breen had chained Chaytan to the twitches suspended from the rafters while Owen Breen forced the iron onto his neck. "It was the smell, it caught me here," Frances said, bringing a shaky hand to her throat. "And the way they had him chained," Frances continued in the low frightened voice. "He could hardly breathe. They stuffed a rag into his mouth. And the noises," she said with the same air of terrified disbelief, "he was grunting and pulling to escape."

Goldie had little time to alleviate Frances' distress. "Where are they now?"

Frances was so horrified by the ordeal she didn't hear Goldie's question or sense her rage. Instead, she began to retell Goldie about the day, how nicely it began with Owen taking her to town as he did each Saturday. "Everything was so ordinary," she said.

There was a traveling show and a carnival atmosphere. Owen and the boys bought a jar of Bertha's homebrewed whiskey. Then Owen left Frances to do an errand, promising to be back in ten minutes.

"I saw him go in the back of Kane's tent," Frances said, referring to the blacksmith's tent. When he didn't return, she went to look for him. She peered into the back of the tent to see Chaytan chained and gagged. "It was the smell," Frances repeated, "the smell of his flesh burning with the hot branding iron."

"Owen Breen branded Chaytan?" Goldie asked.

"Yes," she said, "Lorcan was there too and Timothy Breen."

Goldie went immediately to Aengus' farm, where she found Makawee and Chaytan. Chaytan was lying on his side while Makawee applied paste to the wound on his neck. When Makawee saw Goldie she sighed, and it was a long, weary, sad sigh.

"It will never stop," Makawee said. "They hate so much."

Goldie could not offer any words of comfort. She could only wrestle with a sense of shame that one of her own would commit such a hateful act.

Each account of the branding varied. The blacksmith's son said Chaytan had tried to steal from him. Timothy Breen said Chaytan had it coming to him. When Lorcan returned home from town, Goldie asked him why he did it.

Lorcan rolled his tobacco and stared her squarely in the face. "To show him who's boss," he said calmly.

Goldie slapped Lorcan in the face. She hit him so hard he stumbled back onto the table.

Her father scolded Goldie for defending Chaytan. He reminded her that Chaytan was only an Indian, before adding, "Although he's quite a lucrative Indian, he's still only an Indian."

In the days after the event, Goldie heard how Aengus went to the Breen farm where he found Timothy, who scampered into his house with Aengus in pursuit. Ned Breen tried to spare his son from Aengus' attack. According to Ned Breen, Timothy was no match for Aengus, who pulverized Timothy over their kitchen table. "I swear to Jesus he would have killed him," Ned said. Ned fired his gun at Aengus' feet to stop the assault. "Otherwise he would have bludgeoned my boy to death with his bare hands," Ned said.

The following day, Aengus found Owen on the outskirts of his farm. His front tooth was missing where Goldie had hit him, and his black eye and bruising from Chaytan's beating were almost healed. When Aengus was finished with him, the healing process had to begin again.

Within a few days, when the shock abated, Frances took Owen's side. Her quiet frightened voice was replaced with a tone of defiance. "It's that damn whiskey that Bertha Daly makes," Frances said. "It would turn Father O'Brien into a savage. Someone should do something about her."

"A lot more should be done about Owen Breen," Goldie countered. "That animal," Goldie said, in the customary voice she used when riled, "that beast should be strung up and left to rot on the branch of tree."

Frances began to cry.

Goldie continued, "String him up on a tree in the driest, dustiest part of the prairie."

"Stop it," Frances screamed.

"You know he tried to have his way with me," Goldie said because she couldn't hold it in any longer. "The night of Mam's funeral he came into the barn and tried to force himself on me. I was lucky to escape."

"It's Bertha's whiskey," Frances was crying. "I know she brought that liquor here that night too."

"Didn't you hear what I said?" Goldie asked.

"It wouldn't have happened if Bertha hadn't given them her whiskey," sobbed Frances.

Goldie realized that Frances had to blame someone other than Owen. Regardless of what she told her about the night that Owen had attacked her, she'd always find an excuse to exonerate him.

"Chaytan saved me, that's why Owen did that to him. He couldn't take his beating," Goldie concluded.

Frances was flushed and hysterical, "Bertha's whiskey has killed men."

When Goldie realized how upset Frances was, she stopped. "All right." She walked across the kitchen and put her arm around Frances, yet she had to have the final say. "If that's what you want to believe."

"It is," Frances admitted, crying into Goldie's shoulder. "Mam is dead, and everybody has gone crazy."

Recently, Goldie had had the same thoughts.

When Chaytan refused to return to the O'Neill farm to tame the mustangs, only then did Barry regret the attack on him. Each morning, before he ate his breakfast, Barry looked out at the corral to see if Chaytan had returned.

On the fourth morning, he saw Aengus at the corral instead of Chaytan. Barry went out immediately.

"I've come to claim the broken mustang," Aengus said as he got down from his horse. He took a rope from his saddle and stepped inside the corral. "It'll be his final payment from you to Chaytan."

"I've got eight more mustangs…" Barry said to Aengus. He followed him into the corral, saying, "I don't know who'll break them."

Aengus didn't respond. He put the rope on one of the mustangs and walked it out of the corral without looking at Barry.

"Captain Gallagher will be here in the coming weeks to collect the horses," Barry said in a meek voice. "They need to be broken for payment."

Aengus climbed back onto his horse and attached the mustang's rope to his saddle. "Maybe your son and his friends should have thought of that before branding Chaytan," Aengus said.

"Will you send the boy back to me?" Barry asked.

"It's not up to me," Aengus replied.

"What?" Barry was aghast that Aengus was also taking the side of the Indian. "Whose decision is this?" he asked.

"It's Chaytan's decision," Aengus said.

Barry suddenly stepped in front of Aengus' horse and held the bridle. "We are your family, but you think more of that squaw and your Injun friends."

"You didn't think too kindly of your own brother by selling land that belonged to him to raise the money for America," Aengus said.

Barry let go of the bridle. "How do you know that?" he asked.

Aengus didn't tell Barry that occasionally he wrote to his remaining family in Ireland. News of Barry's misdeed had eventually reached him.

"The Indian thinks more of his brother than you do," Aengus said.

Barry stepped aside as Aengus rode away with the fawn-colored stallion.

That day, Barry could not contain his rage. As he paced the floor, he listed off reams of excuses to hate his only living cousin in this corner of the world. According to Barry, Aengus was deluded, disloyal, although he paused when he mentioned disloyal, saying, "Disloyal for his preference for the savages." Barry had brought his resentments across the Atlantic Ocean from Ireland. "He was the same in Mein, stacking hay for families from neighboring villages instead of helping us." Then, in the same breath, Barry forbade Goldie from ever visiting Aengus' cabin again. "Not so much as your big toe is to cross that threshold," he shouted.

"What about the blankets for Captain Gallagher?" Goldie asked, daunted at the idea of not having her Wednesdays and Saturdays with Makawee and Aengus and Chaytan.

"I'll get someone to build you a new loom, we'll do something, surely to Christ someone knows how to make a loom," he said in a dismissive tone. "That bucko," he said, pointing across the fields, "will have nothing to do with any of us."

Lorcan listened as he stirred the mercury to make his bullets. He offered to sort out Aengus. "I could fix him good for you," Lorcan said in a low, sinister tone.

Barry stopped pacing. "We're in this mess because of you."

Lorcan didn't respond.

"The Indian you branded is more of a man than you are," Barry said. "He made me plenty of money over the last ten years. More money than you ever made me."

Lorcan's face reddened.

Once Barry started, he couldn't stop. "Even little Pedro Dwyer licked you nicely."

Goldie was surprised that Barry knew about Pedro and Lorcan's fight. Although Pedro was small and thin, he'd proved to be wiry and strong. Tired of being teased and bullied by Lorcan and the Breens, when Lorcan tried to dunk him in a trough of water, for the first time Pedro retaliated and had licked Lorcan good.

"You'll sort him out! You can't sort yourself out," her father said, then he tossed his head back and laughed as if the idea were hilarious. "You useless clown."

Two days later, Lorcan left without an explanation. It was the first of many of his sudden departures. He'd been unloading feed from the wagon. Goldie saw him arrive at the house as she was preparing dinner. He retrieved his gun and left. The barn door was left open, with half the bags of feed in the wagon and the other half in the barn.

"He didn't even finish the job," Barry said when Lorcan didn't return that night. He asked Goldie again if Lorcan had said anything before leaving.

"Nothing," she told him.

Timothy Breen told them that Lorcan had gone to shoot buffalo.

"Gone to shoot buffalo!" Barry screeched incredulously. "I have eight acres of trees to plant, and he's gone to shoot buffalo."

Timothy looked nervously at Barry.

"What'll that get him?" Barry asked.

"He'll earn two dollars for every buffalo he kills and sells," Timothy told him.

Barry cursed his litany of bad luck. He cursed Aengus for his Indian-loving tendencies and Captain Gallagher for putting foolish ideas into Lorcan's head about war. He cursed the man who'd told

Lorcan how much he'd earn from killing the buffalo. He cursed the mustangs that restlessly pounded around his corral. Finally, when Barry was out of breath, he looked at the remainder of the untamed mustangs as they kicked and bucked and ate too much, so he opened the corral and released them into the wild.

CHAPTER TWENTY-ONE

1875

It took Barry three days to find a carpenter who could build a new loom for Goldie. He set it up in their old log cabin.

"Are your blankets as good on the new loom?" Barry asked Goldie when he saw the first completed blanket.

"No, Makawee's loom is better," Goldie lied because she was angry at her father's new rules.

"I don't think Captain Gallagher or any of the cold soldiers will notice," Barry said. "Just keeping weaving and stay away from the Turncoat's cabin," he said of Aengus. "Do you hear me?"

Goldie nodded.

Each day, Goldie did her chores and wove her blankets. At night, she changed into her good dress and rode to town to visit neighbors and always called at Aengus' cabin on her way home. She never revealed anything from her home, and Aengus never inquired.

Chaytan changed after his attack. There was a new haste and aggression in his manner. He rarely sat still or delayed for long chats. When Goldie sat with him, his head was always tilted to one side to alleviate the pain of the wound. It was a month before he finally talked about the attack. They were sitting in the barn watching four baby chicks pick at the grain when Chaytan began to talk.

"I thought they'd kill me or take my eyes. When the iron stuck to my neck, I was relieved that it was my neck. Then I was angry that they'd brand me, like I was one of their sheep." He admitted to a new, all-consuming hatred. "I want to hurt them; I want to kill them. I can't think of anything normal anymore, it's them and how I hate them and how I will hurt them when they are alone, all of them."

"Even Lorcan?" she asked suddenly frightened for her brother.

"Him too," Chaytan said.

Although Goldie didn't particularly like her brother's behavior, she didn't want to see him killed either. "Maybe you could spare Lorcan," Goldie said meekly.

Chaytan didn't answer immediately. After a few moments he looked at Goldie and nodded.

Little by little Chaytan returned to his old self. Eventually, when his wound healed, the mark from the Breens' branding iron was covered with a necktie for the rest of his life.

Lorcan returned after a three-month absence. He was dressed from head to toe in black, including a black Stetson hat. Even his gunbelt was black and loaded with shiny silver bullets.

"You left without a word," Barry said. He had just returned from sowing oats. The mud was stuck to his boots and legs of his trousers. He looked at Lorcan wearing his black clothes and hat.

"I just had to see Nebraska," Lorcan replied. He wasn't in the slightest bit fearful of meeting his raging father.

"And now you're back?" Barry said with an air of disbelief.

"Now I'm back," Lorcan said.

"I don't understand you," Barry said, "this will all be yours, and you just go around like…" Barry shook his head in bewilderment. "Like you're a passing visitor," he said, and looked Lorcan up and down, "who likes the color black."

Lorcan laughed.

"Have you anything to say for yourself?" Barry said.

Lorcan had plenty to say, but he waited until he had an audience. When word got out that he was home, the Breens and Dwyers gathered in the O'Neills' home. Lorcan told them all about his adventures. He told them he could shoot thirty buffalo a day, saying, "The gun gets so hot I pour water on it, and when I run out of water, I pass my own water on it," he said. "At night the town comes alive with cards, wine, and women."

The men listened rapturously while Barry stared open-mouthed.

"Is he a half-wit, or is he a half-wit?" Barry asked Goldie later when they were alone.

"I don't know," Goldie said. It was true; she didn't know. She couldn't understand what was missing in his head to lead to such reckless behavior and talk. She imagined, if she were him, she'd work morning and night on the lands he'd inherit. At least once a day, she thought of ways to improve the farm, the most suitable acres for forestry, and how best to rotate the crops. She didn't know if Lorcan had any interest in farming or if he'd prefer to spend his days on the open plains shooting buffalo. A few nights after his return, he answered her question.

Lorcan, Frances, and Goldie were alone on the porch. Lorcan was wearing his black clothes, and the spurs on his boots were gleaming, as were his new guns. Lorcan was sitting in their father's chair with his feet resting on the trellis. He was polishing one of his new pistols. He removed the cylinder and spun it, saying, "Do you hear that?"

"Yes," Frances replied.

Goldie said nothing. She watched him, seeing him as her father saw him, a useless clown who had probably stolen or won the pistol at cards. Admittedly, Lorcan's guns were handsome, probably the nicest, most distinguished set of pistols she'd ever seen. The grip was gold with an array of designs. The rest of the gun was silver with a long shiny barrel engraved with the same design as the grip.

"It rolls as smoothly as a...," he paused and looked from Frances to Goldie, "as smoothly as a pretty good-time lady." Lorcan aimed the gun into the dark night, pretending to follow a target. "Bang, you son-of-a-bitch."

"You've changed since you came back," Frances said.

"How've I changed?" he asked.

"You cuss a lot," Frances said.

"Well, pardon me, Miss Prim and Proper."

"Are you home for good?" Frances asked.

"Can't rightly say," he said, lowering the gun and polishing the barrel.

"So, you don't know if you'll stay or not?" Goldie wanted a clearer indication of his plans.

"It's pretty boring around here. Out there, in Nebraska and other places," he said, waving the gun before him, "it's freedom. Shooting buffalo and riding from town to town is the best way to live. Never felt anything like it in my life." He put the gun back into his holster and sighed with satisfaction, "I can go where I want and do whatever I damn well want whenever I want."

"What will you do when all the buffalo are shot?" Frances asked. "How will you earn your money then?"

"There'll be something new to kill."

"Why didn't you stay shooting the buffalo?" Frances asked. "Why did you come home?"

Lorcan was innocent enough to tell her the truth. "Couple of guys in Nebraska reckon I cheated at cards. Thought I'd come home for a while, let the dust settle, and go back again."

"So, you'll stay for a while, then?" Frances asked.

"Don't rightly know, but in the meantime," he said, then leaned forward in his chair and cupped his ear.

Goldie listened; she could hear horses' hooves approaching.

"Me and Timothy gotta do some living," Lorcan said as Timothy rode up to the veranda. He was grinning. Lorcan stood up, put on his Stetson, and climbed on the back of Timothy's horse. "I'll be seeing you girls."

When the sound of Timothy's horse faded, Goldie and Frances looked at each other and burst out laughing.

On the first day of September in 1875, Makawee gave birth to a baby girl. Goldie was present for the birth.

They called her Winona, *first born*.

Aengus was flushed with emotion when he first saw his daughter. He stroked the infant's face with trembling fingers.

Goldie stayed to watch Aengus make a dream catcher which he pinned to the crib.

The night of the first moon of the harvest, Goldie rode home to her father elated, but was unable to tell him the news.

Each night she'd return to Aengus' cabin and marvel at their infant. "A smaller version of everything," Goldie said, inspecting her small hands, fingers, and even her small sharp nails.

"Small piece of Aengus and me," Makawee said.

"And a small piece of you," Aengus reminded Goldie, "you are her cousin."

Goldie was quietly pleased that a little piece of her blood coursed through Winona's veins.

"All the way from Mein to these glorious hills and great Lakota." Aengus smiled when he said that.

Goldie was present in Aengus' cabin when Blue Feather and his friends called with gifts for the new baby. One of the gifts was an amulet in the shape of a turtle.

"The spirit of the keya is special to us," said Makawee, as she explained the significance of the turtle. Her small finger pointed out thirteen large scales on the turtle's back. There were thirteen new moons in the year and thirteen months in the Lakota calendar. Each moon had twenty-eight days, and on the turtle's back there were twenty-eight scales on the shell.

"This why the keya is important," Makawee explained. "Keya make her safe," she explained.

Makawee placed part of the umbilical cord from the child inside the keya. She tied the amulet to the cradle.

Goldie was fascinated with the Lakota customs. Makawee explained that the amulet would be put away until Winona could take care of it and treat it respectfully. Then it would be given back to Winona to be worn on a costume or ceremonial dress.

For the next week, Goldie stitched a small turtle on each of her blankets.

When her father asked for the significance of the turtle, she couldn't tell him.

Goldie was in Aengus' cabin when Blue Feather talked about the roads the white man made into their sacred hills.

"Long Hair told the world about the gold, so now the wasichu are using his road," he said, referring to General Custer and the trespassing whites.

They mentioned the treaty of 1868 and the promises made by President Grant that they would never again interfere with the Black Hills.

"Wasichu will always lie," they summarized the white men.

"And we will fight," Blue Feather said.

Before the Indians left, Aengus took them to the barn. They attached a sled to the horse and packed the sled with items wrapped in cloth. Blue Feather and the old Indian left dragging the loaded sled behind them.

At the first sign of the snow melt in 1876, Chaytan left. He went with Blue Feather to help his tribe fight the intruders. Goldie couldn't believe that it had come to this.

She hugged him the night of his departure, saying, "Come back safe, and if you see Baby Miriam, tell her I'm coming for her."

He promised he would to both.

She almost cried with sadness at how so much had changed.

"It's a good time for him to leave here," Aengus said after he'd gone, "he'll see the last of the West before it's all gone."

When she returned home sad and lonely, she couldn't tell her father that her best friend had gone to fight his kind of man.

CHAPTER TWENTY-TWO

1875

At the end of planting season on a fresh spring morning in 1875, Frances married Owen Breen. They were the first couple wed in their new church. Frances was eighteen years of age and besotted with her groom. Owen had grown a moustache, which made him appear older than his nineteen years. He was washed and dressed in fresh clothes. Despite being hungry for most of his life, he had a stocky, strong build. When he spoke, his missing front tooth gaped. *I did that*, Goldie thought with pride. There was a sprinkling of red spots on his cheek and his blond hair had grown down to the collar of his shirt. Goldie noticed the new twist in Owen's hair, as if he'd tried to curl it like General Custer's. Goldie wished that Chaytan was in the locality so that she could tell him about her disappointment with Frances' decision to marry the new Custer Curls of Four Oaks.

During the wedding ceremony, Father O'Brien declared his joy at the first marriage in the new church.

"Let our Catholic community flourish and be an example to the lawless nonbelievers of the West," as he referred to the newly arrived, rowdy gold-seekers.

After the ceremony, their entire community returned to the O'Neill homestead for a feast as lavish as the banquet for Neasa's wake. The newly arrived families brought their instruments, and sat in the O'Neill house and admired all that they had achieved. Lorcan wore his black clothes and polished guns. He was happy to tell the new Irish families how to farm, how they should map their land, how they should work, and how they should delegate.

"It's tough, but with a bit of work you can make it like us," Lorcan said with an air of knowing.

Goldie was happy to hear the old Irish songs and the solos on the fiddle that made everyone quiet. Despite the jovial atmosphere, there was an undercurrent of trouble in certain conversations.

Captain Gallagher talked about the Indian situation. "By early next year, every Indian will be living on a reservation. They have until January 31 to return to the reservation."

"What happens if they don't return to the reservation?" Lorcan asked.

"They'll be seen as hostiles," Captain Gallagher said in a matter-of-fact way. "The Army will treat them accordingly."

"You'll whip them good?" Lorcan said.

Captain Gallagher said, "Unfortunately, we'll have to follow orders."

"Will there be another war?" Ned Breen asked.

"Your cousin seems to think so," Captain Gallagher said to Barry. "Aengus is arming the Indians."

Barry considered it. "How do you know?"

Captain Gallagher told Barry that Aengus had been seen buying three cases of guns in Spring Creek, the next big town. "And I know he makes regular trips to Parker Falls buying guns in Cashmore's store." Captain Gallagher asked, "How many guns does one man want?"

Barry shrugged.

"When we go to war it's him against us," Captain Gallagher clarified. "It's the way it is."

"Don't need to be a war for Aengus to be against us," said Owen Breen, the new toothless groom. "He started that war."

"He should be brought to justice," Ned Breen said.

Fueled from Bertha Gallagher's whiskey, Timothy Breen said, "He won't last that long."

Timothy Breen was still smarting from his shameful beating in front of his father.

Under the fading, frosty November sky, they first tossed out the suggestion that men like Aengus were not wanted in their West.

"Shooting him is too easy," Owen Breen said, "string him up."

"One of us has to do it," Lorcan said.

Barry listened without comment, but a look of abhorrence at their unraveling conversation crossed his face.

Goldie thought Cashmore was spelled with a K. She quietly tested the word, *Kashmore, Cashmore*. Goldie decided it didn't matter how it was spelled, the boxes she'd seen were from the gun merchants in Spring Creek. She'd been in Aengus' house when he packed the Indians' sled, only now she knew they were guns. After they'd gone, Aengus always broke up the box and used it for firewood.

The night after Frances' wedding, Goldie noticed more than Cashmore's empty broken boxes by the fire. There was an unusually strained atmosphere in Aengus' cabin.

Aengus was standing quietly by the small window with his eagle feather in his hand.

"Evening all," Goldie said, going straight to little Winona. Each time Goldie visited, Winona was her first port of call. Goldie was fascinated with the infant. With each visit, Goldie noted the subtle changes. Sometimes she found the transformation mesmerizing, like how Winona's eyes followed the sound of Makawee's voice and the strength of her fingers when she clasped Goldie's thumb. Goldie loved how Winona fit into her arms; sometimes her head nestled into the space between her neck and breastbone, and it was as if that space were made for Winona alone. Recently, Aengus jokingly suggested that she find a husband and have a baby. He'd ask if any man was taking her fancy. Although it was all done in jest, he seemed genuinely interested in Goldie's life and if there was any local boy stealing her heart. Goldie's response was always the same, "Still waiting."

There was little said about good husbands and babies that night. Aengus remained at the window looking into the hills, and all the time he kept the feather between his thumb and index finger. Goldie watched him rotate the feather as if the simple action gave him some light relief. Makawee went to him and placed her hand on his back.

Winona was restless in her arms. It was as if even the infant sensed this new air of uncertainty.

Occasionally, Bertha Daly, the great whiskey-brewer, called at the O'Neills' home. She'd bring a tart baked by her mother or a quart of her home-brewed whiskey. Bertha would sit on the veranda gossiping for a few hours before eating half of the tart she brought.

Bertha was the first to acknowledge aloud that Lorcan was a problem. "He's a handsome fellow, but he's just not right in the head," Bertha added.

"He's still young," Goldie said. Whatever her own private thoughts were on Lorcan, she'd no notion of telling anybody outside her home just how *not right* he was.

"I don't know what it is," Bertha continued.

Goldie knew Lorcan had done something to irritate Bertha.

"He shoots his mouth off about all he's done and laughs at the men who challenge him. The same boyo can't take a beating," Bertha said. "An old boy from Parker Falls beat him at poker three times. Then last night I caught him rifling the same man's pockets when he was sleeping off his drink. When I caught Lorcan, he made it sound like I was the thief."

Goldie listened without comment.

"It ain't the first time."

Nothing Bertha said was news to Goldie.

"One of these days he'll fight with the wrong person or play being the big man once too often. A lot of these new kinds of men out here are up to no good," Bertha said in a voice older than her years. "Some of these new folk only want a reason to lynch a man and as sure as I'm here sitting on your veranda eating this pie, your brother will find himself in a fine mess one of these nights," Bertha said, sliding a chunk of pie into her mouth.

"It's mostly harmless," Goldie said. It occurred to her that she was sounding like Neasa, who had never tired of defending Lorcan.

"Not that harmless when he's at the bar telling men that one member of our community is arming the Indians," Bertha said.

Goldie was pleased that their porch was dimly lit and Bertha couldn't see her surprise.

Bertha continued, "Some men don't need encouraging to kill and now that Lorcan is telling people that Aengus Kennedy is arming the Indians, that'll bring new trouble."

Goldie interrupted her, saying, "It's all balderdash," a little too loudly. At all costs, she had to remove the idea from Bertha's mind that Aengus would side with the Indians. There was no gossip as great as Bertha. If Goldie could convince her, then everyone would hear it.

"Lorcan is a liar," Goldie declared.

Bertha looked at Goldie with surprise, her jaws packed with the pie.

"There's no way any white man would supply the Indians with guns. Aengus keeps himself to himself, we all know that," Goldie said.

"Maybe," Bertha said without much conviction.

They sat in silence before moving onto other matters.

"How is Frances settling into the Breens' way of life?" Bertha asked.

"Just fine," Goldie said truthfully. She was also relieved they had moved off the subject of her brother's big mouth and Aengus' rumored gun running. "She's mighty happy."

Frances lived with her new husband and his parents in the Breens' two-story house that was built in the center of their land-claim. The dirt road leading to the cabin was barely wide enough for the wagon. Ned Breen wouldn't waste an inch of land to widen the single lonely road leading to their house. Each time Goldie rode to the Breens to see Frances, she had nothing but pity for Frances' foolishness in marrying Owen Breen. Goldie pitied her living in the Breens' crowded house. The little that Goldie knew about marital obligations, she couldn't imagine the horror of having to succumb to Owen each night.

Much to Goldie's surprise, Frances seemed happy. She enjoyed the lively Breen house with its fleet of large bustling men. She was always talking about a new recipe or showing Goldie their new cabinets that the Breen men had made.

When the house was too packed, they went outside to drink their coffee and Frances talked as enthusiastically about the farm as the cabinets. She'd point out the progress they were making on the new barn, and a new smokehouse, and the irrigation, and the lands where their crops sprouted.

"Owen reckons we'll have a bumper crop this year," Frances told Goldie. "And when the harvest is done, Owen said he'd take me with him to Spring Creek when he sells it."

As they spoke, Owen was on the ladder working on his barn with his brothers. The hammering of nails into wood was the only sound breaking the stillness of the day.

Most of the time, Goldie managed to hold her tongue. She noted when she didn't pass derogatory comments about Owen or call him Custer Curls that Frances was more inclined to reveal their plans and gossip about the Breen family. Frances told Goldie about the little oddities and small bickering among the Breens. She learned that they fought over cards, that all hell broke loose if the boys were not indoors at eight o'clock for the rosary and that Leonora Breen had not spoken to her husband Ned since the day he threw her piano off the wagon train.

"For almost ten years, she's never so much as asked him to pass the pepper or the time of day," Frances said.

Goldie found it hard to believe.

"Have you ever seen them talking?" Frances asked.

"I can't say I have," Goldie admitted as she thought about it then. "Maybe they talk when they're alone."

"It's unlikely. Owen has never heard them speaking since that day," Frances said. "Owen always asks me to talk to him," Frances confessed in a quiet voice. "He said his worst fear would be if I turned silent like his mother turned silent on Ned."

Give it time, Goldie wanted to say. *The toothless Custer Curl will give you plenty of reasons not to talk to him.*

"Is Ned nice to you?" Goldie asked.

"He says nobody can bake a blueberry pie like me," Frances said proudly. "But he doesn't say a lot more," she confessed. "They sure work hard," Frances added, the admiration for her new in-laws clear in her voice. "Ned talks a lot of sense about work. He says nobody will do it, we gotta make the most of this great country that gave us land for next to nothing. Now we work it, work it," she said slapping the back of her hand against her palm.

Frances took on Ned Breen's opinions. Frances believed America was the best country in the world, and she was privileged to be part of such a progressive society that gave opportunities to every man willing to work. It was also clear that anyone who didn't share their opinions was not worthy of the great country.

"The Southerners who refused to be part of the Union are as bad as the Indians," Frances said, quoting her father-in-law. "The Indians who stand in the way of the railroad and refuse to obey are halting our society, and they deserve to be exterminated." The big word sounded peculiar coming from Frances' mouth. "The English didn't offer the Irish anything when they took our land. Not like the American government that offers the Indians $6,000,000 for the Black Hills." Frances repeated the sum of money again in a loud, incredulous voice.

It had been reported in the newspaper that the US Senate Commission offered to buy the Black Hills for $6,000,000. Red Cloud and his non-settled followers refused. President Grant abandoned the 1868 Treaty obligations to preserve the Lakota Territory and ordered every Lakota onto the reservation. The deadline came and went, but Red Cloud and a great many more Lakota did not report to the reservation. Goldie had heard it discussed in Aengus' cabin and what wasn't said there, Captain Gallagher gave his non-biased views.

"Now they're all criminals," Frances said.

Goldie didn't argue the case for the Lakota, she knew it would fall on deaf ears. It was the Lakota's right to refuse to sell the Black Hills. If they dared accept the deal, they might not see the payment. As Captain Gallagher told them that the American's were educated negotiators. The Indians knew that each offering would contain a clause that could make the ink disappear from every treaty they ever signed.

"Every Indian is a criminal including your old *boyfriend*, Chaytan."

Frances used to tease Goldie about Chaytan. It all went over Goldie's head.

Frances continued, "Every squaw and every Injun child who isn't on a reservation is a criminal."

Goldie didn't bother arguing the case of the Lakota with Frances. Instead, she was amused by Frances' animated political talk. She was also a little consoled that Frances seemed happy in the Breen household, even if that meant regurgitating Ned Breen's nonsense.

"And worse than the Indian and more dangerous than any tribe is Aengus Kennedy," Frances added pointedly. "Ned said that Aengus is a threat to all of us, even you," Frances reiterated, her brown eyes wide with a new fear she'd taken on. "He's arming the Indians, buying them guns that will be used to kill us."

The 'us' she referred to were the progressive American people.

"Aengus is a white man who reads his books so he knows what he's doing is wrong in the eyes of God and our country," Frances said before quoting her new father-in-law, "Ned says he's like a black sickness in a field of beautiful yellow corn."

Goldie laughed at Ned Breen's comparison. "A black sickness in a field of yellow corn!" she repeated, tossing her head back and laughing. "Is Ned writing poetry now?"

Then Frances considered what she'd said, and she too began to laugh when she thought about it. Their laughing was infectious until they both had tears in their eyes. "A field of ..." Goldie couldn't continue, she was laughing so much.

"Yellow field..." Frances gasped, unable to finish the sentence, she was laughing so much.

Mrs. Breen came to the back door and smiled in their direction.

Goldie and Frances couldn't shake off their giddiness all evening. When Owen stopped hammering to watch two riders gallop at speed through their land, the girls thought that too was funny.

"Who is that?" Frances asked, standing up for a better view. "And one of them has just lost his hat."

The girls thought the sight of them so absurd, they lapsed into more hysterics.

"Timothy and Lorcan," Owen shouted down from the ladder.

All evening Goldie felt giddy. She stayed for tea at the Breens' and rode home in the wagon a few hours later. It was dusk as she began the steep ascent to her home. She spotted a saddled horse without its rider, and momentarily, she wished Frances were with her so they could continue their howling at the good fun of it.

As she approached the horse, she recognized it as Aengus' bay mare.

She sidled up to the horse and took the reins. Then she stood up in the wagon and looked around her in all directions to see if Aengus was close by. When she saw nothing, she sat down again and patted the horse. "What are you doing out here on your own?" She noted Aengus' rifle was in its pocket in the saddle, then she saw a dark stain on the exposed blanket, just above that on the saddle. She picked at a little dry blood.

She tied the reins to the wagon and went to Aengus' farm. For the thirty-minute ride to Aengus' cabin, she tried to ignore the gnawing feeling that something had happened.

When she rode into the yard, Makawee came out to meet her, her face distorted with despair. "Help me find Aengus," she said. "Something has happened."

CHAPTER TWENTY-THREE

February 1937

F rances Breen was dressed in her nightclothes, and her legs
were slightly apart with her hands resting on the head of her
walking cane. She'd spent the last three days visiting her daughter,
Kate in Montana and only arrived home on the train tonight. The
clock in the hall chimed eight times. Frances Breen's life was orderly;
her built-in timer told her each hour of the day without the chiming
of the grandfather clock. It was bedtime, and she was more tired
than normal tonight after her travels. Although she loved her son,
Wilbur, she'd prefer if his news could have waited until morning.

"Just a second," she said; she wanted everything done before she
could give him her undivided attention. She took her cane, pushed
herself up and walked out of the room, down the long corridor to a
door at the end of the hall. She poked her head in, listened, and
when she was met with the sound of strangled breathing, she closed
the door and returned to the kitchen.

"He's sleeping?" Wilbur asked of his father, whose poor health
confined him to a downstairs bedroom.

"He is," Frances said. She moved the kettle to the center of the range, then eased herself down again. Her nighttime routine never varied: she dressed for bed, looked in on Owen, and made cocoa before climbing the stairs to her own bedroom.

"Now," she said, indicating that Wilbur should begin.

Speaking slowly with concise English, Wilbur told Frances about a phone call he'd received from Bertha Gallagher.

Wilbur quoted Bertha Gallagher, who had said, "There is a man staying here whom you might like to meet."

At the mention of Gallagher's Hotel, Frances' lips narrowed into a long disapproving line. Frances despised Bertha Gallagher and everything her establishment represented. It was a den of iniquity for the local men, a place where the shrill sound of a fiddle could be heard at midday. She was the worst kind of temptation for good-living men. Tonight, Frances was too tired to remind Wilbur of the evil source of Bertha Gallagher's money.

Wilbur continued to tell Frances all the minute details of his story, omitting the name of the man whom he was going to see. He described driving in the rain to meet this mysterious man and those whom he encountered.

"Who was in Gallagher's?" Frances asked.

"Eli Gilmore was sitting at the counter like he hadn't a care in the world," Wilbur said.

Eli Gilmore owed money all over town, including twenty dollars to Wilbur.

"Was he embarrassed?" Frances asked.

"He didn't appear so," Wilbur said.

Frances said, "Eaten bread is soon forgotten."

Wilbur agreed before continuing. He raised his index finger and pointed it to his left as Bertha Gallagher had done when Wilbur entered the hotel bar, indicating where the mystery man was. Wilbur told his mother that the man had arrived on the bus from Denver, and he told her that some people had their doubts that he'd really come from Denver.

"He claims he is," Wilbur paused, "Lorcan O'Neill."

Frances unblinkingly stared at Wilbur.

"Your brother," Wilbur clarified when Frances remained silent.

Frances continued to stare at him.

"Lorcan is alive," Wilbur said.

Frances looked at the kettle that began to gently whistle and then at Wilbur. Slowly, she repeated what he'd said. "Lorcan is alive!"

"Yes, he's in Gallagher's Hotel as we speak," Wilbur added.

"Go back one minute, just one minute." Frances raised her hand and looked toward the floor as if warding off an attacker. "Not possible," Frances said, shaking her head.

"It's possible and it's true. Bertha Gallagher confirmed it, so too did Emilio Dwyer."

"My good God," Frances muttered.

"Lorcan has all the right details about Four Oaks," Wilbur said. "He talked about Goldie's woolen mill, the sheep, their first cabin. He was able to tell me that the hotel where we were sitting was built using wood from the O'Neill farm."

The kettle was whistling louder, but Frances suddenly hadn't the wherewithal to stand up.

"What did he look like?" Frances suddenly asked.

"He is dressed like a fine gentleman with a good suit, although it's not warm enough for our winter, but his face is hard, you know." Wilbur thought for a moment, and continued, "Lorcan looks like the odd hobo who drifts into town. Old, beat up, with runny eyes."

Frances looked toward the whistling kettle.

"His mind seems fine," Wilbur continued, "He even had the same small details about Dad. He said Owen Breen had hands like spades, and the only man to match him was Goldie O'Neill."

Normally Frances would have enjoyed Goldie being compared to a man, but tonight she had other things to consider instead of her uncouth sister.

"He said there were only two families that would ever succeed in Four Oaks, the Breens and the O'Neills."

The kettle whistled louder.

"And then he referred to Baby Miriam and the grasshoppers."

Frances gritted her teeth, so the pain in her mouth from the dentures momentarily lessened the pain of sudden remembrances.

"He mentioned the Indian War, a boy called Chaytan who broke their horses, and a man called," Wilbur paused to recall the name, "Kennedy. A strange first name, Aengus?"

Frances closed her mouth tightly again.

"He said he remembered when Aengus Kennedy went missing," Wilbur said.

"Stop," Frances shouted and raised the palm of her hand again. "Just stop."

Wilbur moved his head back as if he'd been slapped.

The world suddenly seemed to have gone mad, Frances thought. Nothing, absolutely nothing like this had ever happened in Frances' eighty years. Frances could admit, only to herself and maybe privately to her own God, that some very strange happenings had occurred in her own family. She came from a time of violence when the gun and rope were the law of the land, and privately she could admit that sometimes it was abused by members of her own family.

"Mother?" Wilbur was still looking at her.

Frances would rather not think about the occurrences from that time. She'd learned to live in the present, to enjoy all they had achieved. They were the backbone of Four Oaks, her son was the Mayor, her other sons were businessmen, her grandsons were lawyers, her daughters married educated men, and if the West ever became poor again, Frances' family had enough money in the bank to feed themselves for their lifetimes. Many times, she thought of all that they'd achieved from their humble beginnings as Irish immigrant pioneers, but she never revisited those days in much detail. She kept those memories of Aengus Kennedy and Baby Miriam and Chaytan out of sight like a room in a house that was boarded up. A small dark corner that she knew was there, closed off, yet it remained and at moments like this the door swung open and released something bordering on terror.

"Sweet Lord Jesus," she gasped. "The world seems to have gone crazy."

"Mother, are you all right?" Wilbur asked.

Frances sighed, "Yes."

Each decade brought new crazy events like World Wars and

men killing white girls for no reason and an old woman strangled to death in Sundance, unnerving news about a certain sickness and craziness in society, details that normally made her turn off the radio, but Lorcan returning was a different kind of *crazy*.

She leaned in closer to Wilbur, about to tell him her thoughts on the state of the world, before the sound of the kettle almost bore a hole in her head. "It's that damn kettle," she shouted.

Wilbur was transfixed by his mother's behavior.

Frances suddenly found the strength to push herself up. She shoved the kettle off the range so aggressively that some of the boiling water tipped out of the spout and hissed loudly on the hot range.

"Don't speak until I sit down," Frances ordered, then paused, "What did I boil the kettle for?"

"You were making cocoa," Wilbur said. "I'll fix myself a drink," he said, scampering out of the room.

Frances didn't know what she wanted. It was almost nine o'clock, and she'd normally be in her snug bed with her cocoa at this hour.

Wilbur appeared in front of her with a drink in his hand. "So, what do you think?"

"I don't know," Frances admitted.

"You should have a glass of sherry," Wilbur suggested. "On occasions like this, alcohol is useful."

Frances normally had a glass of sherry on Christmas Day, and maybe as a young woman she had a drink on Independence Day, but never in February.

Wilbur got up from his chair again and went to the living room where they kept the drinks. "Medicinal purposes," he said, and raised his glass in a toast.

Frances raised her glass too, although she didn't know what they were toasting.

"I expect we'll meet him tomorrow. You and he will have a lot of catching up to do." Wilbur paused. "At least I'll be able to count on his vote for the next election if he sticks around."

Frances was not listening to Wilbur. She wanted to be alone, she wanted the world to go away, and she wanted her brother to go back to wherever he'd come from. She didn't want to hear names like Aengus Kennedy or Chaytan or Baby Miriam or any reminders from that raw epoch when America was only finding its feet, and as homesteaders they too had to fight their own kind of nameless war.

"Mother?" Wilbur was looking at her.

The past was upon her as clearly as her son's face. She saw her vague beginnings in Ireland, the old homesteaders her parents had been, her marriage and her life in Four Oaks, the great strides for respectability; it was almost too much.

Abruptly, Wilbur stood up, took her glass and left the kitchen. He returned with a bigger glass containing something that smelled a lot stronger than her sherry.

"Drink that quickly," he ordered. "You're in shock."

Frances obeyed. Wilbur was always right.

"The monument to Lorcan's memory is a bit of an embarrassment," Wilbur said. "I could be a laughingstock now that Lorcan is alive. I couldn't concentrate on anything today when I was thinking about it."

No words of comfort would come to Frances. She couldn't think clearly now.

"How were any of us to know that Lorcan was alive?" Wilbur continued, "I still can't figure out why he returned now. He said he got curious, but I think there might be more to it. I thought he might be dying. Although he doesn't look like he's dying."

On and on he talked while Frances' mind returned to the childhood memories in their old cabin on the hills.

"If he is dying, where is his own family?"

Frances loved her son dearly. She had six sons and three daughters. Her older sons were like the Breens, big and bulky and sometimes bad-tempered. Wilbur was different. He was more polished. Frances liked to think Wilbur was like her side of the family. They had manners and knew how to behave, except Goldie of course, but the rest of her family had class. Wilbur was a bookish boy who was generous with his time. He was normally clever; in fact, she saw notable similarities between her son and President Franklin D.

Roosevelt. They both had that distinguished air, both were Democrats, both had brains coming out their ears. In fact, long before President Roosevelt brought America out of the Depression, Wilbur had made the very same suggestions for the American economy. Frances had secretly written a letter to the White House with a detailed list of her son's tactics on the economy. Naturally, Wilbur didn't know about the letter. Both President Roosevelt and her son Wilbur were quick to see situations, but even Wilbur couldn't see that her brother only returned six months after Goldie's death. He wouldn't dare return while Goldie was still above ground.

Wilbur repeated his question, "Where is Lorcan's wife in all of this?"

Frances looked up at Wilbur's earnest blue eyes. "I don't know."

She would not burden her son with her knowledge. Wilbur was born into a privileged time when the American West had established laws and most people adhered to a moral code. Wilbur wouldn't understand how men like her brother would be hanged today, whereas thirty years ago, they were applauded.

"I'd question his mental state," Wilbur said.

"I need my bed," Frances said as she stood up. She never ever cut their chats short but she needed to escape and her bedroom was the only refuge right now.

Frances climbed the stairs slowly and flopped onto her bed. For the first time in years, sleep eluded her. She thought of Lorcan. What did he want? Maybe money? Or he was dying and wanted one last look at his old home? Was it some unsettled score he'd come to sort? When that occurred to her, a slow fear worked its way up from the pit of her stomach.

Frances rolled on her side and pulled the spare pillow over her head. She thought about Lorcan as a boy. She remembered the day of the grasshoppers and her last sighting of Baby Miriam. Abruptly, Frances sat up and fluffed her pillows. She lay back down and turned and twisted and wished the childhood faces of her siblings would go away.

Finally, she sat up in bed. She needed to belch; it was the damned alcohol. Frances was baffled how so many people enjoyed their daily tipple, including Goldie. Frances had seen Goldie with her very own eyes, talkative from too much alcohol on many occasions. At Frances' daughter's wedding, Goldie had stumbled. Frances would like to have slapped her that day.

By twelve o'clock, Frances was not asleep. When the clock chimed one o'clock, Chaytan came into her mind, and she saw him clearly, his face so vivid and the smell of burning flesh when they'd chained him in the blacksmith's tent. It was unlike any other odor. It caught in the back of her throat. She hummed aloud to drown out the memory.

At three a.m., Frances only thought of Lucy. She'd forgotten to ask Wilbur if she knew.

Suddenly, she sat up staring into the dark bedroom, and momentarily forgot about her heartburn. She thought about Goldie bringing home a child whose mother they didn't know. The world was full of unclaimed children. Frances guessed that her oldest son had a child with a local girl of low standing, yet Frances didn't need to bring that child into her life. Goldie was like that, good at picking up strays, and Lucy, that stray, had inherited every red cent Goldie had. For years it had galled Frances. It galled her also that Goldie gave that orphan everything. Frances would say that Goldie made an eejit of herself fawning over the child. Lucy had it all, dresses and toys and music lessons. Then she married Harry, kind of a famous man, and lived happily in New York. Lorcan's returning would be a test to the cosseted Lucy because she knew trouble followed her brother.

"We'll see," Frances moaned into the darkness. "We'll see how the mollycoddled orphan will handle this one."

CHAPTER TWENTY-FOUR

1937

L ucy couldn't say at what point during their afternoon in Gallagher's that she developed a disliking toward her father. It was more of a gradual feeling, like a sheet being slowly peeled back to reveal something ugly.

"He's an interesting old guy," Harry said. He was sitting in front of the fire eating his breakfast with the plate balanced on his knees. Lucy was in Goldie's armchair with Winona's dog on her lap.

"It's hard to figure him out," Lucy said. She didn't want to give a voice to her unkind thoughts of him.

"He's rough and ready but you can expect that from a soldier of his vintage."

"He could hardly remember his wife," Lucy said.

"Naturally, they were probably only together a few short years."

"Probably," Lucy said as she thought about it. Their courtship had probably been brief and with Lorcan's constant absences due to his various postings, they would have known very little about each other. "He almost forgot that I'm his daughter," Lucy said, thinking of his confusion when they discussed her height.

"Because you were questioning him like you were a private investigator from one of those detective novels," Harry said. He finished his breakfast and put the plate on the coffee table. "He sure has some stories to tell about his war days," Harry got up and poured himself a coffee, lit a cigarette, and sat down in front of the fire again. "I never knew that they got paid to kill the buffalo. He said they got two dollars a pop."

He looked at Lucy as if she should find this useless fact astounding.

Harry continued, "Then his stories of working in Fort Niobrara and Fort Laramie and how he'd kept peace with the Indians and his role in the Wounded Knee battle. He comes from the real wild west. I could forgive him his social inadequacies."

At one point while they were in Gallagher's, Lorcan had spotted a picture hanging on the wall. He'd called Bertha to clarify when it was taken. Bertha confirmed it was the day the church was built. "Can you pick us all out?" she asked. Lucy, Harry, and Bertha gathered around and watched Lorcan's large, worn finger slide across the picture, identifying old faces. "Dad, Goldie, my poor Mother," Lorcan's gray head leaned in closer to the picture, "Timothy Breen and poor Kathleen," Lorcan said, referring to Bertha's sister, "she was never right in the head after what that savage did to Timothy."

Bertha's large moon-face frowned with disgust. It didn't stop Lorcan, as he alluded to the days when Gallagher's was a brothel. "He was long gone when this here hotel shook with music and good-time girls."

Lucy could almost see Bertha cringe.

Harry stared into the fire as he smoked his cigarette. "I have to agree with Bertha on one matter," Harry said. "We should invite Lorcan up here. The only way we'll get to the bottom of his plans is if we sit on him for the next twenty-four hours."

"No," Lucy said a little too loudly. This was Harry's second time to suggest it. The idea of sharing her home with a man who boasted about killing Indians and criticizing her aunt and ridiculing the Dwyers didn't appeal to her;

"Why not! I quite liked him. If he came to visit us in New York, we'd be in for a treat," Harry added. "All those war stories, can you imagine the guys hearing an account from a real soldier!"

Lucy looked at Harry and silently wondered how two people could meet the same man and form completely different opinions of him.

Yesterday in Gallagher's Hotel, after Lorcan closed the subject of his past, he was all too happy to tell them war stories. Harry asked about the armory and guns he used during his Army career. He told her about the weapons, and he talked about the modified Springfield 1873 modeled rifle with new bayonets. Harry wanted to know everything, and he even asked if the bayonet was used toward the end of Lorcan's career.

Lorcan said the bayonet was vital. "Of all those I killed, about a fifth was done with the bayonet. When your gun is empty and a man is coming at you," Lorcan had closed his two fists, one in front of the other as if he were holding a gun and bayonet, "then you," and suddenly he jerked his hand forward toward Harry as if bayoneting him.

There was a moment of silence when Lucy thought Harry might have asked too much, and then she realized that Lorcan was enjoying reliving his killings.

"Was it effective?" Harry asked.

Lucy's heart sank.

"Sure was, the bayonet slices and dices them."

Instead of being deterred, Harry began to rattle off statistics that he had read. "A third of all fatalities were from the bayonet. Would you say that's true?"

Then they discussed the bayonet in more detail before discussing earlier battles, high-ranking generals, and their war tactics.

At one point when Lorcan went to the bar, Lucy whispered to Harry that she'd like to leave. Harry promised they'd leave after the next drink. There were several more drinks and several more war scenes described in too much detail, all of which Harry loved hearing.

She was bored and sickened by the evening. She went straight to bed when they got home.

"He must be the last of his kind in the West," Harry continued.

Lucy looked at his photo on the sideboard, the same one that Goldie had removed each time Lucy left Four Oaks. Lucy had arrived unannounced a few times during the last sixteen years, and each time, Goldie claimed the photo had fallen down. Although Goldie told Lucy her father was a great hero, it was all she said. She never shared fond memories of him as she did about other friends, the likes of her father and mother, Aengus Kennedy, and, after once hearing a song on the radio, Goldie told her Sean Dwyer used to sing that song. She told Lucy anecdotes and funny stories, but she never mentioned Lorcan in any of them. Nothing.

Harry interrupted her thoughts. "Although Lorcan never mentioned money, he could still have entitlements." He threw his cigarette into the fire and moved his chair closer to the heat.

Lucy would like to tell him that he'd damage the veins in his legs from sitting so close to the fire.

"I don't know why you're so interested in this house," Harry said, looking up at the smoke-stained chimney. "We'll be gone tomorrow afternoon. Anyway, this house is empty. Who better to give it to than Lorcan? If he wants money, this is an ideal bargaining tool. In fact, I think it's the least we could do. Men like him were overlooked too often."

"This is my home," Lucy said.

Now that Lucy had returned to Four Oaks, she didn't want to leave so quickly. Last night she'd lain awake thinking that the house would be her safe haven, a respite from Harry for a few weeks, or even a month, or possibly forever. Even as she thought about it now, she was looking at the first projects she'd like to do with the house. It needed a good painting, and she'd see about getting the windows sanded and varnished. She was surprised how quickly an unlived-in house fell into disrepair.

"A house needs an occupant," Harry said.

And I am the ideal occupant, Lucy thought.

"I'm sure he has stayed in worse places," Harry continued as if she hadn't objected.

"Please, no, Harry," she said. "Don't even mention it."

Harry looked at her in surprise. "It's only right and proper," he said imitating the country accent. "Only right that we invite our own kin to dine in our home and set their head down on our beds."

"No," Lucy said. "I couldn't bear to listen to more war stories and killing and bloody bayonets."

Harry wasn't listening, he checked his watch and stood up. "Did Wilbur say if we were entertaining or he was entertaining or what was the final decision?" Harry asked.

"You invited the Breens to supper here."

"I'd forgotten that," he admitted. "Well, I suggest you get cracking on the preparations for the meal and clear out as much of this junk as possible, because both of us will be on a flight out of here tomorrow afternoon." Harry said.

"I'm staying Harry, for at least a week," Lucy said. "If you need to return to New York, I'll understand."

He looked at her with an incredulous expression. She knew he was acting. He had sensed her distance. He was clingy, grasping at something that was slowly slipping from his reach.

He stood looking down at her. She held his gaze. They were like two prizefighters weighing up the opposition.

He raised one finger, saying, "We leave tomorrow. I promise I'll come back in the summer."

Lucy shook her head in annoyance, "It's too soon."

Harry saw her despondence. "I promise, this summer both of us will return. Summer isn't that far away," he added.

"I need to get groceries for tonight's supper." She picked up Goldie's car keys and left.

Lucy drove Goldie's car out of the avenue and hesitated, then on impulse turned right and took an immediate left. How better to start the day than a visit to Makawee's home. She also hoped that Makawee would break the habit of a lifetime and tell her what she knew about Lorcan.

CHAPTER TWENTY-FIVE

1876

M akawee told Goldie that Aengus had gone to the river to check his traps that afternoon and hadn't returned.

"I heard gunshots," Makawee said. She looked up at Goldie, her eyes pleading for help.

Goldie took Aengus' mare to search for him. It was dark, but she rode to the river where he kept his traps and called his name. As she trotted up and down the banks of the river, she thought it might be an accident but dismissed it, as Aengus was too well versed in the West to fall into a river and disappear. She thought about Timothy Breen and Lorcan galloping their horses. It was as if they were trying to get away from something. She dismissed the notion and went home to her father.

"What do you mean, Aengus is missing?" Barry asked.

Goldie told him about Aengus' horse and that gunshots had been heard a few hours ago. "I did the neighborly thing and returned the horse," she said, keeping up the pretense that she hadn't crossed the threshold of Aengus' cabin as he had instructed her. "Then Makawee met me and told me that he's missing."

"Since when?" her father asked turning in the chair to face her.

"Since this afternoon."

"An accident?" he asked, getting to his feet.

"There's blood on his saddle and on the horse's blanket," Goldie told him matter-of-factly. "And Makawee heard gunshots."

"Blood and shooting," he sounded almost breathless as he repeated it.

"I have his mare outside. I'm going to return it to Makawee and search at first light." She expected him to object or say something derogatory about Aengus, but he did neither. Instead, he glanced at the empty third chair by fire, where Lorcan usually sat.

Goldie set off at first light on Aengus' mare. She scanned both sides of the river. Her search yielded nothing, even his crude traps were empty.

When she got home that night, Lorcan and her father were sitting in front of the fire. Lorcan was no longer wearing his black ensemble. The farming clothes smelled of sweat and sweet tobacco. He denied he had anything to do with it.

"Timothy and me spent the day in town," he said.

"I saw you galloping through the Breens' farm" Goldie said.

"We were only racing each other," he said.

"You looked like a fellow who was running from something."

"I wasn't running from anything," he said. He sat with his legs crossed, holding a cup of coffee. There was the slightest tremor in his hand.

"What happened to your gun?" Goldie asked. His pistols were on the table inside the door. "The gold is missing from the grip."

"It fell off," he said.

Barry sat in his chair, his elbows resting on his knees and an intensity in his watchfulness spoke of his suspicions.

"I know you had something to do with it," Goldie eventually said.

"Leave it alone," her father suddenly said.

Goldie couldn't leave it alone. She went to the Breens' that evening. Frances was silent and distant. When they talked about

Aengus, Frances only quoted Ned, "Ned says that an accident can happen to the best of us."

"Is that what he thinks?"

"That or the Indians turned on him," Frances said.

When Goldie returned home that night, she saw her father searching Lorcan's room. Goldie also had a look around his bed for his black shirt, which she hadn't seen since the day Aengus went missing.

Ned Breen called a few times during the week, and Goldie noticed that there was more silence than talk. When she left the room, she sat on the veranda and heard their low voices behind her.

Four days after the event, Lorcan left again.

"Guilt," Goldie stated.

"He was going to leave anyway," Barry said. "I heard him telling a man in town he was joining the Army."

After a moment he asked after Makawee, "How are the woman and his child?"

He never mentioned Makawee by name.

"Not good," Goldie said.

Barry put his hands on his hips and looked into the distance.

In the weeks after the event, her father was as at odds with the world. He'd stop his work and look across his land in the direction of Aengus' farm. He'd shake his head before resuming his work.

When Captain Gallagher visited, he asked what had happened. They told him the same story that they told their small community.

"We reckon a simple accident," Barry said.

Captain Gallagher never said if he believed them. "Probably for the best. Aengus would have hung for arming the Indians."

They accepted his disappearance as validation of his death.

They never complimented Aengus' character or dwelled on his small accomplishments as they usually did with the recently deceased. They drank some whiskey and sat in silence.

Captain Gallagher finally mentioned Aengus' harvest and lands.

He spoke to Barry, "You being the next of kin...." He didn't finish his sentence.

"I'd rather the man himself were here," Barry said, surprising Goldie. "Aengus was my blood."

"What about the woman?" Captain Gallagher asked.

Barry shrugged.

"She's got no rights over Aengus' farm," Ned Breen said. "Her nor her kid."

"Get her making the blankets with Goldie, and you'll have a nice earner there," Captain Gallagher said.

When there was nothing more to say about Aengus and each man had pocketed his guilt, grief, and suspicion, their conversation moved onto the Indian War, the gold, the influx of new arrivals, and the approaching spring.

Before leaving, Captain Gallagher asked after Lorcan. "Is he gone to kill the buffalo again?"

"So it seems," Barry said.

Makawee continued to live in the cabin and own the land despite Ned Breen encouraging Barry to send her back to her tribe. Goldie never knew if it was sentimentality or guilt over Aengus' disappearance that led him to treat Makawee fairly.

He sold Aengus' crops and paid her in full. "I suppose it's never too late to do the right thing," he said to Goldie the day he paid Makawee. "We can't turn back time."

He sounded genuinely sorry that Aengus was gone.

Goldie didn't hide the fact that she called on Makawee and Winona each day, and her father never passed any comment. He paid Makawee to come to their old cabin where Goldie had set up her looms to weave her blankets. All of his dealings were done through Goldie; he never spoke to Makawee or referred to Winona.

Barry rented a portion of Aengus' land from Makawee, and planted trees on the land that was between their house and Aengus' cabin.

When at last the trees grew high and thick and the view of Aengus' land was entirely obscured, he said, "Let that be the end of it now."

He hoped new memories would overgrow the old ones. His son's past deeds and his own behavior toward Aengus would fade into the new forest. That part of their history would become shadowy and eventually be unseen forever with nature's new growth. Their unfurling lives would fill in the gaps that the old absences left. The unseen would remain hidden beneath the present; his brother in Ireland and his act of treachery would fade from his sight and conscience.

"It all starts again here and now," he concluded.

For a few years, they found some semblance of peace.

CHAPTER TWENTY-SIX

1876–1889

The following years in Goldie's life blended into one another, although she remembered big occasions that coincided with other occasions.

Frances' first child was born in 1876, a boy they called Edward George. The first name was after his grandfather, Ned.

"Is George after Long-Hair?" Goldie asked, referring to General Custer. She was looking at the newborn in her sister's arms.

"Yes, it is," Frances admitted proudly. "A fine name for a fine American boy," Frances said. Frances continued to adopt the Breens' political stance on everything from continued black slavery to annihilating the Indians. If anything, each year she became more militant. "I suppose you'd have called him Red Cloud, or Walks Tall, or Chaytan?"

"Maybe I would have." Goldie played along, "Or Blue Feather or Makawee if it was a girl."

"You'd really want to find yourself a husband," Frances quipped. "Not that you've much hope the way you go on riding around as if you're a man and drinking whiskey," Frances said.

Goldie wasn't offended with Frances' intended slight. She had no aspirations for a life like her sister. Swapping recipes and being confined to the home appealed to her even less than spending her nights beside a man like Owen Breen.

A few weeks after the birth of Edward George Breen, his name-sake was killed in June, 1876.

"Slain in cold blood," Captain Gallagher told them in a brusque manner. "General Custer went ahead without the rest of the Army to fight a tribe of Indians who were camped at Little Bighorn. He thought he'd take them all before the other regiments arrived." Captain Gallagher was sitting at their kitchen table, where he used the cutlery and table salt to demonstrate Custer's downfall.

"The Indian village was here," he said, sprinkling a little salt in the center of the table. "Custer would have come over the bluffs here," he said, moving the fork forward. "He'd have sent one detachment over the butte to attack the camp from the left, then another would have met them head-on, and the last would have come in behind the village to surprise them," he said, gliding the spoon in an arc. "Then—BOOM," he said opening his hand and fingers wide, sprinkling the salt across the table. "The Indians came at them, wiped every last one out."

Goldie looked at the wasted salt.

"Probably the worst massacre of American soldiers in the West," Captain Gallagher said.

He finished his drink and left. The knives and forks remained askew on the table. In the background, young George Breen wailed for his evening feed, and Goldie thought of Chaytan.

During those years, word spread about Goldie's wares. Captain Gallagher recommended Goldie's rugs for a saloon in Spring Creek. The owner of the Spring Creek saloon recommended Goldie to a wealthy family in Sundance. She supplied a store in Parker Falls, and once a month took a train to see the owner and discuss his order. When Barry saw the money to be made in her expanding business, he built a bigger woolen mill with large dyeing vats, powered by the river.

Makawee remained constant and stoic throughout those years.

She continued to work in the new mill. Although Barry was the profiteer from the mill and weaving, each year Goldie haggled for more money for Makawee, and each year Goldie's request and her father's reluctance became a recurring farce. "Not this again," he'd moan, sometimes feigning boredom, but other times he was amused. Eventually he always submitted.

Despite the passage of time, Barry never spoke to Makawee or asked after Winona. Goldie wasn't sure if he even knew her name.

Makawee's home was a meeting point for passing Indians. When Blue Feather or his Indian friends were passing through Four Oaks, they stayed with Makawee. Blue Feather worked for a rancher in Dakota. "It will allow me time to live peacefully for now," he said. He had given up the fight for freedom. "My people on reservations are not happy, and many people who avoid the law are not happy. This is the closest I'll get to freedom, for now."

Blue Feather kept them abreast of news about Chaytan. For a few years, there was little to report. He had fought with Sitting Bull in the Battle of Little Bighorn when General Custer was slain. Knowing the Army would never stop hunting them, Chaytan fled with Sitting Bull to Canada. "He is free in the Grandmother's Country," Blue Feather said. "One of the few privileged free Lakotas living close to the roaming days."

Blue Feather told them about the sad state of their tribes. Those who remained in America and refused to enter the reservations were met with a different fate. "After surviving the wars and the winters running from the Army, they are dying a slow death as free men. Those on the reservations are prisoners on land they once roamed freely. They are at the mercy of the white man. They can't leave the reservation and if they do, they must carry a pass." He tapped his breast pocket, where Goldie assumed Blue Feather kept his pass. "If one gets sick, everybody gets sick, they die like flies," he held out his hand and wriggled his fingers. "Soon nobody will be left. And those who survive are told to believe in the white man's God and speak the white man's tongue. Those who object are punished, and their rations are stopped." He sighed. "Soon they will all be dead. What we once were will be gone forever."

It sounded wholeheartedly sad, Goldie thought. The proud rulers of the West were condemned to an undignified demise.

Occasionally, Blue Feather would ask if Aengus' body had ever resurfaced.

"No," Goldie said.

Blue Feather knew where their suspicions lay.

Goldie's father had a few good years with bumper crops that changed his finances forever. In 1878, he sowed 100 acres of wheat and 100 acres of oats, and he then got on his knees and prayed for wet Irish weather. When the skies spat out rain, he grinned with elation. That spring, he yielded forty bushels per acre at seventy-five cents per bushel. He made $3,000 and spent it wisely on a riding plow, seed planter, oats, and wheat.

He watched with interest, the new towns springing up in the hills. By 1880, there was Deadwood, Lead, Sheridan, Camp Crook, Hill City, and many more tent-towns. There were more than 10,000 miners living in the hills, their camps perched along the many creeks. At night they drank and by day they panned for gold. As the new arrivals passed through Four Oaks on their last leg of the journey, there was an optimism and haste in their behavior as they paved a road they called *Freedom Road* into the hills. This new kind of immigrant came from all corners of the world. There were cowboys and businessmen, small Chinese men and their delicate womenfolk, polished suited men and their gentrified women, the eager faces of the young, and the tired eyes of the aged. Their town became a hub of activity. The talk of Black Hills Indian War went unnoticed while there was gold to be panned and their fortune waiting to be picked from the bountiful streams in the forbidden hills that still belonged to the Lakota Indians.

Captain Gallagher was quick to seize the opportunity to make money from these new arrivals.

"They need drink and women," he declared.

He left the Army, bought an acre of land from Ned Breen, and built a saloon using timber from the O'Neills' farm. When his saloon was finished, he married Bertha Daly, the nineteen-year-old

Irish immigrant who had a reputation as the finest whiskey-brewer in the West. Captain Gallagher was forty-seven.

"No mountain mule works as hard and darn good as Bertha," he said about his wife on the morning of his wedding.

Bertha was tickled plum with his compliment.

In the fall of 1880, a few miners found a body tucked into the undergrowth a mile from the O'Neills' farm. The miners buried the dead man where they found him. A few nights later, Goldie and her father heard about it when Captain Gallagher called. He told them that the man had been dead for years. "He was only a skeleton. One of the miners tried to pawn off a gold grip from a gun that they pried from his fingers."

Barry stared at the captain without speaking. His eyes were wide and watery in the candlelight.

It was Goldie who asked about the gold grip. "Is it real gold?"

"I don't know," the Captain said. He put it on the table. "I gave the miner two shots of whiskey for it."

Goldie held the grip to the light and saw the fancy design from Lorcan's old pistol. She replaced it on the table. Barry wouldn't look at it. He remained silent when the Captain returned it to his pocket. Barry never mentioned Aengus' name again, just as he never mentioned his home parish in Ireland or the family he'd left behind or the fact that Lorcan was Aengus' killer.

Goldie was grateful that Lorcan remained away during those years. She thought it strange that Barry was also relieved he was absent. It allowed Barry time to absorb Aengus' death without the perpetrator so close at hand.

"Maybe it's for the best that he stays away until he learns to behave," Barry said.

There were times when Barry was jealous of Ned Breen and the fine sons he had waiting to take over the helm.

"None of the Breen boys are gallivanting around the country-side like wild Injuns, only my clown of a son," he often said.

When Pedro Dwyer married the daughter of a Dutch miner, Barry regretted that Lorcan couldn't have done what ordinary men did.

"Pedro and his new wife look rightly odd," Barry said, referring to Pedro's wife, who towered over him. "But she's a fine woman." Barry was baffled when Pedro Dwyer was so successful with the land his father had never farmed.

"Pedro has 500 sheep and the prettiest-looking house in Four Oaks. None of those young Dwyer lads got a good example from their father," Barry said to Goldie as if she had forgotten poor Sean Dwyer. "Yet he's doing mighty fine without any guidance."

At times like that, Barry grew frustrated with Lorcan's irresponsibility. He blamed outside influences for Lorcan's shortcomings.

He blamed Neasa's brother, a man whom Lorcan did not remember.

"He's like that half-mad brother of Neasa's, there isn't a screed of sense between the ears. That's where he gets it," Barry said as if it were fact.

There were times when Barry blamed Captain Gallagher, thinking his talk of killing and war had an affect on the young, impressionable Lorcan. Barry said that Captain Gallagher was nosier than an Irish woman outside a shebeen, and he began calling him Captain Gossip. "Captain Gossip fed that eejit son of mine a load of nonsense."

Barry blamed everyone except himself; at one point, he even blamed the boat ride to America. As the ship had skimmed the waves one particular night, it had flung every passenger from their bed, and one man had cracked his skull.

"Maybe that's what did it," Barry said.

"Maybe. Or maybe not," Goldie said noncommittedly.

After a few years, Barry began to soften toward Lorcan. He held out hope that Lorcan could someday turn out well. "Every young man must sow his wild oats," he said.

Goldie would raise her eyes intolerantly.

"Every man needs a son," Barry said.

Goldie thought she'd get a pain in her face from listening to such nonsense.

Barry eventually said that he'd like it if Lorcan came back. "We'd put all this behind us and forgive him. 'Tis time we all forgave him," Barry said in a cheery voice, still not mentioning Aengus' death.

"Forgave him!" Goldie repeated. "You can do what you want, but don't expect me to be standing on the veranda with a pie waiting to greet him."

Goldie's anger never waned; if anything, it worsened. Sometimes, her anger was so fierce she felt as if it were something tangible, something she could hold in the palm of her hand and pulverize with her fingers. During those times, she felt like galloping to Nebraska or wherever his wild imagination had taken him, to shoot him. She never spoke to Timothy Breen; when they did meet, she behaved as if he were invisible, a nothingness she looked through. The first few times they met, he reddened. Then Timothy became accustomed to her behavior, yet he never again attempted to speak to her.

In early 1881, Timothy Breen married Kathleen Daly, sister of the great whiskey brewer and new wife of Captain Gallagher. Kathleen Daly was smaller and more timid than her strapping sister Bertha, yet she had all of the attributes that made her appear a promising wife.

Barry regretted the fact that Lorcan couldn't have stayed put and married a girl like Kathleen Daly. "One of those Daly women would have made a man of him," Barry said.

Barry had a celebratory drink with the Breens the night of Timothy and Kathleen's wedding. When he returned home, he asked if Goldie would weave a rug for the new couple.

"Similar to the one you did for Frances and Owen," Barry said.

Barry was proud of the fact that every house in Four Oaks had one of her rugs. He delighted in the locals' praise, and occasionally he referenced his daughter's skill of weaving and claimed Goldie's gift went back to the eighteenth century, when Neasa's family had woven for the local gentry, Lord Stratford-Rice.

"Timothy and Kathleen will put the rug into their kitchen where everybody will admire it," Barry added.

"I could do that," Goldie agreed. "But only if I could wrap Timothy Breen up in my rug and set it alight," Goldie said.

He didn't mention a rug for Timothy Breen again, and Goldie managed to contain her anger.

It was decided that the newly married couple, Timothy Breen and Kathleen Daly, would live on Ned's timber claim. Their house was downstream from the O'Neills.' Whenever Goldie happened to be at the Breens' when Timothy was there, she found him intolerable. On her last occasion of being in his company, he had been making plans for his cabin; he wanted a chimney without one whistling gap and a loft.

Goldie's father went to help build his cabin. At night, when he'd come home, he'd volunteer news about the neighbors and what had happened that day. Goldie listened and silently seethed.

A few nights after Timothy had moved into his new house, Goldie saw him leaving late at night. Kathleen was not with him; she stayed alone in the cabin. Several nights when Goldie returned home after dark, she saw Timothy outside his cabin with the lantern and a gun.

"He's terrified," Frances told Goldie about Timothy. "It's all bravado talk about the chimney and the big barns. He is stark-raving terrified out of his wits to stay alone on that farm."

"Why?" Goldie asked.

"Because he thinks the Indians will come after him."

"Why?"

"On account of Aengus," Frances said.

It was the closest that Goldie ever got to an admittance from anyone that Timothy Breen was as culpable as Lorcan for Aengus' death.

Frances told Goldie that Timothy had been reluctant to move onto the property, but Ned had insisted. "Timothy came home twice during the night, and Ned walloped him about the head and sent him back. I heard he slept in the barn here and returned to Kathleen the following morning."

Goldie had not been expecting to hear that.

"His wife is more courageous than he is," Frances said. "She stays alone in the cabin until Timothy comes home and seemingly, it doesn't bother her in the slightest."

After that, when Goldie was returning from town late at night, she'd deliberately ride through the forest, close to Timothy's new cabin. She'd howl like a coyote or hoot like an Indian. When she saw Timothy appearing from the cabin in his long johns and firing his gun into the night, she smiled with amusement at her childish antics. Other times, she felt the old anger resurface, and on those nights when she'd hide in the darkness, she didn't get any pleasure from watching Timothy burst from his cabin with his gun cocked. She had to stop herself from firing her own gun at him, *right between the eyes*, she whispered venomously.

Goldie continued to terrorize Timothy until she grew bored with her own foolishness, and her anger become intolerable to herself.

CHAPTER TWENTY-SEVEN

1882

Five years after Lorcan's departure, he wrote a letter. He told his father he'd spent the last five years in the Ninth Cavalry Regiment in various posts in Utah, Colorado, Nebraska, and Wyoming.

"I've seen the driest land in America and fought in some vicious skirmishes. My efforts have not gone unnoticed, I am now a sergeant. For the past two years, life has been a little easier. I've been posted to Fort Niobrara in Nebraska. We maintain peace on the Rosebud Indian Reservation."

Barry read the letter aloud while Goldie stood in the center of the kitchen with her hands on her hips. When Barry finished reading the letter, he smiled.

"Sergeant Lorcan O'Neill," he said, testing the title aloud. "Sounds good."

Goldie watched him fold the letter. He placed it in the top drawer in their sideboard. Before closing the drawer, he delayed a moment as he stood looking at the folded letter. When he looked up, he was smiling.

A month later there was another letter, and then one letter a week. Goldie noticed how her father's humor improved. When the mail arrived, he'd leave the letter until he'd eaten his dinner. The he'd settle down with a strong coffee and open the letter, as if savoring the best for last.

"He seems to be doing all right," her father said. He wanted to believe all he read in Lorcan's letters. Goldie watched Barry fold the letter twice and put it into the drawer where he kept all of Lorcan's letters.

In the winter of 1882, Lorcan returned. Goldie watched him from the barn. He was dressed in his Army uniform. She noted how he stroked his horse after dismounting; the attentiveness to his animal was something new. As he unbuckled the saddle, she saw her father come out of the house and walk toward him calling his name, a slightly hysterical note in his voice.

"Lorcan, come into the heat," he said, beckoning him toward the house.

They shook hands in the emotionless way men do.

"Leave that to Browning," her father said of their farmhand.

Goldie watched Lorcan walking the short distance to the house. He didn't appear meek or uncomfortable. She often thought that with time she'd feel differently toward him. She saw him as an animal with an unfixable quirk. And she couldn't bear the sight of him. When she entered the house that evening, Barry and their farmhand, Browning and Lorcan were sitting at the table, waiting to be served their meal.

Lorcan nodded in acknowledgement, but Goldie didn't return his acknowledgement. She laboriously wiped her feet on the mat.

That night, Lorcan told them how he'd signed up with the Army six years ago. His first posting had been Fort Steele in Wyoming. He'd played his part in the White River War with the Ute tribe.

"It wasn't always easy," Lorcan admitted.

He'd been shot twice and survived. He told them about the unruly Apache Indians, his many battles, and how he was made a sergeant. Strangely, he didn't have the air of self-importance she'd expected; he seemed mature. Goldie waited for Lorcan to falter, to say something that would indicate his entire story was a farce, that the furthest he had gotten was Nebraska, or that that he was such a nuisance in the Army they'd given him his horse to get rid of him.

Despite her loathing of him, Goldie understood Lorcan. He was impressionable, and he wanted to be a soldier. The idea of marching with men in uniform never faded from his wild imagination. In his foolish young mind, he thought killing Aengus would be a noble act. He was serving his community and country by ridding it of an enemy of progressive America. He saw himself as a hero, as great as General Custer. For years to come, people would point him out in the street and say, "That's him, that's our brave boy who killed the man who was arming the Indians." And more than anything, Lorcan sought the approval of their father. Lorcan's only battle now was to live with his own conscience. None of this brought Aengus back, and Goldie couldn't contend with that part. Although as Lorcan's sister, she loved him, but she could never, ever like him and didn't believe she'd ever find forgiveness. However, watching him now, she had to concede that maybe, just maybe, he'd changed.

Lorcan told Barry that he was home for good. "I'm here to stay."

"Good," Barry said, the lines on his face appearing to soften before their very eyes.

When Lorcan set to work on the farm, Barry noted how he took the time to do the small things that he'd previously left undone. Lorcan hung the tools after using them, swept the barn, and stacked every sheaf of hay.

"Reckon the Ute tribe made him grow up," Barry said of the Indians involved in the White River War.

Although Barry sounded optimistic, Goldie knew that he'd taken his money from his hiding place beneath the floorboards in the hall.

"Best to be sure," Barry said when Goldie asked him. "Even a straight-laced man would be tempted to take a dip."

For a period, Barry hid it in the barn, and then in a hole beneath the porch. Eventually when he was sure Lorcan was indeed a changed man, he returned it to its original place beneath the floorboards in the hall.

"He took it upon himself to sharpen the tools," Barry told Goldie.

When she didn't respond, Barry continued, "Without me even telling him to do it. He did a fine job too," he added as he ran his thumb over the sharpened axe.

In the second month of Lorcan's return, he went to town and didn't come home until the following morning. The old behavior returned. He boasted about the Utes he'd killed. "America can thank the likes of me for opening up their land for homesteaders." As the weeks passed, it appeared that Lorcan was bored with the farm work. He'd spend his free time looking into the distance. When Barry talked about planting trees and the work that needed to be done, Lorcan talked about get-rich-quick schemes. He advised Barry to get out of farming, sell up, and buy cattle. On another occasion, he advised him to go to San Francisco because he had heard that the bay area was lovely.

Barry's initial politeness waned when Lorcan made such suggestions.

"Lovely? What kind of a living will I make on *lovely*?" Barry asked.

Each night, Goldie ate her supper with Lorcan and her father. If she was alone with Lorcan, she wouldn't speak to him.

Three months after his return, when the first of spring arrived, she was sweeping the veranda while Lorcan mended part of the trellis. She heard the sandpiper, and when the sound grew more persistent, she suddenly stopped sweeping and looked in the direction of the river and into the forest. Lorcan noticed and craned his neck to follow her line of vision. Goldie couldn't say what made stop her sweeping, and saddle her horse. She crossed the river and trotted through the forest toward the cave. The only sound was the horse's hooves crunching the twigs beneath his feet and, at interludes, the sandpiper.

When she arrived at the cave, a tall, thin, sickly Indian appeared from behind a tree. Only when he smiled did she realize it was Chaytan.

Goldie dismounted from her horse and went to him. They stood holding each other for several moments until both became self-conscious.

They stepped back to look at each other. Chaytan appeared so much older than when she had last seen him seven years ago.

"What happened to you?" she asked.

"A lot has happened," he said. "I need to sleep, and then I'll tell you everything."

She accompanied him to Makawee's house.

For the next week, each evening Goldie went to Makawee's cabin. Chaytan slept and drank various concoctions that Makawee mixed, using plants to revive his health. When eventually he began to recuperate, he told them about his life over the last few years. He had fought in the Battle of the Little Bighorn and then fled north to Canada with Sitting Bull.

The first year was great, he said, "We were free to hunt and lived as freely as we wanted. We hunted the buffalo and had enough food to last us through the winter. Each night we sat by the campfire without any threat from the Army or whites. The cold Canadian breeze and the joy of hunting together with my tribe were unlike anything I've had. And there were days when nothing happened. Nothing at all, yet on those days there was a stillness here," and he placed his closed fist over his chest. "A feeling of something great inside." He paused to drink the rosemary tea that Makawee had brewed. "Things went bad after the second year. Then the buffalo began to run out and the Canadian Army was fighting with the American Army. Sitting Bull wanted to turn himself in. I broke away from the tribe then and came south on my own. It took me six months to get here." He sipped some more tea and looked up at her. "I am tired, sore, and sick, but I'm happy I did it all," he said with a grin.

When there was nothing more to say, he asked after Aengus. "Has Aengus' body turned up?"

They were surprised he knew.

"I stayed in Spearfish with a Lakota man. He told me."

Over the next three weeks, Goldie filled in Chaytan of all that had happened in his absence.

When Goldie and Chaytan were alone, they talked about Aengus.

"All for what?" Chaytan eventually said. "So Timothy could get his revenge on me and your brother can prove to your father that he's big and brave."

"Probably," she admitted.

Chaytan told her he was going south to work on the cattle drives.

"I'll be paid to roam as far as Mexico to round up herds of long-horn cattle and come north."

She understood that it was the closest to freedom he would find.

Chaytan stayed for three weeks before he moved on.

The morning after Chaytan left, in the spring of 1883, Goldie saw smoke coming from the direction of the forest. It appeared to be coming from Ned Breen's forest. Then it occurred to her that it was Timothy's cabin. She thought of Aengus; the day had the same stillness as when he had disappeared. The slight flurry of the breeze and melting March snow brought the black smoke in coiled clusters to the sky. Goldie rode with Barry in the direction of Timothy's farm. The house was burned to the ground. Two local men were standing at the entrance to the barn, and they spoke in hushed, disbelieving voices.

"Scalded to death," she heard one of them say.

In the barn, Timothy Breen was tied to a beam. Goldie's eyes went immediately to his bare chest which had been branded with an iron. Goldie noted it was the same branding iron he'd used on Chaytan. Timothy's twisted, tortured face told its own story.

Goldie watched Owen Breen's trembling hands as he cut his brother down and covered his face with his coat.

On the morning of his funeral, Timothy's wife was found hiding in the woods. She was delirious and incoherent.

Goldie attended the funeral. Father O'Brien talked about Timothy's brief life, his accomplishments, his wife, and the cabin he'd built. He commented on Timothy's farm and tilled lands. He prayed for his soul and for peace. He also prayed for his wife, Kathleen Daly.

Kathleen was unable to talk about the attack. When Father O'Brien tried to get the details, she started screaming so much, they had to sedate her. Father O'Brien said she'd never be the same. She spent a few weeks living with her sister Bertha and Captain Gallagher before going to an asylum for the insane in Parker Falls.

Three days after Timothy's funeral, Lorcan left again.

Barry was missing twenty dollars from his money box.

"I thought he'd changed," Barry said. "What do I do now?"

Goldie had invested little faith in him. She'd seen him dusting off his old uniform and heard him tell Frances that life as a soldier was easier than taking orders from his father.

"We'll go on as we did before," Goldie said.

"How?" he asked, more to himself. She saw him look in the direction of Aengus' farm and over the thick forest. It wasn't enough to keep the ghosts of the past at bay, and now their presence was stronger than ever.

CHAPTER TWENTY-EIGHT

1937

Frances Breen sat in the rarely used living room at the front of their home waiting for her brother, Lorcan, to arrive. The only sound was the loud tick tock of the clock and Owen's labored breathing. Frances could contend with Owen's breathing, but the grandfather clock was a different matter. She'd never noticed it before. Its rhythmic beat seemed to swallow up the house. She'd like to get up, drag it from the house, and dump it outside. She couldn't really do that; this room was only used when Wilbur entertained politicians or businessmen, and the clock was part of the furnishings. Wilbur had decorated this room. He'd bought the furniture and chosen the wallpaper. Even the lace cloth on the side table was his choice. Wilbur was well-rounded, a man who knew good lace and the texture of well-made curtains. A few times a year they swung open the door of their house for parties, and that damn clock was always admired. Today they'd opened the doors for a different meeting, although it didn't feel like a happy occasion. Frances was nervous. That old uneasiness had returned. She couldn't figure out why she was so uneasy. Maybe it was too much, to hear that her brother was dead and then that he was alive? Or maybe it was that he brought trouble with him; it followed him like a faithful dog. Frances ran her hand across her stomach. It had been years since she'd felt like this. During her heyday, she could deal with it. Back then, Owen was always the source of her discontent. She could tell his humor from his gait. Since his incapacitation, their home life was more peaceful without his wild rages, and the great fear she had lived with had gone. But now that Lorcan had returned, it seemed to bring her husband from his wheelchair to his full height and former strength. The idea was terrifying.

Frances saw Wilbur's car pass the window. Lorcan was with him. It seemed as if she'd stopped breathing. She saw Wilbur and Lorcan walk past the window while they were looking at the lawn. Wilbur was pointing at something. She could only see Lorcan's back. Then he was in the hall, and Frances heard Lorcan's step on the wooden floor. Frances didn't need to look at his face to confirm it was him. He had a cautious light step that could have belonged to a smaller man. He stood at the door, all towering and looming six feet of him. Frances had to look through the map of wrinkles to find her brother. She saw the cleft chin, the long straight nose and wide mouth. Everything else had happened in the last thirty years, the thinning skin that coated his face, the bright white hair, and his eyes which seemed smaller. His suit was good, a contrast to the worn face.

Frances stood up. "You're very welcome," she said, extending her hand.

He smiled as he held her hand tightly. The emotion he couldn't convey was in his handshake. Suddenly Frances felt the tears sting her eyes. So much had happened. When they had last met, they were young and able, and now they were old and gray and more often than not, they were tired.

Frances removed her hand from his grasp, wiped her eyes, and stepped aside so he could see Owen.

If the sight of Owen's shriveled body in a wheelchair surprised Lorcan, he didn't appear so. There was nothing in his expression.

"Hello, old friend," Lorcan said, looking down at him. "Can he hear us?" Lorcan asked Frances and Wilbur.

"'Es," Owen said, the response almost lost in the gurling from his chest.

Lorcan reached out to shake Owen's limp right hand.

Owen pushed Lorcan's hand away.

Frances saw Wilbur's surprise, and his wife Molly's painted red lips formed a perfect O. Lorcan nodded once, as if expecting it.

While the maid fixed them drinks, Lorcan looked around at the large opulent room. The upholstered chairs matched the curtains. The furniture was solid and well-made with expensive wood. There was a chandelier on the ceiling and that damn grandfather clock was unrepentant in its ticking.

"You've come a long way with your mansions and land," he said to Frances and Wilbur.

"And education," Wilbur reminded him.

They sat down in a semicircle.

There was no need for silence while Wilbur was there. He talked about his wife and Molly's family. Her father had come for a visit from New York, and they had liked it so much they bought a ranch in Clover Pass. The conversation moved onto the house, its size, and the furnishings; they even discussed the crystal glass from which Lorcan drank.

Lorcan listened as Wilbur told him about the tumbler glass.

"Molly's parents like to travel. Last year they went to England. They were so impressed with the glassware they shipped back several sets as gifts."

Frances doubted Lorcan was interested in glassware. Frances noted Lorcan's worn fingers holding the sparkling, fine-cut glass. There was more idle chitchat about the side table and even the legs of the table. Lorcan obligingly bent sideways to examine the crafts-manship, and he and Wilbur talked as if it were something remark-able. Lorcan mentioned a carpenter in Texas. Then they talked about Texas. Then their conversation returned to Four Oaks. They talked about the locals, Captain Gallagher and Bertha, the Kellys and the Dwyers.

As the conversation progressed, Lorcan became familiar to Frances and that nervousness subsided. For years, Frances and

Lorcan had been united. Goldie and their father were on one team, she and Lorcan on another team. Goldie looked after Baby Miriam, and Frances looked after Lorcan. The day of the grasshoppers, she had tried to protect him. When the grasshoppers descended, she'd grabbed his hand and fled, and even when their lungs had reneged on them and they couldn't catch their breath, she'd carried him. While the adults lit fires to stave off the grasshoppers, it was Frances who had soothed Lorcan. He'd cried so much that he hiccupped. He was six, she was ten, and that day began their flight from something they could never articulate. Lorcan was never present; as soon as he'd had a choice, he'd left. During her marriage, she'd relived the day of the grasshoppers. She'd confronted a similar fear for many moons when Owen was a capable young man. She'd felt the terror and then relived the calm throughout her marriage. Even Goldie had spent the rest of her life trying to undo what had happened that day.

Just then it all seemed fine. What had she been frightened of? Memories. Her foolish silly memories. A memory could not kill someone, just like nobody died from the snake bite—it was the poison that followed. The poison of yesteryear had long been diluted to become nothing, a harmless drifting thought. What sat before her was her brother, an old man who could do no harm at this stage. They had survived into old age. Her brother was home, alive and well, sitting in front of her, enjoying the glow of family. Then she thought of Goldie. If Goldie were alive, or even the type to reappear as a ghost, she'd lean into Frances' ear and whisper, "You'd convince yourself of anything." Maybe it was true, as it was easier to find the passive route than to confront him. Easier to convince herself that her brother was harmless than deal with the fear. It was easier to be one who pacified rather than provoked. She could pacify Lorcan as soon as she established what he wanted. He probably wanted money or was dying, maybe he'd go back to Denver tomorrow, and they might even write to each other. They could fill long letters about life and their small observations as old people. Lorcan was always discrete; she could confide in Lorcan about Wilbur's wife, Molly, how she never liked to stay at home, and there was always an excuse to go galivanting somewhere else. Molly was wearing a low-cut white silk blouse. She could write to Lorcan about her thoughts on modern women and their immodest attire. Just then she looked at Wilbur, and Frances looked forward to what Lorcan would say about Wilbur in his letter. Today, Wilbur was wearing a blue shirt, and his eyes were as blue as the cloudless sky. Yes, this could have a happy ending after all.

Frances joined in on the conversation. When Lorcan was trying to recall Sean Dwyer's song, Frances sang the first two lines,

"The British fencibles they ran like deer, but our ranks were scattered and sorely battered, For the want of Kyan and his Shelmaliers."

Lorcan tapped his foot as she sang. "I remember it," he said, singing the third line. Molly began to clap in tune.

They stopped singing. Lorcan looked at her and smiled. "Your voice is as clear as ever."

They talked for another hour, and suddenly Wilbur and Molly left Frances, Owen, and Lorcan alone. "You three will have a lot of catching up to do."

Frances poured a fresh cup of tea when they were alone. "What brings you back?" she asked as she stirred the tea.

He didn't answer immediately. "A man gets curious," he finally said. "You just start to wonder about people."

"What really brought you back?" Frances said in a sweet coaxing voice.

He laughed, a short spurt that said he'd been rumbled. "I lost all my crops to the dust, every darn seed was swallowed up. Life hasn't been easy and I've got medical bills and a darn lot of pain," he said, holding up his bent fingers.

"So, money, you want money?" she asked; she could forgive him that. "I guessed as much," Frances said. She was not surprised he was so honest in his reply. He had always inadvertently revealed more than was necessary about his life.

"How did you guess?" he asked.

"You wouldn't come back when Goldie was alive."

"Too right," he said. "She would have put a bullet right there," he said pointing to his heart.

"So, you pretended you were dead."

"I didn't plan on it happening like that. Goldie came looking for me. She frightened the daylights out of my woman in Denver and I just knew she'd never stop until she caught me. I signed up for the Philippines," he said. "During one of the battles I lost sight of the battalion, and then I stayed out of sight until they moved out. The Army assumed I was dead."

Frances took some consolation in the fact that he'd fought in the Battle of Bud Dajo. Briefly she wondered if he'd even been there at all.

"Few months afterward, admittedly after I knew they would have written to you and Goldie about my death, I came home."

It all made sense to Frances.

"I moved around a lot. Two years ago, I returned to Denver. I read in the paper about Goldie's death. A traveling salesman had the Wyoming *Herald*. It was such a fine obituary with all the big words that Goldie wouldn't have been able to read. She never learned to read or write properly."

"She did fine without it," Frances said.

"I still can't believe she paid for the fine sculpture of me," he said. "And the size of it! It must be the biggest statue of a soldier that I ever saw."

Frances had been proud of the fine statue; it was wonderful to tell folks how her brother had fought and died in a foreign land fighting against communism. She'd tell people that they hadn't a grave to visit, and the bronze sculpture was a place for every family who'd lost a son, brother, father, or uncle in a war. For the last thirty years she'd told the same story; it had never varied. Goldie had told her that the best way to cement a story was to tell the same story. "No matter how tempted you are to add bits—don't." Frances had told Lorcan's story for so long and stuck to the same lines that she'd come to believe it and chose not to see the misdeeds he'd committed.

"Goes to show you, Goldie must have had a heart somewhere inside that tough exterior for her to pay for a statue for me."

"She thought you were dead at that stage. And she thought it would be a small plaque. When she saw the size of it, she almost broke Wilbur's back with her walking cane." Frances shuddered at the memory.

"I'm not surprised," Lorcan said. "She was wild, worse than the crazy Injuns in Wounded Knee. Tell me," Lorcan said, "is Aengus' woman still living on his land?"

Frances needed to stop him or whatever little vindictive plan was playing out in his head. "Lorcan, we live quiet respectable lives now. My son is the Mayor, my other sons and grandsons are educated. We're good people now."

"And I'm not?" Lorcan asked.

Frances didn't answer immediately. She looked at Owen, and Lorcan followed her line of vision. Owen was looking out the window, his useless hand resting on the tray.

"None of us expected it to happen the way it did," he said and looked away.

Frances said, "It could all have been avoided. The whole thing could have been avoided." Frances wasn't only talking about Owen's downfall; she was talking about that pocket of their family history that began with branding Chaytan and ended with Owen in a wheelchair.

Owen had played his part in his demise, but none of it would have happened if Lorcan hadn't involved himself. She was angry then. She wanted to say, "Look what you did to my husband."

"I want no trouble," Frances said.

Lorcan shook his empty glass. "I'll have another."

CHAPTER TWENTY-NINE

1937

Most of Makawee's faculties had faded over the years. Those that remained worked slowly. Her sight and hearing were poor; however, man helped bridge the gap with thick glasses that gave her the sight of a younger woman. For her hearing, there was a contraption that had made her laugh the morning Goldie had brought the long vacuum hearing aid. However, it gave her the ability to hear the dog scratch on a quiet day. There was nothing she could do for her slow feet. But what she did possess were those invisible tentacles that allowed her to sense what went unsaid. This week, she felt the unsettled air as if it were a liquid bubbling beneath the layer of wrinkled flesh that coated her thin hands. As she thought about it then, she put her hand on her arm, as if to quell this uneasiness. There were callers at her home who discussed Lorcan O'Neill's return. A few joked about the monument; they said it had come to life and was pounding the bar in Gallagher's Hotel for more drink. They joked about his spirit, that he had returned to settle some old score. Over sixty years ago, Aengus had told her Irish ghost stories, as there was a ghost story for every occasion in

Ireland, with good ghosts and bad ghosts who came back to haunt their wrongdoers. Lorcan O'Neill returning was a different type of ghost story, and she doubted his story had been told in Ireland.

Makawee got up from her perch on the veranda and walked with the aid of a cane through the living room and into the kitchen. She opened the drawer closest to the sink and rifled through papers until her fingers felt the metal. She took out the Derringer. It was one of a set; she possessed one and Goldie the other. Makawee opened the gun and felt for the bullets. It was loaded. She tucked the gun into her pocket and returned to the veranda.

Makawee did not come from this time; she came from a lifetime ago, when nobody but the wind and weather shaped their lives. Once upon a time her people were rulers of the West. Then the corteges of wagon trains arrived, and life changed. Initially, the whites passed through their territory without causing undue harm, but then their numbers grew. Their procession of wagons was like a long meandering snake through the prairies. With time, some of the white men stayed. They claimed land and set roots, and some were afflicted with a sense of ownership of all they saw. Every decade the Indian territory got smaller. Even then, with all they'd acquired, the greedy white man wanted more. A few ventured deep into the Black Hills, the last of the great Indian territory. Those who were caught never rejoined their snaking trains, and their final screams didn't reach the last wagon on the cortege.

Makawee's tribe didn't kill everybody who strayed into their lands. Her tribe brought her stories about a child in their territory with bright red hair. Goldie's strange, rarely seen coloring was a sign of wisdom and luck to the Lakotas. When she ventured onto the Indian lands, they had doubted her wisdom but not her bravery. When she returned again to the hills, some of the braves were so close, that if she had raised her arms, she would have grazed their axes. They'd trained their arrows only to lower them again. She became a curiosity. They watched as she took long strides counting aloud and then stopping to stare into the forest. They watched her from afar as she worked like a man, fought like a boy who doesn't doubt his strength, and sang sweet songs in her father's barn. As time passed, they willed her to live, and one Indian was so eager to see her survive he guided her to the cave the day the grasshoppers came.

Makawee heard a car approach. She put her hand into her pocket and took out the Derringer. If Lorcan O'Neill decided to visit, this time she'd be less forgiving.

The car pulled up at the veranda. "Morning, Makawee."

Makawee almost laughed aloud with both relief and amusement at her readiness to fire so wildly at the unknown car. It was Wakta, the girl who had finally given Goldie a purpose when it was most needed. Makawee saw Lucy hold the car door open, and the dog, Reggie jumped out.

"How are you?" Lucy said.

"All good," Makawee said, sliding the gun back into her pocket.

"I'll make tea," Lucy said, going straight into the kitchen.

She returned a few moments later with a tray, poured the tea, and handed Makawee a cup. Lucy took one of the folded blankets from inside the door and sat beside Makawee.

"Did Reggie do a good job?" Makawee asked, as she indicated the dog that had jumped onto Lucy's lap.

"He sure did," Lucy said, bending forward to plant a kiss on his head.

"You'll spoil that dog," Makawee said.

Lucy was a girl of nature, and it befuddled Makawee how she could live happily in New York City, although Makawee had her doubts about Lucy's happiness.

"I hope that's the end of the mice for now," Lucy said. "Poor Harry is unnerved by anything that crawls."

"Take Reggie anytime you like," Makawee said.

Lucy thanked her. She poured tea and placed Makawee's cup on the stand beside her.

"What are you up to today?" Makawee asked.

"I'm supposed to be sorting through Goldie's belongings today. Harry says we have to go back to New York tomorrow," Lucy took a biscuit and dunked it in the tea.

"Will you get it done?"

"In one day? I could never siphon through a lifetime of belongings that quickly," Lucy said.

"Maybe you'll come back and do it when you've more time," Makawee said.

"Or maybe I've the rest of my life to do it," Lucy said. "Maybe I won't leave at all."

Makawee looked closely at Lucy. "It would be nice if you stayed. You have a fine farm and a house and plenty of looms if you ever wanted to work again." She realized she was talking too quickly. The prospect of Lucy living so close and breathing life into Goldie's old home made her happy. "And you'd have John Dwyer, he never stops asking after you."

Lucy laughed at that. "He's married!"

"Not anymore," Makawee said.

Lucy was surprised. "Did Mabel die?"

"No, she went back to her folks in Chicago. I don't think she liked it much here."

"So, she just up and left?"

"So it seems," Makawee said.

"Poor John," Lucy said, feeling genuine sympathy for his troubles. If any man deserved happiness, it was John. Lucy had only met his wife a few times. "Did she leave him for another man?"

"There was talk, but I don't think so. She was a singer. Who's gonna listen to her singing out here?" Makawee pointed at the hills. "Any news or callers?" Makawee said, inviting Lucy to tell her about Lorcan. She wanted to know if he planned on staying. Would she be sitting on the veranda for the rest of her days looking down the avenue with her gun drawn?

"Only one caller, Wilbur Breen," Lucy said.

Makawee nodded; she didn't care for news about the Breens. Only last week, she'd turned on the radio to hear Wilbur's voice talking about the upcoming election. He was raving about his family's history. Makawee knew that the Breens skimmed over their failures and distorted history to whitewash the truth about some of their kin. With each generation they moved further away from the land toward educated professions. The family idea was that they'd enter politics. "The idea!" Goldie would scoff. Makawee heard from the maid how the Breens talked at length at how they'd better themselves with each generation. Their sons would become lawyers, state attorneys, "And then we'll go all the way to the White House," Wilbur Breen had said drunkenly one evening when he discussed his family's future. In three generations, all trace of the dirt-poor homesteader was gone. What remained of the past was Owen Breen in his wheelchair. The last time that Makawee had laid eyes on him was one Christmas Eve more than twenty years ago. He was in his chair being pushed by one of his refined grandsons. She didn't get any satisfaction when she saw him, because it didn't undo the past or bring back her dead.

"I was in Gallagher's," Lucy continued. "I met Bertha, and she was as welcoming as ever."

Makawee could hear the hesitation in Lucy's voice.

"I met my father," Lucy said.

Makawee waited for her to continue. The dog jumped off her lap when he saw a squirrel and gave chase. They watched the squirrel escape up a tree.

"He's not what I expected. He talked about the war and his battles and the men he'd killed." Lucy stretched for another biscuit. "He's difficult to like."

"Maybe one meeting isn't enough," Makawee said, going against her very core that wanted to warn her about Lorcan O'Neill.

"I think it's plenty enough," Lucy said.

Makawee smiled. Lucy had gotten that behavior from Goldie. She told her that.

"I don't think he and Goldie were friends. In fact, I don't think she liked him," Lucy said.

Makawee remained silent. She thought their history would blow away like the drifting tumbleweed and that she'd never have to deal with him again.

Lucy told Makawee about the photograph that was regularly taken off the sideboard in her absence and replaced when she returned. "When we were leaving Gallagher's, Bertha suggested that Lorcan stay with us in Goldie's house."

Everyone knew Bertha would fill her hotel to the rafters to make money and tolerate the most drunken behavior as long as the men were spending.

"During the conversation, he appeared to forget that he was my father," Lucy said. "I don't know if he's pretending to be my father or if there's another big story that I haven't been told."

Makawee couldn't offer any answers, none that she felt were her place to tell.

"I don't know what to believe," Lucy sighed.

"Will knowing the truth change anything?" Makawee asked.

Lucy considered it, "Maybe it would be nice to know."

Makawee didn't respond.

"Harry thinks that Lorcan is great," Lucy sighed. "And I don't want to say too much to him because, well... I don't know what the future holds or where I'll be living."

"You might not be living with Harry much longer?" Makawee asked.

"I can't commit to anything yet," Lucy said. "That's a secret until I know what I'm doing. If fact, I can't believe I've said aloud what's been in my head for months. And maybe I'll stay here longer or rush back to New York to be with him."

"Maybe it's just a difficult time?" Makawee said.

"Living with him has been difficult for a long time," Lucy sighed.

"I am here, you know that," Makawee said.

"I know that, thanks."

When Lucy was refilling her cup of tea, Winona arrived. "You look like two peas in a pod," Winona said when she saw Lucy and Makawee on the veranda.

"We're having a lovely chat about men," Lucy said. Then she put her arm on Makawee's shoulder. "Makawee is having man trouble."

Makawee pretended to cry into her hand.

Winona smiled at the unlikelihood of her ninety-four-year-old mother having boyfriend trouble.

"Is it lunch time?" Lucy asked, checking her watch when she realized why Winona was home. When she saw the time, she got up quickly. "I'm supposed to be getting food for our supper tonight."

"Kelly's has the best cakes," Winona said.

"Great, see you later," Lucy said, getting into the car and driving away.

Makawee and Winona watched Lucy drive down the avenue.

"How is she?" Winona asked.

"She hasn't warmed to Lorcan and suspects there may be more to the story than Goldie told her."

Winona was standing on the patio looking after the car. "I don't think Goldie thought he'd come back."

"Nobody thought he'd come back," Makawee said.

She felt the gun in her pocket. She could forgive what Lorcan O'Neill had done to Aengus, as he was only a boy then, but what he had done as an adult to her family was unjustifiable.

"If Lorcan shows his true colors, you might have to tell her the truth," Winona said.

They remained silent, looking after the car until it was out of sight.

CHAPTER THIRTY

1888

The O'Neills and the Breens made great strides to become the first families of wealth in Four Oaks.

Ned Breen made his money in timber. According to Ned, there were new towns springing up across the West. Americans needed timber to build their new stores, hotels and houses. Every year, Ned set aside more and more land for forestry until he had almost 700 acres in trees. He worked his sons hard and expected the same ceaseless effort from their wives.

Barry stuck to what he knew; he was a farmer. Each year, he added to his farm. He spent more money on sheep and rotated the crops on his land. By the late 1880s, he owned more than 800 acres. Many times, he compared the size of his American farm to his Irish one. "I could have walked across my farm in Ireland in twenty minutes, and now it would take me a day to cross all I own."

The other surprisingly great source of Barry's income was Goldie's woolen mill.

Goldie had the wool from her father's sheep, and she also

bought Pedro Dwyer's wool. She hired local girls and taught them everything from spinning to dying. Every few years, she needed larger washing cauldrons and dying vats. Mostly, Goldie was contented with her small growing empire, but at other times she was impatient, and she wanted more of everything. Her eyes and ears were always attuned for any new arrivals who had experience working in the woolen mills. Occasionally, she reminded herself of her father and Ned Breen, whose appetite for more was insatiable. At times like that she'd think of Aengus Kennedy, who had asked, *haven't you enough?*

Captain Gallagher prospered with a different kind of money. When the O'Gradys and O'Connors and many Shanahans collected their paychecks, their hard-earned money was passed over the counter to Captain Gallagher. He built a new saloon with a long, shiny, inviting counter. There were card games and a new piano to provide music night and day. Women with powdered faces served drinks and were available to sate a different kind of thirst.

"A scandalous breed of women," Frances clarified, looking at the piano from the saloon.

Captain Gallagher gave his old piano to Ned Breen's wife. He'd heard how she played one on the wagon train. Leonora Breen refused to play it, and it sat in the corner of their parlor coated in a film of dust.

Chaytan returned twice a year. He arrived at night, taking great care not to be seen. During his stay, he remained close to Makawee's cabin. The Breens suspected he was responsible for Timothy's death, and according to Frances, they were gunning for him. Goldie loved it when Chaytan returned. There was always a jubilant air and a hum of unity in the cabin on the night after his arrival. Makawee would prepare a lavish meal and invite Goldie, Blue Feather, and his family. Although a joyous occasion, Aengus lingered in their thoughts.

Each night during his stay, Goldie would call and hear about Chaytan's travels on the cattle drives north. He told her about the arid land of Texas, the giant cacti in the desert, the cowboys who lived for the drive and then spent all they had on whorehouses and whiskey before climbing into the saddle to drive the docile long-horned animals north. He described the sleep deprivation, traveling miles without water, the animals, the camaraderie, and the color of the landscape in the different states he passed through with his cattle.

"I saw the ocean," he told her late one night. "It's bigger than all of America, nothing but water for miles and miles," he said, and stretched his hand in front of him casting shadows on the walls of Makawee's cabin. He told her about the hardship of the trek. "When it gets so hard, all I want to do is roll into the nearest hole and die, then I think about the long grass of home, the soft cool breeze, the smell of the hills," he said, sucking in the air as he spoke, "and then I think of my Goldie. Then I'm happy to leave the ocean and the salty water behind to sit in my old home and tell her how I survived."

She smiled when he said that.

In his absence, Goldie kept notes to remind herself of events to relate when Chaytan returned. Over the course of a few days, she'd go through the notebook with writing that was so illegible, only she could make out the reminders. As she flicked through her notebook, she told him about the Breens and their prosperous farm, her alter-cations with Owen Breen, the piano that Mrs. Leonora Breen refused to play. She told him that her father referred to Captain Gallagher as Captain Gossip.

"And Bertha's as bad. She knows everything, and what she doesn't know, she makes it her business to find out."

She told him about the fresh water in Dwyers Lake. "We bring a picnic and swim there a few times a week."

He liked to hear the little bits of news and her commentary on the locals. "What's in your picnic box?"

"Sandwiches, and Bertha's pie, which is as good as her whiskey," Goldie told him.

Goldie also told him the big happenings, like Lorcan, and how she hoped he'd stay gone this time.

"I don't care if I never again see him," she confessed.

Chaytan didn't need to air his opinion.

They often talked about the Indians and how hopeless their future appeared. In 1888, Chaytan told Goldie about a new movement that was sweeping through the tribes; he called it the Ghost Dance.

"It's our only hope," he told her. He grew animated as he talked about the dancers and how they wore a protective shirt that was said to be stronger than the bullet from a white man's gun. The shirt was made of feathers. "We dance to the left, a slow dance to a single drumbeat," he clapped his hands slowly as he told her. "We dance and dance all night until we fall down. Then we see into the future." Under the candlelight in Makawee's cabin, Chaytan said, "The white invaders will disappear from our lands, our ancestors will lead us to good hunting grounds, the buffalo herds and all the other animals will return in abundance, and the ghosts of our ancestors will return to earth."

Goldie knew that the Indians were torn between two cultures, their own Indian life and the new culture imposed upon them. Nothing had replaced the old lifestyle. They needed to find freedom and they couldn't find that without hope, and through the dance they had found their first glimmer of hope.

"The solution comes from within us," Chaytan said, pointing to his chest.

More than anything, Goldie wanted to believe it, but even to her, it seemed an impossible dream. Their sacred hills were awash with white settlers. Gold-mining towns dotted the old grazing pastures of the buffalo.

Chaytan normally stayed a month, long enough to rejuvenate his body and soul, then he became restless. He'd return to the saddle and ride over a thousand miles to Texas to begin another cattle drive north.

"No sign of Baby Miriam?" Goldie always asked.

His reply was always the same, "No."

The night before he left in early spring 1888, they were alone in the cabin when she asked again. He hesitated before answering.

"Not yet. I'll tell you when I'm closer," he said.

"So, you have heard of someone like her?" she asked.

"Possibly, but I don't want to tell you until I'm sure," he said, "I didn't say anything before now because I know you'll probably go galloping onto the reservation to find her."

Goldie got up from her chair and sat next to him. "You have to tell me," she said. "Where is she? Is it really her?"

"This is why I didn't say anything," he said. "I know you've waited—"

She interrupted him, "I've waited my whole life for this." She paused to consider it. She had always believed that Miriam was alive; she believed it as much as she believed an Indian had guided her to a cave on the day of the grasshoppers and the same Indian had possibly taken and saved her sister. "I've never felt she was dead," she said quietly.

Chaytan sat watching her.

"This could make everything right, everything," she added, almost breathless at the realization that she could be so close to someone actually knowing Miriam's whereabouts. "Tell me," she said.

Chaytan refused to tell her until she returned to her seat opposite him.

Goldie laughed and obeyed.

Chaytan began, "There is a red-haired woman living on a reservation. I heard about her because the local women in the nearest town took her from the tribe. They thought they'd saved her."

Chaytan continued, "They knew she was a captive with her red hair and white skin, so they wanted to return her to her family, but each time they took her away, by nightfall she'd creep away and return to the reservation."

"It has to be her. Where is she?" Goldie could feel the heat going to her face.

"It may not be her," Chaytan cautioned. "There is another red-haired woman with the Skokomish Tribe and another on the Zuni Reservation and probably more that I haven't heard about."

"Where is the Zuni Reservation?"

"This is why I never mentioned it before now," Chaytan said.

"You'll want to gallop onto every reservation around the country at the first whiff of news."

Goldie waited for him to continue.

"The Zuni are in New Mexico. It's not Baby Miriam," Chaytan said. "She's too old."

Goldie had to be content with what she'd heard. She knew she couldn't force Chaytan to tell her.

"And the woman you're referring to now," Goldie persisted, "is she about the same age as Baby Miriam would be?"

"Yes."

"And does she look like me?"

"I haven't seen her," Chaytan said.

"What tribe is she with?"

Chaytan sighed.

"Then I won't ask anything more, just tell me the tribe." Goldie pleaded.

"She is with the Lakota," he said, and looked at her before continuing. "The story goes that she was taken as a child. It would make sense that she was taken by the Lakota because she was taken from here," as he pointed in the direction of the site where she'd gone missing. "Wait for one more month, and I'll tell you then. I'll know her age and more about her in one month."

"This is the closest I've ever come to finding her," Goldie said. She closed her mouth, a determined pout that Chaytan knew well. "One month?" she said.

"You've waited twenty years, one more month isn't that much."

She pretended to agree with him. "In one month you'll be gone, so this is what you will do." she began. "Send me a postcard with the name of the reservation."

"It might not be her and even if I see her, I won't be able to tell if it's Baby Miriam," Chaytan said. "And I don't want you goin' galloping all over the countryside on a whim."

"I think it would be a fine excuse to visit another state."

Chaytan relented, "I'll do that. I'll send you a postcard, but don't get your hopes up."

"If I don't hear anything by the last day of September, I'll take it that it isn't her."

Chaytan agreed.

As soon as he was gone, Goldie burned the notepad with the old notes and started filling a new one.

CHAPTER THIRTY-ONE

1890-1906

Two weeks after Chaytan left, Goldie went to town once a day to check the post office in the hope that his postcard had arrived. Each day she was disappointed. She took consolation in the fact that if Chaytan believed the redheaded woman with the Indians to be Baby Miriam, he would send his postcard.

Some evenings, she'd call to Gallagher's Hotel to visit Bertha and Captain Gallagher. They knew every tidbit of gossip that went on in Four Oaks, from the badly-behaved drunkard to world affairs. Occasionally, Captain Gallagher sat in on their conversations. Goldie had to smile when she thought of her father calling him Captain Gossip. "A darn woman isn't as bad." Her father was annoyed because Captain Gallagher asked after Lorcan. "He was leaning in toward me." Barry imitated the way the Captain would incline his body toward the person he was speaking to and tilt his head when he wanted news.

At the first crisp bite of autumn, as the setting sun cast long shadows across the main street, Captain Gallagher told Goldie that Mr. Kelly was rumored to be secretly meeting up with Mrs. Shannon, Mr. Gilmore lost his entire months wages the previous night during cards and that the Indians had gone mad with their dancing.

"Dancing?" she asked, leaning closer to him and behaving exactly as Captain Gallagher behaved with his head tilted to one side. Goldie was intrigued to hear Captain Gallagher's take on the new Ghost Dance that Chaytan had talked about.

Captain Gallagher said, "Them Injuns reckon they're talking to their dead relatives who are telling them that the white man is gonna go away. They think that the dance will bring the buffalo back along with all their dead relatives."

Bertha sat up straight, asking, "And do their dead relatives come back?"

"No, they do not," Captain Gallagher hollered. "Are you daft in the head! The only way they'll be seeing their dead relatives is if they don't stop 'cause it's making people nervous."

"It's only a dance," Goldie said. "I'm sure there's no harm in it."

"Sure, there's harm," Captain Gallagher said, "this dance is giving them Injuns some crazy hope that don't make sense to anyone except in their minds."

"What's wrong with a bit of hope?" Goldie asked.

"There's a lot wrong with hope," he said, nodding his head knowingly. "You give these people hope, then they hope to be free, hope they can turn back time, hope of fighting and more hope for uprising. Hope is the worst thing you can give them, it's worse than a barn of dynamite. They can't have hope that they'll be anything other than whipped Injuns."

Goldie sighed, saddened at such talk of hopelessness.

"I never heard the likes of it," Bertha admitted when the Captain left them alone. "The Captain is usually right about these things."

Despite the large age gap between Bertha and Captain Gallagher, they appeared fond of each other. Bertha called him Captain, even when they were alone. The air of admiration in her voice was always evident. For his part, Captain Gallagher seemed proud of his wife and how hard she worked. He told Goldie's father that she rose at six, and at midnight she was still motoring around like a farm machine.

"Talking of Injuns," Bertha said, "have you seen the rope in the Breens' barn for the boy who broke your father's mustangs?"

Goldie shook her head.

Bertha told Goldie that the Captain had seen the rope. Bertha leaned close to Goldie, "He seen it with his own eyes. Ned and Owen Breen said that the noose is waiting for the mustang-boy."

It was common knowledge that Lorcan and the Breens had branded Chaytan with an iron; equally, it was suspected that Chaytan had killed Timothy. They knew Aengus' disappearance belonged in the mix somewhere, but few knew where.

"A rope!" Goldie said, not at all surprised at the news.

"As sure as you and me are sitting on this very bench, them Breens are never gonna rest one minute till that mustang-boy's head is in that rope and he's screaming for mercy."

Goldie didn't need Bertha to tell her that.

Timothy Breen's death remained an open wound in the family. It was more than the ebbing tide of grief that drifts in and out; his death was different. It gnawed at his prejudiced father who in turn passed his hatred for the Indians onto his sons. Although the Breens had not laid eyes on Chaytan in ten years, they knew he was involved. The branding iron forced onto Timothy's flesh was a reminder of what had gone on before. If not Chaytan, then, according to Frances, who spoke for the Breens, it was one of his savage Indian friends and somebody must pay.

Occasionally, Frances and Barry asked Goldie if she knew anything about Chaytan.

"Chaytan is probably in Canada or on some reservation starving to death like the rest of the Indians," Goldie quipped.

Owen Breen also asked Goldie if she'd seen Chaytan. "Did you see any sign of that murdering Injun?"

"No, Owen, I only saw one murderer," Goldie said. "He was flayed to hell and back with a branding iron," she said, referring to Timothy.

If Chaytan had been around, she would have told him that she could almost see smoke coming out of Owen's ears.

Owen knew not to ask Goldie again. Despite how rudely and aggressively Goldie spoke to Owen, he always came back for more. He'd call at her home when she was alone, and Barry was in town. During those visits, Goldie never offered him as much as a cup of tea or a drink of water.

That very day when she left Bertha Gallagher and went home, Owen called that evening when she was alone. He said he came to tell her about a new sheep rancher offering good prices for wool.

"When you go to meet him, I'll go with you to make sure you get the best deal," Owen offered.

"It's fine, Owen, I can haggle as good as any man, if not better," she said. She was washing the dishes after dinner. Owen hovered by the door.

"How is it going with the mill?" Owen said.

"What in sweet divine Jesus did you call at my house tonight for?" Goldie asked.

"Just a sociable call," he said and left meekly a few minutes later.

Ten days later he called again.

"We'd have made a great team. You and me," he said.

Goldie shook her head in bewilderment. Owen left.

On the last day of September in 1890, Goldie went into town to check the mail in the hope that Chaytan's postcard had arrived.

She saw Captain Gallagher outside his saloon talking to a soldier. She stopped walking and stood watching them. Only when the soldier turned slightly did she recognize Lorcan's side profile. She was so surprised at the sight of him she forgot about the mail. She bought three items in Kelly's store and rode home.

If her father was surprised to see Lorcan, he didn't appear so.

"What brings you back?" Barry asked.

"It's just a flying visit. I was passing by and thought I'd pop in and say hello," Lorcan said. He went on to tell them that he was on Army business in Hewlett and was now en route to Fort Niobrara in Nebraska.

"You stole twenty dollars from me," Barry said.

"I borrowed it," Lorcan said, and dipping into his pocket, he took out a wad of notes, peeled off a twenty-dollar bill, and laid the money on the table.

Barry looked at the money and then up at Lorcan, "I don't know what will become of you."

"I'm doing fine," Lorcan said.

"What about here?" Barry asked. "Have you any notion of coming home for good?"

"Not just yet," Lorcan said. "There's something brewing on Pine Ridge Reservation, and I need to be back in a few days."

That night, Frances and Owen and their flock of children came for supper.

Despite Lorcan's handsome uniform and fine horse, little had changed. He looked older than his forty years and behaved as immaturely as Owen's oldest son. Lorcan told them stories about his life as a soldier, the near misses and battles and the best saloons in the West. "Denver is my favorite place in all of America," he told them. "In a couple of years, I'll probably sell this place and move there."

"Why?" Owen asked.

"Denver is a happening town, it's on the cattle trail, and it has the finest women your eyes ever did see," he said.

It was the first time that the Breens had little interest in the ramblings of a man who appeared polished on the outside, but with a glimmer into his conversation, he was still the boy who'd marched about in Captain Gallagher's uniform. The Breens were their father's sons, men who lived for farming and accumulating wealth and knowledge about their profession.

They couldn't understand Lorcan's aimless life with boyish stories of luck, wine, and women.

If Lorcan saw the disapproval in their eyes, he didn't pretend. When he was not telling stories or talking nonsense, Goldie noticed that vacant stare of a man who'd seen too much. She shuddered, thinking of the sights he'd seen.

The only time that Owen and Lorcan seemed united was when they discussed Chaytan.

That night their kitchen was noisy with the mass of children and visitors, but Goldie heard Lorcan and Owen speaking on the veranda.

"I believe he's on the cattle drive, I've a crew looking out for him," Lorcan was saying.

"I want him alive," Owen said.

She couldn't hear their entire conversation; however, she did hear Owen mention the noose. "It's got that damn murdering Injun's name on it."

Lorcan was nodding, then he said something that Goldie couldn't hear.

"I'd appreciate that." Owen replied. "Let me know as soon as you see him."

On the morning Lorcan was due to leave, he offered to sell Barry some sheep.

"Sheep?" Barry said. "I thought you were in the Army."

"It's a sideline," Lorcan said. "I've 600 sheep for sale. Do you want to buy them?"

"Ask Goldie, the sheep are her thing," Barry said.

Goldie was alone outside her mill when Lorcan approached her. Not if she was down to the very last thread of wool would she buy his livestock.

Lorcan didn't ask her to buy the sheep. Instead, he had a proposition. "I've got some information that you might like to know."

Goldie looked at him, expecting him to tell her about his flock of sheep that were nowhere in sight.

"First, you gotta tell Dad to give me the loan of $100?"

She waited for him to speak.

"I know where Miriam is."

"Where is she?" Goldie asked, getting to her feet.

"First, you gotta agree to what I ask. I want $100."

Goldie took in the sight before her, Lorcan in his noble Army uniform and oiled hair. He was vain, more vain than their sister, Frances and unlike anyone she knew; he was loathsome. He was worse than Owen Breen, and she told him that.

"Owen Breen is a cur, but at least he's a worker and sometimes even he has manners."

Lorcan was so taken with her reaction, his head moved back.

"You're the worst," she shook her head, trying to find something to compare him with before continuing, "to think that you would barter about your sister for money."

He stood speechlessly staring at her.

"Have you lived such a terrible life that you'd expect me to barter for my sister, or maybe you want me to admire your negotiating skills?"

"You want to find her, don't you?" he said, regaining his composure.

"And don't you?" she asked.

"Not really. I don't know her," he said. "Besides, you can't expect her to come back to us now."

The more he spoke, the more hatred she felt.

"You're a liar, you're a thief, and you're nothing," she said.

"Are you gonna shut up and listen to what I gotta say?"

Goldie only stopped speaking because she was trying to find words to describe him.

"I'll tell you how I know it's her," Lorcan said.

She shook her head in bewilderment at what he was trying to do.

Lorcan continued as if she were listening to him, "There is an Indian captive with the red hair. She's white, as white as you and me, and guess what age she is?"

Goldie wouldn't answer.

"She a few years younger than me. Not only that, but she's tall like you and me. The white women in the town where she lives have rescued her a few times from the reservation but every time they rescue her, by sundown she'd be back with the Injuns again." He stopped speaking, only adding, "Well, are you gonna help me?"

"I hope to God I never set eyes on you again. Now get the hell away from me," she said. She sat down and cracked the loom so loudly that she almost broke the wood.

As much as she wanted to know where Miriam was, she wouldn't help him. She would wait for Chaytan's postcard.

A few hours later, Goldie heard Lorcan and their father fighting. They were on the veranda. She couldn't hear what was said, only her father's voice shouting a litany of curse words.

That night, Barry told Goldie that Lorcan had asked for $100 to bring Baby Miriam home to him.

"And what did you say?" Goldie said.

"I asked him why he waited this long. He couldn't answer me. It would have been different if Neasa was alive or even if it had been a few years ago. I accepted Baby Miriam's death soon after she disappeared. I can't get my hopes up that she's alive and even if she is, she's not one of us anymore."

"She might remember us," Goldie said.

"Captain Gallagher told me that no adult who was taken as a child and returned to their family ever stayed. Every captive returns to the Injuns," Barry said.

They sat in silence, Goldie was thinking about Baby Miriam and her father's reluctance to find her.

Barry exhaled loudly, and she thought he'd say something about Baby Miriam, maybe even that they should see if she's all right.

"Those damn sheep he wanted to sell me," he said about Lorcan, "I doubt there are any sheep for sale. They probably exist in his mind. They're somewhere, maybe in his imagination, but wherever they are, they're not in his possession. Poor man, where did I go wrong?"

Goldie couldn't answer his question.

As it was getting dark, Owen Breen called. He had been in town and happened to be in the post office.

"A card for Goldie," he said, holding it up and reading the back. "I thought I'd deliver it myself." Owen continued, "Do you have a secret admirer you're not telling us about?"

Goldie reached for the postcard, but Owen held it out of her reach. "Rosebud," he said, reading the back of the postcard.

Goldie jumped up and snatched it from his hand.

"Are you somebody's rosebud?" Owen asked.

It explained why Lorcan knew about Miriam, as Rosebud Indian Reservation was only a few miles from where Lorcan was posted.

Barry looked at the card. "Who is it from?"

Goldie shrugged, "I don't know."

Owen tried again, "Tell us his name, Miss Rose Bud, who is he?"

"Well, it sure as hell isn't you," Goldie said, and at that, Barry laughed loudly.

CHAPTER THIRTY-TWO

1890

On October 3, 1890, Goldie and Makawee left Four Oaks on the first train going south. They took a second train east, and then a cab for four miles, and from there they walked for six miles to the Rosebud Indian Reservation. Goldie carried a basket of food, and the Colt pistol in her dress pocket kept banging off her thigh. Makawee carried four blankets tucked under her arms. They walked until they arrived at the reservation. She noticed women and men huddled around open fires. There were tepees and wooden cabins with clusters of children playing outside, yet the overriding air was one of despondency that made Goldie uneasy. A guard pointed Goldie to the cabin where the red-haired Indian woman lived with her family.

As Goldie approached the cabin, the only sounds were her shoes and the swish of her dress as several sets of brown eyes followed her movements. The door to the cabin that housed Miriam was open. Outside, she saw the red-haired captive walking toward a group of men. Goldie followed her. Even as Goldie approached, she knew it was Miriam. She had the same straight-backed walk as their mother before Neasa got sick. Her shoulders were broad, and the red hair was the same red as Goldie's.

Goldie stopped. She watched Miriam hand a bowl to one of the men. He began to eat, then with his eyes he indicated Goldie. Miriam looked around, and she backed away as if she were about to flee, then stopped. Goldie walked toward her until she was right in front of Miriam.

Goldie could see Miriam scrutinize her face. Although they shared the same coloring, their features were different except for the cleft chin. Goldie saw Miriam bring her hand to her chin and feel the indention.

A group of people gathered round them.

For a moment Goldie thought her voice had failed her, she couldn't speak. "You are my sister," Goldie finally said in a voice so quiet, it sounded strange to her own ears.

Miriam didn't speak.

"I am your family," Goldie tried again. She wished for a flicker of recognition or even a smile from Miriam.

Miriam looked down at the children who'd gathered round. She took the hand of the smallest. "This is my family," Miriam said.

"And me," Goldie said, stepping forward. "I am your family too. Your sister."

If Miriam understood, she didn't show it.

"Do you remember?" Goldie said. Her eyes suddenly stung with tears. "Do you remember us?" Her voice faltered, Goldie fought back the rising mixed emotions, the memory of her last sighting of Baby Miriam, the guilt and sudden elation at the sight of her all these years later.

Some kindness in Miriam came to the fore. She saw Goldie's distress and moved toward her. She placed her hand on Goldie's arm.

"I know who you are," Miriam said.

"I am Goldie," she said, torn between shame that she'd allowed her emotions to be seen and an urge to crumple on the ground and cry for what had happened during the lost years. She did neither;

she cleared her throat. "I was meant to mind you, the day of the grasshoppers. It was my fault."

"I don't want to go back anymore," Miriam said as if she hadn't heard Goldie's plea for forgiveness. "These are my people, my family."

Goldie nodded that she understood.

Miriam retreated behind the door and closed it. Goldie left the blankets and food outside the door before leaving.

That night she went home. She pretended to her father that she had been in Nebraska, visiting a hotel that wanted to order rugs. After all, it was he who'd said he didn't want Miriam, she was somebody else now. Goldie silently agreed with him. Miriam had survived to lay her roots in some other country with a race that shared the same fundamental family values as theirs.

Goldie tried not to think about Miriam. But no matter how hard she tried, she couldn't reconcile the fact that her sister was living 250 miles away on a reservation. One month later, Goldie returned to the reservation. When Miriam spotted her, she hesitated. Her expression was like their mother's, at the sight of visitors when there was work to be done. Goldie's visit was an inconvenience to Miriam, yet she invited her in. Miriam thanked her for the basket of food and blankets. The little girl who'd been there during her last visit stood close to her mother, watching Goldie suspiciously. She was a cute little thing with black curly hair.

"How are you?" Goldie asked.

They couldn't make small talk or exchange pleasantries, there was nothing to do. She left the reservation with the same hopelessness, yet she wanted to return again.

"I need to make this right," she told Chaytan, who returned that fall.

"Make what right?" he asked.

Goldie couldn't answer.

"The only way you can make it right is if you can turn back time," he said quietly, "and even you, my bold Goldie, can't do that."

Goldie found it hard to accept what he said.

"You punish yourself for something you didn't do," Chaytan said. His voice was gentle. "You walk for all those miles punishing yourself. She doesn't want you, and you punish yourself and go back again."

Goldie remained silent. She was so intent on making it right that she couldn't understand what he meant.

"Leave it alone," Chaytan said.

Before leaving for Texas again, Chaytan gave her a Christmas present. It was a gun, the smallest, most delicate gun she'd ever seen.

"Is it a real gun?" Goldie asked when she saw how it fit into the palm of her hand.

"Sure, it's a real gun, it's a pocket pistol Derringer. All the fancy women in Texas buy them. They're easy to hide."

On the small curve of the handle, it was engraved: To G, from C, 1890.

Just as Captain Gallagher had said, many of the Ghost Dancers did meet their ancestors sooner than expected. On the last few days of 1890, on Pine Ridge Reservation, 300 Indians were shot dead.

Goldie heard about it from Owen Breen and Captain Gallagher when she visited the hotel.

"There was gonna be an uprising," Owen Breen told her, "the Army had no choice but to shoot them dead or be shot."

"I expect Lorcan would have been one of the boys doing the firing. It's close to his post," Captain Gallagher said.

Afterward, she heard that half of those killed were women and children. A group of boys dressed in Carlisle Indian School uniforms were among the dead. For several days their bodies were left where they had fallen. There was sporadic fighting on the Reservation that the Army had to deal with, and finally, a burial party arrived, dug a pit, and dumped the frozen bodies. The newspapers called it a battle. Those who witnessed it said it was a massacre. It ended armed resistance by the Native Americans.

Two weeks later, when the first postcards with pictures of Indians frozen in the snow went on sale, news reached them about Lorcan's role in the massacre.

Captain Gallagher called with the Nebraska *Herald*. A passing guest had left it in his saloon. He read aloud, "Sergeant Lorcan O'Neill pursued hostiles to a ravine to ensure the safety of his men. He directed his fire at the hostiles, allowing his men access to the battle."

When Captain Gallagher left Goldie and her father alone, Barry looked at the newspaper before rolling it into a ball and burning it.

"Sergeant Lorcan O'Neill has all this land, and he'd rather take on battles that are not his. I'd say the same Sergeant enjoyed following those Injuns to the ravine and shooting every one of them to death." He went to the door of the cabin and looked out at the night, "Captain Gallagher said most of those Injuns weren't armed."

The following January, in 1891, Barry turned sixty-five years of age. Although he was in good health, he began to think of his mortality and his farm.

"Best thing to do with everything I have is leave it to you," he said to Goldie. "Lorcan has no interest. He told Owen Breen he'd sell the farm and move to Denver. I don't know if the money he'd make from the sale would ever make it to Denver. Lorcan would have it long spent." Barry continued in the same melancholic tone, "We don't know what the future holds, maybe nobody will be farming in years to come. The Americans will think of something new to replace everything we know. They talk of steel instead of wood, machines instead of men. We'll always need sheep and wool."

Owen Breen thought his sons would inherit the farm, although he never said it aloud. He was always offering his services to Barry. He wanted to send his oldest son to live with Goldie and Barry. "He is your oldest grandson," Owen reminded him.

Barry knew what Owen wanted. "That bucko is a cute whore like his father. He'd love to get his two feet into my farm and your woolen mill."

Owen wouldn't be deterred so easily. He cautioned Barry about rising crime, "The country is crawling with outlaws robbing trains and isolated businesses." He knew Goldie paid the woolen mill workers on a Friday night. "And if I know, others know. I can send one of my boys to help you on Fridays when you pay the wages."

If anyone else had offered, Barry would have deemed it neighborly, but he was deeply suspicious of Owen, and despite his long friendship with Ned, he had no doubt that both men, in their minds had mapped out what they'd do with every square foot of land that belonged to him.

When their home was robbed, it didn't happen at their woolen mill on payday. Instead, the thief came to her home on a Thursday night.

Goldie was awakened from her sleep by a man standing over her with a gun, shouting, "Where's the damn money?"

Goldie was momentarily frozen when she saw the scene playing out before her eyes. Barry was in the doorway of her bedroom. His face was cut. He appeared old and vulnerable as he held the doorframe for support.

"I'll get the money for you," Goldie said. She put her hand under the pillow and felt the small steel grip of the Derringer. She fired at him twice; the first shot hit him in the neck, and the second hit him in the chest.

She saw him staggering backward and the blood spurting from his neck. She didn't know that a wound could release blood that fast.

Her father crumpled to the floor. It was the first time he'd ever seemed helpless.

In the weeks after the event, Goldie's actions received great praise from certain quarters.

"Best news I've heard all year," Ned Breen said. He wanted to know every minute detail of the attack.

When Goldie was asked about it, she passed it off lightly. "These are the times we live in."

They didn't know that the night after the killing, her hands began to shake. They shook so uncontrollably that Goldie thought they'd never stop. She poured a glass of whiskey that she couldn't lift to her lips. She cupped the jug of whiskey with both hands and swallowed several mouthfuls, then sat in the dark. Only when the alcohol took effect did the shaking diminish. That night, before she went to bed, she saw the thief's face, his determination to find the money, then the surprise when he saw the Derringer pointed at him, and when she'd fired, she'd seen the disbelief on his face. And then submission. One week after the incident, Captain Gallagher called to commend her. He talked about killing. In his indirect way he helped her sleep.

"How long before I stop hearing the sound of the gun and seeing his face at night?" she asked him. Each night the blast of the Derringer woke her from her sleep.

"When you know you done the right thing, it'll stop."

Eventually, she stopped seeing the thief's face and hearing the gunshot.

In her pad of notes for Chaytan, she wrote—Derringer works just fine.

Once life found an even keel again, Goldie's thoughts returned to Baby Miriam. She tried to see what Chaytan meant and willed herself to stay away from Rosebud. Of course, she knew that Miriam had her own life and her own family, and she was more Indian than white, yet knowing all of this and that it would be best to leave well enough alone, Goldie returned to Rosebud Reservation with her Derringer hidden in her skirt pocket. This time she went alone; Makawee didn't accompany her. With the same single-mindedness that saw her accomplish so much, Goldie took the train and walked for one hour. She couldn't accept that she and Miriam could not be friends and that she could not belong in her sister's life. As she trudged through the open prairie, she was adamant that she would get her way.

When she arrived at Miriam's cabin, there was a new family living there. Baby Miriam was gone.

"Gone where?" Goldie asked.

They didn't know.

Goldie gave them the blankets and food she had brought and left. On the train ride home, she turned her face to the window and cried quiet tears of loss.

That evening, when Goldie arrived at Four Oaks train station, she heard that Ned Breen had died.

"He just drifted off in his sleep," Mr. Kelly told her.

Goldie began the ten-mile walk home beneath the gray and amber sky. When Goldie began the ascent up the hill to her home, she began to slow her pace.

How can I make myself stop trying to make it right?

She was aware of nothing, only her sense of loss. She thought of what Chaytan had said, that she punished herself.

I will never again try to find her.

Goldie stopped walking and stood still. She could see the Breens home on her left, and the wind was blowing from that direction.

I can allow her to live in peace.

The enormous sense of loss began to abate. Although the sadness was still weighty, it seemed to make sense.

I can accept that she will never have peace with me trying to turn back time.

There was nothing in sight, only the wind blowing. She realized she was crying again.

Let it go.

Then she heard piano music. For a moment she thought she was imagining it. It was coming from the Breens' house, and the sound of music was carried by the wind. Goldie looked toward the Breens. Mrs. Leonora Breen had finally returned to playing the piano.

Goldie remained where she was, once again caught up in the beautiful sound that came from a woman who could hardly raise a smile. It had been twenty years since Goldie had heard that tune.

When Mrs. Breen stopped playing, Goldie resolved to allow life to take its course.

CHAPTER THIRTY-THREE

1937

Lucy drove to town to buy food for supper. After her chat with Makawee, she felt lighter than she had in months, and felt that surging relief gained by giving a voice to what she wanted and suddenly realizing it was possible. As she glided down the mountain and parked in the main street, she met more old friends, all of whom mentioned Goldie and expressed their own grief for their neighbor. Lucy accepted their condolences. It was as if her grief were not singular, but shared and diluted.

Mrs. Kelly's shop was dusty and dark, yet it was rich with familiarly. Mrs. Kelly, her large bosom resting on the counter, came outside to greet her. She suddenly enveloped Lucy in a hug.

"It's so lovely to see you," she gushed.

While the shop girl packed the box of groceries, Mrs. Kelly asked Lucy about New York and Harry and how long she would stay. Lucy answered all of her questions, basking in the old familiar warmth. When she was finished, the shop girl helped carry out one of the boxes. She tipped the shop girl, and when she turned around, she almost bumped into a man.

It was John Dwyer. Both he and Lucy were surprised to find themselves face to face.

"Hello, Lucy," he said and smiled.

"John, it's lovely to see you," she said, relieved he had never held it against her that she'd rushed off to New York with Harry. The ink on their old letters had long faded, yet here he stood without any resentments.

"How have you been?" he asked.

"I'm good, thanks," she said.

There was a moment of awkwardness.

"You must miss Goldie." he said.

"Yes, it's very strange..." her voice tapered away.

"I know, it just takes time, and it sure isn't easy."

John was still handsome. He had blond hair like his Dutch mother. It was wild and curly, and his face was rugged from the outdoors. She didn't imagine John Dwyer used face creams or wore a thermocap to promote hair growth like Harry did.

Lucy was unsure whether to mention Mabel. "How is the family?" she asked.

"We're all good. You heard about Mabel?"

"Yes, I'm very sorry to hear it. It must be difficult."

He took his hat off and pushed back his hair, "I knew she wasn't happy for the last two or three years. She wanted to be a singer and felt she couldn't do it this far west. She always told me she was unfulfilled."

"That's hard," Lucy said.

"It's harder for our girls than for me. Like we just said, we gotta give it time."

Lucy agreed before asking after his father, Pedro.

"Dad has gone back to his childhood." He tapped the side of his head. "He forgets who we are. Only yesterday he was leaving the house to go to work for Barry O'Neill."

"I'm sorry to hear that," Lucy said.

"It's not that bad," he said. "He seems happy in his own world. I hadn't the heart to tell him that Barry was long dead, and now he is an old man."

Lucy agreed.

"How are the others? Is Emilio still hale and hearty?"

"He became a great-grandfather yesterday," John told her. "We planted a tree for his new great-granddaughter last night." John smiled when he said that.

Like old times, Lucy and John settled into a conversation as if they'd been meeting every week for the last ten years. They began to talk about Emilio's children, whom Lucy knew and was friendly with, including the local sheriff.

Lucy leaned against the car. She'd lost track of time, and right now she was in no rush to head back to Goldie's house.

"How's New York?" he asked, resting against the hood of the car.

"It's certainly not Four Oaks," she said, looking at the wide main street. "I miss home. Maybe its Goldie's death or grief or," she shrugged, "I don't know."

They talked about the small town, the sense of community and the local bickering that was always short-lived. "Because a lot of the time, we're like a big family," he said.

Lucy agreed.

"I've delayed you long enough," he said. "You're having a party?"

"Just a small gathering. You heard Lorcan came home?"

"Yes, I think everybody in the County knows about Lorcan's return. How do you feel about it?"

Lucy thought about it for a moment. Nobody had asked her that. "I met him yesterday." She shrugged. Lucy gathered that the Dwyers had never been fond of Lorcan. She remembered Pedro Dwyer praising Lucy to Goldie. "She must take after her mother," he'd said. It was a harmless remark, yet it questioned her father's character.

"Maybe it's too soon to form an opinion. I've only met him once," Lucy said. She'd like to have told John that she wanted to stay in Four Oaks forever, even if she had to shear sheep for a living.

John nodded. "If you need me, you know where I am," he said, standing straight.

Lucy thanked him and got into the car. She knew that John and all of the O'Dwyers were as solid as Makawee and Winona. She watched him in the rearview mirror until he was gone.

When she pulled up at Goldie's, she noted that the yellow paint on the front door was peeling. If she stayed, she would get that painted too. She paused, deliberating on the color, when the door swung open, and Harry appeared with a face like thunder.

From inside the car with the closed window, she could hear the anger in his voice. "Where have you been?" he said, coming down the steps to meet her. "The Breens will be here in thirty minutes."

She got out and opened the back door. "Help me with the bags," Lucy said, ignoring his rage.

"I have been on the phone since you left," Harry said following her into the house with the bags. "Look at the time," he said pointing at his watch.

Lucy began setting the dining table immediately.

"We'll go buffet style," she said ignoring him. She retrieved plates and cutlery from the kitchen.

Harry was looking at her, waiting for a response. "Did you hear one word I said?"

"What did you say?"

"I said," Harry said, enunciating every syllable, "I have been out of my wits here. The Breens will be here shortly, and I have to go to town to collect your father. You're behaving like we're on some kind of holiday."

"We are on a holiday."

"You might be on a holiday, but I have been working. I have set aside everything to help you, and then since you came here, you're deliberately avoiding me, you're... unloving."

"I believe that happened a long time before we came out here. I have been a loyal wife to you. Can you say you have been faithful to me?" Lucy said.

"How dare you say that to me now?" he said.

"Harry, I want some time away from you." What she'd wanted to say for so long simply rolled off her tongue. "You go back to New York. We'll see what happens then."

"You'll stay here alone?" he asked.

"Yes," she said. She couldn't apologize for how she felt or her need to stay put longer. It was as if she were growing roots from her feet that would pitch her in the small one-horse town, even if the strongest man tried to pull her from here, nothing could uproot her now.

"Then what?" he said.

"I don't know how long I'm staying, but I am staying."

Harry remained where he was with his head inclined forward and an intensity in his expression. Lucy couldn't say if it was anger or disbelief.

"It's not as if I haven't suggested this previously," she added and then began to polish the cutlery.

Harry remained in the same spot staring at her. After a moment he snatched the keys from the table.

"We'll see about that," he said. "I have to go to town to collect your father."

When she heard the front door banging closed, Lucy stopped polishing and released a slow breath. It was another relief, the fact that she'd said it and reiterated her point again. At least while she was away from Harry, she could see her marriage objectively. For years, she had dreamed about this. Quietly, she often imagined explaining her marital status, *I am a divorcee.* In the cold light of day, the disapproval of others had prevented her from ever taking action, but now she felt differently. The shame of being a divorcee no longer troubled her, nor was she daunted at the prospect of living alone for the rest of her days, whether it be in New York or in Four Oaks. She didn't have to decide right now. She began to polish the glasses, then the knives. Goldie's old friend, Blue Feather, had once said that the lesson is learned when the student is ready, and maybe now, she was ready, as ready as she could ever be.

Lucy left the glasses in a neat line. She laid the table with cold meat, bread, vegetables, cakes, cream and tarts. She washed the decanter and filled it with an Irish whiskey. Suddenly she felt a twinge of sympathy for Harry. This evening, she'd make Harry a stiff cocktail. He was better company after he had taken a drink.

Lucy had just finished polishing Harry's cocktail glass when she heard a car outside.

She opened the front door to see the Breens pulling up. Lucy saw Molly, Wilbur's wife, in the back seat of the car. At the sight of Molly waving gamely, Lucy took some consolation that she was not the only one who found her husband tiresome. Molly was increasingly revolted at the sight of Wilbur and living with Frances and Owen Breen. During the summer, Molly had drunk too much one evening and confessed to Lucy that at least twice a day she left the house with the intention of never returning home.

Wilbur got out of the car and took Owen's wheelchair from the trunk. He brought it up the steps and into the hall. Then he returned and carried his father up the steps. Lucy had to admire the Breens. Although Owen's chair was cumbersome, he was brought everywhere. Molly would say that Owen was afraid he'd miss something.

As Lucy was guiding the Breens into the living room and about to offer them a drink, Harry arrived with Lorcan.

Lorcan walked slowly. He came into the living room and stood at the door, his eyes scanning the room. Just then Lucy realized that this was his first visit to Goldie's house.

"Let me take your coat, and then I'll fix you a drink," Lucy said.

As he slid out of his coat, he said, "Thank you so much for inviting me to stay here."

Lucy looked over his shoulder to see Harry arrive. He was carrying Lorcan's suitcase.

"When hard times visit us, we know who our family is," Lorcan said.

Lucy was watching Harry. He wouldn't look at her as he carried Lorcan's brown suitcase upstairs.

CHAPTER THIRTY-FOUR

1937

L ucy did her best to appease and please her guests, but beneath her pleasantries, she seethed with hurt and frustration that Lorcan's suitcase was overhead in Goldie's bedroom. Each time she thought about Harry inviting him to stay, despite her avid protestations, she felt that raw ball of unnamed emotional angst stick in her throat. If she didn't dislike Harry's behavior before tonight, she was revolted by his tactics now.

As Lucy prepared the drinks, Frances Breen thanked her for hosting the get-together. "It's lovely to see you." Frances added.

"You're very welcome, Aunt Frances, it's lovely to see you too," Lucy replied.

Lucy knew they were both lying. "Hello, Uncle Owen," she said, then reached for his weak hand and shook it. She moved a chair out of the way so he could get to the other end of the room where everybody had gathered.

Frances asked for a whiskey for Owen, "No ice."

She had Owen's drink in her hand and held a cube of ice in the serving tongs.

"Without ice," Frances reminded her.

Lucy's hand shook slightly as she placed the drink on the tray of Owen's wheelchair. She was sorry that Frances saw it.

She poured Lorcan a whiskey and made a martini for Wilbur.

"Cocktail for me," Molly said. "But I want Harry to make it in his shaker like he did the last time."

"Your request is my command," Harry said with an upbeat voice. "A Gin Rickey, if I remember."

Harry was beside her now and began to theatrically roll up his sleeves, humming loudly.

Molly beamed as she watched Harry elaborately pouring the gin and squeezing the lime and dropping it into the mixer. Then he began shaking the mixer. He looked at Molly and grinned. In turn, Molly watched him as if he were a magician about to pull a rabbit out of a cocktail mixer.

Molly asked Harry, "Have you been to Club 21 lately?"

Each time they met Molly, she asked several questions about New York, the theaters and shows and musicals and of course, Club 21, where the movie stars and singers frequented. Molly read all the gossip magazines about Hollywood stars and the venues where the famous hung out. She confided in Lucy that she bought every magazine and had to hide them from Frances, who ridiculed her for her interest in singers and stars.

"Actually, we had Lucy's birthday at Club 21 three weeks ago," Harry said, looking at Lucy. He was waiting for her to play along like a united happy couple.

"Yes, there are good jazz bands there," Lucy said quietly.

"Have you seen any stars lately?" Molly asked.

"Bette Davis was there a few weeks ago. Who else did we see recently?" Harry looked at Lucy.

She shrugged; she refused to play along with his farce.

"Hepburn, what's her first name?" Harry said, knowing well that they'd seen Katharine Hepburn. He hadn't stopped talking about it for days.

"Katharine Hepburn," Molly shrieked.

"The very one," Harry said, then he began to pour the cocktail from the mixer into one of Goldie's cocktail glasses, extending his hand high above the glass before presenting the cocktail to Molly. "One Gin Rickey, better than you'd get at Club 21."

As Harry passed Lucy, he placed his hand on her shoulder.

When everyone had a drink, they sat in the armchairs and sofas with the view of the hills. Lucy found herself beside Owen Breen. She saw him looking at a framed sketch of Goldie on the sideboard.

"Ernest drew it," Lucy told him referring to Goldie's husband.

He nodded that he'd heard her but didn't take his eyes off the picture. Lucy often thought Owen would have been better off dead. She couldn't imagine what life was like for him trapped in a body that wouldn't respond to the most basic command. Although she had heard rumors that he was difficult before his stroke, she also heard that his sons, with the exception of Wilbur, had the same angry temperament. Molly had compared living with the Breen men to living beneath Mount Vesuvius. "They can erupt at any stage."

Wilbur and Harry began to talk about politics. They mentioned President Roosevelt's trip to Montevideo.

Lorcan was the only person who remained standing. He had his back to them as he looked at the photos that were displayed on a long sideboard. Lucy watched Lorcan pick up several photos and replace them, while the conversation moved along to other world matters.

They mentioned the recent abdication of the King of England to marry his lover, Wallace Simpson.

Wilbur gave his opinion on the scandal that had rocked the English monarchy. "He's a cad. He chose a divorcee over his obligations."

Molly joined in, "If you were the future King of England, would you have abdicated for me?"

"Yes, darling," Wilbur said, and then looked up and discretely winked.

Everybody laughed. She heard a wheezy chuckle from Owen.

Lucy noticed that Lorcan was deliberating longer over one photo. She recognized the silver frame. It was the photo of Chaytan and Goldie, taken in Sundance at the turn of the century. Lorcan held the photo to the light. When he returned it to the sideboard, he placed it face down.

When everyone had finished their first drink, they moved to the table and tucked into the food. They brought the conversation back to local news. They began to talk about Kelly's store, the fresh cakes, and old Jim Kelly. The conversation progressed to the Dwyers and the Donnellys. Lucy was only half-listening. She knew Harry thought he'd won by inviting Lorcan to stay. He didn't expect her to remain in the house with Lorcan. Lucy considered her options. All was not lost. She had money, enough money to build her own house if she pleased. In the immediate weeks ahead, she could live in Makawee's house. Now she was more adamant than ever that she would leave Harry.

Molly seemed to ask 101 questions about New York. Were the speakeasies closed since prohibition had ended? Did they attend any performances at Carnegie Hall?

Harry told her about the New York Symphony Orchestra's performance at Carnegie and the many concerts they had attended there.

Lorcan had little interest in Carnegie Hall. When he'd finished eating, he got up from the table and went to the bay window looking up at the hills.

"Who rents that land?" Lorcan asked, his finger on the pane of glass pointing at the hill behind the house.

"John Dwyer," Lucy said.

"Pedro's son?"

"Yes," Lucy said.

"I think he rents most of the land from you?" Wilbur asked Lucy.

Harry answered Wilbur's question, "Yes, he rents all of it. My wife isn't a good businesswoman, and I keep telling her that she needs to increase the rent, but she insists on leaving it at a pittance."

"John Dwyer owns over 2,000 acres and rents about the same. He's a clever man," Wilbur said.

They talked about the Dwyers, Pedro and Emilio and their children, while Lorcan remained with his back to them, looking out the window. He was looking to his left in the direction of Makawee's farm.

"Who lives with Aengus Kennedy's woman?" he asked.

"That's the name I couldn't remember," Wilbur said. "Makawee lives alone in the old house. Her daughter lives close by on the farm with her husband and children."

"So, the daughter is still alive?" Lorcan asked.

"She's very much alive," Wilbur said. "She's a fantastic weaver. She made a rug for us recently with matching cushions in the most exquisite autumnal colors."

"And the mill is still going!" Lorcan asked, gliding his finger across the pane of glass to point at the mill.

"I believe Winona manages the mill?" Wilbur said, looking to Harry to confirm it.

"Winona owns the mill now." Lucy corrected him. "She owns the mill and the land that the mill is on."

"Get outta here!" Lorcan said, turning swiftly from the window to face them.

"She has earned it," Lucy said. Goldie had told Lucy that she was leaving all her looms and her mill to Winona. To Lucy, it seemed only fair.

Lorcan shook his head as if he found the news unbelievable. "Christ, Goldie loved those Injuns."

"She sure did," Wilbur said.

"My Dad had a soft spot for them too," Lorcan added. "Remember Chaytan?" he said to Frances.

She held his gaze without answering. Lucy suddenly felt the tension between them.

"Chaytan earned twenty dollars for every mustang he sold. Twenty dollars for an Injun boy!"

"He was a boy who used to break in the horses for our father. He'd sell them to Captain Gallagher, who was in the Army," Frances explained to Harry. "Everybody benefited," Frances added.

"It wasn't right," Lorcan said, "no, sirree, none of that was right."

"We've moved on from all that," Frances said. There was an air of caution in her tone.

"That damn Injun killed your uncle." Lorcan said to Wilbur. "He got what he deserved."

Lucy heard a noise coming from Owen; it was so deep, it sounded feral. The moan escalated until he began to shout, "Wha you no."

Lucy couldn't understand what he was saying. She watched as he began to bounce back and forth in his chair using the only piece of mobility he had left. The glass on his tray smashed. Nobody spoke as the rage escalated. Harry quickly pushed his chair back from him, Molly had her eyes closed and head turned away from him. Lorcan had his head inclined forward, as if he were more curious than abhorred.

"I need to take him someplace quiet," Frances said, releasing the brake and wheeling him toward the door.

Lucy went to help, holding the door open and guiding them into Goldie's office. By the time she got into the office, Owen had gradually calmed until the only sound was his breathless wheezing from the exertion. Gently, Frances wiped the spittle from his mouth.

Then Lucy noticed that his hand was bleeding. "Let me get a cloth," Lucy said. In the kitchen she got a wet cloth and found Goldie's old box of bandages and ointments.

Lucy began to clean the blood from Owen's hand. When she washed the blood away, she saw the tear on his index finger. "It's all right, it's only a small cut," Lucy said. She dabbed iodine on it. "I hope I'm not hurting you," she said, looking up at Owen.

He shook his head. "No," he said.

"I don't think there's any glass in it," Lucy said tilting it toward the light.

"Hank ou," Owen said quietly.

Lucy understood his *Thank You.* "Glad I could help," she replied as she covered it with gauze and a small bandage.

"Horry," Owen said.

"He's saying he's sorry," Frances said.

"No need to be, these things happen," Lucy said, although she couldn't think of when she had ever witnessed anything like that before.

"Irim," Owen said. "Horry."

When Lucy looked up at him, his expression was one of sadness. His eyes were wet.

"Horry, Irim," he repeated

Frances leaned toward him. "Sorry, Irim?" She was trying to decipher what he was saying. She repeated it and looked upward. Frances was reminding Lucy of someone doing a crossword puzzle. "Irim."

Owen forced out his chin and rounded his mouth. "Miriam."

Lucy looked from Owen's face to Frances, whose expression went from puzzlement to shock.

"Miriam," Owen said again. His turned his wet eyes to Frances. "Home," he said.

Lucy watched Frances wheel Owen out of the room. She called Wilbur and Molly to take them home. Lucy held the door open while Wilbur carried his father, and Molly carried the folded wheelchair. Lorcan stepped between them and walked down the steps. For a moment, Lucy thought that Lorcan was leaving with the Breens. He didn't get into their car, though; instead, he sat in Goldie's car.

When there was nothing more to say, Lucy bid Frances goodnight.

Frances didn't respond, but she stood looking at Lucy for a moment. She looked at each of her features as if she'd never seen a human being before, and then she left without a word.

Bewildered by the turn of events, Lucy stood at the front door until they'd driven away. Lucy watched Lorcan start Goldie's car and follow the Breens. After a moment she saw Goldie's car heading up the hill, and then she was surprised to see it turn down the avenue toward Makawee's house.

CHAPTER THIRTY-FIVE

1895

In March of 1895, Barry O'Neill died from an insignificant cut on a saw.

"How could something so small kill him?" Goldie asked as her father's remains were laid out on the table in their home.

"A wound should be cleaned. The poison got into his bloodstream," Dr. Jenkins made it sound so simple.

Goldie and all those who knew Barry O'Neill found it hard to believe that something so simple had killed him. It added to their incredulity about his passing. On May 3, 1895, they buried him in the family plot beside his wife, Neasa, behind the Catholic chapel.

For weeks Goldie had visitors, each taken with the suddenness and simplicity of the death of a seasoned, founding member of their community.

"The Captain is so shaken up, he's been thinking about his own life," Bertha confided in Goldie. "He's gone back to God, saying his prayers on bended knees."

Frances and Goldie called at each other's houses over the following few weeks, both taking great consolation from each other.

They went through Barry's belongings. Together they cleaned out his bedroom, they burned his work clothes, and they kept his good suit to give it away.

"This would be a fine suit for Lorcan," Frances said.

"He may not know Dad is dead," Goldie said.

"He knows," Frances said. "He and Owen are in contact. He's been posted to Fort Logan in Denver. Owen sent him a telegram."

It was almost dark, and they were sitting on the veranda watching the fire coil around the material that turned the flames blue.

"I hope he doesn't come back," Frances said, "ever."

Since their father's death, Frances spoke more freely than she usually did to Goldie. She told Goldie little family secrets. Mrs. Breen was in flying form since Ned died. She'd been writing to her family in New York and burned every single item belonging to Ned, including his Mass missal he'd brought all the way from Ireland.

"Owen reckons that Lorcan enjoys killing people," Frances said. "And I think he does too."

Frances had always been close to Lorcan. It was Frances whom he sought for comfort if his mother was not close by. Like their mother, Frances never tired of defending him. It made Goldie sick to her stomach, and occasionally she told Frances that.

"Are Owen and Lorcan in contact all the time?" Goldie asked.

"Owen wants to find Chaytan. Lorcan says he knows where he is," Frances said.

"Does Owen still want to hang Chaytan?" Goldie asked.

"Yes." Frances continued speaking quietly as she looked at the fire. "Every so often, there is a sighting of Chaytan, Owen goes away for a night. Now my sons accompany him." Frances said, "They paid Lorcan $100 to find him. Lorcan sends a telegram, maybe once or twice a year, telling them that Chaytan is in Denver." Frances sighed loudly, "I dread that telegram, and every time it says the same thing. *Come to Leyden. Sighting.* Leyden is the area where Chaytan visits. Owen and George leave for a few nights."

"Do they think they're close to finding him?" Goldie asked.

Frances turned to Goldie with her thumb and index finger an

inch apart. "This close," she said. "Chaytan calls on an Indian family outside Denver. Lorcan has men who watch the house when they reckon Chaytan will be calling. You know he works in the cattle drives?" Frances said.

"Is that so?" Goldie continued to hide the fact that Chaytan returned to Four Oaks a few times a year. Equally, she knew her closeness with Frances was only temporary. Once their father's clothes were gone and a few months had passed, Frances would be a Breen again.

"They saw him visiting the Indian family on his way through Denver. By the time Owen and Edward arrived, Chaytan had left. They were going to go into the house and burn it down, but Lorcan said to leave it be. They'd lose all sight of Chaytan then. They won't stop until they find him."

Goldie remained quiet as she listened, but the small hairs on the back of her neck stood up.

"Owen said even if he doesn't recognize Chaytan, he'll know him from the brand on his neck."

As the night got darker, Frances shared her problems with Goldie. She told her that she could understand Owen harboring such hatred, but why pass it on to his sons? "Edward has never met Chaytan and didn't know his Uncle Timothy. Sometimes I think Owen and Edward enjoy heading away together to hunt for Chaytan. They visit small towns and drink and gamble. When they come home, they normally sleep through for twelve full hours. Edward thinks it's an adventure."

After two months, life returned to normal. Instead of Frances confiding in Goldie, she reverted to picking out suitors or poking fun at her unmarried state.

"I'll find you a husband who isn't an Indian or a crude Irish miner."

Goldie never took offense even when Frances was serious.

"You'll want to find a husband before you're too old," Frances said, "although you lost all hope of finding a respectable man when you blew the head off that thief. Men don't like trigger-happy women, same way they don't like a woman who drinks whiskey," Frances added as if she were the authority on men and marriage.

Goldie had several suitors, and she was always going to a dance or coming from some social gathering. But her mill took precedence over the idea of romance. By the end of the 1890s, she employed twenty-five people. When the town established a board, Goldie took her place as the only woman on the Town Committee. For forty-three years, she remained the only female member of the Four Oaks Town Committee. New members called her Miss O'Neill, but eventually all called her Goldie.

Chaytan returned twice a year. He continued to ride on the cattle trails from Fort Concho in southern Texas, through Denver, and then to Cheyenne in Wyoming, where they met the rail line. When he arrived in Four Oaks, like always, he came when it was dark and during his stay, he remained close to Makawee's cabin. At night, Goldie and their closest friends congregated to meet him. Over the course of a week, Goldie would go through the notebook she kept in his absence.

They rarely discussed the Indian situation, as it seemed entirely hopeless. By the 1890s, no Indians lived freely on their own land, and even the reservations were being broken up under the Dawes Act. Some tried to adapt to the white man's world. Red Cloud was alive and living peacefully on Pine Ridge Reservation. Some of the chiefs sent their children to the Indian Carlisle School, where they'd learn to adapt to the white man's culture.

When Chaytan returned a few months after Barry's death, he was about to tell her all his news when Goldie stopped him.

"Whoever you visit in Denver, don't go there anymore," she said. "The house is being watched by the Army. They know you're a regular caller and recently you narrowly escaped being captured by Owen and his son Edward and Lorcan."

He nodded indicating that he'd heard her. "Thanks for telling me," he said.

"The rope is still in the Breens' barn but now they'll take you anywhere."

He considered it. "I'll be more careful."

Their conversation resumed, and she told him about Barry's death. "He died from a small cut, can you believe it!"

Chaytan shrugged, saying, "It happens."

Goldie told him all the gossip of the town. When she imitated Bertha Gallagher and Captain Gossip's head tilted to one side for news, Chaytan laughed heartily. She told him about Frances and her advice on marriage and her growing flock of children.

He told her about his travels. The towns that got bigger each time he passed through them. He told her about the men on the cattle drive and his boss and how much money he'd saved and his plans to buy land deeper into the hills.

She no longer asked about Baby Miriam. At last, she accepted that she couldn't force her way into another person's life as much as she couldn't undo the past.

CHAPTER THIRTY-SIX

1901

At the turn of the century, most families lived as they had lived when they first rolled across the plains and stumbled into their Irish colony. Most drank from tin cups, worked hard in the mines that got deeper and continued to throw up gold, and most folks prayed to their God that they'd survive the winter, except the Breens—they had had a great change in fortune. It was so great that they only drank from china cups, or the china cups that survived Owen's rages. More often, they were thrown against the closest wall or at one of his sons or his wife or the hapless maid who told Goldie all the gossip from the Breens' house.

After Ned Breen passed away, his widow, Mrs. Leonora Breen, came to life again. She played her piano, visited neighbors, and got younger with each year. She wrote to her wealthy family in New York, telling them about her life and what had happened after she came west.

Mrs. Breen's brother, Jasper Livingston, came to visit. Her family was made up of wealthy bankers and businessmen from New York. They grew so fond of the area they bought a ranch with a lake for fishing and built a mansion, the first of its kind in the area. For three months in the summer, Jasper Livingston, his pretty wife, and their young son, Harry Livingston, came to Four Oaks for fresh air and country pursuits. As far as Goldie could gather, the Livingstons and their consort of monied friends talked a lot of nonsense about Broadway plays, politics, and investments.

The Livingstons secured timber contracts for Owen's lumber yard. Frances confided in Goldie that they couldn't keep up, they were so busy. "He's rolling in it," she said of the money Owen was making.

In 1900, Owen Breen was the elected mayor of Four Oaks and continued to sit on Four Oaks Town Committee. He looked more and more like his father with each passing year. His face grew bigger and redder, and the crease joining his eyebrows grew deeper, making his nose appear longer. The only great difference between the late Ned Breen and his son Owen was that Owen learned to spend money. Owen bought expensive suits, he bought a false tooth, and he built a big house. He had barbeques and parties and invited businessmen and 'important people,' as Frances said. Owen Breen behaved as if he had more money than the Livingstons.

Frances was proud of their success. Occasionally, her accent would change as she talked about her big strong sons and beautiful daughters. She picked out suitors for her daughters, only those with an education, and even better if they had politics in the family. Owen and Frances mapped out a future for each child, one would take the original farm, another would take over the lumber yard. The third son was clever; they'd sent him to college to study law.

Frances told Goldie their plans as if they were set in stone. "We've done well," she said raising a toast to the new year with her new bone china cup.

At the Breens' New Year's party, she accepted a dance from Ernest Garcia, a new arrival in town. When he asked her to dance a second time, Frances told Goldie not to get her hopes up.

"He's too educated for you," she said, as if that settled the matter.

Goldie danced with Ernest a third time, and when he joined the

Town Committee the following Thursday, she sat beside him. Like everyone, Ernest addressed her as Miss O'Neill on the first evening. Thereafter, it was Goldie. Each Thursday she admired him from afar. He had little to say at the meetings. Often, he was like an amused bystander. When Owen Breen was animated and his false front tooth bobbed up and down, Goldie saw Ernest smile. Goldie learned that Ernest came from Dallas, Texas. He'd made money in investments. His recent investment was a ranch outside Four Oaks, and he bought and sold the same longhorn cattle that Chaytan brought up from the south. He chose to live in Four Oaks because it was central, had a railway line, and had vegetation suitable for cattle. Ernest had gone to college, and he could sketch people with an inordinate likeness.

During one of the committee meetings, she thought he was taking notes, but later, when they delayed leaving to speak, she saw that he'd sketched Mr. Kelly. Ernest had drawn his thick bushy eyebrows and captured Mr. Kelly's perpetually disorganized state.

Each night they waited to talk after the meeting. Goldie found out something else about Ernest Garcia each time they met. He was born in Dallas, drank red wine, had one son who was eight, and his wife had died in childbirth. He worked as a cattle rancher; however, he had had great success with various investments in other businesses. He'd moved north for greener pastures for his cattle and to be close to the railway lines.

She thought about his soft voice, and his unassuming easy manner. It surprised Goldie that she spent as much time thinking about him as she did.

One afternoon she saw him riding close to her home, so she invited him in for tea. That day he sketched Goldie. She was unsmiling in the drawing, and her eyes were fixed, yet it was flattering. That day they talked well into the afternoon. She invited him for lunch on Sunday, and every Sunday thereafter.

"It's grown on me," Ernest said about Four Oaks. "I thought I'd miss the city, the noise and variety and the anonymity, but I don't. Something unexpected has replaced everything I thought I needed."

They took the horses out for a trek into the hills. They visited the same sights that she visited with Chaytan. She showed him her woolen mill and introduced him to Makawee and Winona.

"These are my best friends," she said.

If he was surprised that her best friends were Indians, he didn't appear so. He shook their hands and expressed his pleasure at meeting them.

They began a routine of sitting together at the committee meetings and afterward they'd delay leaving in order to talk. Occasionally, he'd ask about the members in their community. Goldie told him about Captain Gallagher, that he'd fought in the Indian Wars; she told him about Pedro Dwyer, how he'd turned their rundown farm into a fledgling business when he was still a boy. She told him about the piano that was thrown from the wagon train, and that she had a brother who sought adventure instead of farming. Goldie wasn't forthcoming with all her stories; she never told Ernest about Baby Miriam. When Ernest commented on Owen Breen's denture that occasionally slipped down when he spoke, she didn't tell him that it was she who'd knocked out his tooth. She was surprised he'd learned a little about her without her telling him. When he asked about the man she'd killed, she told him it was a necessity.

"It annoyed me, the whole business of it," she said dismissively.

Ernest asked her about Chaytan. "You were friends?"

She knew Owen Breen was spreading gossip.

"Yes, we were great friends. I love him like a brother." She told him how he came to their farm to tame the mustangs. "Each day, he'd get closer to the wild animal until he had it trotting around the corral like a well-behaved dog. It was magical to witness," she added, "you'd like him."

Goldie showed Ernest the gun he'd brought her, the Derringer that was so small she doubted it would work. "It saved my life."

In the fall of 1900, Goldie was forty-three when she left Four Oaks on the train and traveled to Dallas to see the crowded streets and tall buildings and to marry the Texan. She married Ernest Garcia in a small church in the presence of his son, Gabriel, and Ernest's sister and her husband. They stayed on the fifth floor of a hotel in the center of the city. Goldie watched as the night edged in and the lights of the city grew brighter. Slowly they made love to the sound of trotting carriages and the bustling city below them.

For five days, Ernest took Goldie to see his old friends and the many sights of the city. Goldie saw the tall buildings and elegant stores that catered to the wealthy Texans. She went to the famous stores, Sanger Brothers and A. Harris. She examined their rugs, noted the material and price, and then bought one. On their last day, Ernest bought a camera and they went into the desert to see the cacti. Goldie was surprised they were was so tall. It was the only photo from their wedding and honeymoon, a lone picture of Goldie beside a desert cactus. At night their exhausted bodies found a different energy.

On the second-last morning of their stay, Ernest woke up to find Goldie sitting by the window with her suitcase packed. "We must leave and return to Four Oaks, the noise of this city is deafening," she said.

When news reached Owen and Frances Breen that Goldie had married the Texan in Dallas, Owen threw one of their china cups against the far wall of the living room. The maid who witnessed his outburst couldn't tell Goldie if it was bone china or fine china.

"Those 820 acres and her weaving mill will all go to that damn southerner," Owen bellowed.

CHAPTER THIRTY-SEVEN

1902

G oldie and her new groom enjoyed a few happy years. They were different people; Ernest was quiet and reserved, Goldie was outspoken and familiar. Ernest was rational and calm, and Goldie was fiery and sometimes irrational. When they argued, their disagreements were over before they began. For all their differences, they complemented each other.

All seemed surprised at Goldie's decision to marry Ernest Garcia. It didn't fit with the Goldie they knew. They couldn't reconcile the woman who seemed interested only in weaving and managing her mill with the woman who walked arm-in-arm with the handsome, educated rancher.

Frances called at Goldie's home and watched agog as she baked an apple tart.

"You never baked when Dad was alive," Frances said.

It was true, Goldie had cooked dinner but never baked. "This is me now," she said, tickled to see Ernest enjoy her efforts.

Ernest was appreciative and some would say, more besotted with his wife than she with him.

"What next!" Frances said, unable to get used to seeing her sister behaving like every other woman in Four Oaks.

Goldie bought a loveseat that was placed on the porch. Frances stood gaping at it for a few minutes before speaking. "What are you going to do with that?" she asked.

"I'll probably just fling my boots at it," Goldie said sarcastically.

Frances warned her to enjoy the early days, "Because they won't last. Love waxes and wanes."

"So be it," Goldie said.

During the summer nights, Goldie and Ernest would sit on their loveseat and talk. She could never say what they talked about, only that there was always something to talk about.

When Ernest realized that Goldie was almost illiterate, he offered to teach her to read.

"I'd be happier if you taught me about making investments," she said. Goldie was impressed with Ernest's insight about money and marveled how he could get such a high return from his ventures.

"But wouldn't you like to learn to read and write?" Ernest persisted.

"No interest in the wild world," she said with an exhausted sigh.

He was amused at her single-mindedness. Instead of teaching her to read, he taught her all he knew about investing in everything from coal mines to property.

At night he'd read the paper aloud.

Ernest was a moderate. When he read the news articles, he didn't get angry at the injustices of the world. He moved onto the next article unaffected, while Goldie saw the unfairness in a different light. When a politician who defrauded his local community was spared jail, Goldie said his hand should have been hacked off, and then said, "Not his hand, his whole arm."

Ernest would lower the paper and listen with an amused expression when Goldie vented her rage.

A criminal who strangled a woman in Ohio, "Deserved the worst kind of death."

"What death would my genteel wife give him?" Ernest asked with the same amused expression.

"Burn him alive," Goldie said, beginning to see the funny side of her death sentences.

When Ernest read about the Wounded Knee Battle and that the soldiers who fired into the crowd of unarmed women and children were given medals of honor, Goldie was not amused, she was apoplectic.

"It was a massacre and not a battle," she declared. "Every one of those men who fired at Wounded Knee should be lined up and shot to death instead of giving them medals of honor,"

Ernest looked over the rim of his glasses as Goldie poured her wrath on the Army.

Goldie never mentioned her brother, who was at the front of the firing squad; she castigated him without naming him. "Medals of honor! Sweet divine, sometimes this country is crazy."

"Moving on," Ernest said, turning the page of the paper.

When they retired to bed, Goldie did not deem her marital obligations a duty; it was a pleasure that she anticipated.

Goldie's home remained an open door to old friends. Most nights, there were visitors and a bed was offered to those traveling any distance. When Blue Feather called with his family, he was greeted with the same warm welcome as when Ernest's family had arrived from Texas. So too was Emilio Dwyer, who became the county hangman. Goldie introduced Ernest to all her old family friends. She'd feed and water her guests with the warmest of hospitality.

"Have you hung a woman yet?" Goldie asked Emilio Dwyer each time he called.

"Not yet," he said, "but the day that happens, I'll come straight to tell you."

Goldie was always curious about the crimes that warranted the rope. What had they done? Did they show any remorse?

Emilio had said they did, "Every man shows remorse when his neck is going into a noose."

"Do they ever whisper anything to you before the trap door

opens?" Goldie was teasing, "Do any of them tell you if they've a crock of gold hidden in the desert?"

Emilio said, "Only thing they do is swear and sweat and some even ask for their mama."

It was Emilio who told Goldie that Lorcan had married a widow and was living outside Denver on her farm. "She's a schoolteacher with two sons. Small and mighty pretty," Emilio said.

During those years, Goldie was untroubled by Lorcan. He was another ghost who had drifted out of her sight. She wished him well but wanted nothing to do with him. "Good for him," she said when she heard of his marriage.

When Chaytan returned, Goldie deliberated over telling Ernest that Chaytan was a regular visitor to Four Oaks. She was afraid to reveal to anyone that Chaytan came and went to Four Oaks since Timothy's death. Added to that, she refused to break with tradition even if she was a married woman—she wanted to sit up all night talking. In the end, she told him the truth, and she even told him that her brother had killed Aengus.

"And Chaytan is rumored to have killed Timothy." Goldie refrained from telling Ernest that she too believed Chaytan had killed him, or that he was in the area the morning of Timothy's death. She told him about the rope in the Breens' barn. Before she told him the next part of the story, she stood up from her loveseat and retrieved an old missal. She stood in front of him with the missal, saying, "Before I say anything you must swear on this holy missal that you'll keep this a secret forever."

Ernest was intrigued with the story. "I swear," he said. "And you know you don't need me to swear on a Mass missal to keep a secret."

"I know," she said. "I just want you to understand how serious this is."

He waited for her to tell him the secret.

"Chaytan has been coming home for years. He is in Makawee's cabin now waiting for me to visit." She showed him her notebook, none of which he could read.

Ernest was disappointed he wouldn't get to meet Chaytan, but he accepted it. "Go and visit your friend," he said. "And tell him I don't bite, and he's always welcome."

She kissed Ernest and left for the night.

Goldie told Chaytan all about Ernest, her wedding, and her loveseat.

Chaytan was as surprised as everyone else with the changes in Goldie's life. When she finished talking, he said, "Where is the real Goldie?"

"I know, isn't it a hoot?" Goldie went on to tell him about Dallas. "The streets were so wide and the buildings so high I thought I'd fall backward from looking up," she said. "Give me my little house on the side of the hill any day."

"Would you like it if children came?" Chaytan asked.

"Yes," she answered again. "If they come, they come."

Chaytan and Goldie talked until the sun peeked over the horizon.

"Is Baby Miriam still alive and well?" Goldie asked.

"She sure is," Chaytan said. "She's doing fine."

"You tell her if she needs anything, all she need do is ask."

Chaytan said he would.

During those years Goldie was content. The guilt she could never let go of lightened but never entirely disappeared, although Goldie took great comfort in the fact that Miriam was happy where she was.

Nobody was surprised when they saw the Texas longhorn cattle on Goldie's land. She showed Ernest the great caves where she'd first seen the etchings. Ernest was a businessman and talked about inviting tourists to see the ancient drawings. Goldie refused to allow gaping tourists into her cave.

"Why not?" he asked. They were in the cave looking at the drawings with a flashlight.

"Because they're sacred," she told him.

"Sacred to whom?" he asked, surprised by her reverence.

"Sacred to me," she said. "Those pictures have been there for thousands of years, and I hope they're there for another thousand years."

The townsfolk speculated how much land and money Goldie and Ernest had between them, and some of the less kindly folk talked about her greed.

"You'll be as rich as me," Owen Breen said to Goldie.

"We have our health, Owen, isn't that worth all the tea in China and all the money in the world?" Goldie said, knowing an evasive comment would aggravate him.

Goldie's first love was her mill. She told Ernest she didn't care if everything was taken from her, as long as she could sit at her loom and escape into her craft for a few hours each day. "I'll survive," she summarized.

Goldie spent most of the day working with Makawee and Winona. By 1902, her blankets and rugs were in stores all over Wyoming and the Dakotas. The looms got bigger as the demand increased. She loved the process as much as she had all those years ago when she first sat at Makawee's loom.

Winona had married one of Blue Feather's sons, and they had a little boy.

A year after their wedding, Ernest built a new home for Goldie and him. It was a large imposing house with a wraparound veranda. Upstairs, there were four bedrooms, and each had its own balcony. There were two latrines, which was unheard of, one upstairs and one downstairs.

Captain Gallagher flushed the toilet upstairs and listened, remarking, "Well, I'll be damned."

Each Thursday night, Goldie continued to sit on the Town Committee where she remained the only woman. Goldie was happy to bundle up the unhappy parts of her past and send the parcel down the river forever. Several times, she reminded herself of her father all those years ago when he talked with such gusto about the American West, a place where there is no history, only beginnings. There are no towns and nothing to root us to its past, only the future we make for ourselves. Like him back then, when they'd slowly edged across the West, and he'd been pleased to leave his past behind him, only then did Goldie understand his need to press forward.

CHAPTER THIRTY-EIGHT

1902

Although their lives were largely happy, they were not without tragedies. In 1902, Pedro Dwyer's oldest son was killed when he fell out of a tree. Everybody knew little Mikey Dwyer, and the sight of his still corpse in the coffin tore at their hearts. Later that same year, Goldie gave birth to a daughter, and she called her Neasa. The infant only lived for twenty-one days. Goldie never knew how she got to be so fond of someone who was in her life so briefly. For many months that year, she was consumed with little Neasa, before time helped her forget the weight of her sadness, and life's tragedies moved onto someone else's home. In the late spring of 1905, Goldie heard that Owen Breen was at death's door after suffering a stroke.

Pedro Dwyer brought her the news that he had heard that morning. "Owen and his oldest son. Edward were on business in Denver when the stroke happened. Edward is inconsolable."

What seemed like a simple event was more complicated when Goldie called on Frances.

Frances was tight-lipped. "We don't know anything yet. He's in an infirmary in Denver. He had a stroke."

Just as Pedro said, their son Edward was inconsolable. He was as disheveled as the days the Breen boys had come to Mass with the muck dripping from their feet.

"It all happened so quickly," Edward cried into his hands.

"It was a stroke," Frances shouted above his bawling.

Frances was to travel to Denver the following morning to see Owen. Goldie offered to accompany her.

"Kate and Billy will come with me," Frances said informatively.

The Breens were clannish and secretive around Goldie but with Owen's stroke, they were even more secretive. Goldie believed there was more to the story.

Two weeks later, Owen returned home. He had to be carried off the train and placed into a buggy. Everybody said it was a terrible sight.

"He went to Denver an able-bodied man and came home on a stretcher," Bertha Gallagher said.

They marveled at the danger of a stroke and how it could cripple a man as badly as a wagon falling on his back. Then Goldie heard that the maid had to dress his wound.

"His head had been stitched," the maid told Goldie.

Goldie reported the story to Ernest, who listened with interest.

"Since when do stroke victims have bleeding heads?" she asked.

"Never," he said.

They considered it.

"What was he doing in Denver?" Ernest asked.

That night Goldie told Ernest the truth about her brother, Lorcan. She told him that he had pursued more than adventure. She was surprised to hear herself using her father's terminology. "He has a peculiar quirk," she said, pointing to her head as her father used to do. She told him how he'd been commended for actions during the Wounded Knee Massacre.

Goldie told Ernest that Lorcan had been posted to Fort Logan in Denver, and that he knew that Chaytan visited a house outside Denver on his way home from the cattle drives, and that Lorcan routinely informed the Breens. "The only reason any of them go to Denver is to capture Chaytan and hang him."

When she'd finished talking, he pulled her close to him and kissed her forehead. "Leave it sit for a few weeks, and we'll look into it."

There were nights when Goldie forgot about her dead daughter, she was so suspicious of the Breens. Goldie did her utmost to find out where they were, but nobody spoke. "They're worse than a crowd of tight-lipped criminals," Goldie said. Even Wilbur, who was six at the time repeated the same line. "My dad had a stroke."

As the spring advanced into May, Chaytan did not return. Each week Goldie noticed the changing landscape as they drifted into summer; she saw the dried earth cracking from the sun and the animals sheltering in the shade, but there was no sign of Chaytan.

Makawee was also concerned, as were Winona and Blue Feather.

"Nothing yet?" Goldie would ask.

Makawee would shake her head.

In the end Goldie stopped asking. They'd looked down the hill at the town and as far into the distance as their eyes could see.

Ernest and Goldie made plans to go to Denver in September 1905 if Chaytan hadn't returned.

In the first week of September, Emilio Dwyer called.

"You're as welcome as the day is long," Goldie said, getting to her feet when she saw him riding into her yard. "Where are you coming from or going to?"

"Just passing through. I've been in Sundance, and I'm on my way to Cheyenne."

Goldie set a place for him at the table and served a hearty meal of fresh bread and cold meats. After they'd eaten, Goldie poured three whiskeys, and they sat outside on the veranda to enjoy the last of the fall sun. They talked about the local news. At that point, Captain Gallagher's continued survival was noted, so too was the hotel as it made great strides toward respectability. When they talked about the changing times, Emilio told them that he'd soon be redundant as the hangman.

"They got new ways to kill a man now instead of hanging him. Now you just give a man some gas and send him to sleep. Easy-peasy," he said.

"It's too easy-peasy." Goldie added, "Make them dangle at the end of a rope."

"That's my girl," Ernest joked.

Emilio laughed.

"Have you hung any woman lately?" Goldie asked.

"Not lately," he said. He took a moment and hesitated.

Goldie watched him closely

"I been thinking a lot about you, Goldie. I lied when I said I was passing through. I came here deliberately to talk to you." He picked at his nail as he spoke. "Three months ago, I got a call to go to Denver. I heard they had an Injun who was supposed to have killed a rancher. I believe the Injun might have been your old friend, Chaytan."

Goldie looked at him slowly. As the sun slowly sank behind the hills, Goldie heard about Chaytan's last hours.

"Lorcan brought him into town. Owen Breen's son was there too. The day of the hanging, I heard they found Chaytan in a house outside Denver. They surrounded the house and shot the owners dead. Then they got your friend alive. He was shot once in the shoulder, but the wound wasn't enough to kill him. I didn't rightly know what was happening, only Lorcan showed me the judge's signature. That's all I needed. But when I put the noose on the Injun's neck, he called me my name. He said, 'Tell Goldie that I am dead'."

"Chaytan is dead?"

"Yes, he was hung in Denver about three months ago."

Goldie felt Ernest holding her hand.

"I sure am sorry I couldn't come sooner," Ernest said.

Goldie closed her eyes. "Dear God, no," she murmured quietly.

"I know you're friends with Makawee and would want to tell her the news," Emilio said.

"Yes, I'll do that," Goldie said.

"He's been gone from here for years?" Emilio asked.

"No, he used to come back twice a year," Goldie said. "We remained great friends."

"I'm mighty sorry, Goldie." Emilio said.

"It's all right, Emilio, you didn't know."

Goldie heard Ernest and Emilio's voices but not what they said. She felt the sadness coat her as if it were something physical.

Goldie was aware of Emilio's voice.

"Left me rightly cold," Emilio said. "Next day I heard what had happened. They surrounded the house belonging to an Injun family outside Denver. They shot the woman and man of the house dead."

"Was Owen Breen there when Chaytan was hung?" Ernest asked.

"No, he was being tended to by the local doctor. He took a bullet to the side of his head. His son was there, and he wanted a picture taken to show Chaytan at the end of a rope."

"Did he get his picture?" Ernest asked.

"Yes, he got his picture."

Ernest refilled their drinks.

"I know Lorcan is your brother, and the Breens are kin to you, but they sure are wicked men."

Goldie nodded in agreement. Her rising anger was quickly smothering her sorrow.

Goldie told Makawee and Winona the news. While Makawee sobbed tears of grief, Goldie's anger deepened. At the sight of Makawee's aching loss, Goldie quietly damned her brother to hell. Without telling a soul, that same day she took a train to Denver with her loaded Derringer. She'd find her godforsaken brother and make him pay. In Denver, she went to the Army fort and was told that Sergeant Lorcan O'Neill was on a three-day leave, but the solider did tell her where he lived with his wife. Goldie hired a buggy and went to the farm. On her way she passed through Leyden. She remembered that was the place where Chaytan visited. The telegrams that had arrived from Lorcan mentioned *Leyden*. Goldie cracked the whip and imagined the surprise on Lorcan's face when he would see the gun pointed at his forehead. At Lorcan's home, she met his wife, a small fair woman with large, light blue eyes. His wife didn't invite her in. She could see childrens' toys over her shoulder.

"He's out for the day," his wife said. She stood at the half-opened door.

Goldie believed that Lorcan's wife was lying. She put the palm of her hand on the door. She was going to push it open and force her way in until she saw a pair of eyes peep around his mother's skirt. He was a little boy only up to her waist.

"Tell him Goldie called," she said before leaving. "I'll be back tonight."

She returned that night and crept around his barns and his home, she peered in the windows but only saw his wife and two little boys. Goldie made four more trips to Denver, all of which yielded nothing. On their last trip, there was a new family on his farm. She learned that his pretty wife had died, and the farm had been sold. On her return home to Four Oaks, she thought about her Lorcan. Would she have killed her own brother if she'd found him? Or was it all a farce? A journey to make her feel as if she were doing something constructive? She dreamed about killing him, about meeting him outside a bar and putting her pistol to his forehead and firing. Would she really have killed him if she'd found him? In the end, it was somebody else who killed him.

In April 1906, she received a telegram from the Army informing her of his death in the Philippines. She had just served dinner when the letter arrived.

Ernest read the formal notice aloud. The letter stated that he'd been missing in action, "presumed dead during the Battle of Bud Dajo."

Goldie listened without speaking. Ernest left the letter on the table beside her. On impulse, Goldie snatched the letter, got up from the table, opened the stove, and jammed it into the flames. "That's the end of him, thanks be to Christ," she said, returning to her seat at the table. She looked at the steam rising from the potatoes and the lamb, and realized that suddenly her appetite had left her.

Later that evening, she regretted her hasty decision to burn the notification of Lorcan's death. She felt out of sorts. One minute she was sorry, and the next she was relieved. She became melancholic during the evening. "What's it all for?" she asked Ernest.

"The Battle of Bud Dajo is part of the Moro Rebellion," Ernest began.

Goldie interrupted him, "No, not the battle." She was unsure what she wanted to say. "Like, what is life all about?"

"He was your brother," Ernest said. "Regardless of how we dislike or disapprove of family members, it affects us deeply when they die."

Goldie didn't want to have that kind of conversation about death and feelings. She went to the Breens to tell Frances the news. Frances behaved like a grieving widow, and Goldie had to tell her to get a grip on herself.

Frances continued bawling, "We'll have to do something, we'll have a Mass for his death," she said between sobs. Frances' daughter Kate was there, nodding in agreement.

Goldie left quickly and called on Makawee and Winona. She thought she'd enjoy telling them, an audience who would be pleased with the news.

Makawee, Winona, and Blue Feather didn't take any consolation from Lorcan's death. There was no great rejoicing or satisfaction that the man who was instrumental in Chaytan's death met his own death on a battlefield in an unfamiliar country. There was a moment's silence, and then Winona put her hand on Makawee's back, and Blue Feather looked into the distance. "I'm sorry, he was your brother," Makawee said.

Their dignity stopped Goldie from castigating him like a fishwife.

A few weeks after his death, she received a sympathy card and a photograph of Lorcan from the Army. For some peculiar reason, Goldie didn't burn the photograph. It had been taken shortly after the Wounded Knee Massacre. Goldie threw it into a rarely used drawer and slammed it shut.

One year after the events of Chaytan's hanging, Owen Breen remained as incapacitated as the day he'd arrived home on the train. Each month they expected him to die, but like a disease that lingers, Owen remained. Goldie took some comfort at the sight of him propped in his wheelchair. Admittedly, there were times when she felt sorry for him. The world was passing him by as day rolled into another, yet his body made no signs of recovery. After the initial few months, Frances seemed mostly unaffected by his incapacitation. She thrived as the matriarch of her family, the one who took center stage in her home.

Life continued. Goldie attended her committee meetings and worked in her mill. Under Ernest's guidance she learned about investments and was generous with earnings. She donated to local causes, and occasionally sent money to charities far removed from Four Oaks. She also gave money to the Divorce Campaign.

"Why the Divorce Campaign?" Ernest asked.

"Why not?" she said.

"Are you thinking of divorcing me?" he jokingly asked.

"Never," she said.

When an orphanage for white girls in Denver requested a donation and identified one of their charges as her niece, initially she thought it was a ploy to extract money from her. She asked Ernest to write to them requesting an explanation. The orphanage duly responded that the late Sergeant Lorcan O'Neill's daughter, Lucy, a four-year-old girl, was in their care.

Goldie's initial response was that the four-year-old girl called Lucy "could damn well stay in their care." She couldn't see past her anger at Lorcan.

Ernest reminded her that the orphanage was not looking for her to adopt the child, "only a donation to help."

For weeks she thought about the girl. When she saw Pedro Dwyer's son, John, she thought of Lorcan's child. It also occurred to her that her daughter, Neasa, was born around the same time as the orphan called Lucy, her niece. Then she'd quickly make herself think of Lorcan and her detestation of him.

"Your blood," Makawee reminded her. They were sitting on Makawee's veranda. Makawee's grandchildren were playing in the yard. Their high-pitched laughter reached Makawee's and Goldie's ears. "They're blood," Makawee said pointing at the children. "Blood is blood, regardless of what the father did."

And so it began, Goldie returned to Denver for a different reason this time. Makawee accompanied Goldie to the orphanage. During the first trip, Goldie made it sound like they were only going to look in on the child. At the orphanage, she asked to see Sergeant Lorcan O'Neill's daughter. When Lucy was led into the parlor, she stood in the center of the room silently eyeing Goldie through dark cautious eyes. Little Lucy was so small and vulnerable, swallowed up in the large parlor. Goldie gave a donation to the orphanage and fled, but she was more troubled after seeing the child. Goldie and Makawee went to a saloon near the railway station, and Goldie ignored the glares from the onlookers as she ordered a soda for Makawee and a whiskey for herself. She downed the whiskey and remained pensive for the ride back to Four Oaks. Eventually, she spoke when the train was gliding between the familiar bluffs of Wyoming. "Curiosity is a terrible thing," she said. She was angry, rebuking her own curiosity that had taken her on a 300-mile trek to spend five minutes looking at a child, only to turn around and go home again. Goldie returned to Denver once more and took Makawee with her.

"Don't know why I'm doing this." Goldie muttered. "It's not as if I liked Lorcan."

Makawee told her the child could not be responsible for the sins of the father.

The second time Makawee and Goldie went to the orphanage, Goldie took Lucy back to Four Oaks.

CHAPTER THIRTY-NINE

1907 – 1933

During the next three years, Goldie, Ernest and Lucy were a happy unit. After the initial adjustments, they slotted together as if they'd been a trio since the beginning of time. Lucy attended school in the mornings and during the afternoons, she worked with Goldie in the mill where she had her own chores. On Saturday's they went visiting neighbors and family and sometimes they took the train to the next town because the passing scenery and chugging sound of the train was a novelty for Lucy. On Sunday's they went to mass, although Goldie wasn't religious, it was a sociable event, and afterwards had their dinner in Gallagher's Hotel. Lucy had little time for dolls but loved animals. Ernest bought her a pony and Blue Feather gave her a puppy which Goldie stipulated must remain outside. Gradually the puppy moved from the porch to the hall to the living room until it had its own place beside Lucy's chair. Before bed each night, Lucy would sit on Ernest's lap as he read her a story. Goldie would listen to Ernest's voice as it rose and dipped to match each character. She marveled at his effortless theatrics and that Lucy was so engrossed in the story. There were times when even the dog appeared peaceful as he too listened to the story. Sometimes Goldie marveled at her own life, the little unexpected gifts that were sent her way, and sometimes she enjoyed the simplicity of the story.

In 1909, when Goldie's beloved Ernest was killed in a farm accident, she was devasted. She told Makawee that she felt as if her heart had been ripped from her chest by a cruel God. It was Lucy who helped to rouse Goldie from her grief. Two weeks after his death, when Goldie sat forlorn in her living room, Lucy appeared beside her. "I'll mind you," she said, stretching her arms around Goldie's neck and planting a kiss on her forehead. When they went to town, Lucy took Goldie's hand. There were times when Goldie felt as if their roles were reversed and Lucy was the reassuring parent. It was then that Makawee and Blue Feather's family began to call her *Wakta*, Hope. Lucy gave Goldie hope for the future and eased the pain of the present. During those days when they pressed forward into a new beginning, Goldie hoped that an easier road had been paved for Lucy and her generation. As the years passed and Lucy grew from the little girl to a young woman, Goldie noted similarities between Lucy and Goldie's mother Neasa. She had the same gait as Neasa, and she'd tilt her head to one side when she was concentrating. On a few rare occasions, she also thought she found sweet similarities between Lucy and Lorcan, daughter and father. When Lucy won Four Oaks Beauty Pageant, Goldie was so proud she commissioned a photographer to take Lucy's portrait in her winning dress. Goldie bought eight portraits and dotted them around the house until Lucy found it too embarrassing and removed all, except one.

When Lucy began seeing John Dwyer, Goldie was overjoyed. She couldn't have wished for more. World War 1 was just ending and it seemed as if peace and goodwill prevailed. Goldie would lie in bed at night daydreaming about Lucy and John's wedding and their house and how many children they'd have. She imagined their children would have brown hair because John was fair and Lucy was dark, their children would be a good mixture. The oldest boy would be called Pedro after John's father. If they had a daughter they might give her a fancy American names like Crystal or Dorothy.

When Harry Livingston appeared, Goldie's daydreaming about fancy names ended, there were more pressing concerns. "I swear as sure as I'm sitting here on this veranda, Harry Livingston is not the man for Lucy," she told Makawee who listened to Goldie's concerns and reminded her that Lucy's husband was Lucy's choice. "Well, I know," Goldie pointed to her chest, "John Dwyer would make a better husband and is a far better man that that vain, New York toff."

When Lucy married Harry and went to live in New York, Goldie cried. As a child she'd never cried but in 1921, she cried so easily and so often, she confided in Makawee that she thought her eyes would roll out of her head with all the crying. Makawee reassured Goldie that her eyes wouldn't roll out of their sockets. "If the tears are there, let them come. Its only natural."

Eventually Goldie accepted Lucy's choice. Each Christmas Lucy and Harry returned to Four Oaks, and for the entire month of August, Lucy returned without Harry. Goldie often tried to read between the lines of their marriage but only saw contentment for the first few years. When Lucy showed no sign of conceiving a child, Goldie wasn't upset. "She's still you and divorce is legal."

When Goldie had the telephone installed, it allowed Lucy and her to talk regularly. Each Friday afternoon, Goldie sat by the phone waiting for Lucy's call. Lucy would tell her about her week and where she'd been and what parties or concerts she had attended. It was on one of those Friday afternoon's in 1929 when Goldie was sitting by the phone waiting for Lucy's call when Emilio Dwyer visited. Normally she'd be pleased to see Emilio but not when she was expecting her call from Lucy. She made coffee and sat with the door open so as she'd hear the telephone in the hall.

"I come with some strange news," Emilio began. "I believe Lorcan isn't dead but living in Oklahoma."

As Goldie stared unblinkingly at Emilio, he told her that he'd heard a wild rumor a few years ago during one of his trips to Denver that Lorcan O'Neill owned a farm in Oklahoma. He had bought cheap land to grow wheat. "First time I didn't believe it, but then I heard it again from an ex-soldier, then a few months ago I heard his name mentioned again. I made enquiries and, sure enough, he's above ground and breathing God's air like you and me."

As Goldie's coffee grew cold, she learned that Lorcan had lived in at least three states during the last twenty years. He continued to play cards and remained friends with some of his old army buddies.

When the phone in the hall rang, Goldie didn't answer it, instead she tried to recall what the telegram said all those years ago. Dead? Presumed dead? Missing in action?

Eventually Emilio said, "I knew you'd want to know."

She thanked him and he left at dusk. As day gave way to night, Goldie remained sitting in her chair in the living room. She speculated if he was still a threat? He wasn't a threat to her but if he outlived her, he might be a threat to Lucy? He was possibly a threat to Makawee. What then? She thought about Aengus and Chaytan and Baby Miriam, and then she thought about her advanced years. She was too old to take on this battle again. She remained where she was, speculating and writhing in uncertainly until finally she realized that it was dark outside and she was cold and suddenly hungry, yet she remained sitting in her armchair until she felt the clawing hands of fear envelop her, then she stood up and packed her bag. The only way to deal with fear was to meet it head-on.

Over the next four years, Goldie made several trips to Denver, Kansas and Oklahoma looking for Lorcan. Each time she got a forwarding address and when she arrived to each location, she suspected he'd moved on or was hiding. There were times when she felt as if she was still chasing Baby Miriam, it had that same sense of unfinished business to her trips. Sometimes she thought she only wanted to talk to Lorcan. She wasn't sure what they'd talk about, maybe how all of this began and if he could, would he turn back time? There were times when she felt as if she was propelled by something other than her own vengeance. Sometimes she enjoyed packing her bag and leaving just for the pleasure of the train ride. She liked to see other people and eavesdrop on the conversation. It made her feel young, as if there was a lot more left to do and see. When she saw the impact of the Great Depression in the big cities with half-starved women and men, and children in rags, she was grateful she was old and not a mother trying to feed her hungry young. Once or twice she packed her bag knowing she wouldn't meet Lorcan, yet she went again. She wanted to feel as if she was doing something.

"Let your God deal with Lorcan," Makawee said, waving her hands towards the skies.

Goldie didn't have Makawee's trust in God. She tried, but as quickly she felt her God wouldn't strike Lorcan dead and that she had to take it into her own hands. She'd dwell on Lorcan's crimes and allow the old uneasiness and anger to return. She never ruled out killing him. She was old, her years in prison wouldn't be long and even if they executed her, it was painless now according to Emilio Dwyer. There were times when she scolded herself for foolishly gallivanting around the countryside on some aimless vendetta. "Stay at home and stop your nonsense," she said as sat in her hotel room in Rolla, Kansas looking out at a white house on the brow of a hill in the distance. Behind the house, there appeared to be a mountain, or a cloud, she wasn't sure. She wiped her eyes and tried to refocus. It was then she realized, it wasn't a mountain but a dust cloud that turned the afternoon to night. It was almost reminiscent of the day of the grasshoppers, but this moving mass didn't descend, it edged slowly toward her. She got off the bed and went to the window and stared with a morbid fascination as the dust cloud advanced towards her. It swallowed up the house and came nearer and nearer. Goldie was so fascinated with the scene playing out before her eyes, she forgot about Lorcan and the purpose for her visit. She remained in her bedroom until the dust cloud came to meet her. It obscured everything until the brown gritty dust stuck to the window, like a malevolent force, it seemed as if it was wanted to force its way into her room and suffocate her too. She put her hand to her neck. The pane of glass was suddenly filthy with Gods earth. She pitied the window cleaner, and the farmers who lost their crops and the generation coming behind her, those men, women and children who had to wage their war in this dustbowl. The following morning she left on the train. For the duration of the return trip to

Four Oaks, Goldie couldn't peel her eyes away from the window. She saw the roof of a cabin, the remainder was hidden beneath the dust. She saw land and machinery swallowed in the same dust. Where the dust and dirt hadn't accumulated, the land had been swept clean of topsoil. She spotted a dead animal close to the tracks, it had suffocated from the sand, along with a thousand dreams of prosperity and hope.

"How was your journey," Makawee asked when she met Goldie in the mill the following morning. "Did you see him?" she asked of Lorcan.

Goldie was inspecting the newly dyed wool in her office. She put the wool on her desk and sat back, "No, I saw something different, something that will change everything." She told her about the dust cloud, its great menacing size and the damage it left in its wake.

Makawee looked at her doubtfully.

"Its true. They call them dust storms. It changes everything, farming and rural life will never be the same." Goldie declared. "I got thinking how we spend years trying to make things right. We spend years hating and hunting to right the past. Really, its all for nothing," Goldie picked up the dried wool and felt the texture. "From dust to dust, and ashes to ashes, isn't that the way we'll all go?"

Makawee nodded.

"I'll be gone from here some day and then a different kind of dust cloud will probably finish my unfinished business."

CHAPTER FORTY

1937

M akawee sat on her veranda and closed her eyes. She tried to determine the direction of the wind. Her tribe had long talked about the winds, the cold north wind brought by the bear, and the south wind brought by the gentle fawn. Makawee's favorite was the east wind brought by the moose, because it blows its breath to chill young clouds as they float through the sky. The image of the kindly moose stayed forever. Tonight, it was a west wind, brought by the panther which was destructive and harsh. Makawee was prepared for what the wind brought, although she had not always been this prepared. She couldn't remember if a west wind had been blowing when she set up home with her first husband, Chaytan's father. Her time with him was dominated by terror. He was a scout for the enemy. She never knew what became of him after he left them some time in the mid-1860s. Makawee believed that the gentle south wind had brought Aengus to her. She had years of peace with him and then the sadness of his loss was almost as great as the sadness of her son Chaytan's death. She could not look back on her life without remembering that pain. When Goldie came one

September morning over thirty years ago to tell her that Chaytan was dead, she'd felt his death before she heard the news. Makawee took consolation that Chaytan had known freedom like his ancestors until he was hanged by Lorcan O'Neill, the man who was instrumental in the greatest sadness that afflicted her life.

Since Lorcan's return to Four Oaks, Makawee thought about the winds of the past more than the winds of the present. In her mind, she went back to her childhood tepee, riding a horse over the bluffs, and sometimes the images were so clear she could see and smell the buffalo meat boiling in a clay bed. She saw Chaytan's face, as a boy and then as a man.

In the weeks after they heard that Chaytan had been hanged, Goldie seemed to take his death worse than anybody. She went into a rage that nothing, only Lorcan's death, would contain. Goldie had gone to Denver almost as soon as Emilio had left. She didn't even tell her husband. She packed her carpetbag and put her Derringer into her pocket. "I will find him," she told Makawee. She hired Indians and bloodthirsty ex-Army men to locate him. They rode out to his farm in Denver where he'd married the widow. Like Lorcan waiting for Chaytan, Goldie waited. She called on the widow a second time, a third and a fourth time. Eventually, Goldie learned that Lorcan had been posted to another war at the other side of the world.

Makawee felt the steel from her Derringer. It was in her pocket and warm from the touch of her hands. The dogs sat in their beds on the floor of the veranda. She saw the small one open its mouth and yawn.

Makawee had been taught that an animal will always come back to the place where it found easy prey. The same applies to man. They will fish in the abundant streams and hunt where the animals are plentiful, and the bully will return to the victim to satisfy his need for domination. Lorcan will go to the root of his discontentment.

The dog roused itself and strolled into the yard. She saw its head cocked as it looked in the direction of the avenue and the second dog did the same. Both stood with their ears pricked. She heard a car approach, and then it stopped. Makawee listened but only heard the deep growl from the dog nearest her. Then it ran, and its bark was menacing. Makawee took the Derringer from her pocket. She had thought about this day for years. Since the day Goldie told her that Lorcan was alive, she knew he'd come back if Goldie died first. She'd never wanted revenge for Aengus' death. Aengus had known that he was courting danger by arming her tribe. However, Chaytan's death was different. Makawee resolved that if Lorcan ever came back to Four Oaks, she'd shoot him. She sat and waited for the intruder to make himself known. The dogs were barking. She knew the little one would bite his ankles. That's all they'd do, bark and nip. He wouldn't be harmed.

Makawee saw a white head approach her. The dogs were still barking, running at his feet and then backing away. He came closer until he was standing five feet from where she sat. He was outside the trellis of the veranda.

"Hello, Makawee," he said.

It was the voice that she recognized; it was deep and damaged, yet it was Lorcan's voice.

As determined as Goldie had been, Lorcan was warped. The boy had a bad strain. A bit of cajoling would have worked, nurturing the few gifts he had or patting him on the back occasionally, but Barry O'Neill hadn't gotten that quality to give away. His son picked up the determination of the O'Neills, the same determination that saw Barry O'Neill planting forty acres of trees in eight weeks and becoming a wealthy man, the same determination that saw Goldie trying to right a wrong she believed was her doing. In fixing the past, she'd made good the present, but not Lorcan, he couldn't forget that his father was unable to see his potential. Instead, Barry had praised Chaytan because he made money for Barry, and money was Barry's god. Lorcan was still the boy who fought his wars, and yet it brought him nowhere, only back to the scene of his first battle.

"I believe those Injuns in Leyden told you the truth about Lucy," Lorcan said. "I'm mighty pleased you never told Goldie what you knew."

If Makawee were younger and Lorcan O'Neill had not taken so much from her, she'd tell him that his father was dead, and there were times when he had been a good son. If he hadn't killed Aengus or hung her son Chaytan, she might even have offered him some kindness or told him with the wisdom of age that at some point we forge our own future.

"Are you gone stone deaf, Makawee?" he asked, and he took a step closer. The dogs' barking escalated.

Lorcan could have come with good intentions. Maybe an apology for killing Aengus or justification for Chaytan's hanging, or he possibly had come for a neighborly chat. She wasn't going to find out. She put the Derringer between the rungs in the patio and aimed.

LUCY FOUND HARRY SITTING ALONE IN THE LIVING ROOM. HE WAS IN the armchair with his hands jointed on his chest and his drink on the arm of the chair. He began to comment on the night. "I thought Owen was going to die before our very eyes tonight. Seemingly, it's a common occurrence."

Lucy was standing at the window looking out at the evening as darkness elbowed its way into the dusk.

"I'm so pleased that the Breens are one family I'll never again have to meet," Harry continued. "Between Owen and his frenzied tantrums, Wilbur holding court about autumnal colors of rugs, and Frances like a martyr spoon feeding Owen, it's a damn circus."

Lucy wasn't listening. As she passed him, he stretched for her hand. "We'll be home tomorrow. I'm sorry that I had to invite Lorcan to stay, I simply couldn't have your father staying in a hotel."

"I am not going back with you," Lucy declared.

"We've discussed this," Harry said and smiled patiently at her.

Lucy repeated what she'd said before leaving. She ran out the front door and cut through the vegetable garden, and then she ran through the grounds of the mill. When she reached the road, she almost ran into an oncoming car. She stopped, breathless; she was waiting for it to pass as she looked down the avenue leading to Makawee's house.

"Do you need a ride?"

It was John Dwyer. Lucy sighed with relief when she saw him. She got into the passenger seat, asking, "Will you take me to Makawee's?"

"What's going on?" he asked as he turned left and powered down the avenue.

Lucy explained that Lorcan had gone to Makawee's house. "It's probably nothing, but..."

John drove faster.

It was then that they saw the flash from a gunshot. They arrived to see Makawee with the gun in her hand and Lorcan lying on the ground.

Lucy went immediately to Makawee. "Are you all right?"

"I'm fine," she said.

At the other side of the patio, Lorcan O'Neill took his last breath, splayed on the earth beneath the sharp east wind.

CHAPTER FORTY-ONE

After the shooting, John Dwyer called the sheriff. Lucy stared at Lorcan's remains.

"It's too late," John said removing his jacket and covering Lorcan's face.

Lucy hesitated before guiding Makawee into the house. It seemed macabre to sit on the veranda with her dead father sprawled at the other side of the trellis. Nobody spoke while John made tea. They sat soundlessly around the fire.

"What happened?" Lucy asked Makawee.

Makawee emitted a long, tired sigh. "I don't know where to start."

"Start at the beginning," Lucy said.

"I'm gonna leave you two to talk while I watch the body." John took his tea outside to give them privacy.

Makawee began her story at the beginning, when Barry had employed Chaytan to break his mustangs, and how the grasshoppers came, and Baby Miriam disappeared. Makawee didn't stop until she got to the point of Miriam's life when she'd left Rosebud Reservation.

"We knew Miriam's movements because Chaytan had kept

track. He liked to keep an eye on her for Goldie's sake and see that she didn't need anything. He also struck up a friendship with her husband and was a welcome guest at Rosebud and when they moved to Leyden outside Denver, the same applied. Twice a year on Chaytan's return from the cattle drives, he called at their home, and he'd stay a few nights before facing the long journey to Four Oaks. Sometime in the mid-1890s, Lorcan was posted to Fort Logan in Denver. He spotted Chaytan and when he realized where he stayed, he posted soldiers to keep watch on the house in his absence. The Breens wanted him alive."

"Why?" Lucy asked.

"Because they wanted the pleasure of hanging him."

"So, the house where Chaytan visited was Baby Miriam's house?"

"Yes," Makawee replied.

"Did Lorcan know that Baby Miriam also lived in the house in Leyden?" Lucy asked.

"No, Miriam was more Indian than white. Tired of whites trying to save her, she used the henna plant to darken her red hair and she wore the clothes of an Indian woman. She was unrecognizable to him at that stage, and naturally she didn't know who he was." Makawee continued, "Each time there was a sighting of Chaytan, Lorcan sent a telegram to the Breens. In the spring of 1905, when Chaytan was returning, he called again at the house in Leyden. This time Lorcan was quick enough to have predicted Chaytan's movements. The minute he saw him, he sent his telegram to the Breens, who arrived that night. With the help of some of Lorcan's Army friends, they surrounded the house and opened fire. There were two adults killed in the house that night. There was one soldier killed, and Owen Breen was wounded." Makawee pointed to her head. "Here. It's why life as he knew it stopped that day."

"Wasn't it a stroke?" Lucy said.

"No, Frances had to say that, because it didn't bear well when she wanted to be respectable and her husband was caught trying to settle an old score."

"Sounds about right," Lucy said of Frances.

"Did the Breens and Lorcan capture Chaytan?"

Makawee nodded. "Before they hung him, Chaytan told Lorcan that his sister, Miriam, was one of the dead."

"Lorcan killed Miriam?" Lucy said.

"Miriam may not have died from his gun, but she died because of his actions. Before they hung Chaytan, he told them. No matter what Lorcan had done in his past, he could never forgive himself for the final act." Makawee stopped speaking for a moment. "So Lorcan tried to compensate in the only way he could. Chaytan also told Lorcan that Miriam's child was hiding in the bunker in the house." Makawee stretched across the narrow table and clasped Lucy's hand. "Some good grace must have lingered within Lorcan because he returned to the house in Leyden after witnessing Chaytan's hanging. Lorcan placed you in the orphanage in Denver."

"Me?" Lucy said.

"Yes," Makawee said. "You are Miriam's daughter."

Lucy remained looking at Makawee.

"And your father was a Lakota Indian," Makawee added.

Lucy remained quiet for several moments before asking, "Why did Goldie not tell me?"

"Because she didn't know, and I never told her. I learned all I know from those who survived."

"If Goldie hated Lorcan as much as she did, why did she adopt me when she thought I was his daughter?"

"Goldie hated what he did and the man he had become, and more than anything, she hated what he represented, but she loved him. He was her brother."

"Goldie never knew I was Miriam's daughter?"

"That's right," Makawee said. "I never told her because I didn't want to bring up the past that had drifted away. There were days when Goldie believed that Miriam's disappearance was not her fault."

"But Miriam's disappearance wasn't Goldie's fault," Lucy said.

"Aengus told me that he heard the blame in her parents' tone in the days after Miriam's disappearance, and if he heard it, as a child Goldie heard it too. It's difficult to unlearn a belief like that, those type of accusations stick forever," Makawee pointed to her head. "But when she adopted you, she was content. By telling her that you were Miriam's daughter, it would have opened the old wounds, and I don't know if Goldie had it in her to fight that battle again."

Lucy was silent.

Makawee said, "You helped her heart soften toward him. She often said the only good thing Lorcan ever did was to produce you."

Lucy smiled at that.

Outside they saw the flashing lights of the sheriff's car. They sat in silence.

CHAPTER FORTY-TWO

The sheriff examined Lorcan's body before it was taken away. He found a Derringer in his pocket, the sister of the gun that Makawee had used. The sheriff was Emilio Dwyer's grandson. In the privacy of each Dwyer home, when the cruelty of young men was discussed, they whispered the comparison to Lorcan O'Neill. Those who had not seen the mustang-boy with their own eyes told their children and their grandchildren about a boy who came to the O'Neill farm to break wild mustangs. When Lorcan O'Neill reappeared, they whispered about Chaytan's death and Lorcan O'Neill's hand in it. Sheriff Dwyer wasn't surprised when he saw Lorcan.

He helped Makawee give her statement. "You were defending yourself and your property, ain't that the truth?" The sheriff tried to put words of self-defense in Makawee's mouth. He wrote as he spoke. "And you were scared out o' your wits?"

"I didn't get time to be scared," Makawee said.

The sheriff stopped writing his notes and looked at Makawee, advising, "It's best you say you were scared outta your wits."

Makawee agreed. "All right, I was scared outta my wits."

They sat in silence as Sheriff Dwyer added a few more lines to the statement. He read the last words aloud, "The approaching man didn't identify himself. He came out of the dark toward me, I was scared outta my wits on account of all the news of killings on the radio. I asked his name but he wouldn't say. Then I fired. It was self-defense. I was defending my property. Sign here," he held out his notebook.

Makawee hesitated.

"An X is fine," Sheriff Dwyer said.

That night Lucy stayed in Makawee's house. They talked until the early morning. She slept in the chair and when she woke the following morning they talked some more. They lapsed into long silences as they dwelled on all that had happened.

Lucy suddenly broke one of the long silences by asking, "Did Goldie know that Lorcan had not been killed in the Battle of Bud Dajo?"

"Yes, she only found out about eight years ago that he was alive," Makawee said.

"Did Goldie try to find him?"

"She sure did. She returned to Denver and Kansas and Texas several times with her Derringer in her pocket. Four years ago, she stopped looking for him."

"Did she forgive him?" Lucy asked.

"No, Goldie went to Kansas and saw one of many dust storms, and it changed her. She told us about the dust clouds bigger than mountains that inched across the land. She said the storms were like the end of world."

"She told me about that," Lucy said. "It was the beginning of the dustbowl."

They sat in silence, Makawee recalling the past and Lucy understanding the present.

Winona brought them breakfast and together they reminisced until late afternoon. When Lucy returned to Goldie's house, Harry was gone.

Two days after Lorcan's death, it was decided that he would be buried in Denver. Frances Breen paid for the coffin and went to the railway station when it was loaded onto the carriage. She claimed she was too poorly to make the trip to Denver for the funeral.

"You must mind your health," Bertha Gallagher said.

Frances agreed.

"So, what happened?" Bertha asked.

Frances gave Bertha a reproachful glance. Not only was she a money-grabbing, whiskey-brewing woman of ill-gotten money, she was being overly familiar and downright nosey.

"An accident," Frances said before moving away from Bertha.

The morning Frances heard that Lorcan was dead, she sat opposite Owen and asked him why he had apologized to Lucy about Miriam. It took over one hour for him to tell the full story. She didn't know why she felt so bad when she heard that Lucy was Miriam's daughter. It didn't even bother her that Lucy's father was an Indian. She just felt bad, that's all she could tell Owen.

"Right here," she said, placing the palm of her hand on her chest, "I feel so bad, right here."

At the train station, the locals sympathized with Lucy. She didn't correct anyone who offered their sympathies for her father. Lucy kept up the pretense that Lorcan was her father. It seemed too long-winded to explain to anyone, other than her family, that her mother was the child taken on the day of the grasshoppers. When the train pulled away, she met Frances. Lucy was the one to do the sympathizing then.

"He was your brother, and I'm very sorry," Lucy said.

Frances held her hand a moment longer but didn't speak.

There were no charges brought against Makawee.

Two months later, Molly Breen left Four Oaks. Lucy heard that she eventually returned to New York. She'd been seen at Club 21 with Harry for a period. A month after her departure, Wilbur won the election with a landslide victory. The town sympathized with him after his wife left. He devoted the rest of his days to political endeavors in his local town. In December of the same year, Owen Breen died. The towns people marveled at his will to live; a stroke victim who survived for thirty-one years.

Lucy dusted off Goldie's old loom. She wanted to see if she could remember how to weave as Goldie had taught her. She referred to the reminders stowed away in the corners of her mind and the many instructions taught in the Lakota language. Lucy had forgotten how much she enjoyed it.

In 1939, while Makawee was sitting on her veranda enjoying the cool east wind, she slipped away taking with her the last vestiges of the days of the free roaming Indians. She was 98 years of age. That year, Lucy stitched two inverted figures on her rugs.

In 1940, Lucy stitched a turtle into her wares to celebrate the birth of her daughter. She was christened Grainne Dwyer after Goldie. Lucy lived out the rest of her days in Four Oaks with her husband, John Dwyer, and their daughters.

The End

ACKNOWLEDGMENTS

To Brian Sheridan, Eilish Rafferty, Margaret Scott, Marian Healy and Pauline Clooney from The Mill Lane Writer's Group for continual encouragement and solid advice.

To Eileen Keane, for friendship and listening to my long-winded plotlines.

A special thanks to Pat O'Brien, for reading the early drafts and advice.

Thanks to Debra Hartmann at The Pro Book Editor who went beyond the call of duty.

To Ann Seipel for her dedication.

And, finally, my heartfelt thanks to you, the reader.

ABOUT THE AUTHOR

Olive Collins grew up in Thurles, Tipperary. She has always loved the diversity of books and people. She has travelled extensively and still enjoys exploring other cultures and countries. Her inspiration is the ordinary everyday people who feed her little snippets of their lives. Her debut novel, *The Memory of Music*, was an award-winning bestseller. *The Tide Between Us* has continued to ride high in the charts since its release in 2019, attaining No. 1 in numerous categories at Amazon.

If you'd like to hear more or receive Olive's newsletter, please log onto www.olivecollins.com

HISTORICAL BACKGROUND

The Irish and Land: Land ownership for Irish men was one of their greatest aspirations. Most were tenant farmers who were at the mercy of fluctuating rents, and their lease could be changed or terminated, and the families evicted at any time. America and The Homestead Act allowed them to buy 160 acres for eighteen dollars.

Irish Colonies in the West: Until 1922, Ireland was governed by England. The Irish were second-class citizens in their homeland and obliged to adhere to English laws that kept the Irish oppressed. They aspired to own land and self-govern. By moving West and establishing their colonies, they hoped to become their own masters, live in peace and thrive.

Grasshopper Plague / Rocky Mountain Locust: The locust swarms were an ongoing problem for the farmers until the late 19th century. Sightings often placed swarms in numbers far larger than any other locust species, with one famous sighting that estimated the swarm at 198,000 square miles in size (greater than the area of California). When the swarms struck, they scoured the fields of crops, the trees of leaves and removed the paint from tools. They even devoured the clothing and quilts that the farmers threw protectively over the vegetable gardens. A farmer's wife called Kansan

Viets claimed to have had the clothes eaten off her back. "I was wearing a dress of white with a green stripe. The grasshoppers settled on me and ate up every bit of the green stripe before anything could be done."

Navajo Blankets: Written records establish the Navajo as fine weavers for at least the last 300 years, beginning with Spanish colonial descriptions of the early 18th century. Few remnants of 18th-century Navajo weaving survive, however the most important surviving examples of early Navajo weaving come from Massacre Cave at Canyon de Chelly, Arizona. In 1804, a group of Navajo was shot and killed there, where they were seeking refuge from Spanish soldiers. For a hundred years, the cave remained untouched due to Navajo taboos until a local trader named Sam Day entered and retrieved the textiles. Day separated the collection and sold it to various museums. The majority of Massacre Cave blankets feature plain stripes, yet some exhibit the terraces and diamonds characteristic of later Navajo weaving.

Caves beneath the Black Hills: There are several caves beneath the Black Hills. The famous ones are Jewel Cave and Wind Cave. Jewel Cave is the third longest cave in the world, with 200 miles of mapped passageways. Wind Cave is the sacred site for the Lakota. They believe they and the buffalo emerge from Mother Earth to live together. A man was employed to map the cave, but he was unable to complete his task.

Gold and The Black Hills: The United States government recognized the Black Hills as belonging to the Sioux by the Treaty of Laramie in 1868. Despite being within Indian territory, and therefore off-limits, white Americans were increasingly interested in the gold-mining possibilities of the Black Hills. For years, men had gone into the hills searching for gold. In 1887, a rock was discovered with the following inscription, "Got all the gold we could carry our ponys all got by the Indians. I have lost my gun and nothing to eat and Indians hunting me." It was dated, June 1834.

Wounded Knee Massacre: It was a massacre of nearly three hundred men, women and children of the Lakota people by soldiers of the United States Army on December 29th, 1890, on the Lakota

Pine Ridge Indian Reservation in South Dakota, following a botched attempt to disarm the Lakota camp. Thirty-one soldiers also died. Twenty soldiers were awarded the Medal of Honor. In 2001, the National Congress of American Indians passed two resolutions condemning the military awards and called on the U.S. government to rescind them. In 1990, both houses of the U.S Congress expressed "deep regret" for the massacre.

Dust Bowl: On April 14, 1935, known as "Black Sunday," twenty of the worst "black blizzards" occurred across the entire sweep of the Great Plains, from Canada south to Texas. The dust storms caused extensive damage and appeared to turn day to night; witnesses reported that they could not see five feet in front of them at certain points. Robert E. Geiger happened to be in Oklahoma that day. His story about Black Sunday marked the first appearance of the term *Dust Bowl*. The Dust Bowl intensified the crushing economic impact of the Great Depression. Roughly 2.5 million people left the Dust Bowl states during the 1930s. It was one of the largest migrations in American history. Oklahoma alone lost 440,000 people to migration. Many of them, poverty-stricken, travelled west looking for work.

https://olivecollins.com/

ALSO BY OLIVE COLLINS

THE TIDE BETWEEN US

1821: After the landlord of Lugdale Estate in Kerry is assassinated, young Art O'Neill's innocent father is hanged and Art is deported to the cane fields of Jamaica as an indentured servant. On Mangrove Plantation he gradually acclimatizes to the exotic country and unfamiliar customs of the African slaves, and achieves a kind of contentment.

When the new heirs to the plantation arrive from Ireland they resurrect the ghosts of brutal injustices against Art. He must overcome his hatred to survive the harsh life of a slave and live to see the emancipation which liberates his colored children. Eventually he is promised seven gold coins when he finishes his service, but his doubts his master will part with the coins.

One hundred years later in Ireland, a skeleton is discovered beneath a fallen tree on the grounds of Lugdale Estate. By its side is a gold coin minted in 1870. Yseult, the owner of the estate, watches as events unfold, fearful of the long-buried truths that may emerge about her family's past and its links to the slave trade. As the skeleton gives up its secrets, Yseult realizes she too can no longer hide.

THE MEMORY OF MUSIC

One Irish family – One hundred turbulent years: 1916 to 2016

Betty O'Fogarty is proud and clever. Spurred on by her belief in her husband Seamus O'Neill's talent as a violin-maker and her desire to escape rural life, they elope to Dublin. She expects life there to fulfil all her dreams.

To her horror, she discovers that they can only afford to live in the notorious poverty-stricken tenements. Seamus becomes obsessed with republican politics, neglecting his lucrative craft. And, as Dublin is plunged into chaos and turmoil at Easter 1916, Betty gives birth to her first child to the sound of gunfire and shelling.

But Betty vows that she will survive war and want, and move her little family out of the tenements.

Nothing will stand in her way.

One hundred years later, secrets churn their way to the surface and Betty's grandchildren and great-grandchildren uncover both Betty's ruthlessness and her unique brand of heroism.

Winner of The Annie McHale Debut Award

https://olivecollins.com/

CPSIA information can be obtained
at www.ICGtesting.com
Printed in the USA
LVHW050517150321
681562LV00020B/754